Dale Mayer

Hide'n Go Seek

Book 2
Psychic Visions

i

HIDE'N GO SEEK
Dale Mayer
Valley Publishing
Copyright © 2011

ISBN 10: 0987741144
ISBN-13: 9780987741141

DEDICATION

This book is dedicated to my four children who always believed in me and my storytelling abilities.

Thanks to you all.

ACKNOWLEDGMENTS

Hide'n Go Seek wouldn't have been possible without the support of my friends and family. Many hands helped with proofreading, editing, and beta reading to make this book come together. Special thanks to Amy Atwell and my editor, Pat Thomas. I had a vision, but it took many people to make that vision real.
I thank you all.

CHAPTER ONE

Death shouldn't be so greedy. Everyone came to him eventually.

Kali Jordan surveyed the wet gray rubble, her heart aching with sorrow. Three days ago this giant pile of debris had been a small but thriving Mexican town. Today it was a deathtrap.

Thunder rumbled across the mountain. She squinted at the black clouds gathering on the horizon. Already the weather and location had hampered rescue efforts with fog preventing the helicopters from landing.

The disaster site had been treacherous before the earthquake, yet if the approaching storm deluged the area as predicted, search and rescue conditions would deteriorate even more.

Rubbing her throbbing temple, she dropped her gaze to the crumpled mass of concrete and glass ahead of her. So many people missing and, as always, so little time to help them. Shiloh, her long-haired Labrador Retriever, had worked this same quadrant all morning with the concentration and focus typical of her breed. This afternoon, however, her tail drooped. Kali could relate.

Strong muscles bunched as Shiloh jumped up to another boulder. Her bright orange K-9 SAR vest stood out against the dusty gray backdrop. Even dirty, the vest was striking enough to be visible. Although Shiloh's fur was an unusual fox red, the grime had an equalizing effect, coating everyone and everything with a uniform layer of dust.

An aftershock rattled the ground, shifting the pile under the dog's sturdy feet. Shiloh scrabbled to stay upright.

Kali's heart stopped for a second, her breath catching in her throat. The earth stilled. Shiloh caught her balance and kept going. Kali waited an extra moment before exhaling. She didn't want to be here.

Many disaster sites had huge influxes of help from the global community. Many sites had organization, management of some sort, experienced people to move resources and offer assistance to the survivors. Many sites – but not this one.

Kali and Brad, along with Jarl and Jordan, another set of old hands in this game, were one of the few groups on the spot. The roads had washed out after their arrival, hampering the army's efforts.

Right now everyone else was working on a different quadrant. Her intuition – her grandma called it the Sight – had insisted she search here. She'd learned a long time ago to listen. But that didn't mean she liked where it sent her.

Shiloh barked.

Ignoring her headache, Kali hopped over the mess of ripped supports and roofing. Shiloh barked again, then sat on her haunches, head high. She wagged her tail, sweeping away the dirt around her.

She'd found a survivor.

Excitement bloomed. Unbelievable warmth surrounded Kali's heart. A miracle, after three days in this heat, and one sorely needed to boost the exhausted search and rescue volunteers' flagging optimism. A rush of adrenaline sent her surging up the next pile of rubble.

A large block shifted, tossing Kali sideways. She scrambled to recover her footing. Shiloh yipped, her version of 'are you okay?' Kali grinned at her when she'd righted herself.

"I'm fine, girl. Not to worry."

Jumping onto a different cement slab, Kali climbed ever higher, to where Shiloh waited.

"Hey, Kali, what have you got?"

Turning, Kali spotted her best friend and fellow SAR member Brad, with his German Shepherd, Sergeant.

"Shiloh's found a survivor here." Kali reached for the next handhold.

"Really? Hang on. I'm on my way." With his long strides, Brad covered the height differences in the piles within seconds. Sergeant passed them both as he jumped up to join Shiloh. He barked and sat on his haunches.

"Good Lord, this is great to see." Brad's voice brimmed with energized exhilaration. Holding out a hand, he helped Kali up and over a broken wall. "We passed that all important forty-eight-hour window this morning. I hate this stage of the search."

"Especially here." From her high position, Kali stared at the surrounding chaos while she caught her breath.

Both dogs whined.

Groaning, she started climbing again. Her muscles ached with tension. The rubble shifted again. "Shit," she whispered. "It's touch and go."

"I know. Slow and steady. Let's assess whether we can do this on our own or if we need to bring a crew over."

Not that there were many crews to call.

Disorganization ruled here. Survivors scrambled in desperation to find their lost family members, along with the few volunteers who had made the trek to help. Volunteers were invaluable on disaster sites. Silent unsung heroes as they often made their own arrangements and covered their own costs in a bid to help out.

The army would probably arrive in time to organize recovery operations. Meanwhile, everyone was doing what they could at a location where just being on site was a huge risk. The ground trembled with aftershocks several times a day, shifting the wobbly debris under their feet.

Kali finally reached Shiloh. Digging into her fanny pack, she removed Shiloh's reward, her black-and-white, well-chewed teddy bear. Shiloh gently grasped her cuddly toy before bounding to ground level where she lay down to rest, her bear tucked under her chin. Brad sent Sergeant to join her.

Peering through the helter-skelter heap of broken flooring and walls, Kali heard a faint voice. She studied the small pocket of darkness off to the left. "Hello? Is anyone there? Can you hear me?"

The tiny feminine echo bounced upwards. "*Si.*"

Kali let out a whoop. "It's a child. Brad, call for help."

Brad searched the surrounding area to see if anyone was within shouting distance. Several people scrambled toward them. He signaled for assistance then turned back to her. "A team is on the way. Does she speak English?"

She shrugged. Peering into the dark opening, Kali squinted at what appeared to be a young girl in the murky shadows. Slowly, a small face came into focus. A small hand waved up at her. "She's pointing at her leg. Ah. I see it now. Her leg is broken just below the knee." Kali called to the girl, "What's your name?"

The weak high voice trembled in a new spat of Spanish.

From Kali's poor Spanish, she thought the child said her name was Inez. She could only hope Inez was old enough to understand what had happened and not panic. Although if Kali were the one stuck in that hole, she'd be panicking plenty.

The girl stared up, fear and hope warring on her face. Kali's heart ached. She looked so tiny. So alone. She had to be terrified. Hell, Kali was terrified.

Needing to help in some way, Kali tried to reassure the child by speaking in a calm steady voice. "Take it easy, Inez. Help is here. Don't try to move." The little one might not understand the words, yet the smile and easy voice would help her to relax.

A noisy hub of activity heralded the arrival of several other workers. Lilting voices flowed as singsong conversation bubbled between the suddenly animated girl and the crew. A hubbub of activity commenced. Brad grabbed Kali's arm, pulling her out of the way.

She frowned, but let herself be moved. She didn't want to leave Inez alone. She was too big to squeeze through the opening to the frightened child.

On a separate slab twenty feet back, Brad and Kali watched as the crew went to work. The crowd on the ground swelled as news of a survivor spread. Spanish and English mixed into a confusing yet understandable wash of conversation. Kali tuned out most of it, staying focused on the yawning pit that held the promise of life...and the threat of death.

A buzz of excitement rose as one of the smallest rescue team members descended on ropes. The opening was ringed with hardhats as everyone leaned over to watch. Kali shivered. Instinctively, she backed up several more steps, shifting to a different piece of cement. Brad followed.

"What's the matter?" he whispered against her ear.

"There're too many of them, too much weight. This could cave at any moment."

Brad frowned as he surveyed the straining men muttering into the cavern. "There haven't been any major tremors for hours now. Maybe it's all over."

Kali snorted, her eyes never leaving the action before them. "Right. And this could be a warm up for an even bigger one." Telling herself everything would be fine didn't help much either. Her instincts said otherwise. Holding her breath, she waited for someone to surface. It seemed to take hours. Kali knew the broken leg would need to be splinted. She knew the child would need to be secured into a harness. Fear knotted her gut. She knew all that. It didn't matter. A chill clutched her heart. She wanted to yell for the workers to hurry.

The earth grumbled again, a deadly reminder of the risk they all took.

The band of workers stood, heaving on ropes. Slow painful inches at a time, the crew struggled to raise their load. The top of a head popped into view, followed by a very dirty, tired face with a pained smile shining through the grimy tear tracks. Cheers erupted from the crowd. The girl waved as the rescue team worked to bring her up the last few feet. Finally, her splinted leg rose into view.

Kali gasped, her breath catching in her throat, her hands clenching and unclenching as fear dug its own claws into her more strongly. The child was almost there. Almost safe.

A hard tremor rippled through the region.

"Oh, God, no," she whispered. "Please, not."

The crowd cried out. Their yells morphed into screams of horror.

Grating sounds mingled with shouts and screams, followed by heavy grinding as rocks slid against each other, building to that one final destructive crash.

Kali screamed, falling to one side as tons of shifting material sent her tumbling. Debris rained on top of her. Curled into a ball, she held both arms protectively over her head, crying out as a small block smacked her left arm. She thought she heard a cracking sound, but she was too busy scrambling toward Brad, who'd been tossed several feet below.

"Brad. Brad! Are you okay?" Holding her injured arm against her chest, she leaned over him. Her heart stalled, then raced with relief when he swore and opened his eyes.

He struggled to sit up, shaking off the stones and dirt covering him. "I'm fine." He took several deep breaths before struggling to his feet. "Your arm, is it bad?"

She dismissed it with a wave of the hand on her uninjured arm. "It'll be fine."

Shiloh barked.

Tears of relief filled Kali's eyes. She searched the area and spotted her several yards away, Sergeant at her side. Thank God, they were fine.

Brad helped Kali to stand. She winced. "Better your arm than your head. Come on. Let's get away from this hell hole."

Kali realized suddenly that they'd ended up close to ground level. A horrible silence had fallen.

Of one mind, they pivoted to see how the rescuers had fared.

A horrible sense of knowing clutched Kali. She yelled, lunging forward only to be caught and held tight in Brad's arms.

"No, Kali. You can't go there. It's not over." His arms tightened as she struggled against the truth.

The heap surrounding the black pit that had held the little girl was gone. Dust floated several feet into the air, blurring their view. The walls of the pit had imploded then heaped with more concrete and twisted steel, burying the area under tons of new debris.

As the dust cleared, there was nothing to see.

No equipment.

No rescuers.

No little girl in a rope harness.

They were all gone.

CHAPTER TWO

Kali closed her eyes in a useless effort to ignore her surroundings. She hated hospitals, drugs, even doctors. Her parents had died after a car accident killed her father outright and left her mother barely hanging on to life for a few days before she succumbed to her injuries. Kali hadn't been in a hospital since.

Today she'd had little choice.

After the disastrous loss of the rescue workers and that poor little girl in Mexico, Brad had taken control. He'd determined her arm was badly sprained, shipping her home with Shiloh crated and at her side. He'd stayed behind to continue the rescue efforts. Numb with shock, Kali remembered little of the trip home. Dan, her boss and mentor, had been waiting for her at the airport, his sparse gray hair sticking straight out in all directions as usual. He'd driven her directly to the hospital. Kali had been beyond arguing. Good thing, too, her left forearm was cracked, just below the elbow.

The painkillers Brad had stuffed down her throat prior to loading her on the plane accounted, in part, for her silence since landing. The loss of the little girl, Inez, hurt her beyond words. The loss of the rescuers was another painful reminder of the dangers inherent in her profession. Those poor families.

Kali had seen more death than eighty percent of the people in the world. She hadn't had much experience with the process, just the aftermath. A hot tear leaked from the corner of her eye. That poor child. In her mind, Kali could clearly see the grimy smile and the excited wave as Inez surfaced.

So much loss. The tears dripped faster. Kali hated breaking down. The litany of reasons she worked disasters repeated like an old broken record. *To save the people I can, bring closure to the families, and stand for the victim.*

"There, there, dearie. Are you in pain? The doctor's going to be here soon. We'll get that arm casted in a couple of minutes. Then you can go home and rest."

All nurses should resemble grandmothers. This one oozed comfortable reassurance that gave Kali the impression everything would be all right. That was the problem with impressions. They lied.

She wasn't sure anything would ever be okay again. Despite the many disasters she had experienced, the many rescues she'd participated in, she'd never been faced with a survivor dying the way this child had. And had never been this badly affected. Naïve? Maybe. Those who survived were always rushed away to a hospital. Sometimes they succumbed to their injuries, but they did so where Kali wasn't watching. Of course those deaths had hurt. But they hadn't been as up close and personal as seeing this child vanish before her eyes.

During the plane ride home, she hadn't managed to quell the disquieting sense that maybe she should have stayed and searched through those cement slabs herself. Maybe the other rescuers had missed an opening, a crevasse somewhere. Maybe Sergeant had made a mistake. Maybe life had survived in that heap of unforgiving rock and concrete.

But life wasn't fair. When Brad had called Dan to pick her up at the airport, he'd filled him in on the details. Details that hadn't included a happy ending.

Kali wiped her eyes with her good arm, staring despondently at the wet streak across her sleeve. She had to stop thinking about it.

The middle-aged doctor strolled in. "Kali, the x-rays look good. You just need a cast to immobilize it and time to heal." The doctor's smile was both gentle and understanding.

The nurse beamed as if she'd created this happy outcome by herself. Kali stared at them both, dazed. So what if her arm was a simple break? It was still broken. She still wouldn't be able to return to Mexico or help Inez.

The nurse escorted Kali to the treatment room. Twenty minutes later her left arm sported a deep-purple cast. Dan hovered, asking questions and pestering Kali to stay awake. He snatched up the prescription when the doctor handed it over and said he'd get it filled at the hospital pharmacy.

Kali wanted to get home and be alone with Shiloh, who currently waited in the truck. Dan returned within minutes a small white package sticking out of his pocket. "Let's go, kiddo."

Conversations flowed around her, bits and pieces floating through her awareness. Something about shock, see her doctor and rest. Kali rose and followed Dan blindly. Shiloh barked as they approached, her tail wagging hard.

"Sorry for the long wait, sweetheart." Kali hugged her tight, giving her a good scratch on her ruff. "We're going home."

Home meant a fifteen-minute drive south of Portland's center to her house on the coast. When they arrived, it was all Kali could do to make it up the front stairs.

Dan put her pain meds on the table, then hauled in her gear. Shiloh bounded inside, barking once.

Kali stood at the bottom of the stairs, weaving on her feet. Pain, drugs and exhaustion blended toward an inevitable collapse.

"Kali, can you manage a shower or do you want to wait until later?"

They both looked at the purple fiberglass cast on the one arm – with the clean white fingers poking through – and then at the other not quite so clean arm.

"Sleep first, then a soak in the bath," she whispered.

"Let's get you upstairs."

Like a mother hen, Dan laid down a blanket to protect her sheets from the grime coating her hair and skin. Turning back to Kali he helped her remove her boots.

"I'll grab you a glass of water, while you get undressed." Dan walked into the bathroom while she struggled to shimmy out of her soiled jeans and t-shirt before crawling under her duvet. She pulled the covers up to her chin.

A moment later, Dan returned to place a glass of water and her pills on her night table. "Get some rest now. I'm going to the center for a few hours. I'll check on you later."

Shiloh, ever the opportunist, jumped up beside Kali and curled up into a ball. Kali rolled over to elevate her injured arm on the dog's shoulder and closed her eyes.

Dan turned off the lights. Before leaving the room, he added, "Look after yourself, Kali. Everyone has to deal with death and disaster in their way. Go easy on yourself. You did your best. That's all anyone can ask of you."

With that he walked away, his footsteps fading away in the distance.

All anyone could ask of her? What about what she asked of herself?

***

Today sucked. One more day in a long series of the same. Clouds gathered overhead. They suited his mood.

"Hey, Texan. I wanted to thank you for your involvement here." Adam spoke around the cigar butt in his mouth.

Texan? He'd worked hard to minimize that drawl. Still, if that's what this guy saw, it was hardly an insult. He could tolerate it, identify with it even. He sat on one of the many large rocks that dotted the unforgiving terrain. Brown dusty bushes similar to the sage brush found across Texas dotted the Mexican hillside.

The rescue teams had taken a severe hit with that last quake. Seven rescue workers and the little survivor from the original quake, dead. Kali Jordan injured and shipped home. Her departure had hit them all hard. Especially him. Even though she'd laugh if she knew.

Chaos had ensued in the short term, depression, and lethargy in the aftermath. Things had yet to be reorganized. No one cared anymore, apathetically accepting what life dished out. It was as if the simple beliefs from the locals had come true. He cast his thoughts to the old woman he'd found on the first day. She'd clutched his hand, speaking in broken English as she died. What was it she'd said? Something about it being God's will? The earthquakes, their punishment for a lifetime of sins?

Now, hours later, shadows blanketed the area. People littered the ground. Not moving, not talking, just staring into the emptiness of their lives. He looked over at Adam squatting under low hanging branches, smoking. Blue white fog winding upward through the leaves.

What an idiot. Adam was one of the lucky ones, pulled free early on. He should have been dead, and could have been maimed for life. Instead, that caring old woman had died and Adam had survived with only a cracked wrist. A break that still allowed him to move the cigarette to and from his mouth. Disgusting. Adam made him feel old today.

God, he hurt. He'd worked the south quadrant of the main center. Mostly houses. Mostly dead inhabitants. Shifting on the rock, he tried to ignore the other man. Fatigue had taken over as despair settled on his soul. He closed his eyes, grateful for the last few moments of daylight.

Adam wouldn't leave him in peace.

"That's a good thing you did here, helping everyone out like that. Good job." Adam spoke around the butt in his mouth.

Another stream of smoke drifted his way. What a filthy habit. Nodding in response to Adam, he narrowed his eyes and waved off the smoke. Adam's skin was scored with wrinkles and his bloodshot eyes would have fit a man who'd spent decades searching for the bottom of a bottle – not a man in his mid-twenties. "Did you ever consider giving up smoking? You got a second chance today. Don't you want to make the most of it?"

"I'm going to. Tonight I'm going to find me a hot woman, and I'm going to fuck her until *she's* almost dead." Adam howled, his open mouth showing yellowed and missing teeth. Evidence of heavy tobacco and probable drug use. The drug of choice here was marijuana, wasn't it? Or maybe it was cocaine? Not that it mattered, Adam hadn't taken care of himself before the disaster and had no intention of doing anything about it now.

What a waste.

"Remember the rescue angel, you know, one of them SAR people like you? Now I wish I could ride her tonight. Those long legs, wowzers. That walk of hers should be illegal. Definitely put a spell on my poor pecker." Adam frowned at the lack of response. "You should know the pair. The furry bitch is Shiloh. Don't know what the two-legged bitch is called. She must be from one of them foreign Nordic countries."

Staring off into the darkening sky helped tone down the rage in his belly. His fists clenched. How dare this asshole talk about Kali Jordan like that? Of course he knew her. Not as well as he'd like to. He'd worked on many sites with her. Besides, with so many rescue totals to her credit, it was hard not to know of her. She was famous. She was special. His grip on his temper slid. His stomach knotted, barely containing the bubbling acid in his gut. The bastard had no right to even speak of her.

"Hmmm mmm. Adam took another long drag of the cigarette barely clinging to his lips. He cackled then coughed, loud wheezing rasps driving up from his belly. His red-rimmed eyes lit with unholy amusement. "A couple of centuries ago, she'd have been burned at the stake for that walk of hers. I'm gonna catch me some shut-eye and dream of a witch." With a carefree wave, Adam flicked the still burning cigarette to the dirt before returning to his shadowy hollow. Within minutes, guttural snores wafted out from the burrow. The dust settled on top of him, even as the light evening shadows crept over him as he slept.

A witch? Watching Adam sleep, he tasted the word, rolling it around in his mouth. Hardly. Kali's skills were hard to explain, harder to understand, even for those who did the same work. Her record unbeaten. How many jobs had he done? How many times had he wondered why Kali was always so blessed in finding people when he was the one who prayed? He was the one who honored Him. He'd tried to emulate her, hoping for similar success – without much luck. Now another reason surfaced. One he hadn't considered.

Did she have unworldly skills? Nah, surely not. She epitomized everything good in a person. Could it be that she was too good? Maybe Adam's interpretation was right on the mark.

It would explain why she had such phenomenal success.

Troubled, he realized the more he tried, the less anything changed. He worked hard. He went to church. He believed in the good of all people. So why, with all the effort he put into his work, did it never make a difference? It needed to make a difference. *He* needed it to make a difference. Otherwise, why was he here? Why was anyone here?

Studying the ground, his gaze narrowed in thought. That old woman from his first day was never far from his mind. She'd been so peaceful with her death. It was her time, she'd said then. He'd thought it unfair. What if he had it wrong? What if he had it backwards?

What if this act of nature, this earthquake, was really an act of God? What if God created these *natural* disasters to call home the people He needed, when He needed them? What if they weren't the horrible accidents everyone said they were?

Once he latched on to that train of thought, he couldn't let it go.

God had created this planet and put Mother Earth in charge. She carried out his orders. Therefore, it followed that if she'd created this earthquake, it had been with God's consent. If that were what God wanted, saving these people buried by rubble was going *against* His wishes.

He sat back stunned. He looked around to see if the sky had turned purple or the trees had suddenly grown upside down. After all, his whole belief system had just flipped.

Glancing over at Adam's burrow, he could see a bare foot sticking out from the overhang. Adam was the type of person he'd been rescuing these last few days. Sure, there had been a couple of children included in the group, yet several had been single, asshole males like this one.

"Why? Why bother?" He looked up to the sky for answers. "What do you want me to do, Lord?"

All these years he'd been told that God was the creator of all. He believed it…knew deep inside it was true. His faith had been the mainstay of his world. So, then God had to be the creator of this earthquake. How simple. Why had he never made that connection before? If God had made this earthquake happen, it was because He wanted these results. He wanted these people to die. And if He wanted it, He had to have a good reason. It was not Man's job to wonder or to question why.

God had called these people home.

Just as the old woman had said; it was God's will.

He straightened, his face brightening with enlightenment. By SAR's intervention, these people hadn't followed God's orders. He suddenly understood. These people needed to go home. Search and rescue work was going against His will. The best of them, being the worst of them all – Kali.

This new understanding reenergized him. That's why nothing he'd ever done had made a difference – he'd been doing the wrong type of work. He hadn't understood.

He walked over to where Adam slept. So stupid, so careless of the life he'd been graced with. No appreciation.

"Hey, Adam, wake up!" The Texan nudged Adam with his foot. Adam moaned and rolled over; his snoring continued, unabated. He kicked harder.

Adam opened a bleary eye. "Huh?" At that moment he sneezed. A thick black wad of tobacco-reeking snot splattered the Texan's work boots.

Staring at Adam, the Texan scrunched up his face in loathing. "That's disgusting." His leg lashed out, the tip of his steel-toed boot connecting with Adam's chin. Adam's head snapped back. He groaned once, then fell silent.

Kneeling, he studied Adam for a long moment. This was almost too easy. Shoving the brush to the side, he slid both arms under Adam and rolled him over and then over again. It took several more rolls before Adam's unconscious body settled at the bottom of a shallow ditch at the edge of a small hillock. Using his hands, he cascaded dirt and rock on top of the prone man.

Adam moaned as small rocks bounced off his cheekbones and forehead. His eyes opened, then slammed closed as dirt rained on top of him. He flipped his head to the side, sending dirt flying. He rolled over. Using his elbows as levers, he tried to push upward. He was kicked back down, landing on his belly. Bigger rocks pounded his back. He lurched lower under the blows. "Wha...t?" A small boulder crunched hard on his shoulder, sending him flat to the ground. Adam shook his head as if to clear it. He turned to stare, pain and confusion evident in his gaze. "Why...why are you doing this?" Blood trickled from his temple and scratches razed his neck.

"You weren't meant to survive. You were meant to go home."

Another large rock hit Adam's skull, dropping him in place. The dirt piled higher. Adam could still draw a breath, but blood bubbled from the corner of his mouth.

The dirt pile, now with a large hollow gouged out of one side, collapsed, sending yards of dirt tumbling onto the still form below. Not satisfied yet, Texan kicked, shoved and scooped the balance of the small mound until it reformed above Adam.

His chest heaved when he finally stopped. Sweat rolled off his face and soaked his back. The summer heat sweltered, thickening the air, making it hard to breathe. Dust filled his nostrils and eyes. He bent over to regain his breath. After a couple of minutes, he turned to search the area. It was deserted.

Of course, it was.

God was on his side.

What was that old saying, ashes to ashes, dust to dust? He'd sent Adam home – where he belonged. Underground.

He smiled, a beatific reflection of the new glow surrounding his soul.

He'd passed his initiation. Now his vocation could begin. Satisfaction permeated his being. He'd found his calling.

Simple, reasonable, perfect.

CHAPTER THREE

Six months later

Kali came to a sudden stop, staring at the deserted landscape.

Dust whirled around her on scorching dry wind, adding yet another layer of filth to her face and clothing. Lord, it was hot. She lifted her hard hat to wipe the ever-present sweat from her forehead. Her nostrils flared at the smell of decomposition and despair. Moving carefully, she stepped over a broken plastic doll, its head crushed by rocks. A table leg jutted from under a cracked window half covered in construction paper depicting a hand-drawn map.

This pile of rubble had once been a small school. Now death surrounded her. A week ago, school children had laughed and played here, smiling their joy to the world. Bodies of twenty-two children had been recovered since.

Her lower lip trembled. She gripped Shiloh's harness even tighter. Children's deaths were the hardest. Especially after Mexico. Before that disaster she had been able to keep death at a distance. She might as well have been wrapped with cotton batting, protecting her, giving her space to function in the face of so much pain. Now the images of her past pulled at her, keeping her awake at night. The cotton no longer insulated or distanced her.

Everything was worse after Mexico.

Especially the Sight. Stronger, clearer, more insistent.

The instinctive pull had morphed into a knowing she couldn't ignore. It demanded her attention. Sometimes she saw dark-colored ribbons. Other days she saw shadows. There appeared to be little in the way of consistency. The only definite here was that it was changing. And whatever was happening was getting stronger.

Kali pulled her drenched t-shirt away from her breasts as sweat continued to trickle. Grabbing her water bottle, she took a healthy swig. The place had a desolate appearance with gray dust coating everything and everyone. A landslide in the Madison River Canyon had taken out part of the town center of the small community of Bralorne, Montana.

Most volunteers worked on the other side of the hastily established rescue center that served as a command post. It also served as refreshment area and medical center. She chose to search in this direction. The Sight hadn't given her an option.

Whup whup whup. The sound reached its crescendo as a helicopter crested the treetops and approached her. Drawn upward by the propeller, dirt was swept into a swirling storm that engulfed her.

"Shit." Kali dropped to a crouch, wrapping her arms around Shiloh, tucking both their heads low as the chopper passed. The dust settled slowly; still Kali stayed hunched over. Their eyes would suffer the most from the filthy air. Normally, the helicopters didn't come in so close. Her safety vest should have alerted the pilot.

Straightening, Kali reached for her water bottle again, this time pouring some into Shiloh's mouth. Carrying a recessive gene, Shiloh was an odd, long-haired crossbred in a world of short-haired Labradors. Another reason the two had bonded instantly. Both were oddities in their respective worlds.

Taking a firm hold on her frayed emotions, she tuned in to the weird energy calling her. She'd given up calling 'it' intuition. It had become so much more. Right now, the ribbons were twisting.

Dark tendrils beckoned her. She caught her breath. The murderous threads, black and violent, rustled in the space between life and death. More north. Taking several large steps forward, Kali stopped again to listen to the whispers.

Stop.

Kali bowed her head.

Facing her, lay something she found all too familiar – with a twist. A twist she'd only started to better understand since Mexico. Mexico and little Inez had provided a defining moment in her life.

The whispers spoke again – called to her. Insisted she follow them. It was rare for the Sight to be this strong, this insistent. She shifted her feet, easing the ache from standing too long. At least her heavy, steel-toed work boots grabbed the uneven ground with the solid grip of experience.

She looked around, then filled her mouth with water, to rinse away the grittiness.

Shiloh whimpered at her side. Death depressed her friend. Kali frowned, rubbing the back of her hand across her forehead. Didn't it depress everyone? Kali stroked the top of Shiloh's silky head.

"It's okay, sweetheart. We can't help him anymore, but we *can* bring him home to his family."

Him? Kali tilted her head in consideration. Yes, the victim was male. That knowledge sat confidently inside her soul. Another fact. Her intuitive hunches had become something she could count on as fact.

She didn't understand how her skills worked or why. Kali also didn't know the best way to use them or how to shut them off. She could only accept that they were there, refusing to be ignored.

Kali had morphed into a divining rod for violence – man-made violence. She had no trouble finding this victim.

And this poor man had been murdered.

***

Grant Summers leaned back against his high-backed office chair and rubbed his temple. Working for the FBI always meant tons of paperwork. On days it went smoothly, he could burrow in and dig himself out. Then there were days like today. Delay after delay. He'd yet to get anything off his desk. Instead, dozens more red-flagged problems had joined the pile. He'd be lucky to clear it before the weekend.

His stacked inbox caught his eye: Big, brown manila envelopes, too many to count; white business envelopes, too many to care; and a magazine. Now *that* he could handle. Grabbing it out of the stack, he grabbed five minutes for something unrelated to his cases.

It was the latest edition of *Technical Rescue*, compliments of his brother in Maine. Rob wanted Grant to return home and resume the type of work they'd both done once, long ago. Grant chose to stay up-to-date on the industry and the idea percolated in the back of his mind that maybe one day...

Turning to the Table of Contents, he scanned the listed articles. He paused. His breath caught and held as his fingers raced through the pages to the name that had caught his eye. To a picture in the center of the page.

Kali Jordan.

The same damned baseball that had hit him seven years ago socked him in the gut again. Time hadn't diminished her impact. His breath whooshed out on a long sigh as he feasted on the picture. Fatigue dripped from her features, dust coated her from her work boots to her hair drawn back in a no-nonsense ponytail. Obviously photographed on a disaster site, her dirty rescue vest dominated the picture. Tired, proud, Kali stood strong on a boulder, her dog at her side. A sunset colored the background.

Damn she looked good. Older, sure, but then so did he. Was her hair darker? He remembered a sun-kissed gold layer over deep rich brunette locks. And long. God, he loved long hair.

She wore a pained I'm-doing-this-for-the-cause smile. She had heart, that girl. And as he recalled, she was no media hound.

He'd first met her years ago at a conference where she'd been a guest lecturer.

He'd been fascinated. The stomach punch at the first sight of her had been illuminating. He'd been new to auras and chakras and had never understood the various terms for the different psychic abilities back then, but even he hadn't missed the emerging sensation of rightness between them.

But *she* had.

It had been hard. In his head, the rightness of it was natural, automatic. She'd been *the* one. The perfect match. The synergistic yin to his yang.

Except – she hadn't been free.

That realization had stunned him. How could anything so perfect not work out?

He shook his head at the painful memories.

For seven years he'd had that gut feeling that it wasn't over. It couldn't be over. It might not have been the right time back then, but there would come a time when it would be right. Yet what if he were wrong? Had he let life pass him by while he waited – for something that might never come?

He stared at the picture and wondered. Would that time *ever* come? He'd avoided committed relationships, always wondering...always waiting.

His cell phone rang, yanking him out of his reverie. He reached into his pocket and checked the number. Stefan. Of course. Stefan slept when he wished, painted when he wished and channeled incredibly strong psychic abilities the rest of the time.

Grant leaned back in his chair and lifted his feet to rest on top of his desk. What did his wily friend have to say today? "Hey, Stefan."

"You're wondering right now if you're going to see her."

Grant slammed his feet down on the floor as he leaned forward. "Shit. What?" He closed his eyes in frustration. His free hand pinched the bridge of his nose. Being friends with Stefan meant his mind was his friend's to read. Sometimes that became very irritating.

"But not today?" Stefan snickered.

"Oh, shut up."

"The answer is 'yes, you will. And soon.'"

Grant loosened his tie, swallowing heavily. His mind spun at the endless questions forming.

"She has the Sight but has no idea how strong she is. Ask to see her paintings."

With that cryptic statement, Stefan rang off. Grant frowned. Damn. Stefan was right ninety-nine percent of the time. What's the chance that this one time – the one time he was desperate to have Stefan be right – he was wrong?

***

Kali swallowed, her throat rasping like aged sandpaper on stone as she avoided looking at the mounds of rocks and crushed buildings around her. She was stuck in Bralorne. Hours filled with organized chaos had slipped away since she'd located the buried victim. Kali had continued to search for survivors, always keeping an eye on the crew and gathering throng. Now she'd finally allowed herself to be drawn to the drama like the rest of the crowd.

Shiloh whined. Kali tore her gaze from the heavy equipment sitting beside the open pit. The smell of death was hard to get used to – even for a dog. Knowing what it was didn't help. In fact, it almost made it worse. Still when it was your life's work, what choice did you have?

Except to wear a mask and breathe through your mouth.

Tugging once on Shiloh's bright orange lead, Kali took several steps back. The crime scene people needed more space. At least that's what she thought they were. Their white coveralls carried no labels, but proclaimed them 'official'. She was grateful they'd arrived to take over.

The crowd immediately swarmed forward to fill the gap she'd left.

"When did this crowd arrive?"

Kali twisted to face Brad. "Just after you left." She offered him a tired smile and wiped the dust from her eyes. "What took so long?"

Brad held out a tall takeout cup. "I was waiting for Jarl to show. I don't know where he took off to. That guy's a bloody ghost when he wants to be. Besides I brought this back for you. Forgive me?" He wafted the full cup under her nose. "Tall, dark and black?" The warm cup passed to her hands.

Kali moaned in delight. "Coffee. Oh, thank God. I'm so cold."

"It has to be ninety-two degrees. How can you be cold?"

With her fingers hugging the coffee, Kali blew at the steam coming through the small opening. "I'm exhausted," she admitted. "I don't seem to have much energy these days." She shot him a worried glance. "Jarl's gone missing? Again? What's with him? He's been acting different lately."

Several men jostled her, almost spilling her coffee as they made their way past.

Brad patted her shoulder and pointed to a spot away from the action. Shiloh who walked in front of them dropped and sprawled in a small patch of shade. A huge boulder provided a place to sit and enjoy their drink in relative peace. Kali sat with her legs crossed, while Brad stretched out his six-foot length. Covered in dust and both in jeans and black t-shirts – except for their bright fluorescent vests – they could have been any two tired people.

"Jarl could be struggling today. This gets to you after a while. We have to remember tomorrow is a new day."

Kali exhaled noisily, staring at the heat waves rising around them. "I don't know. We work so hard to free these poor survivors, then to have this happen?" She eased her sore body into a more comfortable position. "I don't understand how someone could do this. It's senseless."

Brad frowned. "Like what? Who? What did I miss?"

Kali motioned toward the commotion in front of them. "I don't know exactly what happened here, but remember the guy we found several days ago? Stephen? The one with the broken left arm that had been pinned between the two cement slabs?"

Brad narrowed his gaze as he considered her description. "Yeah, I remember. Construction worker or something similar. What about him, outside of the fact he's damn lucky to be alive?"

With a tight smile on her face, she said, "That's the problem. Someone decided he shouldn't be. Alive, that is."

Brad shot her a startled look. "What?"

Kali swirled her cup, watching the black brew slosh around. Brad deserved the full explanation. He'd been in on the poor guy's original rescue. "Shiloh signaled when we were walking through here a couple of hours ago."

She glanced over at him. "Heaped on one side appeared to be freshly turned dirt. I requested a crew to check it over. When we found the clothing we went into recovery mode, thinking this was a slide victim. It didn't take long to realize we were wrong."

"Wrong?" Brad frowned, a crease forming on his forehead. "What could be wrong with finding another victim?"

Kali stared up at him, the ghosts from too many disasters, accidents and deaths swirling through her mind. "This one was murdered."

**

How was the 'best of the best' now? Standing quietly, the Texan watched as Kali wandered along the temporary road, Shiloh ever at her side. His position was perfect. Close enough to keep abreast of the running conversations but far enough away to mask his interest in what was going on.

He'd orchestrated this lovely little mess, so why shouldn't he enjoy the results? After all, this was his debut. Well, his *public* debut.

People surged forward when the recovery team brought out the victim. The crowd's gasps and cries were his well-earned accolades.

Shifting his weight, he slid his hands into his dusty jeans pocket.

He hadn't realized how much he would enjoy hearing and seeing their reactions. How much he would enjoy being the only one who truly understood. How much he would enjoy being God's inside man. His stomach had roiled initially at the hands-on work, but he'd never been the squeamish type and he'd gotten over it quickly. Besides, practice had improved his technique. Less messy.

He straightened, rolling his shoulders as a sense of freedom washed over him. A heartfelt sigh gusted free. Such a difference this had made in his world. A small smile played at the corner of his lips. Life was good.

Kicking the loose dirt at his feet, he considered returning to the temporary command center, except that could mean missing something good here.

He watched Kali and Shiloh again. She'd almost reached the center. Several people stopped to talk to her as she walked. Everyone loved her. A little girl offered Kali a flower and a hug for Shiloh. He frowned with disgust. She'd been blessed with a model's body, a dancer's grace and a queen's regal air. Only he knew her now. It had taken him a bit, but he'd finally seen the light. She had no soul. How dare she defy God's plan? Shooting a dirty look in her direction, he refocused on the scene going on around him, determined to enjoy the fruits of his labor. He could bide his time. There was a natural order to everything.

Her turn would come...and soon.

CHAPTER FOUR

Four days later

Kali awoke early. She ached deep inside. A weariness, a heaviness weighed on her as she lay in bed. Now if only she could go back to sleep.

There was such joy in saving a life. She could only liken the experience to what a doctor must experience in an Emergency. When one case offers little hope - yet a miracle happens, and the patient survives. Heart-wrenching, painful, satisfying.

It was easy to understand why Brad went on a bender after some of the bad rescues. Still, it was hard enough on his wife with him racing off to disasters around the world, without adding days of wallowing in it, as well. Several others, like Jarl, used God to help them get through the pain. Other rescuers depended on the people in their closest relationships to help them heal.

Rolling over, she dropped a hand over the side of her bed, reaching until a cold nose nudged her palm. Grateful for Shiloh's presence, she stroked the dog's furry head – the two of them inseparable as always.

"Let's go for our run, Shiloh, before it gets too hot."

Shiloh's ears perked up, her head cocked to one side. She barked once.

It took a couple of minutes to change into a black tank top and matching shorts and to pull her hair into a ponytail. Running on the beach was unlike any other type of jogging. It was much harder. The first couple of times she'd thought the run would kill her. Time and practice had improved her speed and technique.

Now she loved it. She'd lived in Oregon all her life – on the coast for the last year. Now she couldn't imagine living anywhere else.

Kali and Shiloh navigated the fifty-odd steps down the cliff to the rocks and sand. Large boulders and crashing waves dominated this part of the coast. The sound of the ocean was always noisy and boisterous, adding extra energy to anyone lucky enough to be near it. Another reason for running here. No matter how little she might want to run beforehand, as soon as her feet hit the cold, moist sand they gained a will all their own to send her speeding along the waterline. Today was no different.

Shiloh barked and danced in circles, and Kali laughed. The miles churned under their feet as she dodged the tidal pools. They ran daily, when their schedule allowed. Staying fit was mandatory for rescue work. Besides, she loved the way running made her feel.

Thoughts tumbled around in her head as she looped back over several miles of beach. It was a good thing the tide was out, or she wouldn't have been able to go as far. The beach narrowed to a strip winding between the rushing water and majestic cliff face. The slope was unstable there. Made so by tumbling rocks and sand.

By the time they'd returned to the cascade of rocks below her stairs, Kali was covered in sweat. Life thrummed through her veins. She gasped for breath as she slowed to a walk and stretched her upper body.

The sun slipped behind the clouds. It gave her a brief respite from the sun and helped her cool down faster. She walked up the stairs and across the long wilderness stretch to her yard.

A small white envelope sat on her back doorstep.

She searched to see if the person who'd delivered it was still around. There was no sign of anyone. It hadn't been there when she'd left. At least she didn't think so. Wiping her sweaty hands on her shorts, she picked it up and flipped it over and back again. No return address and only her first name printed in ink on the front. Written in all capitals, it appeared more businesslike than personal.

Weird.

After unlocking the kitchen door, Kali stepped into the kitchen before ripping the envelope open. A small folded sheet of paper fell into her hand. She flicked the paper open and read aloud.

Game on
Start of round one
I hide and you seek, see
- it's simple
If you don't find them in time
- they die
So use those unholy skills
- and see
Are you really so much better
- than He?
Get ready, because it's
- Game on!

Kali dropped the letter on the table and backed away, almost stepping on Shiloh. What the hell was that? Her heart raced and it was all she could do to stay calm. She wiped her sweaty palms on her t-shirt. She studied the letter from a distance, searching for some clue to identify the sender. No signature, no letterhead, no watermark. Nothing. Reaching for the envelope again, she searched for clues she might have missed. Nothing. The note was printed in the same style as her name on the envelope, blocky hand-printed letters, only *not* all capitals this time.

Shit.

She took several deep breaths as confusion and disbelief argued with fear. Common sense righted itself. This couldn't be real. It had to be a sick joke. Giving herself another moment to calm down, Kali reread it, this time slowly, trying to analyze the words – and the meaning behind them.

What *game?* Who was going to do the hiding and what was being hidden? It sounded like a child's game. As part of her SAR work, she found people all the time. Did this person know her personally? Know of her? Know her enough to understand the type of work she did? Was the person a psycho or a sicko? Hard to tell. Best-case scenario, this was a stupid prank. Worst-case scenario...well she didn't want to go there.

That question about whether she was better than *He* made her stomach drop. They couldn't know. She closed her eyes. *Don't panic. Don't panic.*

Added to that line was the fact that the letter had been delivered to her kitchen door. Talk about scaring the crap out of her. The letter writer knew her – in ways she didn't dare contemplate. It might have been a coincidence that she hadn't been here at the time of the delivery, except she couldn't stop wondering if she'd been watched and the letter delivered after she'd left. The fine hairs on her arm stood straight. Unable to stop herself, Kali relocked the back door then ran to make sure the front door was locked too.

What the hell should she do now?

She had to inform someone. She'd never sleep again if something bad came of this and she hadn't spoken up. That it could be nothing more than a bad joke, didn't matter. Ignoring the letter and the envelope, she put on a small pot of coffee, then headed to the shower. She did some of her best thinking under hot water.

Twenty minutes later, her hair still wrapped in a towel, she walked out onto her deck and took a bracing gulp of her freshly poured java.

Kali stared blindly out at the garden, considering her options. The simplest answer was to call the police. They might come and inspect the note, take her statement and possibly make a couple of inquiries. Still, they weren't likely to do more until something else developed.

All she really had was a piece of ugly fan mail.

Great.

Or she could call Dan. In the twenty-something years since starting the Second Chance SAR Center, he'd received several threatening letters. Dan *was* the center. He was as well-known as Kali, maybe more so. Had he received a similar letter? She reached for the phone.

An hour later the sound of crunching gravel drew her to the front porch. Beside her, Shiloh stood alert, barking madly at the unfamiliar large black truck. Kali narrowed her gaze as it parked beside her Jeep. As she watched, Dan stepped down from the passenger side, waving at her. She relaxed against the doorframe.

"Hi, Kali." Dan's smile reassured her further. She waved back before turning her attention to the driver. Tall and slim, dressed in jeans and a black stretch Henley, he looked big, dangerous and vaguely familiar. Her stomach twisted. Energy stirred inside. A faint zap crackled between them. She puzzled on it as he fell into step behind Dan. The two appeared opposites. Dan had wizened into a small gnome of a man, while the larger man resonated health and purpose.

Dan gave her a quick hug. "I called an old friend for help. This is Grant Summers."

Kali welcomed them both inside. She'd known Dan a long time and couldn't remember hearing the other man's name before. Nudging the door shut, she led the way through to the deck. "Can I get anyone coffee? It's fresh."

"Always, thanks." Dan beamed.

Grant shook his head. As she walked into the kitchen to find another mug, she glanced back. Grant watched her, an odd look on his face. Kali flushed. She'd seen him before, yet more than that, her energy knew him. Did he sense it too? From where? When? Her stomach pulsed. Which was crazy – she didn't know him, yet she *knew* him.

31

The two men had taken seats at the outside table. "Here you go." Kali placed the mug in Dan's waiting hand. "Careful, it's hot."

"Thanks, Kali."

"No problem. I was ready for another cup myself." She motioned to the letter on the table at Dan's side. She'd placed it there earlier. "There it is."

Dan reached for it, when Grant interrupted, "Read without touching it – just in case."

Glancing over at Kali apologetically, Dan read the letter aloud.

When he stopped, Kali spoke, her tone wry. "It's covered in my fingerprints. Honestly, I never considered that issue."

Grant moved over to study the envelope beside the letter. "Is this the envelope it came in?"

"Yes. It has no markings either, other than my name."

He gave a short nod. A muscle in his jaw clenched and unclenched like he had a twitch.

Under lowered lashes, she studied his lean face and narrowed gaze. Jet black hair matched by imposing brows and squared high cheek bones led to a chin that said capable and strong-minded. This was not someone to cross. So still, so stern, she couldn't read him. And if she'd seen him before, surely she'd have remembered that air about him.

Yet his energy synced with hers. She didn't really know what that meant. Her energy and Dan's were comfy together. She'd always figured it was because he'd treated her as the daughter he'd never had, giving her the opening to treat him as the father she'd lost.

Grant's energy was different. Warmer. Hot. Sexual? Maybe. Except it was more than that – she recognized an instinctive surety…a knowing. She couldn't really explain of what or how. She'd never experienced this with anyone else.

He glanced up and his deep brown eyes locked onto hers. Time stopped. Energy leapt, pulsed between them. She forgot to breathe.

"Is there something wrong?"

She blinked. Heat washed over her neck and face. "Oh no, sorry. I didn't mean to stare. I thought I recognized you from somewhere." Dan looked over at her, curiously. Kali averted her face and moved to the red cedar railing where she took several bracing gulps of air. She was an idiot.

The men's conversation droned on in the background, helping her refocus on the more important issue – the letter.

Still, why had Dan brought Grant here? She spun around to study the two men. Her narrowed gaze logged the inner strength and confident air of the bigger man, then she remembered his comments on fingerprints.

"You're a Fed."

Grant and Dan both stared at her.

"What makes you think I'm FBI?" Grant asked, studying her face.

She snorted but managed to meet his gaze calmly. "Everything. It's written all over you."

Dan jumped in. "You're right. He is. After we spoke, I called him to get his take on this. We rarely get a chance to visit, so I suggested he come with me to see the letter. He's not here in any official capacity."

Pursing her lips, she leaned against the railing, her gaze traveling between the two of them. "So, what do you think?"

Glancing from the letter to her, he gave a small shrug. "Definitely personal. This could be serious – or it could be a prank."

Kali widened her gaze. "I'd figured *that* out on my own. What else can you add?"

His narrow gaze studied her. "You think this is for real?"

"I'm concerned that it *might* be," she stressed. "What if it is?"

"Then we'll deal with it. In the meantime, there's no way to be certain. I'll take the note and have it checked for fingerprints. Chances are it's clean." He motioned to the envelope. "Same for that." Glancing up, he added, "Show me where you found the letter."

Kali walked ahead of the men and through the kitchen to her back doorstep. "It was there. Resting flat on the top step."

Grant stepped over the spot and took stock of the area. "Gravel all around the house. No footprints. Cement steps, but the delivery person didn't have to step on them to drop the letter. If you didn't see the person who delivered it, and there's no other evidence where the envelope was found, then there's little we can do at this point. I can search the files for similar cases. Other than that, it's a waiting game."

Kali crossed through the kitchen to the deck, where she slumped back into her seat, baffled. "You mean there's nothing I can do?"

"I have to admit, this letter is a bit unnerving." Grant's gaze narrowed in consideration. "I'm leaning toward it being a real threat."

She choked. "That's not the answer I was hoping for."

"On the off chance that this isn't a joke gone wrong, I need to ask a few questions. If you don't mind?" Grant tilted his head, his dark compelling eyes studying her.

There it was again. That same ping of recognition. Why? Keeping her voice calm, casual, she answered, "Of course not."

"Does this letter mean anything to you? It talks about this being a game. Do you know of, or have any idea where that game idea is coming from?" At the violent shake of her head, he continued. "Rounds. Any games that have rounds? Competitions with rounds?"

Surprised, Kali glanced down at the letter. "No. I don't. Nothing about finding people is fun or playful. Most of the time the experience is horrible, depressing and full of disappointment."

"Don't think of it that way. Think of it more competitively. Back to the wording here. It says I hide and you seek. I'm presuming that is your search and rescue skills being called into play."

She shrugged. "I don't know. Probably."

"It's simple." Grant continued to read.

"The hell it is." Kali didn't see anything simple about it.

"And if you don't find them in time, they die. Not good. Who or what are *them*? And how could we find out?" He pursed his lips, studied the letter, her face, then the letter again. "Definitely a competition. Do you know anyone who is jealous of your reputation?"

"My what?" Startled, Kali glanced at Dan for help. "What reputation? And why would that matter?"

Grant explained. "I understand from Dan that you and Shiloh are considered one of the best teams in the Search and rescue field." He glanced at Dan. "That you recently received several awards and a rather large monetary gift."

She shook her head slowly. This wasn't real. It couldn't be. "I'm good, yes. So are hundreds of other teams. As far as I know, I don't have a *reputation*." Kali blinked several times, trying to clear the fog his question had created. "That money went to the center to help offset the costs from all the emergency trips. We have to pay for flights and supplies ourselves more often than not."

"You were written up in several magazine articles."

Puzzled, she glanced at Dan. "I was?"

Dan answered, "A couple of times. Once as part of the team and you've been mentioned several times in write-ups on the rescue work we do."

"Sure, but so was everyone else."

Dan shrugged, adding, "Shiloh won that contest. You were interviewed over that."

"But," she protested. "That was last year."

He wrinkled his face. "Still counts."

"I need a list and preferably a copy of articles where you or the center have been featured. We don't know what might be important here. It seems obvious that this person is jealous or thinks you undeserving of your reputation. It's almost a challenge of some sort. Prove that you are good as everyone says you are." Grant looked up at her.

"Challenge? Prove myself? That sounds so wrong." The whole concept sounded wrong. "I'm not the one saying I'm good. That's what other people say. More to boost morale than anything. The media plays up the successes at disaster sites. There's so much pain and suffering, no one wants to focus on the many losses." She hunched her shoulders, hating the influx of memories.

"I don't think it matters who said what. What matters is that this person believes what's been said. Supposedly, people are going to die if you don't participate. It sounds very personal to me."

Kali massaged the building tension at the base of her neck. This was unbelievable. "So, because he wants to make this a game, I have to play, too?" Running her fingers through her hair, she added with a touch of humor, "At least we know he's male."

Dan tilted his head, a puzzled frown between his brows. "How can you be so sure?"

Kali snorted. "This is classic male 'my penis is bigger than your penis' – the old I'm-better-than-you-are kind of male competitive behavior. The mano a mano style of competition. A shrink would get that immediately."

Grant appeared interested in his notebook again, a muscle twitching at the corner of his mouth. "I imagine one would," he admitted dryly.

With a smirk, Kali leaned back, feeling marginally more in control.

"Now according to the letter, he said you're to use your mad skills. Even more troubling is that your skills appear to be competing against God. He - written with a capitalized H - is likely to mean God and brings the possibility of a religious fanaticism in play here."

"As if he's seeing himself as God?" Dan asked, shock and disbelief in his voice. He sat there with his hand to his throat, his face pale and aged. "That doesn't sound good."

Grant nodded. "Definitely a possibility. Although he might also see himself as a messenger, a servant of God. Back to the mad skills part, does that mean anything to you, Kali?"

She swallowed hard. "I'd have to guess my search and rescue skills."

Her face froze in place. Her breath caught in her chest. This letter writer couldn't know about the Sight. No one knew. Hell, *she* didn't know much about the visions. Her stomach knotted and the band around her temple tightened with each question. Somewhere along the line it all became too much and Kali dropped into silence.

"And the worst line of all is the last one. Game on." Grant stared off in the distance. "I'd interpret that to mean whatever this is, it's *about* to start."

Dan added, "Or it has already done so and we just don't know it yet."

Kali shuddered. Shivers wracked her spine and a horrible feeling of impending doom filled her heart, boding no good for whatever was coming.

The men left soon after, taking the evidence with them.

Kali closed her eyes in relief as they walked out.

Mad skills. Surely, that was conjecture.

It had to be. Nothing else was possible.

***

As he walked to his car, Grant forced himself not to look behind him. The energy tug telling him to return to her, was hard enough to deal with. His heart made a small jump for joy.

Kali Jordan.

She'd changed. Not surprising. Life hadn't been easy on her. Maybe it was due to the circumstances or what life had dished over time – now she appeared distant. To him she looked every bit as stunning as the first time he'd seen her. She'd been addressing a large group of government employees during a training seminar. A refined beauty with a ready smile, she'd been energized about her topic, her face animated with excitement, her hands waving wildly to make her point. Passionate.

She still was, only more restrained.

Stefan had been right. Again.

She was an incredibly strong psychic but quite undeveloped. Dan hadn't mentioned *that* fact. But then, he might not know. He wasn't the most intuitive type around. Grant wasn't either. If it hadn't been for Stefan, Grant might have missed the signs telling him to look deeper.

Only Stefan *had* told him. And with that tidbit, he'd taken a deeper look using the techniques Stefan had taught him. He'd seen something that made him and his almost nonexistent skills pause. He could see her energy. Lavender and teal color waves flowed around her like a breeze. So unusual a color and so rare for him to see the energy at all, he couldn't help but enjoy the vision.

Grant started his truck then waited until Dan finished buckling his seatbelt.

"So what did you think?" Dan asked.

"I'm not sure. It *feels* ugly."

"Horrible letter."

"Does she not have a partner?" Grant glanced curiously over at Dan, who grimaced. He didn't want to let on just how badly he needed to hear this answer.

"She's a loner most of the time now. Her last long term relationship was years ago. The guy turned out to be a greedy son of a bitch. She dated for a while but nothing serious. Then something went wrong on a site in Mexico. She's been locked emotionally ever since. She won't date or socialize. Hell, she won't even have coffee with the regulars at the center anymore. Just hides away in the offices."

Grant shot a quick glance Dan's way. "Hmmm."

"Oh no. Don't think she's involved in this nasty letter business. There's no way." Dan stuck his chin out. "I'd stake my life on that. Kali lives to serve."

Grant pulled the vehicle onto the main road. "I didn't say she was. However, someone wants her to play the game – willing or not."

"We don't know that yet. I'm hoping this is a hoax."

"Time will tell."

From the corner of his eye, he could see Dan settle deeper into his seat with a heavy sigh. Grant frowned. How old was Dan now? Grant tried to remember what he knew of his father's old friend. He had to be mid-sixties at least. Could even be a decade older.

It had been a while since they'd spoken. What a way to reconnect. Kali Jordan.

He grinned. She had reacted to him... *Dare* he hope she'd remembered him? Dare he hope she'd felt the same tug he had? Dare he hope it was the right time – finally?

CHAPTER FIVE

Sleep wouldn't come. She'd gotten up once already to double-check the locks on every window and door in the house. Shiloh whined softly. Kali stroked the dog's head, helping them both to relax. Glancing at the clock, she wondered if it was too late to call Brad. Her best friend had been in and out of the town on various jobs these last few days. She didn't want to burden him with this nightmare, but she really needed to talk to him. Giving in to impulse, she dialed his number.

"Hello." The cool voice of Brad's wife always made Kali wince. Susan was iced wine, Kali was beer. Susan was a first class traveler in life, and Kali could always be found in the back with the dogs. Susan was grace, poise and perfectly turned out. Kali was jeans, t-shirts and hair pulled back in with hair scrunchie to stop it from bugging her. Sure, Kali cleaned up nice for special occasions, but she didn't start each and every day as if cameras would be following her. The two women were as different as caviar and hot dogs.

"Susan, it's Kali. Is Brad there? I need to speak with him."

There it was. That awkward drawn-out silence whenever she called lately. Kali tried to shake off the icy disdain directed her way but damn it was getting old. The two women used to be friends. Somewhere, somehow this last year that had all changed. Whether it was from Brad's extended drinking binges, Susan's wish for him to leave the industry or something else, Kali didn't know. At one time she'd tried to find out. The icy wall had been in place ever since.

At the continued silence, Kali double-checked the clock. Ten at night wasn't late, was it? "Susan?"

"He's not here, sorry."

Click.

What the hell?

Kali stared at the phone. Now she really wouldn't be able to sleep. What a bitch. She allowed herself a moment to mentally vent, then pushed Susan firmly from her mind, focusing instead on Dan's visit and his FBI buddy. Could anyone just pick up the phone and call the FBI? And she couldn't even begin to sort through the weird sense of connectedness she felt with him. Her mind tripped over the questions about the letter writer, all without answers. Time passed while she just lay there, covers up to her chest and a cup of chamomile tea sitting forgotten on the night table beside her.

A stranger could know *of* her. She wasn't proud or boastful, but she knew her name had been bandied about by those in the industry. A private person in many ways, she still attended conferences, spoke at charity events and had written various reports submitted to SAR organizations all over the world. The trust fund set up after her parents' deaths, while not huge, provided sufficiently for her modest lifestyle and allowed the money from her appearances to go to Second Chance. She worked as hard as anyone to keep the center running.

Though she wasn't famous, she was known. She sighed. Her headache slowly returned. Grant could be right. This was personal.

Her gut quivering, Kali threw off her covers, turned on a lamp and retrieved a notebook and pen from her dresser. Scrambling back under her duvet, she turned to a clean page and titled it 'Competitors.' Enemy was too strong a word.

Throwing her mind back ten years, she skipped from disaster to disaster to the odd conference, and training sessions. She wrote a list of every person who'd been mean, cutting or jealous of her. Those who had been openly antagonistic received an asterisk beside their names.

Then on a clean page she repeated the process, this time listing every person she thought was incompetent or dangerous on the scene and those she'd been forced to file complaints against.

Both lists ended up surprisingly short. She frowned and highlighted the couple of names that might be worth checking further. Several hadn't been around in years, and still others had left the industry.

Completing that task was like pulling a plug in her mind. She yawned then her eyes finally drifted closed as sleep overtook her.

Caught in a dream state, Kali walked across the remains of a cement city where buildings lay crumpled like tissue. Steel and glass littered the surface where agonized screams for help came from people buried alive, waiting for rescuers who would never come. Their screams echoed in her head. With her arms wrapped tightly around her chest, she scanned the devastation. It was too much. She couldn't help them all. Even as she stood there, the earth grumbled, sending her into an abyss opening beneath her feet. Twisted metal caught on her legs; stones tumbled on her head. She panicked as she tried to get free of the collapsing rubble. Something clamped her heart and squeezed. She flailed her arms and struggled harder. She cried out her terror.

And woke up.

Kali jerked upright, fighting against the endless darkness. Her blankets lay on the floor and the sheets tangled tightly around her legs. Her heart slammed against her ribs. A light film of sweat coated her skin. She shuddered. Her chest rose and fell as her breath gasped out into the empty room. The cool night air wafted over her already clammy skin, raising goose bumps.

"Oh, God."

Shiloh's warm furry head brushed her arm, a wet nose nudging her shoulder.

"Hello, sweetheart." Kali kicked the sheets to the bottom of the bed and swung her legs over the edge of her bed. She needed a drink of water. Sleeping pills were not an option. She hated – *hated* – drugs of any kind.

The warmth slowly filtered back into her body as she paced her room, trying to slow her racing pulse and catch her breath. Sleep was done for the night. It was three a.m. But it was morning somewhere in the world. She needed to take her mind off this mess. She needed her paints. She walked through to the second bedroom-turned-studio. A blank canvas awaited her on the easel.

She donned her favorite smock over her pajamas and grabbed her mixing board. Shiloh took up her usual position at the doorway – beyond spatter range. Kali couldn't help reaching for black and dark purple. With the brush in hand, she felt her emotions gather strength, reaching for release.

Kali drowned in the maelstrom. At her easel she experienced no hesitation, no decisions of what to create or how. Her brush moved in smooth, sure strokes. A little more here, a dab over there – her brush quickly filled in details. Somewhere along the line, she got lost in the image swirling in her brain.

Then she stopped.

Her hand hovered in mid-air, the brush ready for yet another stroke. She sagged, barely managing to stop herself from falling to the floor. She dropped her materials on the table. Without gazing at the picture, she wiped her hands on a nearby rag, removed her smock and headed back to her bedroom. Her mind felt like a bucket with a large hole in it, completely drained. The steps to her bed took forever.

Shiloh plodded slowly beside her. That was the last thing she remembered before collapsing on her bed already asleep.

***

The chime of her phone penetrated the fog inside Kali's mind. Stirring, every muscle heavy and sore, she reached for the handset.

"Kali? Are you there?" Dan's thin reedy voice gave her the shivers

"Yes. I'm here." Her voice came out scratchy, as if rusty and unused.

"There's another letter. It was on the doorstep of the center this morning. It has to be the same guy." Excitement rolled through the phone line, disturbing Kali's senses. Clearly, this drama excited Dan. He sounded almost *pleased*.

Kali frowned in dismay. "Another one? At the center? Huh?" She cleared her throat, hoping it would clear her mind. "What does it say?"

"It's simple. The first part is just two words – Game on."

Game on. Dread gripped her throat. That could only mean the game, whatever it was, had started. She'd been included, whether she liked it or not.

Something twigged. "What do you mean – the first part?"

"Yeah. The rest of it...and I sure hope you understand this...says, 'Kali's the pro. She'll know what to do.'"

"But I don't," she wailed. "Dan, I don't know what to do!"

"Well, he seems to think you do."

"Well, he's wrong," she snapped, throwing back the covers to jump out of bed. "As far as I know, he's just another of the many loose screws wandering planet Earth. Have you told Grant?"

"Yes, he's on his way in."

She strode to the bathroom, shuddering at her image in the mirror. Purple bags. "Look, I'm just out of bed. Call me if Grant has anything to add to this. I need a shower – not to mention a chance to think."

"Good idea. I'll talk to you in a few minutes."

What a mess. Again, she had to consider that someone had been watching her house. Why else would this guy take the second letter to Dan's center if he hadn't watched Dan and a stranger arrive here...and leave with the first one? Unless he wanted the center involved in his game? And Dan?

Twenty minutes later, dressed and depressed, Kali made her way to the kitchen. She fed Shiloh on the deck in the morning sunlight. Running her fingers through her shoulder-length hair, she remembered last night's painting. She headed to her studio to take a look. She'd almost reached it when apprehension washed over her.

The door was closed.

She never closed the door after painting. It wasn't good for the wet canvases. Besides, the room only had a small window, so the paint fumes built up fast. A frown wrinkled her forehead. Had she simply forgotten? She had been deadly tired last night.

Bolstering her courage, she pushed the door wide and flinched as the fumes rushed out, stinging her nostrils. "Oh gross."

Holding her breath, Kali crossed to the window, shoving it as far open as it would go. Fresh air surged into the small space. She'd love a huge studio, except painting wasn't exactly a full time career for her – no matter how much she'd like it to be. It was a release she relied on when depression and madness overcame her soul. Maybe later, when she no longer did rescue work, she could indulge her art as a creative hobby instead of as an outlet for pain and turmoil.

Walking around the easel, Kali stopped mid-stride.

The painting stood where she'd left it. With surreal and strangely enticing clarity, blacks and purples and browns popped off the canvas. Heavy paint splotched at places, then thinned and stretched across the top.

She stepped back and frowned. Up close, the heavy amount of paint applied to the canvas resembled a distorted nightmare. Not surprising. Still, she caught a glimmer of an intentional design. She tilted her head and looked at it from a different angle. Nothing changed.

Sniffing the air, Shiloh ambled into the doorway.

Kali smiled down at the dog. "Not very sweet smelling, is it?"

She glanced back at the jumble of colors and stilled. There. She studied the abstract mess, letting the colors move and form to reveal the image hidden within.

Shivers slid over her spine.

Oh my God.

No way.

Kali blinked. It was.

There was no mistaking the image of a person buried under small bushes. Civilization of some kind crouched on the horizon, with a series of rough rock formations soaring behind the bushes.

"What the hell?" she whispered.

Kali was not a great artist, by any means. Blind escapism kept bringing her back to the process because it worked. She painted with wild abandon. The paint, slapped on canvas with no thought, discharged her emotions. For some reason it always worked.

And it always looked like shit.

This, on the other hand, was ingenious. Sure the subject matter was gruesome; however, given her volunteer work, it was not unexpected. Especially after she had found the letter.

The artistic abandon was still there. The paint was so thick in spots the picture was almost three-dimensional. The terrain had depth and movement. The light was dark and terse, yet still shone with gruesome clarity – and this was way beyond her artistic abilities.

"It's fucking brilliant."

It was also scary as hell.

***

It had started. Finally. He couldn't stop beaming. And he'd learned to be a master of keeping his feelings to himself. Six months. For six months he'd been moving forward, taking tentative steps to clarify his path, bringing events into alignment and planning. Always planning. Finally, he'd reached the stage where he would deal with the abomination called Kali. She couldn't be allowed to continue with her Godless ways.

Hunkering lower into his makeshift bower on her neighbor's beachside gate entrance, he used his high-powered binoculars to keep an eye on Kali's cedar house. He had a perfect view of both the back entrance and a large chunk of the sundeck. She'd been storming in and out of the house all morning. Something was up.

He smirked. He was up.

With a quick tug, he delved in his backpack for his water bottle and the granola bars he always kept handy. He should have brought popcorn for the show.

Pushing an evergreen branch aside, he studied the road to Kali's house. She'd chosen the property for the privacy and beach access. Even better, the corner of both properties led to a pathway along the edge of the cliff. He'd have to examine those possibilities later.

The heavily wooded properties, while designed for maximum privacy, afforded him a secure blind. And one far enough away from Shiloh's incredible nose. Settling into a more comfortable position, he relaxed, prepared to wait and watch. He had time. He wanted to make sure he got this right. She was a jumping-off point – the supreme test, so to speak. If he rose to the challenge here, then he knew he could handle all of God's work – whatever that might be.

CHAPTER SIX

The small plane bucked in the heavy winds.

Kali stared out the window, happy her stomach had learned to adjust to turbulence years ago. Dark gray clouds glared back. She hated flying through storms. The lightning hadn't started...yet. Not her idea of fun.

But necessary today. An apartment building had collapsed on the outskirts of Sacramento, California. Sixty apartments lay in rubble. With the collapse occurring during the small hours of the morning meant the building had been occupied.

The only good thing about it was it took her away from the letter mess. She'd dumped it in Grant's and Dan's capable hands. Part of her felt guilty. A bigger part cried with relief that she had a viable excuse to leave.

She couldn't do anything about the game, regardless of what the author of the letter thought, but she *could* help these people in Sacramento. Her choice had been easy.

Thankfully, Grant and Dan had agreed.

Search and rescue teams were en route. Kali yawned. The call had come pre-dawn. As always, her bag and Shiloh's traveling kit both lived in the front closet, ready to go. Two and a half hours later they'd been airborne.

Several others had made the same flight, with Lauren, Brad and Todd in the back with the dogs while Jarl and Serena were up front getting briefed. The quiet in the plane was thick. They all knew what was coming. No matter how much preparation time was available, no one was ever ready.

Once they arrived on site, the first nine hours passed in a blur until she reached the end of her endurance. She was tired and dirty, dispirited. Shiloh didn't look much better. The Labrador Retriever's beautiful coat was gray with dust, her eyes sad but valiant.

"Come on girl, one more corner, then we'll take a break." That was a unique aspect of these special dogs. They were always willing to go on, always willing to give a little more. Shiloh wagged her tail and headed forward. Kali followed. They were working the far left quadrant. She'd been given the map coordinates, but her brain was too tired to remember the numbers. What she'd really love was a full bottle of water. Dust clogging her nose and throat made her eyes run.

Picking her way carefully through the debris, Kali walked on ground level. Shiloh climbed up to walk atop the closest cement block. She sniffed around the exposed area before climbing higher.

"Kali?"

The voice was faint yet insistent. Kali pivoted to find Brad calling – Lauren at his side.

"The first teams are returning. Come and get something to eat and drink."

Kali waved acknowledgement. "Shiloh, come on, girl. Break time." How many times had she said that to this brave dog over the years? Breaks didn't always happen. During huge disasters like earthquakes the rescuers slept when they could, ate when food was available and kept bottled water on hand at all times. Time was always against them.

Kali and Shiloh strolled along the cleared path to the safety zone where sheets of canvas had been set up as tents for a makeshift command center. It offered some small comfort from the hot sun and provided a steady source of water and medical aid.

Kali gave Shiloh her much deserved meal and water in the shade beside Lauren, who'd already found a spot out of the way.

Picking up muffins and coffee for herself, Kali collapsed on the ground between them. Kali studied her friend.

Lauren had aged. Weariness pulled at her dust-streaked face.

"How are you doing?" Lauren asked. Her German Shepherd, Halo, lay quietly beside her. She reached over to scratch his ruff.

"I'm okay. Just tired." Kali shifted to get more comfortable. "Shiloh's holding up well."

"At least we made it on site fast this time."

Kali studied what was left of the original structure.

This building that collapsed should have been condemned for shoddy construction. Everyone was trying to make a buck and no one wanted to put out the money to get the job done right. With the tough economic times, families were screaming to get in, glad to have shelter of any kind. Babies and children, parents and grandparents, all piled in together to save money.

Now glass shards twinkled in the sunlight, an added danger for the rescuers. Huge tents had been set up to shield the dead until they could be tagged and removed.

For Kali, one of the most difficult elements was the noise. Steel groaned under the weight of moving heavy concrete next to the workers screaming instructions. Loud wailing could be heard at the tents. A sudden crash sounded. Kali jumped to her feet, spinning around. As she watched, a loader lost a chunk of cement, adding a second crash to her frayed nerves. Rubbing her hand over the back of her neck, she shuddered and slowly resumed her place beside Lauren. Loud noises always made her jump at a disaster site, since they often meant more death and destruction.

"I'm getting too old for this shit," murmured Lauren, her eyes closed.

Kali smiled gently. In her late forties, Lauren was married with four boys – all gone from the nest. She was as sturdy and as dependable as anyone Kali had ever met. Every crisis they'd worked though, Lauren always said the same thing.

"I mean it this time." She laughed lightly and kept her eyes closed.

"Then quit. If your heart isn't here, maybe you need to be doing something else."

"Oh, my heart's here. That's not the problem." Looking older than she ever had before, Lauren lifted her water bottle for a long drink.

Kali glanced at her in concern. "Sore and tired?"

"No, I could handle that. At least I always have." Lauren shifted to a sitting position. "Not sure what it is. It's almost as if my soul says *enough*."

Kali's lips twitched. "Interesting way to put it."

"I know. I'm searching for an alternative description because it sounds nebulous, but that one feels right." Lauren sent her a sidelong glance. "How are you doing these days?"

The letter business flashed into her mind. Immediately, Kali squashed that thought. Lauren couldn't possibly know anything about it. She was asking about Kali's recovery from Mexico.

"Better. It's taking time. However, I am getting there." And she realized with surprise that today those words rang true. They weren't just a pat answer to stop others from asking personal questions. She really was on the road to recovery. She shifted back, relaxing yet a little more. Progress.

"Great." Lauren reached over and patted her knee. "You're a good person, Kali. Don't ever forget that."

A shout of excitement from the site disrupted the quiet lull. The noise was unmistakable. Rescuers had found something. Kali's energy surged and it was all she could do to stay put, not wanting to add one more person to clog up the area. Lack of coordination on these incidents was a nightmare – as were the onlookers. Desperate family members crowded for that first glimpse, and gruesome curiosity drew others close enough to see the dead. Finding survivors was a victory for all of them.

The noise continued to build into cheers and clapping.

Lauren stood, hope breaking through the fatigue on her face. "They must have found someone."

"That would be excellent. I'm tempted to go and see, but there's such a crowd now."

"Look, there are Brad and Todd."

Todd loped toward them, a huge grin on his face. His near seven-foot frame gave him a distinct advantage over the crowd. Almost a foot shorter, Brad powered along beside him. Vibrant energy beamed off them both.

"Hey, they found four people. All from the same family. Two kids, a baby and mom."

"Wow, that's fantastic." Kali hopped to her feet, giving them both a big hug. "How are they physically?"

"Cuts, bruises and possibly a broken bone or two." Brad watched the crew bringing the last of the children out. "They nearly didn't make it. Someone upstairs had to have been looking out for them." His smile dimmed.

Kali caught his change in expression and understood. Rescues missions were difficult for everyone.

"Even better," Todd said, "the kids said they heard people next door, too. So they're going to try and open up that pocket next."

Brad interjected, "That part of the building slid sideways, missing the weight of the rest collapsing on top of it. There's real hope of more survivors."

The volunteers returned to work with renewed enthusiasm. They worked long past the fall of darkness and even further – past point of exhaustion. They slept in relays. Industrial spotlights flung their weird yellow glow, magnifying shadows around every corner. By dawn, exhausted determination ruled as they forced one foot in front of the other.

Soon rescue would turn to recovery.

The building had sprawled and shifted like a sliding deck of cards, with the center of the building taking the worst damage.

The rescuers were focusing on the outer areas, where the odds of finding survivors were the greatest.

With no new survivors found since the two neighbors next to the family of four, most of the teams knew in their hearts that they were in recovery stage. Though there was always hope, there was talk of some of the teams heading home soon. After first aid checks, several of the survivors had slept out here with the rescuers, waiting, hoping that family members and friends would be found. Many were silent, frozen in place with shock and despair as the workers toiled on.

Kali tried to give them hope. She'd seen miracles happen. She never let herself forget that.

She returned to the rescue center. The local coffee shop had delivered huge urns of coffee and someone had dropped off cases of donuts, muffins and cookies. A sugar rush to boost the caffeine. Great. She had moved beyond tired and was happy to have sustenance. She'd gone from adrenaline junkie to numb endurance.

Just like Shiloh and everyone else here.

Standing beside Todd, Brad held a hot cup of coffee toward her.

Accepting it, she studied his weary face. Brad rarely missed helping out when he could. He always seemed to be one step ahead of her, anticipating her needs, her wants. She loved that about him. That he was a compassionate, sexy male with an endearing crooked grin didn't hurt either. She was just damn glad attraction hadn't gummed up their relationship. They were good friends. Best friends.

He needed to take a break. The stress and exhaustion had to be getting to him. She frowned, knowing he'd race for the closest bottle of booze when this was over.

Brad poured himself a cup of coffee before choosing a blueberry muffin. "They haven't gone into recovery mode, but it probably won't be long."

Todd stared across the huge area of destruction. "There's talk of some of us heading home soon. More equipment is coming to move the rubble. Should be here within the next hour or so."

Brad grimaced. Professional crews could handle much of the clean up along with local search and rescue crews. Almost thirty-five bodies had been recovered. Kali had no idea how many survivors were still buried. Due to the circumstances, they might never know. The building would have to be bulldozed and moved off while the authorities did their best to determine the lists of those that had and hadn't survived.

As she stood quietly enjoying her coffee, a twinge of energy bounced up her spine and latched onto the base of her brain.

Where it tugged – hard.

Kali casually looked around. Lauren spoke quietly with Brad. Todd had moved to the first aid area and appeared to be in a heavy discussion with the medics. She glanced in the other direction. The streets were full of crews and equipment, the noise deafening. Shiloh was in her crate in a tent behind Kali, sleeping. She'd worked hard these last days. Kali didn't want to disturb her unnecessarily.

Excusing herself, Kali walked away from the disaster site. The apartment had been the last building on the block. A large wooded area lay behind and to the left. A thick wall of trees started fifteen feet from the pavement, making it hard to see any deeper.

The tug happened again.

She frowned.

The tug turned to a yank.

Kali strode forward. Dark waves rolled off in the distance. Waves most other people had no idea existed.

She passed a couple standing wrapped in each other's arms. She walked by unnoticed. At the green edge, she stopped for a moment, checked her direction and walked forward a few more steps. The waves had slimmed, twisting and curling in anger, the remnants of a violent act left behind. She frowned. Hands on her hips, she pivoted in a slow circle, an ear cocked for the whispers. Ah. There.

She walked to the right about twenty feet and stopped again, searching for a physical sign, something to point to other people.

A small ravine, taken over by trees and brush, dropped in front of her. She surveyed it first, then discovering where the ground had recently been disturbed, she walked closer.

And froze. The waves of energy became more defined, separating into wide, twisting black ribbons. All centering from one spot.

Shit.

Another one.

CHAPTER SEVEN

Kali closed her eyes as different visions poured through her mind, mixing, churning into a bizarre picture of someone's life. Someone laughed, a grim smile, then the image flashed to someone else crying with pain. Bizarre colors swept through her mind. She struggled to orient herself. Sacramento. Apartment collapse. Murder.

Her nostrils flared, already smelling what Mother Nature hid. Decomposition. It took minutes of focused deep breathing before her senses returned to normal.

She wandered toward the center, her thoughts consumed with the next problem...disclosing it without anyone knowing about her talents or putting herself forward as a suspect. This required Shiloh. And maybe a witness or two.

The coffee station had emptied of people. Kali poured herself another cup of java, even though her caffeine intake had her floating already. Then she went to check on Shiloh.

As she came into view, the dog whined, her paw lifting to the wire front gate, her chocolate eyes beseeching. Perfect, Shiloh needed a walk. Time to find a witness. Kali's gaze darted in one direction then the next. Time was of the essence. There. The two women enjoying donuts at the edge of the center had stopped to talk to Shiloh this morning. Now if they cooperated, she could get this thing done.

Unlocking the cage, she hugged Shiloh, laughing as he gave her face a wash. "Let's go girl. Walk time."

Shiloh woofed and danced at her side, wagging her long plume of a tail. Kali snapped on her lead. Shiloh sobered. "Yeah, you know already don't you, sweetheart?" The two headed over where the ladies were talking quietly. The older lady, dressed all in denim, went to pet Shiloh, then stopped and looked up at Kali for permission

"Sure, you can pet her. She's not on the job now."

"She's beautiful."

Shiloh wagged her tail, her nose in the air, head tilted to one side. A perfect lady accepting her accolades.

The other woman, sporting long pigtail braids, asked, "How old is she?"

"She's seven." Kali gave the two women a friendly response. "Do you two live close by?"

They both nodded. The older lady answered. "We live a couple of blocks over. We wanted to help in some way."

Kali understood. "I'm sure everyone appreciates what you're doing."

The younger woman smiled warmly. "I'm Doris, by the way. It's been good to be able to do something. This is so horrible for the families."

"Do you want to stroll over this way a little so Shiloh can relieve herself?" Kali walked a couple of steps, still speaking with them. "In cases like this, it's the survivors I feel bad for."

The two ladies fell into step beside her, tired but happy to carry on the conversation.

"Those poor people." The older woman spoke angrily. "The apartment was supposed to be torn down in the spring, only the landlord managed to keep the matter tied up in the courts."

"The guy's just plain mean," said Doris. "We all knew people had moved into the building, but since most had lost their homes and jobs, we didn't want to make an issue of it. I'm one of the lucky ones. My husband is a policeman, so he's employed, but we have so many friends in trouble. Marian here..." She patted her friend on the shoulder. "Her husband was laid off at the beginning of this recession. He found a new job about a month ago, right?"

Marian glanced over at her friend, her face grim as she nodded once.

The conversation kept the two women busy and walking in the direction Kali needed to go. So far so good.

As they moved closer, Shiloh's ears perked up. They were at the green edge now, not far from the ravine and its grisly prize. Bending, she released Shiloh's lead and checked her working harness over again, tightening the buckle. Shiloh understood. Using hand signals she commanded Shiloh to go search.

The dog bounded into the brush. She jumped onto a fallen log before disappearing into the underbrush on the other side. Dew drops fell, splattering widely from the disruption. Birds scattered. A cacophony of beating feathers and bird cries rose to the treetops.

As the other two women continued to talk, Kali kept an ear tuned to the conversation and both eyes on the dog. Shiloh lifted her nose and went into action. It didn't take her a minute before she stopped at the exact spot in the ravine and barked several times. Then she lay down, her nose buried beneath her paws.

Both women stopped, twisting to stare into the woods.

Leaving the women, Kali hurried toward to Shiloh, stepping carefully over the underbrush and fallen wood. "I'm coming Shiloh. Hang on."

Patting the dog on the back, she whispered, "Good girl, Shiloh." Taking a treat from the pouch at her waist, she held it out. Shiloh whined, bolted the food down, then replaced her paws over her nose. She whined again. Kali kicked herself for forgetting Shiloh's teddy bear. Shiloh liked her teddy bear anytime. She *needed* it after finding cadavers.

Kali studied the area. Whoever had done this had taken advantage of the natural decline to the ravine and heavy brush, basically tumbling the bank over the body. It was a lot of dirt – many hundreds of pounds. If that person had been alive initially, they wouldn't have been for long.

"What's wrong?" Doris called. The women were curious, yet unconcerned, not understanding a working dog's signals. Not that other rescue workers would, either. Due to her special skills, Kali had been forced to create unique signals for Shiloh that could adjust to the different situations.

She glanced over at the women. "Shiloh says she's found something."

"Oh." They both ran closer.

Kali yelled, "No." She held her hands up. "Stop. Don't come any closer. We need to call the police. Do either of you have a cell phone?"

Both women immediately held up phones, shock on their faces. One phoned the rescue center and the other phoned her husband – the policeman.

***

Another successful mission and another successful experiment. Kali had failed beautifully.

Now Texan – and damn, he liked that moniker – had proof she was using unnatural skills. She had to have been to find the body this far away from the site. That had been his mistake with the Bralorne victim – he'd buried him on site where her finding the victim could have been accidental. And he couldn't have that. He'd needed a definitive answer. Now he had one. There could be no mistake here. Satisfaction permeated his soul. He'd caught her...and now she would pay.

Pleasure rippled through him. Safely tucked in the middle of the crowd, he watched as Kali sat and waited, unable to leave. The crime scene surged with waves of people. He carefully hid his smirk. Once again, she didn't appreciate the effort he'd put out for her. That was okay; this time she wasn't meant to. She would though. Eventually. They had time. It wasn't like he was going anywhere.

He studied Kali's face. Fatigue had aged her. Covered in dust, she sat hunched over, weary patience holding her upright. No longer a perfect princess.

Her night wasn't over yet either. The police were still going to want to talk to her. Again and again and again. He chortled.

Damn, he liked pissing her life down the drain.

***

Kali wondered how much longer. With the police short-staffed due to the apartment crisis, it seemed like she'd been waiting forever.

She knew the victim had been murdered. She even thought she knew how. She didn't know why or by whom. And that's where the problem stood. She'd considered volunteering more information to the police; only they were quite capable of finding out the cause of death on their own and would do it regardless of what she had to say.

She didn't understand much about these psychic tugs, except that they refused to be ignored. It wasn't as though psychic abilities came with an instruction manual.

She'd blundered along in the beginning. Visions had begun to slip into her head, sometimes of the victim's life or their death, usually vague and always as confusing as hell. Even when she wasn't on a disaster site, but sitting and watching television, the newscaster would mention a murder and Kali would receive a quick flash, a picture of the dead person. Even worse than knowing all that, was not being able to discuss it with anyone.

Her last freaky painting was a puzzle, too. So was this letter business. With any luck, Grant would solve the problem while she was away. She'd wanted to mention it to Brad but couldn't find the right moment. There'd been no time and too many ears to hear what she needed privacy to say.

Her butt had gone numb from sitting for so long. Kali sighed and shifted again. Most of the other teams had flown home. She thought she'd seen Lauren and Todd still working, but had no idea where Brad and Jarl had gotten to.

Powerful lights turned on suddenly, brightening the atmosphere. Another police cruiser arrived. Kali watched, hoping this would end her wait. An older, grizzled officer walked toward her.

"Hi, are you Kali Jordan?"

Kali straightened in relief.

"Sorry, you had to wait so long. Let me take your statement and you can go home."

The process was over in a few minutes

"Kali! Jesus, there you are."

Kali spun to find Todd running toward her, a ragged look to him. She could relate. "Hey. Am I glad to see you. I was afraid everyone had left already."

"I saw you talking with the police, what the hell happened?" he asked, concern shifting away the fatigue in his face.

Kali winced. "Just the norm. Shiloh found another body."

Todd frowned, staring in the direction of the collapsed apartment building.

"No, not here." She pointed toward the direction she'd walked away from. "Over there. I walked Shiloh over to the woods to relieve herself."

Todd shook his head. "She shouldn't have been working there."

"Nope, she shouldn't have. You know yourself that it's hard for the dogs to separate from the intensity of a disaster site and the surrounding areas. Besides, what's the chance of another body that far from the site?" She linked her arm with his. "I'm glad you're still here."

"Lauren has left and I'll be leaving soon. A couple are staying behind." He searched her face. "Can you leave now?

There's another flight in…" He glanced at his watch. "In an hour and a half."

Kali groaned. "I so want to be on it." She bent down and scratched Shiloh behind the ear. "Yeah, you're ready to head home, too, aren't you girl?" Shiloh wagged her tail and licked her hand. "Come on then. Let's pack up and get the hell home."

Straightening, she realized the night had gone quiet. If she hadn't been staring blindly in the direction she might have missed it. Murmurs wafted through the crowd, growing in volume as one of the crime scene officers carried out something large and awkward. As he placed it in the back of the van, she caught a better glimpse. Her blood ran cold.

Tucked in a clear bag, tagged as evidence, was a large metal tank of some kind – shaped almost like an oxygen tank.

CHAPTER EIGHT

Kali pulled the Jeep onto her gravel driveway, parking at the front of her house. She frowned when she noticed the dark truck parked to one side.

Grant. And a stranger.

This she didn't need. The door opened and Grant stepped out. Shiloh barked. Kali murmured to her, "I know. Bad timing, huh?"

Still, Kali had a hard time dragging her gaze away from the tight faded jeans that accentuated his muscled thighs. And the cream golf shirt stretching across his chest didn't help either. She swallowed. She might not want him here, but he was definitely eye candy.

The twinkling front bay windows of her house caught her attention. The rest of the world danced with the dawn of a new day, whereas she...she felt like shit. And probably looked it, too. She'd been gone for days and had spent the last twenty-four hours in the same dirty clothes, with her hair covered in dust and her skin gritty as sandpaper. Lovely.

The flight home from California had been postponed by a good six hours. She thought it was Friday. Her inner clock was beyond screwed. Thank God Dan had been waiting to pick her up when she'd finally made it in. She could have begged off the next step, too, except she'd been doing this for far too long to shy off work when everyone else was exhausted. Together, they'd transported gear and animals to the center for unloading in the large garage. Later, equipment would be washed and sorted...checked to see if it was safe to reuse, and kits restocked.

First, the team needed rest. Janet, a long-time volunteer and dog trainer, had sent Kali home. Her good humor had been a balm to Kali's stressed nerves.

Right now, all she wanted was sleep.

Grant strolled over as Kali let Shiloh out of the Jeep, then headed to the back for her gear.

"Good morning."

Shooting him a quick glance, she reached for her grubby travel bag. "Well, it's morning. I don't know about the good part. It's a little early for a visit, isn't it?"

He reached inside the cargo area and lifted her bags in a smooth easy motion before she had a chance to argue. She turned to face the second man and her brain stalled. Christ he was gorgeous, cool and classy, with Adonis type features. He wore black jeans and a silver knit shirt tight enough to show the rippling muscles with every movement, but not so tight as to label him a player. He nodded his head in her direction, a small smile playing on the corner of his mouth. "Good morning."

Holy shit. The warm chocolate voice rolled through her ears and down to her tummy. She couldn't pull her fascinated gaze away. She must look like an idiot.

She didn't need this. She needed rest. No matter how many male models Grant put in her path today, nothing was going to stop her from heading to her bed – alone!

Grant passed her on the way to the front door, his spine stiff, his movements clipped, bags carried easily in his hands. Sure, he hadn't been up for the most of night, she thought, disgruntled. Slamming the Jeep door shut, she made her way to her front door. If Grant wanted to ask questions, he was going to have to let her shower and eat first. Hell, no. Better to give him what he needed then collapse. Besides, what she really wanted was another look at her painting.

"Just put the gear by the back door, please. I'll clean it up later." She tossed her keys on the counter and faced him and the hunk who had walked in behind him. "I have to feed Shiloh. You have about five minutes after that before I collapse." She turned her attention to rummaging up a meal for the dog. With Shiloh happily wolfing her food down, she faced the men. "What's so important that you had to come this early? And who's your friend?"

Grant crossed his arms and leaned against the counter. "Stefan is a consultant for law enforcement. He knows about the letters. I thought he should be here to hear today's discussion first hand." He cast a glance at Stefan, then turned his gaze back to Kali. "You were part of an investigation down in California yesterday, I understand." He regarded her intently. "At the apartment collapse. Apparently you found a body."

Shit. How had he known? And so fast? Was there anything the FBI didn't know?

She turned to face him, widening her gaze in what appeared, she hoped, to be casual interest. She kept her gaze on him, refusing to be sidetracked by the mind-blowing Stefan. This time there was no mistaking Grant's assessing look. Brushing her hair back off the side of her head, Kali realized just how weary she'd become. Grant and then bed.

Her eyes widened. No, not together. She blinked as her hormones stood up and shook free of months – hell, years – of dormancy. No way. They had a hell of a nerve rearing their heads right now.

Slamming a lid on her unruly libido, she met his gaze calmly. "We found several victims. I presume you're talking about the last one that Shiloh found separate from the disaster site."

He raised one eyebrow. "Can you tell me about that, please?"

Dan had probably told him. Then again, bad news always traveled fast, and anything linked to her name probably had been flagged. It took a few moments to explain. When she fell silent, he studied her for several long seconds. Kali stared back, refusing to let this man unnerve her. Still, he was an imposing figure, causing her belly to quiver uncertainly.

"They've identified him."

"Oh, good." Exasperation crept into her voice. "Does that mean I can go to bed now?"

"He was one of the survivors from the apartment complex. And he'd been buried alive."

"Oh no!" Kali's stomach heaved and she closed her eyes briefly. "That tank. Christ. I saw a tank tagged as evidence when they loaded it into the van I didn't understand the implication." Kali's shoulders sagged, defeated by such a horror. "Why? Why would somebody do that?"

"I don't know. That's what I'm trying to find out."

"You?" She frowned. "Why you?"

"Because I wanted in on this one." He shifted casually.

"You work in California?" Kali was really confused now. Why would the FBI in Oregon be concerned about a local murder from California? "I don't understand."

Leaning forward, he pinned her with a gimlet eye. "Can't you see a potential connection between the letters and this murder?"

Kali grabbed the closest chair, sitting before she collapsed. As the realization set in, she slumped lower. Thoughts frantically rushed through her mind, only to circle around in endless loops of confusion. The letters... "No," she whispered. "I mean it's hard *not* to think of them. Still, I didn't make the connection – it's a different state."

"Understandable." He pulled out a small notebook and sat down opposite her. "So now...let's focus."

For the next half hour, Grant *questioned* her. Kali felt more like she was being interrogated. By the time he was done, she felt like a wet dishcloth hung out to dry.

Stefan never said a word. Quiet he might be – stoic he wasn't. His gaze locked onto her with unnerving intensity. She struggled to ignore him.

"Good. I think that's it. Except I need a list from you of every person you recognized in Sacramento. Dan has given me a list of everyone who went from the center."

Kali struggled as the world she thought she knew shifted again. "You think it's one of us? A rescuer?" Defeat tinged her voice.

"I think it bears reviewing. The person has to be in the know somehow. I'm going to be at the center for a week or so, posing as a visiting SAR member from Maine." He stood up and stretched.

The golf shirt pulled across his massive chest, showing every muscle. Then there were the tight-ass pants. Why was it Grant made her throat constrict and the nerves in her stomach dance? The consultant, Stefan, was better looking, with some indefinable charisma she'd never seen before.

But it was Grant that interested her.

It was Grant's energy that surged toward her whenever they were close together.

It was Grant's energy that made hers brighten.

Forcing her gaze back up to his face, she swallowed a couple of times before trusting her voice. "Are you experienced enough in this field to answer the type of questions that come up?"

Grant dropped his arms to his side. "I volunteered with my brother for years. He works out of a center in Maine. Both training and rescue work."

"Then maybe we could use you regardless of the real reason. We're always short staffed."

"Good to know. I'll be around, if you get called out again, let me know where you're going to be." Pulling a card from his wallet, he dropped it on the table beside her.

Kali's face froze. Was that the same as *don't leave town?* "I can do that," she whispered.

Something in her face caught his attention.

"Tough couple of days, huh?"

"Yeah, just a bit." Intense weariness made it hard to get up.

Stefan spoke, smooth velvet that momentarily hid the punch of his question. "How's the painting?"

She froze for the second time. "How do you know I paint?" she murmured, her heartbeat knocking so loudly against her rib bones, she was sure the men could hear.

"You just confirmed it." His gaze locked onto hers. So intense she couldn't break away. It was as if he were trying to see inside her mind. She blinked...and he broke the connection. She'd been released only because he let her go. She exhaled slowly, a fine tremor wracking her spine. It should have scared her. He should have terrified her. Instead, she understood. She didn't know if she'd passed or failed whatever test he'd administered, but she knew he'd been assessing her.

Beyond strange.

She gathered her strength and stood, stumbled slightly, catching herself on the side of the table.

Grant reached out to steady her.

Energy zinged her.

She jerked back reflexively. He frowned. She bit her bottom lip.

His hand stayed in the air before dropping to his side. He studied her quietly.

Heat flamed her cheeks. Bravely she met his gaze. "Sorry, I didn't mean that the way it looked; you startled me."

With a curt nod, he accepted her excuse and turned to walk away, a slight clip to his step.

Stefan stayed behind. She glanced at him, expecting anything but what she saw – compassion. He reached into his back pocket and pulled out his wallet. He handed her a business card. "Here's my card. You're going to want to call me."

Kali watched the two men drive away. She'd handled that badly. She hadn't been able to stop herself bolting from Grant's touch and the freakin' scary need to touch him. She couldn't explain it anymore than she could explain the need to feast her eyes on him. Attraction was one thing. This was something else yet again. She didn't want to care about anyone. Not anymore. It hurt. And she'd had enough hurt lately.

The trouble was her hormones weren't listening.

She glanced down at the card in her hand. Stefan Kronos. Consultant. Psychic Investigator.

What the hell?

***

Grant pulled onto the highway heading back into Portland. Kali lived in Sorenson, a hiccup of a town nestled between Salem and Portland. By rights it should lose its town status as it had been all but eaten up by Portland's growth. He drove seamlessly in and out of traffic, his mind caught on Kali's last comment. And her reaction to his touch. Now that had hurt. He'd only been trying to save her from a fall.

He'd felt the zing. Reveled in the energy. She'd bolted from it.

And not in a nice way. How could something that powerful *not* be right?

Damn. His hormones went into overdrive every time he thought of her. Yet when he was *with* her, he went into professional mode. Calm, quiet and dependable. Not exactly every woman's dream.

He needed her to feel the same way he did.

"She does." Stefan spoke for the first time.

Grant snorted, easing the car into the other lane. "Really? How come she couldn't take her eyes off you, then?"

"Only at first meet. She got over me pretty quickly."

The smile in Stefan's voice had Grant studying his friend's profile. Grant wanted to believe him.

"And you need to."

Staring back at the highway, Grant realized he needed lots of things, but Kali in the middle of this case wasn't one of them. Kali in his arms, Kali in his bed, or how about Kali in his life? As if.

His logical mind struggled with the whole logistics of the Sacramento murder. It would be physically challenging to pull off alone. Moving bodies required a physical strength and a level of fitness few people had. The oxygen tank added to the weirdness factor. Although Kali was in great shape, she couldn't have lifted a man the size of the Sacramento victim. If she had a partner – maybe. A partner would open the suspect pool to include almost anyone. Something else to talk to the profilers about.

Working with Kali on this case would be like diving into a game of 'hide and go seek' with the devil. Finding buried victims was going to be a challenge. She needed to stay strong. If the press found out about this...not fun. And with her undeveloped psychic power... He knew all too well what happened to people who couldn't control that. Most of them ended up in mental institutions or committing suicide.

Stefan could help her.

"I left her my card. She needs a bit of time."

He would have to watch how she handled this mess.

"You're in trouble here. With her."

"How bad?" Grant couldn't *not* ask.

"Bad." Stefan leaned his head back against the headrest and closed his eyes. "She's very powerful. Untrained, not in control and her system surges with physic awareness."

"That's not necessarily bad, though, is it?" he asked cautiously.

As if almost asleep, Stefan murmured, "No, not bad. Except she's keeping secrets."

＊＊

Once awake, Kali lay still for a long time. The last few days had finally caught up with her. Shiloh snuffled and rolled over beside her. "Hey girl. You're as whupped as I am, huh."

Maybe it was time to quit. What had Lauren said? 'It's almost as if my soul says enough.' Kali had to admit a part of her felt the same way. She hadn't handled this last mission very well and finding a murder victim definitely added a nasty ending.

She rolled over and checked her clock. Noon. Kali yawned and stretched. Shiloh stretched her paws across the pillows, burying her nose against the blanket. A lady in all ways. Kali laughed. Not.

She hopped out of the bed, opened the glass doors for Shiloh in case she needed to go out. Having an upper deck with direct access to the backyard was a nice feature to the house. So was having a doggy door in the laundry room. Shiloh could take care of her own needs while Kali slept. Enjoying the clear blue sky for a brief moment, Kali walked inside to shower. By the time she finished getting dressed in cotton capris and camisole shirt, Shiloh had joined her. The two trooped into the kitchen, feeling rested and more ready to take on the day. Hopefully without the letter writer's interference. She didn't dare call him a stalker – even in her mind. That sounded more ominous than she could deal with.

Kali stopped. Energy pulsed from outside her kitchen. Someone sat on her deck, someone in a black suit. Grant. Again.

Shit. Her stomach jumped, her aura pulsed in welcome. *What the hell?* She so didn't need this. Or want this.

And if she kept repeating that, she might actually believe it.

What could he possibly need now? She opened the French doors and stepped into the afternoon sun.

He immediately stood and faced her. Grim lines etched his face.

Her stomach sank.

"Hello. Sorry if I kept you waiting. I gather you forgot to ask me something this morning?" She yawned as the fresh air caught her. "You could have just called, you know." She stretched. "I feel so much better. It's amazing what a little sleep can do."

A quizzical look came over his face. "So you should." He studied her expression. "I didn't come this morning, I was here yesterday. It's Saturday."

Kali stared at him in shock. "No way. I only slept for a couple of hours, at most."

"No, you slept all day and all night. I was here yesterday," he said firmly.

Her stomach growled. Maybe she *had* missed three meals. She spun on her heels and turned on her laptop. She put on a pot of coffee while the machine booted up. When done, she checked the date. Damn. No wonder she felt good.

Grant stood in the open door. "Do you believe me now?"

"I guess I needed more rest than I thought." She shrugged dismissively, brushing past him to cross the deck. "I can't say I'm surprised. These last few days were pretty hellish." Kali walked over to the railing to stare out at her half-wild yard – so different from the dust and grayness of the Sacramento site. She took a deep breath, loving the musky scent of the evergreens, warm and heavy from the hot sun. It was good to be home.

She turned to him. "Will you have coffee? It should be ready soon."

"Sure. Thanks."

Returning with two cups, she held his out. "I seem to be doing this a lot. So, tell me, now that we have the social niceties out of the way, why are you here this time?"

"Dan received another letter."

Kali's stomach clenched. Suddenly she didn't feel quite so well. Carefully placing her mug on the table, she returned to the railing, trying to find balance in the craziness. Turning to face him, she leaned back against the wood and narrowed her gaze at him. "Why Dan again, I wonder?" She winced. "Not that I want the letters here. Believe me, I'm happy to put some distance between them and me."

He glanced at his mug and back up at her. "That's not going to happen. And the most likely reason for delivering the letter to Dan is that the writer knew either you wouldn't be here to receive it or that you wouldn't be awake in time to find it." He took a sip of coffee. "Or maybe he's trying to discredit the center. Or directing the suspicion toward it and away from something else? We don't *know* anything at this point."

Kali rubbed her temple. God, what a horrible thought. "So many people would have known I was out of town. Also, anyone could have watched the house and seen me come home and collapse. And that's just creepy." Shivers rippled over her spine. That had 'stalker' written all over it. She tried to refocus. "Putting that aside for the moment, what did this message say?"

"It said, 'First round to me. Round two begins soon.'"

Kali's knees buckled. Grant hastened over to steady her, his arm curving around her back. "Easy, Kali. Take it easy."

She leaned into him, welcoming something solid to grab onto in a world that had suddenly shifted. Flashes of color flared, sparked between them. She blinked. Embarrassed and more than a little stunned, she pulled away and retreated to the closest chair.

Yesterday she'd pulled away. Today she'd leaned in, then pulled away. She was an idiot. Talk about sending mixed signals. Grant was still speaking.

"I'm sorry. There was no easy way to tell you." He studied her face intently.

She shook her head, a broken laugh escaping. "It doesn't matter. I would feel this way regardless."

"Maybe."

She considered his strong face. She'd thought he had brown eyes. Right now, they looked as black as the dead of night. She swallowed and leaned back. Grant straightened. He walked away for a moment, then came back.

"Have a drink of coffee. It will make you feel better."

She stared blankly at him. "Coffee?"

He held out her cup. "Here, drink. Do you have any brandy?"

"Brandy? Uh no, I don't think so." Kali accepted the cup, then closed her eyes briefly and took a deep breath. She needed to get a grip. "I'll be fine. I just need a minute."

Grant took a seat beside her, his cup of coffee in hand.

It took a few minutes before she trusted herself to speak again. "One more time, what did the letter say?"

Slowly, Grant enunciated, "First round to me. Round two begins soon."

She shuddered.

"Do you think the victim in Sacramento was his first?"

He studied her face. "I don't know. The timing, situation, people involved could all work. However, it's too early to be sure." Turning to look up at the bright sky, he added, "It's also possible there's a different victim. One we haven't found yet."

Another victim? Christ, weren't there enough already? "I can't even begin to contemplate that scenario." She struggled to reason through the message. She'd been so happy to put this from her mind. No longer. "So, if – and it's a big if – this first victim were the Sacramento victim, it would mean the killer was there when I was there – or close by."

"And possibly for the same reason you were – only he had a hidden agenda. So the question remaining now is who was there with you? Any chance you wrote that list of everyone you recognized there, did you?"

"No, I went to bed right away." She sighed. "You said Dan wrote you a list of the workers who went from our center. Besides, those people, there were teams from other regions. And the many volunteers who weren't SARs." She took a sip of hot coffee, hoping it would warm the block of ice forming in the pit of her stomach. "Overall, there would have been more than a hundred people involved. Tracking them would be next to impossible. Besides, anyone could have flown there and done this. We weren't all that far away from home. Honestly, someone could have driven there and back in the time I was stuck there."

Heavy silence settled between them. Kali couldn't even begin to understand the mindset of someone who could do something like that. Why? She certainly had trouble with the center being targeted, but that someone had involved her in this nastiness...well it didn't make sense.

"Think carefully. Do you know anyone who could do this?"

A strangled laugh escaped. "What a horrible thought." She stared up at the sky. "I started *a* list after I gave you the first letter. I have to tell you, everyone on it is ridiculously normal."

Grant stared at her soberly for a long moment. "So were the worst killers in history."

Frustration boiled deep inside. It festered, turning her stomach sour. "Why is he doing this?" she whispered. "What does he want?"

Grant laid a soothing hand on hers, squeezing gently. Sparks flashed. Amazed, she watched them spark and then become absorbed into both their auras. Why? She couldn't begin to understand the timing for this new awareness. So much in her life was screwed up – and all at the same time – making everything hard to sort through...and even harder to understand. Acceptance was a long way off.

She released her death grip on the armrest, her knuckles pasty white already. She sighed, relaxing her shoulders. Her stomach burned with remnants of the revulsion slivering through her.

"What matters is that you realize and accept that this is happening. And..." he paused mid-thought, stretching out his long legs. "He knows you very well, which means you know him, too."

That scared the crap out of her. She liked normal. She liked predictable. She liked routine.

She sure as hell didn't like killers who issued challenges. She hopped to her feet.

"I'll be right back." She strode to her bedroom to retrieve her notebook. As she returned, she handed it to him.

"What's this?"

She picked up her cup and walked back into the kitchen, continuing to talk. He followed. "My lists. I tried to think of any known associates that might have a problem with me." She hitched a shoulder. "I don't know how well I did."

He flipped through the pages. "This gives us a place to start. If you think of anything else, call me."

"I will. Is there...anything else I can do?"

"Possibly. We're forming a small task force that will coordinate with several different local law enforcement agencies. The FBI is working with the Sacramento Police to process the evidence from this latest murder. Time is in short supply. We need to know everything we can before he strikes again. Therefore, we need to know what you know."

"Except, I don't know anything." Kali closed her eyes briefly. "I wish there was a way to predict his next victim...and why he would choose a particular person."

Grant loosened his tie. "There isn't yet. We'll know more once we plow through the material we've collected. Then we'll have to wait. For forensic information. For autopsy results. For the handwriting analysis. For a profile." He stood. "If I need anything else, I'll give you a call. Do I need to remind you to lock your doors, watch out for strange cars and keep your cell phone handy?"

She winced. "I will. Thanks."

The house felt empty after he left. Empty. Cold. A chill had settled into her soul. Her stomach growled, again. Kali opened the fridge and rummaged for anything that hadn't spoiled. Something wrinkled and brown sagged in one corner and something blue in the other. Lovely. Shiloh barked once.

"You're hungry too, aren't you girl. We both lost a few meals." Kali opened cupboard doors. "Yours is easy enough." She would prefer to feed Shiloh a raw food diet, but the constant traveling and rough conditions made that impossible. Kali opened a can of food and portioned out crunchies to go with it. Putting them together, she gave the mix a good stir before offering it to Shiloh. "There you go, sweetheart. I added a little extra to help with those sore muscles."

Rummaging for ingredients, she rustled up a quick cheese omelet and toast. She'd have to go shopping before she could eat again. Taking her plate outside, Kali sat in the sun and slowly ate her first real meal in days.

Knowing the letter writer might be watching her even now, she tossed her hair back, and took another bite. She refused to let the thought of him drive her away from the simple joy of being home and sitting on her deck. That didn't make her stupid. Her cell phone sat beside her coffee cup.

She sighed and leaned back, grateful to be home.

People were funny. She'd seen what people called 'home' all over the world. Some were gorgeous million-dollar houses on the ocean with private waterfalls and their own airstrips. Most often the homes were commonplace – four walls and a roof with a middle class family trying to make a living and enjoy life while they were doing it. Then there were the rest. The smile slid from her face. She'd seen cardboard boxes sheltering complete families. She'd seen platforms with big leaves for walls and she'd seen dugouts into the sides of hills that held multiple families. In every case, the shelter meant just as much to those people as the million-dollar homes did to their owners. Usually more.

A shelter represented home, security and a place to call their own.

When Mother Nature destroyed homes, she didn't discriminate. They all fell to her will.

Disturbed by the sad memories, Kali took her empty dishes to the sink. In a few quick seconds, she had the kitchen clean. Drying the last dish, she paused.

The painting.

She'd forgotten about it.

Finishing up quickly, she walked down the hallway. The door was closed again. She couldn't remember if she'd left it that way or not. Damn she hated the shakiness that slithered through her.

Stupid. She pushed it open and strode in.

Christ.

Power streamed toward her, waves pouring off the canvas. The force of it stopped her in her tracks. Determined, she stepped forward a couple of steps. She frowned. No way. She leaned closer. She studied the detail, the accuracy, the emotion. The life. She shook her head. No. It wasn't possible. Digging into her memory, she compared those images with the painting. She blinked several times. There could be no doubt. Grim foreboding slipped down her spine.

The picture took on a new ugliness.

The panicked finger marks scraped into the dirt wall, as if the victim had tried to dig his way out, hadn't looked odd before. She'd seen this countless times. It was a natural reaction for anyone buried in rubble.

No, it was the tiny cylinder tucked into the image that made her blood run cold. As did the faint tube running to the victim's nose.

There could be no doubt.

The person in the painting had been buried alive – intentionally.

Kali knew there were too many similarities to discount, regardless of how ludicrous. The painting, the scene with a dead body and the oxygen tank, depicted the murder victim she'd just found in California. Not a similar scene but that same one.

Kali lifted a hand to her aching temples. That meant she'd painted this before the murder had happened. Wait. She thought about that for a moment. Was that right? Did she know when that poor man had been buried? No. Grant hadn't offered a time of death or a time line of any kind.

One thing she did know was that this painting would be hard to explain, particularly if anyone knew when she'd created it. On impulse, she bent forward to check something else. No, there was her signature.

So, she'd actually created this. Now if only she knew how? And what should she do about it?

CHAPTER NINE

Kali avoided the center on Saturdays, if she could. Today, Dan had called asking if she could come in to help with the accounts. He'd been snowed under since Sacramento and as usual, his bookkeeping had gotten out of hand. The parking lot was half-full when she arrived. With mixed emotions, she parked at the front by the stairs. Chaos reigned outside the building, making her tired and energized at the same time. Dogs could be seen and heard everywhere. And that was comforting. Normal.

In a way, this really was home.

Shiloh barked and bounced from side to side in the back. Kali opened the door of her Jeep. Gathering the leash and her purse, she walked toward the front door.

"Hi, Kali."

Elizabeth, a regular visitor at the center, stood at the top of the stairs with a tongue-lolling Newfoundland pup slouching against her leg.

"Hi, Elizabeth. This place is chaos today."

Elizabeth laughed. "That's Dan's doing. He organized weekend training classes for those of us that work. I signed up Jefferson." Elizabeth motioned to the dog at her side.

"Hey, Jefferson, when are you going to grow into those feet?" Kali grinned, then couldn't resist bending down and hugging the beautiful teddy bear. Jefferson took immediate advantage, swiping her face with his huge tongue. Kali laughed and used her sleeve to dry her face. "How did he do?"

Elizabeth winced. "He's the biggest suck of the class. Does anything for a cuddle and remembers none of the lesson five minutes later."

Kali grinned. She could just imagine. "Have you seen Dan?" she asked, her hand scrubbing Jefferson's thick black ruff.

"Nope. I think he's hiding. Starting these extra classes has ruined his peace and quiet." Elizabeth tugged on the dog's collar. "Let's go home. It's good to see you, Kali. Take care."

"You, too." Kali watched Elizabeth coax the Newfoundland toward her van, before she turned and walked into the center. She greeted several other people on her way. Dan would be in his office. She knew he preferred the old days when the center was more about rescues and less about dogs. He often forgot that he hadn't built a business, he'd built a community. People came to socialize – themselves and their dogs.

She appreciated his call today. Helping out should keep her mind off the damn letter writer. A win-win situation.

At the open doorway to Dan's office, she watched him stare at reams of paper in his hands. Wrinkles creased his brow; a brown color tinged his jowls. He looked unhealthy. Her heart lurched. She wasn't ready to lose him. He'd been a mainstay of her life for years now. She couldn't image life without him.

"Hey, Dan. Nice trick if you can manage it."

Her absent-minded friend lifted his head, confusion clouding his face. It cleared almost instantly. "Oh, hi, Kali. Thanks for coming. What was that about a trick?" He ran his fingers through his hair, making it stick out at odd angles.

Kali sat on the spare chair, Shiloh at her feet. "Hiding in your office. What's the matter? The center too full for you right now?"

His sheepish grin slid free, brightening her spirits. "You could say that. It's crazy out there. We've got obedience classes going on right now. I used to enjoy Saturdays. I enjoyed the center more when it was smaller, too." He dropped his pencil and leaned back. "You had a rough go this time, I hear. And made the headlines again with the Sacramento disaster." At her grimace, he added, "But then, what else is new, right?"

Dan fixed his gaze on her as if wanting to say something else. His eyes were piercing, yet sad. The salt and pepper hair that she remembered had turned to snow white. The wrinkles of his face sagged, reminding her of a topographical map. Every job he'd worked had contributed to those heavy lines. This man had heart. He'd spent a fortune of his own money helping others and keeping the center going. Mostly, the center survived on government grants, contracts, training classes and private donations.

Instinct prodded her to look closer. Something deeper was going on. She waited for him to continue.

"You know, I've seen some nasty sites in my time. I've also learned more than I'd like about what one person can do to another. This letter business..."

Kali winced. She so didn't want to go there if she could help it. "That mess is bad news; I know." She hesitated. "Is something else bothering you?"

Dan wrinkled his forehead, a heavy sigh escaping. "It's probably nothing. Not like he hasn't done it before. Brad still hasn't reported in from Sacramento. He shipped Sergeant home that last night, isn't answering his phone and he hasn't been seen since. Susan's called several times already today."

"Oh no. Not again." Kali didn't know what to think. Brad often disappeared for a day or two, particularly after a bad disaster; still it was rare for him to let Sergeant travel alone. "If he's gone on a bender, he wouldn't normally check in for several days."

Brad's drinking binges often lasted three to four days. His wife hated them and usually called his friends to see if he'd bunked on their couches. Susan hadn't called her yet. Apparently they weren't friends anymore. Truthfully, Kali couldn't remember if she'd checked her messages when she woke up. Grant's visit had thrown off her routine.

"I wouldn't worry yet." Kali injected hope into her voice.

"You're right. We'll give him a day or two to check in." Dan's face lightened, the wrinkles eased as a happier look appeared on his face.

"Let me know when he calls." Shiloh nudged her hand and Kali refocused for a moment on her furry friend. Shiloh always knew when she was upset. "I'll worry until I know he's okay."

"Me, too." Dan's fingers played restlessly with the stack of papers in his hand. When he looked up at her, the dread revealed in his eyes shook her. "I don't know, Kali. I'm not sure what's going on, but I've got a bad feeling about this."

So had she. That didn't change anything.

***

The kitchen door lock snicked open. Kali had been gone for hours. She'd probably gone to the center again. He knew he could be cutting it close, but he'd wanted to deliver his gift in person.

Careful, he placed the plate on the table and tucked the note half inside the wrapping. His gift stood out like a centerpiece. She couldn't miss it.

Perfect.

Backtracking to the door, he stopped. Her car lights would be visible well before reaching the house. He'd have lots of time to get away. What could it hurt to look around?

Decision made, he headed straight upstairs to her bedroom. He opened her dresser drawers, neat stacks of cotton underwear lay inside, his black gloves a strong contrast to the pristine whiteness. The need to touch the smooth cotton was a temptation he couldn't afford. Slamming the drawer shut, he opened the next and the next. He moved toward the large closet, examining clothes and shoes layered inside. Only then did he allow himself to focus on her bed.

He sighed. A cream duvet covered the chocolate sheets, with one corner turned back as if in invitation. As if. He forced himself back, angry as lust twisted against his purpose. She was the devil's tool, and the sooner he proved it to the world, the better they'd all be.

He walked downstairs, determined to erase the intimate picture of her bedroom from his mind. He cast a quick glance at the plain but comfortable living room with several arm chairs and couches arranged around the well-used fireplace before heading down the hall. He passed the laundry room and main bathroom. The next door was closed. Curious, he pushed it open.

A studio? She painted?

Her easel stood in the middle of the room, a sheet tossed over the top. Unable to resist, he walked over and lifted the sheet.

And jumped back.

He hissed his fury. Witch. Evil spawn.

Control, cold and clinical, returned his focus. He had to study her work – to know his enemy.

And that knowledge sealed her fate.

***

Kali enjoyed bookkeeping. Seeing the overall picture of the financial state of the center, stable and growing, gave her such a great feeling. She was part of something good, worthwhile. And she needed the distraction now. She couldn't get Brad out of her mind. She'd tried to call Susan several times, only she wasn't picking up. Kali had left messages. Susan hadn't returned her calls.

She thought about the teams she'd met in Sacramento. Her industry was relatively small and the dogs and handlers, well known. Who could have stayed behind and worked with Brad? It took her a few moments, then it hit her. Jarl.

Pulling out her cell phone, she dialed his number. No answer. She left a message. She hoped he'd call her back. Their ten-year friendship had hit the rocks late last year when she realized he'd been pilfering little things from the center. He'd stopped after she'd confronted him about it. Their friendship had taken a hit for a while. Still, things were cordial now.

Kali picked up a receipt, read it and placed it down on a pile. She snatched it up again, reread it and placed it on a different pile. She needed to get a grip or she'd really make a worse mess of the accounting than Dan.

Her mind refused to let go. Someone was killing people. Could Brad have somehow run afoul of this killer? She closed her eyes. Please don't let him have been a victim of this killer. She didn't even want to think about Jarl in the same light. That he hadn't returned her calls yet, surely didn't mean he'd been kidnapped, too. This nightmare was making her crazy.

No. Brad had to be drowning his sorrows. Like the last time and the time before. He'd check in soon.

Determined to complete the job, she reached for another handful of paper. This load had phone bills mixed in with several crumpled restaurant receipts. One for take-out Chinese food. Burger King. Stamps and envelopes. Kali groaned. Damn, Dan had entered the last batch of figures. That usually meant she had to review all his postings. Another hour of trying to read his writing. Honestly, he shouldn't be allowed close to the bookkeeping.

"Kali, good to see you." Janet stood at the doorway a big cheery grin on her face.

"Janet." Kali threw her pencil down on the desk in relief. Any interruption was welcome at this point. "Hey, thanks for finishing the cleanup from the last trip. I appreciate it."

"No problem. You were exhausted and I was glad to help," Janet said, leaning her tall willowy frame against the wall. "Besides, Brenda was hanging around, so I put her to work, too."

Kali rolled her eyes at the thought of her cute bouncy friend being put to work by Janet. Brenda loved to help out – for a little while. She wasn't great on sticking around. Janet, on the other hand, was one of those rare individuals who could see what needed to be done and then do it.

Janet's happiness seemed so genuine. If only Kali knew her secret. Janet was like a breath of fresh air and her light-hearted laughter was just what Kali needed right now. "Still smiling I see."

"Of course. Life is too short for anything else."

Kali avoided that topic. It was easier to present a front of peaceful contentment than to open up about the unsettled emotions chewing up her insides. Life was too short. And she had too much death in hers, as it was.

"What are you doing today?"

"The new guy is helping me this afternoon. He worked at the Maine center years ago. He does have a magical touch with the dogs. If he works out and stays around, we should consider hiring him as an instructor."

Kali blinked. New instructor? Maine? Jesus, Janet was talking about Grant.

Janet glanced behind her to see if anyone was close enough to hear, before she stepped further into the office. "Did you see him? Oh, my God." Her eyes gleamed with humor, her voice a conspiratorial whisper. "He's stunning. That tall-dark-and-take-charge look always does it for me." The tall redhead fanned herself and rolled her eyes, a huge grin on her face.

Kali sat back and watched her as-good-as-married friend rhapsodize over Grant. Kali didn't dare voice her opinion. She'd give herself away, for sure. Besides, she didn't need to say anything. Janet was right. Grant was stunning. And a little unnerving. "That good, huh?"

"Oh yeah, that good." Janet looked furtively behind her again. "Not only that, he's going to be here full-time." Her face split in huge smirk. "I'm about to volunteer every day."

"So much for Dennis." Dennis was Janet's police officer boyfriend. They were perfect together. Both would do anything for a person in need.

"Maybe not. Dennis wouldn't mind if I played a little." Mischief lit up her deep brown eyes. "I won't ask him about it, though. I'll just go ahead and snag this guy. Maybe, we'll have a threesome."

There was no help for it. Kali laughed. The thought of Dennis letting anyone close to Janet was comical. He was loving, possessive and never let her out of his sight when he was off duty. Even on duty, he called her several times a day. "I can't imagine Dennis with another guy."

"Well, I'd be in the middle of course. So technically, it wouldn't be Dennis with another guy." She jutted out one hip in an exaggerated imitation of deep thinking. "This has possibilities. Hmmm."

"Jeez, woman. How am I going to get any work done with you putting those damn images in my mind?"

"You need to laugh more often. You're serious these days. As if the weight of the world is on your shoulders. You need some fun in your life." She grinned. "Jesus, I bet you haven't been laid in months."

Like she needed thoughts of Grant rolling around in bed mixed up with her bookkeeping. Kali narrowed her gaze. "Like I'd tell you. You'd just post it on the bulletin board."

"How about I post a job ad for someone to apply for the position?" Janet wiggled her eyebrows rapidly, sending Kali into fits of laughter.

"What ad are you looking to post, Janet?" Dan had arrived, unnoticed, behind her and stood in the doorway.

Janet half choked. "Nothing, Dan. I'm just hassling Kali."

"That you are," declared Kali. Energy hummed into the room. Grant. She didn't need to see him to know Grant stood behind Dan. A lightness she was starting to recognize and respond to filled her.

"I brought someone for Kali to meet." Dan looked expectantly at Janet.

Janet took the hint gracefully. "I'm heading out. I'll talk to you later, Kali." Smiling coyly at Grant, she sidled past the two men and left.

Dan moved inside the office, whispering, "I wanted you to know Grant's going to be—" He looked behind him and dropped his voice further. "You know...around."

Kali barely withheld her smile. If it weren't for the deep worry lines on Dan's face, she'd almost think he was enjoying the cloak and dagger event. As much as she hated the reason for it, it was good to see the normally frail man energized by something.

Studying Grant's casual jeans and a white Henley, she could see he'd fit in perfectly as their new instructor. He didn't need power suits like he'd had on this morning – power radiated off him. His persona came across as large and in charge. Comforting. And attractive.

Power had a seductiveness few women could ignore. "Hi, Grant. Welcome."

He studied her face intently before nodding as if satisfied at something. "Thanks. By the way do you help out with the classes?"

Kali looked over at Dan. "Sometimes. If I'm needed. It's not what I've been doing lately, but I've taught in the past. Why?"

"Just wondered how many people know you well and how many might know of you?"

She groaned. "You're after another list of names, aren't you?"

He tilted his head in acknowledgement.

Kali reached for her bag and the list she'd started. "This list is those people I could remember seeing in Sacramento, I put an asterisk beside those that that aren't fans of mine and vice versa."

"Everyone loves you." Dan was nothing if not loyal.

A half laugh escaped. Kali shook her head. "If only that were true. You know perfectly well that some people resent me."

"They just don't understand."

It was Kali's turn to nod.

"Don't understand what?"

Both Dan and Kali looked at Grant, surprised at his question. Dan looked over at Kali. "Does he know?"

She wrinkled her nose at him. "I'd have thought so at this point."

Dan turned to face Grant. "Kali is financially independent. Some small minds would like to blame her success on her wealth. You know, she can afford better equipment, do more advanced training. Things like that." He straightened his back. "I, for one, would be lost without her help."

Grant studied her for a long moment.

Kali flushed and stared at the stacks of papers piled high in front of her.

"Has anyone ever said anything about it to you?"

Startled, Kali looked up at him. "Pardon?"

Pulling out his notebook, Grant asked, "Has there been anything more than usual grumbling. Like arguments? Threats?"

Kali and Dan exchanged looks. "No. At least none I know about." She looked over at Dan. "Have there?"

He shook his head vigorously, sending tuffs of hair flying in all directions. "No, I don't think so."

"Okay, but if you do remember anything let me know."

"Will do." She waved toward the stacks of paper on the desk. "Dan, this is the biggest mess yet."

"I'm sorry. I tried to stay on top of it, but...it ran away from me."

"Yeah." Kali groaned. "It always does. Take off, you two. I've got work to do."

The men left.

The soft hum of warm energy hung in the air. Reminding her. Teasing her.

Did she really want to open her heart again?

And was it already too late?

CHAPTER TEN

Kali worked on the accounts late into the evening with Shiloh sprawled at her feet. Dan had tried to send her home at one point. She told him she'd rather finish than come back tomorrow.

When she finally locked up, the sun had set and the intense summer heat had dissipated slightly – a welcome relief from the stuffiness of the office. Shiloh perked up in the fresh air. She explored the brush and pranced through the cool grass.

"It's past time to go home, isn't it?"

Kali yawned as she unlocked her Jeep, holding the door open for Shiloh to jump into the back seat. As she threw her purse to the passenger side, a rustling noise sounded by the trees to the left of the front stairs. She spun around. Jesus. Her heart pounded as she searched the deepening shadows. "Hello?"

The outside light from the center cast a yellow glow that barely reached the edge of the parking lot. A half whine, half growl slid from Shiloh's throat. With a last nervous glance, Kali scrambled into the front seat. "Let's go home, Shiloh."

Cranking the engine, Kali locked the doors and peered through the tinted window. Nothing. The eerie sensation of being watched would not dissipate. Kali left the parking lot and drove toward home. She kept one eye trained on the rearview mirror. She didn't think she was being followed...yet couldn't shake the sensation she was.

Uneasy enough to not want to go to an empty house, she drove instead to a late-night coffee shop at the mall and parked close to the patio seating. Kali clipped Shiloh's leash on and walked to the takeout window before choosing a seat close to her vehicle. Hating that she'd let a simple noise unnerve so badly, Kali hugged her latte and tried to unwind. Several tables were full. A couple of teenagers sat off to one side, heaps of whipping cream topping their concoctions. A man sat at another table with an open laptop, working diligently on something.

"Kali?" someone called, startling her. "Wow, I haven't seen you in a long time."

Squinting into the gloom beyond the cafe lights, she finally recognized the speaker. "Jim. How are you?" Kali was happy to see anyone she knew right now, even a stocky, fun-loving, very ex-boyfriend. She thought he'd gone north to work on the oil rigs. "I haven't seen you for a couple of years. How are you?" She motioned to the empty seat. "Join me."

"I've only been back in town a couple of months." He grinned down at her, spinning a chair around backwards and straddling it. Dressed in jeans and a lightweight plaid shirt, he looked like he had filled out some since she'd seen him last.

"That's great. I'm sure your mom is delighted to have you home." She watched as Shiloh greeted Jim like the old friend he was, before sprawling at her feet again. Kali relaxed some herself. Jim was safe. He could never be the letter writer.

As soon as the thought crossed her mind, she questioned it. Did she know that for sure? How? Jim could have changed. For that matter, how well had she known him to begin with? They'd had a hell of a fight before they split. A fight that hadn't been easy to resolve. Kali had bolted from the fight, from the relationship, from him. Then again, that had been years ago. And their relationship hadn't been serious back then. They'd both known it. The breakup hadn't hurt either of them. They'd seen each other enough since then to know they'd both moved on to new relationships. It was actually nice to consider that they could visit on a friendly basis now without all that 'relationship' stuff to interfere.

Shiloh grunted and stretched on the cement, reminding Kali that if anything was wrong with the company, Shiloh wouldn't be so relaxed.

They spent a pleasant hour catching up on their years apart. Then the conversation lulled.

Slowly that same sense of unease returned. She sat nursing her empty coffee cup, stalling. She wanted to see Jim drive away before she headed home. Stupid, she knew, but that didn't change how she felt. Her cell phone rang. She frowned. Who'd be calling at this hour? Pulling it out of her pocket, she didn't recognize the number. "Hello."

"Kali. Are you all right?" Grant asked.

"Ahh, yeah," she said, hating the instant relief washing over her at the sound of his voice. Her world righted itself. The sense of unease slipped away. "Why?"

"Because you look like you're trying to get rid of the guy at your table." His voice deepened, sending delicious shivers along her back.

"Where are you?" Kali smiled apologetically at Jim, and continued to search the area around her.

"Close. I'll walk your way in a couple of minutes. Feel free to act like I'm an old friend," he said and hung up.

She stared at the phone in her hand. For the number of times she'd seen him lately, he almost was an old friend. And how had he known where she was?

As she glanced at Jim, smiling reassuringly at him, another thought occurred. If Grant was that close, maybe he'd been the one following her? No, that didn't make sense. He had no reason to.

She searched the parking lot and patio again. Grant should have shown up by now.

Jim stood. "Home time. You take care of yourself, you hear?"

Kali waved good-bye and watched Jim walk away – unsettled again. His exit seemed abrupt, making her once again suspicious of him, though moments ago she'd been wishing he would leave. God, it was horrible thinking like this about people she'd known for years.

There'd never been an energetic connection between any of her past friends and lovers like she had with Grant. There'd never been this sizzle. That reaction was for Grant alone.

She watched as other people came and left.

Grant didn't show.

Sitting long past the time manners would dictate, she finally had enough. She considered phoning him and decided against it. As she walked to the Jeep, her phone rang again.

She checked the caller ID. She didn't recognize the number. She ignored it, not wanting to be sold any more free trips to Costa Rica. It rang again as she unlocked the Jeep. Same number. She ignored it again. Then she reconsidered, chewing on her bottom lip. It could be something important. Calls at this hour were often emergencies.

As she reached to answer, it stopped. Figures.

Kali put her key in the ignition. It rang again – from the same number. "Damn it."

Shiloh whined.

"Sorry, Shiloh. I'll answer it this time, okay?" She hit the talk button. "Hello?" No answer. "Hello?"

Still no sound. Then a faint coughing chuckle sounded in her ear.

"What the hell?" Kali stared at her phone then held it to her ear again. "Who is this? What do you want?"

The same chuckle sounded again, followed by a distinct click. They'd hung up. Kali searched the darkness as she turned the key to start the engine. Placing her phone in the holder, she hit the automatic power lock on the door. She knew locking her doors would not stop her creepy phone calls – however locking them did make her feel marginally better.

Where the hell was Grant, anyway?

Someone pounded on her driver door window. Kali shrieked. Shiloh barked. Her heart banged against her chest as she peered into the night – and saw the swirls of energy.

Grant.

She closed her eyes as relief and anger rolled through her. "Where the hell have you been?"

Grant motioned for her to roll the window.

Relieved, and now mildly pissed, she lowered the glass.

"Take it easy."

"Take it easy!" she snapped. "I'm getting freaky prank phone calls and—" She unlocked her door and pushed it open, forcing Grant to move back. "You were supposed to be here close to an hour ago."

Stepping out of the car, she stormed away a few feet to stand staring at the stars, hands on her hips. Damn it.

"From the beginning, please. What's made you so jumpy?" he asked, concern warming his voice.

Just hearing that caring helped. Kali closed her eyes and focused on Grant's energy. She drew in two cleansing breaths as she regained control. The last thing she wanted was for him to think she was so easily rattled. In truth, tonight she had been. She wasn't proud of that fact. Until this letter writer mess was over, she didn't think there was much she could do about it.

The next deep breath and the knot of tension in her spine loosened. She turned to face him. "Several things," she said. "It started when I left the center. A noise in the bushes rattled me, Shiloh didn't like it much either. Then I thought I was being watched as I left."

Grant's eyes narrowed and he frowned at her but didn't interrupt.

She continued, "Not wanting to go home to an empty house, I came here, where I met Jim. That worked for a while. Then the visit got weird. You called, he raced off, and I sat here waiting for you." She glared at him. "Only you never showed up." She took another deep breath. "When I finally decided you weren't coming, I headed here to my Jeep when three phone calls came in, one after the other. I didn't know the number and chose not to answer the first two calls." She rifled her fingers through her hair before meeting his eyes. "I answered the third call." She caught his frown. "There was no answer at first, then some weird laughter before the asshole hung up."

Grant held out his hand.

Kali frowned. "What?"

"Let me see your phone, please."

Blasting him a fulminating look, she walked to the Jeep and pulled the phone from its holder. Handing it over, she added, "Then you scared me half to death."

Grant wrote down the number of her mystery caller. "No, I didn't. You'd already scared yourself half to death before I ever got here. I only knocked on your window." He passed her the phone. "I'll have this number checked."

"The laughter sounded weird, almost mechanical."

Shiloh, still in the Jeep, barked. Kali opened the driver's door and sat half-in and half-out in a way that allowed her to put a calming hand on Shiloh's neck. "It's okay, girl. It's just a crazy night." She turned so she was sitting properly in the driver's seat and reached to pull her door closed. "What happened to you anyway? Why didn't you show?"

Grant moved and closed it for her. "I followed your friend."

"Jim? Why?"

"I saw him leave and thought his timing a little suspicious. So, I followed him to a bus stop and waited until it he got on a bus to downtown Portland." He shrugged. "Then I came here to find you freaking out."

"Okay, I resent that." She hadn't been that bad, had she?

"Almost freaking out, then," he amended with a small grin.

Damn that smile. It did make her feel better, though. The heavy surge of emotions had taken its toll on her energy levels. Kali looked at the shadows surrounding them and shivered. The warm energy wafted between them. It wasn't enough to dispense the darkness. "I'm going home. I've had quite enough of this for tonight, thank you."

"I'll follow you home."

"Why?"

"So that you know no one else is."

"Oh." That made sense and made her feel stupid at the same time. "Okay, thanks." She turned the key in the ignition.

"Just a moment." He pulled out another business card. "Keep this in the Jeep. And call me the next time you think you're being followed."

Kali tossed the card in the coin holder on the dash. "I hope I won't need it. I never thought to call you tonight. What if I'd been imagining things?"

He snorted. "Better to call and be embarrassed over nothing than not to call and get into trouble."

She sighed. She knew that. "Except, it's not me he's after."

He bent down and looked her in the eye. "What makes you say that?"

"He's taking victims to challenge me. If I'm dead, there's no fun in it for him." She allowed herself a moment of relief. She was right. She could feel it. This asshole didn't want her – at least not yet.

"That may be – only this guy's not rational. You can't attribute normal reasoning or behavior to him. He could switch in a heartbeat and decide that it's more fun to hold you captive for a month or two."

A month or two. She gulped. That was *not* something she wanted to consider.

Grant continued, "And what about when he decides the game is over? I'm sure he has final plans for you, too."

Oh, God. That didn't bear thinking about. Kali avoided answering by shifting into reverse. True to his promise, Grant stayed behind her the whole way home. As she neared the house, she couldn't decide if she should invite him inside.

Still undecided, she watched to see if he'd park or, now that she was home safe, leave again. Locking the vehicle, she headed to her front door, not wanting to appear obvious.

Shiloh sniffed the long pampas grass by the front steps, enjoying the fresh air. Behind her, she heard Grant's door slam and the crunch of gravel as he followed her. She unlocked the front door, pushing it open for Shiloh, who wiggled in ahead of her.

Shiloh howled and raced down the hall.

Kali stepped inside. Shiloh stopped at the entrance to the kitchen and started barking madly. Kali halted, fear demolishing what little calm she'd regained earlier.

Grant raced forward. He grabbed her arm and tugged her onto the front porch behind him. "I'll go and check. Stay here until I tell you it's safe."

Kali's eyes widened. Good. She wasn't a hero.

"Call Shiloh back."

Kali called Shiloh to her and snagged her collar. Both retreated to the front porch. Together they watched as Grant, gun out and ready, took several deliberate steps into the hallway, assessing the scene. He reminded her of herself on a SAR mission. Survey, assess, identify, catalogue the elements that need to be dealt with before moving forward. At the kitchen, he stopped.

Exactly where Shiloh had stopped.

He glanced at her, still huddled under the outside light, before he entered the kitchen.

She waited. And waited. Finally, she couldn't stand it anymore and called out, "Grant. What is it?"

He reappeared, talking on his cell phone – as usual. Completing his call, he closed his cell phone. "I've called in a team."

Kali swallowed hard. "What's wrong? What did you find?"

"A package with a note from our letter writer."

Her stomach clenched. Nausea stirred in her stomach. The killer had been inside her house. She'd left it locked up. Shit. She forced herself to ask, fearing the answer, "What's in the package? And what does the note say?"

Grant sighed. "Kali..."

She held up her hand. "Don't. Don't try to protect me from this. It's way too late for that. To stay sane, I have to know what I'm dealing with." She closed her eyes for a moment. Opening them, she said, "Now, what did you find?"

"A bloody gold and emerald earring."

Kali swallowed hard as relief rushed through her. "I don't know what I'd imagined it could be, but I hadn't expected something as benign as an earring. That's good, right? This poor woman could be still alive. Right?" Kali felt a little better at his nod. "And the note?"

"I only read the part that showed – without touching it. It said something about, Round Two to me. Someone close is gone forever. Now it's on to Round Three."

CHAPTER ELEVEN

"Round Three?" Kali squeaked. Shock reverberated inside. Not possible. How could they have missed round two? "Are you serious?"

"That's what it says. I haven't moved it yet. There could be more to the message."

"What happened to the second round?" Kali closed her eyes, pain washing through her. She leaned against the wall, grateful for something stable. If only she had something to grab onto emotionally. "He's already kidnapped, buried and killed someone, and we didn't even know about it? Didn't even know this person was missing? How is that possible?"

Grant slid his hand through his hair, exhaustion and frustration in his voice. "Unfortunately, it's all too easy to do." Hands resting on his hips, Grant stared, grim-faced, into the vast blackness beyond the yard. "Kali, I need you to look at the earring. You might recognize it."

She stared at him wordlessly. Through her own shock and disbelief she could see years of experience in scenarios like this one etched in his face. His job had to be harsh to live with. The things he'd seen. The things he surely wished he'd never seen.

She took a deep breath. "Show it to me."

Pushing the door open wider, he led the way. "I don't want you to disturb anything. I'll take you to the entrance first." He led the way down the hallway, pulling on thin latex gloves from his pocket as he went.

His broad frame blocked her from entering. "First, take a good look at the kitchen. Can you tell if anything has been disturbed?"

Kali perused the room. Nothing popped out at her. Except for the item on the table. She took her time, then finally said, "I can't see anything odd from here." At his nod, she drew a deep breath, then walked to the table.

The earring lay on a paper plate. No napkin, no wrapping, just a mistletoe pattern marred by the contents. Through the flecks of dried blood shone a stunning starburst earring with a half dozen emeralds. From its position, she couldn't tell the type of closure. It appeared to be a post style. The deep yellow color of the metal made her think it was real gold set with real stones. She didn't know for sure.

Bile rose in her throat. Kali swallowed hard. Her eyes flew to the note tucked slightly under the plate.

The sheet of standard printer paper had been cut in half; the message printed again in block letters, but this time in black ink. She couldn't see anything to indicate the location, identification or where to start looking for the owner of the earring. Neither was there anything to denote the identity of the letter writer.

Unless something else were written on the note. Her hand at the ready, she glanced over at Grant. He stopped her and used gloved fingers to pull the note free.

"Round two to me -
Did you even see that someone is missing?
She's a beaut and she's a charm,
Love her, leave her and no one to release her.
Back where she belongs — free
Even better, she's where she should be
Now, it's on to round three."

"Oh God," she whispered.
"Does that mean anything to you?"

Kali shook her head, incapable of speaking for a long moment. Finally, she cleared her throat. "The 'no one to release her' part, I'm presuming means she's contained in some way. As I search for buried victims, I can only assume she's also been buried. And, yes," she added bitterly, "I know we can't assume anything with this psycho. Back where she belongs? That could mean all kinds of things – and none of them nice. But free? Since when is death, death through being buried alive as the other victims were, an avenue to freedom? And what does it mean that she's where she should be? She should be buried? Dead? She should be dead?" She stared wordlessly at Grant. "Chances are good that no one *will* find her because I don't even know where to begin looking for her – so she will be dead."

"Do you recognize the earring?"

Kali shook her head, studying the emerald design. "I don't remember it." She shifted her position, trying to see from a different angle. *Have I?* When was the last time she'd even noticed other women's clothing? "Sorry. I'm not really one that notices that type of thing."

He nodded. "Understood. What about the note? The killer must think that means something to you."

"Sure. It means this asshole has taken some poor woman and I'm supposed to help her. But I *can't.* I don't know how," she cried out. She gave her cheeks a quick scrub. "Sorry. I didn't mean to lose it."

"Shh. It's understandable. Stop kicking yourself for it. Let's focus on what's here. See if we can find anything useful. The earring has older styling, like something worn by a mature woman. The jewels, if real, are expensive. Someone had money."

"Or had a *friend* who could afford it. Not to mention it could have been a family heirloom handed down."

"True."

Kali stared at the plate with morbid fascination. As much as she wanted to turn away, she couldn't. The cheerful seasonal print contrasted so sharply to its contents. "Does the plate have any significance?"

He shrugged. "Possibly. It may have been a convenient way to deliver the item, or it could signify something much darker, uglier. Does anything here give you an idea of where you'd go to look for a person?"

Kali glanced at the plate, then away again as her stomach roiled. "No," she whispered in despair. "Nothing."

Grant gave her a brief hug. Energy warmed and sparkled between them, not energizing but soothing. For a moment, the chaos faded. Safety surrounded her. Then he dropped his arms as if realizing what he'd just done. "Let's change tracks. Who has keys to your home?"

She barely tracked the conversation. Bereft of his heat, so brief and so tantalizing, Kali couldn't help but wonder if he felt anything of the energy that hummed between them. How could he when he'd stepped back so casually. Did he hug all the women?

"Kali?"

Blinking, Kali focused on his face, grateful for the momentary shift back to reality. "What?"

"Who has a key to your house? Who would know you weren't home tonight? Who knows the layout of this house?"

Kali's mind raced to grasp something concrete. "Many people have been in here over the years but I haven't given out spare keys to friends and lovers, if that's what you're asking. I don't do that. I'm gone constantly and Shiloh always goes with me. I don't have plants that need to be watered or other animals to be taken care of, so I don't need anyone to check on the place when I'm not here."

"What about Dan? Does he have keys?"

Kali frowned. "Sure, he did. I'll have to ask him if he still has one. I stored a bunch of stuff for him while the center was undergoing renovations. Most of the boxes were kept in the garage. The financials were stored in the spare room."

"I'll check with him. That thread leads us back to the center again." He paused. "Do you think this," he pointed to the earring, "could have been worn by someone from the center?"

Her gaze followed his movement, nonplussed. The question had to be asked. She understood that. Really, she did, but to contemplate who might have worn the earring meant acknowledging that someone she knew could be the victim...waiting in eternal darkness for rescue.

That the murderer was likely to be another person she knew was beyond thinking about. Too much had happened recently. Kali couldn't wrap her mind around it. She didn't want to. She wanted it all to go away.

Not that it was going to.

"Of course she could be from the center. If you're asking in a roundabout way if I know who the wearer was – the answer is no."

"What about anyone else from the center? Julie? Brad? Jarl? Do any of them have keys?"

She reared back. "No. I don't think so." Bringing up Brad's name just brought up the fear. She took a deep breath and asked, "I can't help but wonder if Brad could be the missing victim. He was working the Sacramento disaster with me, but has been missing ever since."

Grant opened his mouth to respond, but it was his beetled brows that had her rushing in to say, "I know he goes on benders after a rescue. So I know it's probably nothing, but..."

Grant reached out and squeezed her shoulder. "Take it easy. We don't know what – if anything – has happened to Brad. Dan told me and I alerted the local authorities in Sacramento. If he's there, we'll find him."

A nerve twitched in her cheek as she struggled to hold back the sudden tears. "I didn't even know that he was missing until today. I would have found out yesterday, if I hadn't slept the day away."

He nudged her toward the double glass doors and outside. "Let's go sit on the deck until the team comes."

Kali let him lead her onto the deck and her favorite chaise where reality hit her all at once. "Oh God. The bastard probably taunted them. Saying I'd be looking for them. They'd have been waiting for me. Hoping I'd come to save them. And I never even knew they were missing." Tremors washed over her. Grief brought tears to her eyes. "Now there could be another one."

Grant swooped down and grabbed her by the shoulders, giving her a light shake. Energy flipped off them at his movements. Yet he didn't appear to notice. "Take it easy, Kali. You can't blame yourself. You didn't know."

"But maybe I should have." Bitterness colored her voice. "You already said that the Sacramento victim was likely to have been his first." Haunted, she stared into the night, as if the surrounding darkness would offer up the answers she needed. "Do you think the earring is from the round two victim or from the round three victim?"

"Stop. It's. Not. Your. Fault. Got that?"

With effort she tried to listen to him. Not just listen, but hear his words. Rationally, she knew it wasn't her fault. And that didn't matter one bit. She bowed her head, rested it against his chest, letting his confidence and calm seep into her soul.

And with it came anger. A deep down pissed off fire that ripped through her – burning, cleansing, firing up her soul. She lifted her head. "You're right. He's responsible. He's been playing on the fact that I consider the center as much mine as Dan does. I'm not there out front like he is, but it's my life's work. Any failure at the center or any loss of life feels personal. Like I should have done something to stop it."

"But you couldn't."

"Exactly."

After a moment she glanced toward the kitchen, then she said, "It would help if we had a time line. Like when the victim went missing. To narrow down which SARs workers were where, although I can't imagine any of them being involved. I slept for a day and a half to recover. There's no way another of the rescuers could have kidnapped and murdered someone in the same time."

"Unfortunately, a couple of hours would have been long enough." Grant checked the time on his cell phone.

She dropped back into her deck chair, her emotions churning inside. She needed her sketch book or, at least a piece of paper. Something to dump the tension winding up inside. "Would you get my sketchbook bag? It's hanging in the hall closet." As Grant walked back inside, Kali let her body relax slightly; there was no relaxing her mind.

Shiloh nudged her hand, a soft whine escaping. "Hey, girl. I know, someone was in there who didn't belong. Not nice, huh?" She gently scratched the dog's head. "If only you could talk. I wonder what you could add to this."

Her blue cloth bag landed in her lap. She dug through it, withdrawing the sketchbook immediately.

Grant eyed her curiously. "What are you going to do?"

Her art was deeply personal and not something she cared to share. Need clawed at her. The need to dump the images in her mind. The need to find a peaceful center again in the midst of the chaos. "Doodle. It helps me to calm down when I'm feeling overwhelmed." She shrugged dismissively, hoping he'd take the hint and leave her alone. "No big deal."

Choosing a pencil, she opened the book to the first page. She loved a new sketchbook with its pristine blank pages waiting for her creativity. Within moments Grant ceased to exist. She let her fingers flow and move, transforming the page to a jumble of emotions. She knew the result would be garbage. That wasn't the point. She needed to pull the plug and let her mind drain.

Once she paused, arrested by sounds in her house. Twisting, she could see Grant in conversation with several men. The team had arrived. Fear, pain spiked again. Kali picked up her pencil, her hand moving at a furious pace.

"Kali?"

She stopped and tried to refocus on the face in front of her. "Grant. Are they done?"

"Not yet. A team is searching the property, but we need you to do a walk-through to make sure nothing else was disturbed. Are you up to it?" He held out a hand. "We'll also need your fingerprints to rule them out from the ones collected tonight."

With Grant's help she stood, her stiff muscles a sure sign she'd been in one place for too long.

Kali stretched, closed her sketchbook and dropped it on the table. She followed Grant into the house. Putting on gloves, she went systematically through each room, standing first at the doorway, then walking in and checking drawers and cupboards. Everything appeared normal and undisturbed. At her bedroom, she opened dresser drawers, night tables, even her cedar chest at the foot of her bed.

Her walk-in closet appeared normal, disorderly and disorganized...but normal. "I don't think anything has been disturbed," she said. "Everything looks untouched."

"Okay, that's good. Let's check the rest."

They moved downstairs to her studio. Shit. She hadn't considered they might need her to go in there. The door was also closed. Again. "Lately I've been forgetting to leave this door open." The possibility that the killer had been inside and closed the door on her made her skin crawl. She shoved that thought away.

Uneasy, though she didn't know why, she opened the door and stood still, her gaze sweeping her small studio. Her painting stood on the easel, a drop sheet draped over the top. She tilted her head. Had she done that? She might have. The rest of the room appeared undisturbed. The paints sat where she'd placed them. The spills and smears had been there before. She really needed to clean up in here. Checking the door, she found her paint smock hanging on a hook where she'd left it.

Kali pivoted to return to the kitchen, hoping to avoid her easel.

"Don't you want to check that the painting is untouched?"

Double shit. No, she really didn't. Kali glanced at it, then at Grant. "No. I don't really care if the intruder touched the painting, and if he didn't, then nothing has changed."

"Please. We need to know where he's been and what he might have done."

Kali bowed her head briefly, then sighed. He was right. She walked to the easel and lifted the cover. She flinched. It was the same as before. She dropped the sheet and walked out. "He didn't touch it."

Grant didn't say anything. "Can I see?"

She froze. "Why?"

"Your reaction as much as anything. I want to know what caused that pained expression." Not necessarily true.

"Maybe I'm just a bad artist." She tried to quell her nervousness. When that didn't work, she nibbled on her lower lip. Would he understand the significance? Or would it throw suspicion on her?

"Please."

Kali knew she could refuse. The painting certainly didn't come under his jurisdiction – at least she didn't think it did. A refusal *would* arouse suspicion. She didn't want that. Neither did she want to explain the picture. She couldn't. Finally, she walked over and flipped the drop cloth over the top, turning so she could see his instinctive reaction.

Confusion. Intensity. Then comprehension.

He stepped closer. "Bloody brilliant, yet bloody horrible at the same time."

"Now you have the explanation for the look on my face," she said lightly, reaching for the drop sheet.

His hand stalled her movement, his gaze never leaving the painting.

"You must have awful nightmares." He retreated a step.

"You have no idea." She stared at the victim in the painting, knowing a second person could be in the same situation even now. Bile crept up her throat.

She could sense him studying her and the painting, shifting back and forth. Yet he didn't ask. It surprised her, but she was grateful. It was a temporary reprieve. He wouldn't be able to leave it alone. Not forever.

At least he didn't know she'd painted this *before* her Sacramento trip.

CHAPTER TWELVE

An hour later Kali sat on the porch and hugged a cup of fresh coffee while Grant's team worked over her house. She'd lost track of time. Surely bedtime had come and gone hours ago. She wrinkled her nose at Grant and yawned. His energy clung close to his body. He was tired, too. "What? Sorry, I was miles away."

"I asked if I could look at your sketchbook," he asked gently, sitting beside her. "That painting you did was damn powerful. I don't think I've ever seen anything like it. Remember Stefan Kronos, the consultant that came with me a couple of days ago? He also uses art to purge his demons."

She paused, uncertain where this conversation was going. "I imagine many people do," she said cautiously.

"Of course he's different in another way, too. He's a psychic. He often paints his visions. It helps him set the details."

Her breath caught and held. "He left me his card. Something about him being a psychic consultant?"

Grant nodded. "And famous. His success rate is phenomenal. He works with law enforcement all over the world." He shifted casually in his seat. "Of course, that work is often the source of his demons."

She considered the point. "The disasters are the reason I paint. Occasionally I paint for pleasure, but it's more an outlet for my pain, instead. If I draw something, it's concrete and clear and real. Once it's on canvas, it's out of my mind. If I leave the stuff in my head, it rolls around in an endless rewind."

"Sounds like the system works." He reached for the sketchbook, paused and looked at her.

She nodded, returning to blowing gently on the hot brew in her hand.

He flipped back the cover to the first page and stopped. "Kali?"

"Huh," she looked over at him.

"Is this the picture you worked on today?"

"As it is the only picture in there, yes, I'd say so. Why?"

Grant quickly leafed through the rest of the pages before returning to the front of the book.

"Do you remember what you drew?" His curiosity was palpable enough to make her uneasy.

"I didn't draw anything. It's just doodles. An outpouring of pent-up images and emotions."

"Where do these images come from?" His voice held an odd tone.

She looked over at him. "Like I said, my SAR work supplies a never-ending film of horror stills. Why?"

He stared at her intently, ignoring her question. "Do other people know about your art?"

She leaned her head back and closed her eyes. Surely there was something more productive for him to do. "Probably. It's no big deal. Artists are everywhere."

"Kali?"

She opened her eyes to find him holding the sketchbook in front of her. At first glance in the poor light, she couldn't make anything out. "I can't see in this light."

"Sit up. Look." Urgency threaded through his voice. He changed the angle of the sketchbook.

Shifting forward, she took another look.

And froze.

"Oh my God," she whispered.

In stark black and white, dominant strokes depicted a woman in a fetal position, jammed inside a box of some sort, and buried under the ground. A pipe extended upward to the surface to let in fresh air. Blood dripped from a head injury. The woman appeared to be unconscious or...dead.

Kali shook her head. "I didn't draw that."

"Didn't you?" he asked, leaning closer to study her face. "It's the only picture in the book."

She glowered at it. "I suppose I *must* have – but I didn't realize what I was drawing at the time. Not sure I believe it now, either," she muttered. Her pencil *had* moved at a furious pace. She'd let everything pour, not caring if it made sense or not. Like her painting sessions, she'd hoped to lose herself in another world when her physical one had became too much.

And just like the painting sessions, something very unexpected had popped out. Reaching for the drawing, she studied the details intently. She bolted upright.

"Oh no." Her shocked voice faded to silence. Her fingers clenched around the pages.

"What?"

"I know this woman." She tapped the picture with her finger, unable to tear her eyes from the sketch. Then she stopped and frowned. "I *think* I know who it is?"

"You do? Who is she?" Grant leaned forward and peered closer to the sketch. "How can you identify her from that little bit?"

"Her name is Julie." Kali choked back the emotion threatening to overtake her. "I'm not sure, though. Her hair looks like Julie's, the line of her nose, the body shape." She studied the sparse details. Doubt crept in. "It's hard to see when she's bundled up like that. It could be her." Tears sprang to her eyes. She swiped them away. "Julie comes to the center a lot. She likes to help out because she's a survivor herself. She was in Thailand when the tsunami hit in 2004." Kali looked over at

Grant. "She's a very sweet lady. About 35 and single – at least I think she is."

"Do you know where she lives?"

"Close to the center. That's all I know. Dan will have her contact info."

Grant pulled out his cell phone. Kali reached across to grab his arm. "What are you doing?"

"Going to call Dan and ask."

Her fingers clenched on his forearm. "Because of this?" She lifted the book. Her painting prodded at her memory too. She'd never drawn or painted anything like these two images before. She wasn't about to count on them being right, though. Far from it. And there was no way she'd have bet this picture depicted Julie. It could represent any small-framed woman or teen.

He paused, his gaze going from the book to her. He shrugged. "Yeah."

Shit. "Uh. This is just a sketch. Something I drew while I was upset." She shook her head. "It's not a photograph. It's just a combination of random drawings. It probably means *nothing*."

Closing his phone, he took a deep breath and faced her. "Where did that image come from, Kali?"

She stroked a finger along the edge of the book. Her gaze locked on the image rendered with horrible clarity. "My mind?"

"Kali, is there is something you want to tell me? You know you can, right? I'm not going to judge you."

Uh-oh. Here it comes. She shifted uncomfortably. He could say what he wanted, but that didn't mean she believed him.

"I've worked with Stefan a long time."

She wrinkled her nose. Stefan the psychic. Maybe Grant would comprehend. Still...

"Kali, surely you recognize what's going on?"

She swallowed hard. She didn't know how it had happened, but for the first time she had to talk about something she'd kept

113

hidden from everyone. He stared at her so patiently, his gaze seemed so understanding.

Did she dare?

How could she not? "I've never spoken of this to anyone."

He reached for her hand, cradling it in his large capable ones. His thumb stroked the side of her fingers gently.

"You're psychic?"

There. He'd asked her a direct question. She sighed heavily. "Honestly? I don't know what I am. My grandmother called it the Sight. She had it, too. I see things. Know things."

"Paint things?"

She half-laughed. "Apparently. And sketch them, too."

"Can you explain what happens to you? How you perceive the information?"

She shrugged. "Not really. It's been changing so much I don't have a handle on it. When I think I understand how it works...it changes. Sometimes, I just know things. Sometimes, I see ribbons of energy that point me one way." She frowned. "That painting in my studio is a first. I woke up in the morning with paint on my hands and a faint memory of my actions." She stared into his deep eyes, more than a little unnerved by what had happened. "I went into my studio and there it was."

His eyes widened. "Wow."

She gave him a lopsided grin. "Yeah."

"Is it the same way with your sketches? You just close your eyes and draw?"

"I don't know. Now that you mention it, that does seem to be my process. I close my eyes, as if I'm asleep." She thought about it. "All I can say is this is all new to me. Six months ago, I was working a different disaster. We lost a lot of people, including a little girl that Shiloh and I found. The loss really affected me. After that, all this stuff," she tugged one hand free to wave at the sketchbook, "went wild. Before then I had some inkling of where to search for victims on a site, just an instinct that told me where to go. I could find my friends' lost jewelry, keys, pets when I was growing up. It was always minor stuff. Now..." She shook her head, unable to finish the thought.

Silence hung between them.

"Then maybe we should give it free reign and see what comes." He straightened, still holding her right hand. Waves of energy slid off him and toward her.

"Huh?" she eyed him and the energy curiously. The more time they spent together, the easier their energy blended, almost joining into a single color. Odd. Comforting. Intriguing.

But he'd gone from being a friend to being an agent in that nanosecond it had taken her to understand. And that switch – no matter how intriguing their energy match – was disconcerting. Now he was making calls...again. He dropped her hand and stood up while he talked on his phone. Then he strode inside to his team.

Kali stared at the sketch. Just when she'd figured he'd forgotten about her and the stupid picture, he returned, all business again.

"Kali, Dan's headed to the center to find Julie's contact information. Apparently she moved recently. We're going to meet him there."

Kali jumped to her feet. It didn't matter that it was past one o'clock in the morning. Shiloh watched her, waiting for the signal to say she'd be coming along. She'd be needed if Kali had to search, but that would mean figuring out where to start looking. It would, however, be nice to have her with them. She packed up the sketchbook and pencil to bring along, just in case.

"It's not likely to be Julie, you know." She muttered glancing sideways at him. "Just saying."

"Maybe it isn't. Let's find her and we'll know."

"The doodle might mean *nothing*," she told him. "I'm not Stefan. I don't do this stuff."

"And it might mean everything." Grant's lips curved in a grim smile. "I'm willing to take a chance. We'll take my car."

***

Kali followed Grant, letting Shiloh into the back seat. Moonlight danced between the clouds. A chill had settled in. They pulled into the center a few minutes later. Dan's car was already there. Kali pulled out her keys and opened the front door. "Dan?"

"I'm in my office," he called back.

Shiloh raced toward him.

They walked in to find him frantically searching through drawers and stacks of papers; his sparse hair sticking out at all angles as usual. "I can't find it, Kali."

"Find what?"

Dan lifted another stack of papers before dropping them again. Frustration marred his face. He tugged at his shirt collar.

Was he still wearing pajamas?

"The volunteer list. The one with all the names and contact information on it."

Kali frowned. "The last time I saw it, you were carrying it and updating the information as you saw people. That was before Sacramento."

"Right. Several people had moved recently, Julie being one of them. Damn. Where did I put it?"

Kali stared at him, a growing pit of darkness in her gut. The list was important, and she had a good idea why it was missing. Then a new idea struck her. Horrible, but a possible explanation as to why Julie might have been targeted. "Dan, are there just names and phone numbers on the list? Or does it have more personal information?

He looked up at her, puzzled. The usually vague expression sharpened. "It has names and contact information. So addresses, phone numbers, emails and some information concerning their volunteer status and what areas they worked in. Also information on their readiness to leave at a moment's notice. So if they had kids, did they have a caregiver lined up? Or did they live alone; did they work for a living; were they retired and could they come to help out at odd hours? You know we come in and out of here all the time. Some people are good with that. Others only want to help out on weekends." He shrugged. "We need more volunteers. We've had major changes here, so I was trying to see who was available to do what and when. Like always."

Oh God, if the killer had somehow gotten that list, he'd have information on Julie that he might not have gotten anywhere else. "Did Julie ever talk about her time in Thailand?"

"Often. You know it helps victims to share their experiences. Even though it's been years for her, it still helps to have someone listening, who understands."

Kali scrunched up her face and glanced over at Grant. "There wouldn't have been anything on that list to indicate she'd been a survivor from another disaster – would there?"

Grant went still. Kali kept her gaze casual but firmly locked on Dan.

With one hand running through his hair, sending the spiky mess into a new formation, he said slowly, as if thinking it through. "I don't think so...it said that she lived alone, worked at the bank, her hours, work number." He paused, an odd light coming into his eyes, before adding, "And that she would prefer to not be called on Thursday, as she meets with her online support group that night."

Online support group night? Kali shot Grant a quick look, to find him staring at Dan, a hard look in his eyes. She could just imagine how he'd feel about that level of information missing on so many people. "That's fine," she said to Dan, watching as his shoulders sagged slightly, relief washing the dread out of his eyes.

She didn't want to discuss this here. "Wait." Dan came to a stop, his eyes widening as if his brain and thoughts just clicked. "You're thinking the list has something to do with the letter writer?"

"I'm *afraid* it might. It's just one of many possibilities."

Dan nodded. "Then we better find it." He walked to the filing cabinet by the door. He *was* wearing pajamas and shoes.

Kali lowered her voice as she spoke to Grant. "Julie was a survivor from a disaster. So was the last victim in Sacramento. He'd survived the apartment collapse. Could that be a link? That letter said something about *even better, she's back where she's meant to be* or something."

"So since they survived a disaster they should be returned to the state where they were found?" Doubt colored his voice. "Both being survivors of a disaster is a link. Whether it's pertinent in this case, I don't know." Frustration glinted from his eyes.

"I don't know that they'd have to be returned to how they were found, but consider that the Sacramento victim was buried under the rubble of the apartment collapse. He was found buried close to the same location. Hell, the oxygen tank could even represent air pockets from the building that collapsed." She frowned. Damn it. They didn't have enough information. They needed more on the second victim. Whoever that was.

"It's also likely to be sheer coincidence that Julie and the first victim are both survivors. The first could just have been a victim of circumstance. In the wrong place, at the wrong time. We know nothing about Julie at this point."

Damn him and his logic. Kali's mind tumbled over the possibilities. Then she noticed how silent the room had become.

Dan stood stock-still, eyes wide, jaw slack as he stared at them. "Oh, God. You think she's been snatched. Where's that list? Damn it to hell. I figured you needed to talk to her. That she knew something, someone...damn me for being an old idiot. Shit." He frantically pulled out files, looking for the right one.

"Don't you have her number in another place? On your cell phone, in the bills, somewhere?" Grant's hands fisted on his hips.

"Dan, you have a master list on the computer, don't you?" Kali strode over to the desk and pushed the power button. It would take a minute or two to load.

He shook his head. "That's the old one. That's what I was trying to update the other day."

Typical Dan. Still, she could understand. Sometimes she had trouble with priorities, too. Any other time the contact list wouldn't have been critical. The log-in screen came up.

"Dan, come log in. This is your computer, not mine."

"What? Oh, yeah." Dan stepped up to the keyboard and pounded out a series of numbers and letters.

Kali waited impatiently as the computer finished booting. Then she navigated to the main directory.

"Here it is." She double-clicked on the document, her fingertips pounding out a rhythm on the desktop as it opened. There. "Okay. What's Julie's last name, do you know?"

Dan leaned over her shoulder. "Taylor. There. Wait, you just passed it. Go back."

"Okay. Here she is. We have her old address, old phone number of..." She rattled off the number to Grant, who wrote it down. Kali quickly rattled off the cell number, too. Both men snatched up phones and started dialing.

"No answer." Dan said. Grant was talking to someone. They both waited until he was done. "Grant?"

"I have her new phone number and address." Even as he spoke, he was re-dialing. Everyone waited to see if Julie would pick up.

Kali absentmindedly stroked the top of Shiloh's head. She watched Grant's face as he left a message on her answering machine.

"Let's go," she said. Grant headed to the door.

Dan looked at her, confusion wrinkling his face. "Go where?"

"To her home."

"Did she have a vehicle?" Grant asked abruptly.

Kali shrugged. She had no idea.

"Yes, she *does*." Dan stressed. "But I don't remember what."

"We'll find it. Let's go."

Kali was already through the door and heading back to Grant's car. "Dan, I'll call you if we learn something." She snapped her fingers. Shiloh came running.

Dan trailed behind them. "Is there anything I can do to help?"

Kali started to shake her head, then stopped and considered. "Pray?"

Dan shuddered. "Call me when you find her," he cried as they drove away.

***

They arrived at Julie's townhouse within minutes. Kali jumped from the car before Grant had the engine off. Racing to the front door, she pounced on the doorbell. Then rang it again. The brick townhouse remained dark and silent. Where had Grant gone? She searched the surrounding area, spying him walking through the parking lot to stand behind a small red car.

"Is it hers?" she asked.

"I'm having the plates run now."

She watched as he checked the parking space number. It matched the townhouse number. They both walked around the car, as if it would give up the answers they sought. Grant's cell phone rang.

"Right. Okay. Yeah, I'm going in. No. Yes. Fine."

Grant put away his phone and approached Julie's front door where he knocked first. Then again. Then he called out, "Julie? This is the FBI. Answer the door, please."

Silence. He pulled out a small tool and had the door open within seconds.

Kali watched, astonished. "Isn't that illegal?"

"Not if we have just cause. The car is hers." He pushed open the door and stepped inside.

"Julie," Kali called out behind him. "Julie, are you home? This is Kali."

"Julie?" Grant ran up the stairs two at time. Caught up in his energy, Kali raced after him.

There was no sign of Julie.

But she'd been there. The bedclothes lay crumpled, half on and half off the bed. Several days' worth of clothing decorated a rattan swivel chair. Untidy but normal-looking.

Grant strode over to the night table and turned on the lamp. A halo of light filled the room. Grim lines wrinkled his forehead as he assessed something on the floor.

"What is it?" Kali whispered.

"Blood."

His words punched her in the gut. "Oh no." Her imagination took flight. Now all she could think about was that Julie was missing and possibly injured, and Kali was trying to find her, with no idea where to look. Shit.

Panic set in. Julie didn't deserve this. Kali had known her for years, yet she didn't really *know* her. She was a great woman who'd already survived so much. Kali wished she'd taken more time to visit with her. After Mexico, Kali had ignored the people around her, the changes going on in the world and especially at the center.

She stood in the middle of Julie's bedroom and held her throbbing temple. "Think, damn it. Think," she whispered. Where could Julie be? What was the chance she'd be doing something ordinary like visiting friends or staying over with a boyfriend? Just because she wasn't home didn't mean she should hit the panic button. And yet...Kali's nerves refused to be calmed. She spun around looking for a jewelry box. "What's the chance the matching earring is here?"

Grant frowned but checked the dresser and night table. A small one sat open in the top drawer. Kali walked over to see. No missing earring.

"It makes sense that the earring wouldn't be here. If he has her, she's likely to have started out wearing both."

If she'd been taken, she couldn't be far. There'd been no time. Or had there? When had the earring been delivered? She'd been at the center for hours, followed by at least two hours at the coffee shop. So where could he have taken her within...say an hour's drive? Although, even that was an arbitrary time frame.

"What are you thinking?" Grant asked, the phone open in his hand.

"I'm sorting through possibilities." Kali motioned out the window. "If the letter writer has her, this isn't exactly the easiest place to kidnap or bury her. Presuming he buried her. There are always people around – someone should have seen him. She's small, but surely he's still going to be noticed carrying a body, isn't he? She might not have been in the box until she was buried."

"If she didn't walk out on her own. We'll have to get a team out to canvas the neighborhood in the morning. It's in the middle of the night, but if we're lucky, someone saw something."

"But chances are we won't find them in time to save her." Kali couldn't keep the bitterness out of her voice.

"This is not your fault," he reminded her firmly, a gentleness in his eyes.

Kali wanted to believe him. Shaking her head, she struggled to concentrate. "My brain understands, my heart, however..."

"I know."

His voice soothed her tattered nerves. She welcomed the comfort, but the deepening connection between them confused her more. So much for locking people out. Grant had wormed his way inside.

"Let's stay focused," Grant said. "*If* she's been taken, and, yes, we're jumping to a conclusion here, where could he have taken her?"

"Anywhere. Everywhere. Within an hour's drive, there are millions of places to bury someone so they'd never be found." Places flashed through her mind, ditches, fields, gardens, empty lots. The opportunities were endless.

"You found the last victim."

"Sure. But I was already on the scene with a SAR dog in hand." She threw her hands up in frustration. "That was the right location with the right tools. Yes, I have Shiloh with me now, only she won't be able to help unless we can narrow the location."

"Okay, now think. He knows you and how you work, so he must be expecting you to do something. There has to be a clue somewhere."

"Yeah, somewhere." Tears of frustration turned her voice into a croak. Damn it.

"What about your sketch? Can you identify a location from your picture?"

"Maybe," she said, relieved to have something constructive to think about. "I can take another look." Grant retrieved the sketchbook from the car while she waited at the front door. Using the bright kitchen light, they studied the details.

"No mountains or major identifiers." Grant bent over the map. "It's hard to pick out anything."

"I know," Kali whispered. "Yet..."

"What?" Grant straightened, his sharp gaze zeroed in on her face. "What do you see?"

"It feels familiar." Kali reached out and motioned toward the slope and ground cover surrounding it. She chewed on her bottom lip. "But I can't be sure."

"What about it looks right?"

"It's hard to explain. That single line captures Julie's profile." She pointed it out. "This line here captures a hill on one of the training areas we use for cadaver training."

"You have a special training area for that?"

Kali shook her head. "It's not full of dead bodies or anything. It's where we run training exercises for the dogs, especially young ones."

"Would you have trouble finding Julie there?"

She understood what he meant. "No, Shiloh can separate live from dead and, although it may take her awhile, she will eventually find everything buried, dead or alive." She pressed her lips together, thinking. "It would be a good hiding spot, because the ground is easy to dig." Kali dismissed her words with a head shake. "Then again, it's an area that Shiloh knows well so, this wouldn't be much of a challenge."

"Maybe the challenge is to find the location, knowing you'd have no problem finding the body."

Kali recoiled. "What time is it?"

"Just after two in the morning."

"Sunday morning. Already."

He put his hands on either side of her face. "Focus for a moment. Is there anything else in the picture that calls to you? Anything recognizable?"

Kali closed her eyes against the tumultuous thoughts crowding her head. Opening them, she stared at the picture one more time. Instead of seeing something new, the picture cemented the location in her mind.

"She's there." Kali knew it in her heart. Julie was buried somewhere in their training ground. "I need to go home and get my gear."

Grant held the front door open. "I'll pull a team together. And I'll get a uniform over here to wait in case she comes home. Just in case this is a wild-goose chase." He headed for the car, already talking on the phone while Kali waited impatiently. Before opening the door, he asked, "Directions?"

Quickly relaying them, Kali hopped into the car, wishing he'd hurry up. Her heart pounded and her palms started to sweat. Julie was dying. Kali knew it, even though she couldn't prove it. Urgency morphed into panic – they weren't going to be in time.

Tears blinded her.

Grant drove back to her house. He glanced at her several times, and Kali appreciated his concern...and his silence. She needed time to collect herself.

Back at her house, lights blazed because Grant's people had never left. Kali shook her head at how far her life had slid out of control. Shiloh barked. Kali bent and hugged her tight.

"Okay girl. Let's go to work." Kali quickly gathered up a vest, Shiloh's lead and some dog treats. As an afterthought, Kali filled a couple of water bottles and stuffed several granola bars in her pockets. It took a moment longer to find Shiloh's teddy bear. She tucked it inside her jacket.

A fine-edged focus calmed her by the time she'd finished. *Time to go to work.*

"Ready?" she asked Grant on her way to her Jeep.

"We're right behind you."

Kali held the door open as Shiloh jumped into the back. Kali slammed the door, hopped into the driver's side and took off, spitting gravel in her wake. The training ground was a good twenty minutes out of town. Wooded areas and meadows dotted the hilly terrain there. Shiloh's playground.

As she drove, she had to wonder who knew the industry and the center well enough to know their training ground's schedule, setting their plans in motion when they wouldn't be disturbed accidentally. Detailed records were always kept of who had been where, and used what for each training session. Who knew enough to access the schedule?

Kali's cell phone rang as she pulled onto the highway. Shiloh whined, an odd note in her tone.

She pushed the button, leaving the phone in the holder on her dash. "Hello."

Eerie laughter filled her Jeep.

"Hello? Who is this?" Kali snapped.

"You're too late." The strangled whisper ended with a click as the line went dead.

Kali's heart stalled. "Oh, God. Shiloh, please tell me that doesn't mean what I'm afraid it means." Her hands started shaking. Shiloh whined and nudged her nose against Kali's neck.

Leaning forward, Kali rummaged through the front cubbyholes for Grant's card. Damn it. Where was it?

There.

Keeping one eye on the empty highway, she punched in his number. Grant," she said, "the killer just called me." She quickly relayed the conversation. "It had that same mechanical sound as the voice from the other night."

"Chances are he's disguising it. It's easy to do with today's technology. My team will have traced it. I'm betting it's a dead end again."

Tears collected in the corner of her eyes. "Shit." She pounded the steering wheel. Frustration and anger warred with grief and sorrow, all of them threatening to collapse her very foundation.

"Keep steady, Kali." Grant's voice sharpened. "Let's stay focused. There's always hope."

"But what if I'm wrong and she's not even here?"

"Then we're wrong and we have to accept that. None of it means you're to blame."

Kali sniffled. She checked her rear-view mirror, noted the steady headlights of the FBI following her and changed lanes. "The turn-off is ahead."

"We're right behind. Let's see this through to the end."

Kali hung up and made the turn. "Right. To the end then." Shiloh woofed behind her.

She parked beside the small shack that served as a basic shelter against the elements, and hopped out. Shiloh scrambled behind her. Kali snapped Shiloh's working leash on, then turned to the huge area ahead of her.

The other vehicles pulled in beside them in a flurry of dust. Kali ignored them, grabbed her flashlight and stepped out. Shiloh urged her left. Kali had considered snatching up a piece of Julie's clothing, but that wasn't Shiloh's forte, and if the victim wasn't Julie, Shiloh's focus would stay on that scent, potentially missing a different victim.

Shiloh barked once, lowered her head and got to work. The flashlight was dim and the heavy cloud cover made the terrain treacherous. She hadn't taken the time to put on her work boots and her runners slipped on the leaves littering the ground. Kali scrambled up the short incline, her hands digging in the thick natural loam. Behind her, the sounds of the team trying to follow chased her. Shiloh tugged hard on her leash. She wanted to go. Kali didn't dare let her run free. She'd never be able to track the dog in this dense blackness. Instead, she picked up the pace giving Shiloh more lead.

Left, then a little more to the right, around the trees and into a clearing on the right. An eerie glow shone. Kali blinked. The light was gone. She blinked again, opening her psychic senses. There it was. She turned toward a soft tumbled hill. Kali unsnapped Shiloh's lead. She bolted forward. Circled the hill once, twice and whined.

"What is it girl?" Kali reached the hillock and didn't need her flashlight to see the dark purple glow. "This is it, isn't it?"

Shiloh barked once, then lay down, her head on top of her paws. Kali jogged the last bit toward her. She could hear the sounds of the men catching up behind her. She ignored them, trying to understand Shiloh's reaction. It was unusual. And it gave her hope.

Kali shifted her vision, allowing the psychic threads to light up further. In the darkness, they held an unmistakable luminescence. Only they were dark, deep colors in snaky thin threads, acting unlike anything she'd seen before. They snuggled low to the ground, weak and reedy instead of reaching upward.

She frowned, trying to understand. Noises rustled ten feet in front of her and off to the left. Kali sucked in her breath. What was that?

"Grant?" she yelled into the blackness. An odd sound burst through the brush in front of her. Kali spun around. "Grant, are you there?"

Heavier thuds clumped into the eerie darkness before fading away. Kali's heart thudded in panic. Oh, God. She hadn't been alone. Kali snapped off her light and hunkered down in the darkness, motionless beside Shiloh.

"Kali!" Shouts sounded behind her.

"Here!"

The men's high-beam flashlights broke through the blackness, picking up Shiloh and her. Kali stood up, pointing in the direction of the receding footsteps. "Grant, someone was here. He took off that way."

Men scattered.

Grant grabbed Kali's arm as she moved. "The men will look. Now," Grant took a deep breath. "What did you and Shiloh find?"

"Shiloh," Kali stressed, "stopped here."

Grant used his flashlight to survey the ground. "It's been disturbed recently." He shifted position, scooping the dirt away with his hands.

Kali joined him. "It looks different from my sketch."

He glanced over at her. "Does it?"

"There's no air pipe."

Grant stopped for a moment, then shone his flashlight over the area in a quick perusal as Kali continued to dig frantically at the end where she knew the head would be. "No, there isn't." He resumed working beside her. Two other men with shovels joined them. Grant pulled Kali back. Exercising caution, the men went to work. There was no time for proper procedures. Julie's life hung in the balance.

"Look," Kali cried out.

Flashlights beamed in her direction and locked onto where she pointed. A piece of plaid fabric shone in the light. A shirt. Shovels were tossed aside as careful hands scooped and lifted, clearing the dirt from around the head area. Grant followed the shirt to the body underneath, sliding his hands underneath. He tugged a body upward. With effort, he pulled it free. First a pinkish arm flopped out and then another as the dirt grudgingly slid to the side, unwilling to give up its secret.

Kali stood fixated on the chaos, Shiloh cuddled up at her side. The lights created weird shadows in the sky as men went to work on the victim. An oxygen tank landed off to one side.

Kali's heart stopped. She closed her eyes briefly. "Is it Julie? Is she still alive?"

Just then, the sea of men parted.

"Grant?"

Grant stepped back a pace as the light flashed on the victim's face. Kali stared. It wasn't Julie.

It was a man.

***

That had been too close. Hidden in a hollow less than two miles away from the craziness, Texan struggled to control his breathing. Crap, he shouldn't be this winded already. He went for much longer on disaster sites. He hadn't expected panic to steal his strength. Groaning, he rolled over and flopped on his back. Dampness soaked into his shirt, cooling the raging sweat he'd worked up. Kali's black magic was strong. Scary strong. If he hadn't seen her painting, he'd never have believed how strong.

His heart had pounded so badly when he'd heard Shiloh coming up behind him he'd been afraid of having a heart attack. When Shiloh worked, nothing threw her off. He'd bolted, as far and as fast as possible.

No easy feat in the dark.

Tugging his jacket loosely over his chest, he coughed once, then twice. He'd take just a minute more. His car was quite a distance away yet. The last thing he needed was to run into a roadblock. The dark would hide him for hours until the searchers brought in high-powered lights and really got to work. He had to be long gone by then.

He'd survived this far by being careful and faithful to God's plan. He wasn't about to screw up now.

Damn Kali, anyway. She'd gotten lucky this time. He'd underestimated the strength of her evil. Forewarned was forearmed. Next time, he'd plan better and make damn sure she came out the loser.

CHAPTER THIRTEEN

Kali stood, a silent island amid the sea of men surging in the eerie moonlight. Where was Julie? And who was this poor man?

Someone bumped her, jarring her to awareness. She looked around. Grant's men blended with paramedics, at least she thought that's who they were. Having led the way the whole time, she'd had no idea how many people Grant had called in, until she was drowned in the sea of people. High-powered lights had been set up, throwing weird shadows across the area as men moved about their tasks. Energy wafted high in the night sky. Colors flung and retracted with the movements of the men. So many men, so much energy. She blinked several times and tried to shift her awareness away from her own personal borealis. Nudging the agent closest to her, she asked, "Is he alive?"

Looking up at the sky beginning to lighten ever so slightly, he gave a small shake of his head. "No." His voice dropped to a low whisper. "But he's still warm."

"Oh God," she whispered, pulling her light jacket tighter. That explained the low to the ground and barely black visible threads amongst the brighter waves. It also explained Shiloh's reaction. Crouching down, she hugged Shiloh, who lay with her teddy bear under her chin. Shiloh understood. Kali buried her head in the thick pelt as hot tears pooled. They ran and mingled as sorrow overwhelmed her. They'd been so close, so fast. Had almost saved him...almost.

Where could Julie be? And if Kali had gotten this wrong – was Julie even missing? Some psychic she was. Kali sniffled softly as she stared out in the night.

The picture clicked into her mind, drawing her attention back to the missing air pipe from the victim to the surface of the ground. She'd been so sure the picture had depicted this location, yet she'd found someone else. God. Another victim.

She reached for her phone. Damn, she'd left it in its holder in her Jeep. Stupid.

Grant came up behind her. "Not exactly the end we'd hoped for."

She flushed at the reminder and stood swaying in place, so tired and confused that nothing made sense. A firm hand grabbed her and tugged her forward. Before she realized it, she was tucked close to Grant's chest. She accepted the gesture as tears threatened to fall. Not Julie. A stranger. Some poor soul buried out here all alone. Her lip trembled then firmed. "No," she whispered. "Not exactly."

"Kali, you're beyond exhausted." Giving her shoulders a gentle squeeze, he added in a voice that made her want to weep with its tenderness, "It's over. Let's get you home."

It would never be over. "It's not over. Julie is still missing." Kali opened her eyes and stared at him. "Who is he?" she asked, grief warring with the pain in her voice.

"We don't know yet." Turning her slightly, he pulled up her vest zipper before stepping back, putting a slight distance between them.

"I'd hoped—" She swallowed, her throat dry and rough. "I really hoped to find someone alive."

"We all did." Nudging her gently in the right direction, he led her forward. "Let's get you home and into bed."

Kali didn't fight him. "I doubt I'll be able to sleep." A choked laugh escaped. "We can't forget about Julie. We have to find her."

"And we will. I'll have a team continue to track her down. Don't worry about it now. We'll handle it. You need rest."

She did need sleep. Having burned through the adrenaline rush, she had nothing left. Maybe come morning everything would make sense. "The caller was right." The words blurted out on their own. The emotion threatened to overwhelm her. She stumbled, righted herself and then stumbled again, her feet like ungainly blocks of wood. "We were too late."

"I know. Take it easy. We're almost there." Grant's voice echoed from the shadows.

Kali kept moving forward. Her eyes focused on the shifting beam of light as it moved over the uneven ground. They passed several team members carrying gear one way or another. Grant spoke to them. Kali kept moving forward. She wanted to go home.

After another ten minutes Kali recognized the small shack and the outline of her Jeep.

Thank God.

Shiloh, quiet for the whole trip, barked once as they approached the parking lot. "Yes, Shiloh. Time to go home." Kali opened the back door of the Jeep for Shiloh before collapsing into the driver's seat. She leaned her head on the perforated steering wheel cover. And caught sight of her phone.

She checked for messages.

Julie's voice, faint and reedy sounding, came out clear. "Kali, what's going on? Call me back."

Relief overwhelmed her. "Kali." Dan's voice signaled the next message. "Kali, I found Julie. She's fine. She went to the hospital last night for a bad nosebleed. She's home now. I hope you get this." The next message was an exact repeat.

Grant crouched and leaned in on her driver's door. "So now we have the answer to the Julie mystery. And yes, we'll have someone go talk to her. Warn her, just in case... Okay?" At her tired smile, he added, "Kali, let me get someone to drive you home."

"I'm fine, just tired." She shook her head. "And I'd rather be alone right now."

Grant stood, understanding evident in his expression. "Call me when you get home." He started to turn away but stopped.

"Remember, I set up surveillance on your house, so don't worry and sleep well."

Kali lifted an eyebrow. How easily she gave up her prized privacy. Her mind was numb, on overdrive, and yet nothing fit together in there. Too exhausted to sort this out, she stopped trying.

All she could focus on was that it wasn't Julie. Julie wasn't in danger. She'd never been in danger. Or was she? What about her painting? She'd painted that before they'd found the victim in Sacramento – if it even depicted that victim. She was good at what she did, finding people. As a psychic, she sucked. Big time. Her earlier sketch and even her painting were nothing but twisted meanderings of an exhausted mind.

Confusion, fatigue and she'd admit a little shock linked and twisted everything together. She needed rest. Then she'd sort this out after a few hours.

Putting the Jeep into reverse, she backed out of her parking spot, stopping when Grant walked toward her again.

"You two did really well tonight. Don't forget that."

She whispered to the dark empty interior, "So why do I feel like such a failure?"

***

"Damn it." As soon as Kali turned onto the highway, Grant regretted not driving her home. She might want to be alone, but she probably shouldn't be. He was needed here. Yet he couldn't shake the bad feeling in his gut. He wasn't really psychic, with effort he could see some energy, like Kali's, but he'd learned to trust his intuition. He called to one of the junior team members returning with equipment.

"Grab a car and see that Kali gets to her house safe and sound." He pointed to the taillights disappearing down the road. Grant watched the second car peel out after her. With a marginally better frame of mind, he returned to the crime scene. Clouds whispered across the moon, giving the night a surreal look.

That went along with the surreal events of the night.

Thomas approached. "I don't know, Grant. You sure collect weird friends."

Grant laughed, a sound at odds with the scene open around them. Still, he appreciated the easing of the macabre tension. "That I do. Have you ever seen anything like this?"

Thomas, his demeanor grimmer than usual, said, "Never. To imagine one person carrying this guy all this way is pretty unbelievable. He is small and wiry, but still...unless he was forced to walk in at gunpoint."

"I mentioned that to Kali. She said the training is not only extensive, but also intensive, with some people becoming fanatical about their fitness levels. She said this level of fitness wasn't out of line with some of the stronger people."

"Then those are the ones we should be focusing on." Thomas glanced over at him. "Did she really draw a picture of this scene?" He waved his arm to the controlled chaos going on around them. "Cause that's beyond bizarre."

"I know. I need her to connect with Stefan. He could help her a lot."

"I have to ask." Thomas hesitated. "I know you don't believe it, and that people are working in the background to verify it, but are you absolutely sure she isn't involved? It wouldn't take much for an artist to draw this image if she'd participated in the events."

Grant knew Thomas well. They'd worked together for over a decade and often spent time off, together. He'd been Thomas's best man three years ago. In fact, Thomas had attended the same seminar where Grant had first laid eyes on Kali. They'd spoken about it several times.

"I'm asking you, both a friend and as an FBI agent, do you believe Kali is innocent of any wrongdoing here?"

"Yes." Simple, clear and the truth. "She had nothing to do with this. In fact, I'd wager my career on it."

"You realize that's exactly what you're doing?"

Grant stared calmly back at his friend. "I am and that's fine. She didn't do this. I know it, and the truth will prove it."

Some of the rigidity slipped off Thomas's shoulders. He slapped Grant on the shoulder. "Good enough. So who the hell did?"

***

Kali wished she could have slept longer. Sandpaper hid under her eyelids, and her muscles ached after her midnight run. Shiloh joined her, limping, her joints moving stiffly as she walked into the kitchen. Last night had been hard on both of them. They needed a week of physical and mental healing time.

In the kitchen she turned on her computer and checked her answering machine as she waited. Pressing the play button, she listened to the messages. One from Dan, updating her on Brad's disappearance – no word on his whereabouts. The next was from Brenda, who wanted to do lunch now that Kali was back from Sacramento. The last two were business calls.

Kali wasn't up to returning any of them. She forced herself to the beach for a short run to loosen up her legs. She couldn't shake her awareness of the security Grant had provided for her protection. Just to make sure, she checked that her cell phone was tucked in her pocket.

She'd just made it back to the bottom of the steps when the phone rang.

"Kali, it's Jarl. You called yesterday?"

His thick European accent came through loud and clear. Still gasping for breath, it took a moment before she could speak normally. She started to walk in a circle to cool down. "Hi, Jarl. Glad to hear you're home safe and sound."

It took her a moment to remember why she'd called him. All thoughts of Brad had been forced from her mind after the crazy midnight hunt.

"Except I'm not home yet. Should be there tomorrow. God looks after those that do his work."

Kali frowned. Though she didn't share his beliefs, she was happy to leave him to them. "Did you see Brad over in Sacramento this last week?"

"Sure I did," he said comfortably. "Why? What's the problem?"

"He's gone AWOL again. I was hoping you might have seen him after I left."

"That I did. Saw him a couple of times, in fact. That Sergeant of his is hell on wheels with cadavers, isn't he?"

"Isn't that the truth?" Shiloh was better at finding live victims, Sergeant had made a name for himself in recovery operations locating the dead.

"Time is still messed up for me. All this traveling and weird hours. If you're wondering when I last saw him, it was right after you went home. I passed him outside drinking with some of the locals." Jarl's disapproval laced his tone.

"He does struggle with his demons. It's the work we do."

"Aye, a man's got to do what he's got to do."

"Okay, well, I thought I'd check." Kali had hoped for better news.

"Let me know if I can help you with anything else."

Jarl rang off, and Kali climbed the steep set of stairs cut into the cliff.

Showered and refreshed half an hour later, she poured a glass of orange juice, then sat down at her computer to check her emails. Forty-two. Several were spam telling her how to enlarge her penis. She snorted. As if. Even with her email filters, she received several a day. There were a couple of work-related emails, one from The Picasso Gallery owner who carried a few of her prettier paintings. Good news. They'd sold the last painting and wondered if she'd be interested in placing more with them. A good idea, if and when life returned to normal and she could actually think in terms of *pretty* again.

She clicked on the last email. No sender listed. She frowned. "The game is up. If you don't tell, I will."

Kali could feel the tension build inside of her. "What the hell?" she whispered. As she scrolled down, her shoulders slumped and tears came to her eyes when the picture came into view.

The picture showed a dead or dying man, an oxygen mask on his face.

It looked like the man they'd found last night.

Kali reached for her cell phone and called Grant.

"Finally woke up, did you?"

"I have an email from the killer."

Grant's voice snapped to business mode. "I'm on my way."

Kali signed off and returned to the kitchen. She put on coffee and turned her attention to food. Anything to stay busy and keep her mind off that email. Besides, Shiloh had missed enough meals. Searching the fridge, she realized it had to be a skinny omelet and toast again for her.

Shiloh dug into her breakfast with gusto. Kali ate hers more slowly, her mind now locked onto her weird sketches.

If they'd come at any other time, she'd have assumed they were an outpouring of ugly memories. Yet they'd proven vital in sending her, for all the wrong reasons, straight to the wrong victim – but a victim nonetheless.

Kali stared at the Julie sketch, as she'd come to think of it, even though it had led to a man and not Julie. It looked the same as it had five minutes ago – if anything, a bit freakier. She'd used it as a map straight to a dead body last night. That would freak anyone out.

She needed to take another look at her painting.

Kali opened the door to her studio, grimacing at the mess. Tubes and brushes were now sitting amongst her paints, fingerprint dust covered most surfaces and her stack of canvases had fallen askew.

Snatching up a cloth from a cupboard under the counters, she quickly put things back to rights. While she worked she puzzled over the time frame. It really bothered her.

Turning her attention to the canvas, she flipped back the cover, struck anew by the power streaming off the painting.

Then it hit her.

She'd done this painting *before* she'd traveled to the apartment disaster in Sacramento. If, and it was a big if, she'd done the same thing again, it meant that her doodle of Julie, should have happened *before* Julie was snatched. Then, theoretically, Julie should not have been kidnapped...yet.

Which meant she was in danger even now. Thank God, Grant had left someone at her house last night.

And she needed to talk to him.

But it was a hell of an assumption to think this sketch had anything to do with her oil painting. Or that either picture depicted real-life murders, which brought her full circle to one indisputable fact. The last sketch *had* led them to a victim.

Hearing the crunch of tires, she raced to the front door. Grant walked toward her as a second vehicle pulled in behind him.

She sighed. How was it that he could appear handsome despite his exhaustion? She sighed. "You don't look like you got much rest."

"Thanks for reminding me. Where's the coffee?"

"In the kitchen," she answered tartly. "Go get a cup."

Leaving Grant to direct his men as needed, Kali walked straight out to the porch with her cup, biting her lips to keep from blurting out her fear about Julie. She'd give him some time before she dumped that on his shoulders. "The email is up."

From the porch, she heard another vehicle arriving. More of his team, she supposed.

Turning, she found Grant standing in the doorway. "Did you get the name or email of the sender?"

Grant shook his head. "I can't, our specialist..." He nodded toward to the man she could barely see behind him. "Should be able to."

"Does he have to take it away? I need my laptop."

It was Grant's turn to shrug. "Probably." Frustration colored his voice.

"Did you learn anything about last night's victim?" She hadn't wanted to think about him, and therefore hadn't been able to put him out of her mind.

"Yes and no. His ID said David Stewart. A fifty-year-old trucker. We're waiting on confirmation but there's no reason to doubt that's his name at this point."

Kali stared at him. "A trucker. How did this guy get to him?"

Grant looked up into the sky and then dropped his gaze to her. "We don't know. Or what the connection is to the killer or to the other victims.

Bitterness rose up. "We don't know very much at all, do we?"

"Without you, he could have been left there for a long time." Grant reached out and squeezed her shoulder gently, before dropping his arm. "You brought him home. For that, we are all grateful."

Tears rose, surprising her. How could such a simple touch comfort her? Disturbed, she blinked the tears away, rubbing the back of her neck, feeling a stiffness she hadn't noticed earlier. "He'd have been found soon anyway, since we do regular training there."

"The killer probably counted on that."

"Only it happened sooner, rather than later through dumb luck." Kali looked over at him. "We focused on that stupid picture."

"Regardless, we did hit the right destination."

"But not in time." The bitterness returned.

"Chances are David wouldn't have survived anyway."

Kali stared at him in shock. "What? I thought we'd just missed saving his life."

"That's what we all thought. His head injury was severe and the oxygen mask hadn't sealed around his face. The coroner should be..." Grant looked at his watch and finished, saying, "Doing the autopsy right now."

Kali's cell phone rang. Turning away slightly, she clicked it open. "Hello."

"Hi, Kali. Did you get my message?"

"I did, Dan," she answered. "Sorry for not getting back to you sooner."

She could hear the happiness in his voice. "No problem. I'm calling about Julie. We upset her last night. Can we give her a better explanation now?"

"Ask Grant. Here."

Grant raised an eyebrow and accepted the phone. "Hi, Dan."

Kali shut off the rest of the conversation and headed to the far end of the deck where she could catch a glimpse of the ocean through the treetops.

Grant joined her a few minutes later. "We're done here. The email was sent through a special server and that account has been closed already. I doubt we'll get anything from it." His voice shifted, becoming brisk. "I need you to take another look at your sketch to see if you notice anything else we can use."

"Damn it, Grant, I've stared at it for hours already. I thought it was Julie. Honestly, I'm still afraid it is – or will be – Julie."

Silence.

"You think she's the *next* victim?"

Kali turned, propped one hip against the railing and closed her eyes, her head bowed in thought. "I don't know what to think." That was the truth. At least as far as it went. She'd refrained from telling him one tiny little detail. He'd freak.

"Yet something is bugging you."

She gave him a sideways look. "I think it's fair to say that a lot is bugging me."

He narrowed his gaze. "You know what I mean."

Wrinkling up her nose, she admitted, "I might not have told you everything."

That same eyebrow shot up. His cheeks hollowed as his chin firmed. When she didn't speak, a glint came into his eye. "Speak."

Kali didn't know how to begin.

"Kali? Please."

She nodded. Reaching up, she ran her fingers through the strands, collecting her thoughts. "It's about my painting."

He glanced in the direction of the studio. "That painting?"

"Yes."

She hesitated, then the words erupted from her mouth. "I painted it before I went to Sacramento."

He blinked. Then he got it. "Precognitive painting?"

Kali stared at him. "Is there such a thing?"

With a half laugh, he asked, "You tell me?"

"It was only when I got home from that trip and took a closer look that I understood."

"Except we don't know when that victim was kidnapped. Does the rest of the painting fairly represent the scene you found down there?"

Mute, she considered the question. "Yes, it does. So now I have to wonder if this Julie sketch is something similar. I'm just too new to this psychic stuff to know."

"Has this happened to you before?"

"Drawings like this? No. Never!" *Or had it?* She frowned pensively. Would she have recognized other paintings for what they were? Not likely. "At least I don't think so? I've drawn for years, like I told you. I've never mentally connected the image to a specific event before. Especially not something like this."

"Could *they* have been precognitive in nature?"

"I don't know."

"Maybe you should check?" He studied her features curiously.

Kali spun around and headed to the small studio, Grant at her heels. Opening the door, she walked in. "Uhmm, .there should be some around here somewhere." As she talked, Kali opened cupboards and drawers. The big storage closet held her overload of art supplies and it was full, very full.

"Wow. Maybe check your artwork from the last couple of years. Your precognitive skills could have been developing for a long time."

The smaller closet contained an organized stack of her sketchbooks. "Maybe when this mess is over and I get a minute." She turned to face him. "Still *if* I'm right, Julie could be the *next* victim."

Grant's eyes narrowed, his focus shifting inward. She could almost see him tick off each point in his head. "We'll talk with her."

Kali closed her eyes briefly. "Thank you. I should have considered it earlier, but, honestly, it only crossed my mind just before you arrived."

He snorted. "And when were you supposed to think of it? You drew the picture last night. We found the trucker within hours and you've caught a few hours of rest. There hasn't been any extra time. Stop with the guilt trip. We'll speak with her."

He strode to the front door. "I'm going back into town. I'll call you later."

Kali felt torn as she watched him leave. She connected to the nasty turn her life had taken, yet he was comforting to have around. He'd become a rock in her world of quicksand.

She hadn't thought she'd be willing to lean on anyone else again after so many years alone. True, it was a rare disaster where she didn't break down at least once. Death and hopelessness did that to a person when blended with exhaustion. Dan had lent his shoulder a time or two, as had Brad. Her heart swelled. God, she missed him. Though she wasn't as tough as everyone assumed, she always pulled up her socks and carried on. She was no quitter.

So what now? Grant had set up security, surveillance but she hadn't asked him about new locks. That she could do. The last thing she wanted was another visit from this asshole. She should have done it earlier. Kali picked up her phone and by promising to pay extra, she secured the locksmith's promise to come out within the next hour. That done, Kali noted down things she had to do.

Talk with Julie.

Catch killer.

Figure out what she wanted from Grant.

But no pressure, Kali!

***

Julie wandered through her town home, hating the sense of vulnerability. It was hard to believe the night could have gone so wrong. Her nosebleed last night had been so bad she'd gone to the hospital. She hated hospitals. She hadn't even been able to drive herself there.

And to come home to have an officer waiting for her...

She sighed. Surely she had a forgotten bottle of wine stashed somewhere. It didn't matter what time of day it was. Finding out everyone thought she'd gone missing was bizarre, and Dan's explanation had been over the top.

Kidnapped, for heaven's sake. They'd really lost it with that assumption. And what about coming in and searching her place? In a small way she felt violated. Better make that in a big way. It no longer held the same comfortable hominess. Her house was full of energy – their energy. She'd need her feng shui specialist to clean it out properly.

Dan had been so apologetic that he'd made her laugh. He reminded her of her father, his actions coming from the right place, even if Dan appeared to have lost his head. He was the epitome of the forgetful professor. Harmless.

Kali was downright scary. How could she do the type of work she did with such eerie calm? Julie shook her head as she opened her fridge.

Wine. That would take the edge off. She popped the cork, breaking off a little into the bottle in the process, and poured herself a hefty glass. Carrying it out to the porch, she chose a seat in the shade.

A sparrow hopped through the garden, pecking away at the ground. Julie smiled at its antics. She'd like to be so carefree. According to her shrink that wouldn't happen until she 'made peace' with herself. Julie snorted before taking another hefty swig of her drink. The place was a connection to what she'd experienced. The SAR center an irresistible lure, a chance to connect to people who understood. Most people couldn't understand; the people at Second Chance did.

As far as she was concerned, she didn't need a shrink; she needed a new life. And she'd been hoping that was in progress.

Until this.

Julie shuddered.

Men in her house. Going through her drawers, her bedroom, her papers and her life. Yuck. She knew they believed they had just cause. It was supposedly for her benefit, still… Her personal space was everything to her.

Checking her watch, she realized it was time to get dressed. Her new man should be here soon. They were going out for lunch and to the conservatory. She hadn't yet decided if this would be the night. She'd held him off so far, wanting him to work for it a little. In her opinion, women gave in too easy these days. Then the guys became spoiled and expected the same treatment all the time. Julie loved a good romp, but not because it was expected of her. Besides, the guy was married. It's not like he wasn't getting it on a regular basis.

Julie preferred her men married. Short term and private, with no complications. Her phone rang. Checking the caller ID, she smiled. "Hi," she sang into the phone. "Are we still on for lunch?"

CHAPTER FOURTEEN

Damn drawings. Since when had her barely existent extrasensory skills extended to paranormal artwork? Was there even such a label? Or did she have the dubious distinction of being the only weirdo who created 'kidnap art'?

Kali reached for the cold iced tea sitting beside her on her patio table. Grant had been gone an hour, and her thoughts had already dropped into chaos.

Her phone rang. Grant.

"Last night's victim died of a heart attack," he said brusquely. "He'd most likely been comatose for hours."

"What? What about the head trauma? Being buried? Lack of oxygen from the dislodged mask?" Kali had a hard time taking it all in.

"All of that would have sped up the process, but what I'm saying is you couldn't have saved him. He was a dead man anyway."

Relief and pain washed over her. Poor guy. At least he wouldn't have known what was happening. Shit. "So, if he hadn't had that heart attack, he'd have been there waiting for us?" Relief vanished. Shakes wracked her spine. God, if he hadn't died, he could be still lying there, waiting in agony and terror, wondering if his life were over. Understanding hit. "We weren't meant to find him that fast."

A heavy sigh slid through the phone lines. "I'm thinking the same thing. That's why the killer felt safe being there. We were supposed to look for the owner of the earring."

"How does he think I'm going to find these people?"

"What's the chance he knows about your paranormal skills?"

"Not likely. I don't talk about it. At all."

"Feel free to contact Stefan if you want to talk."

Right, the psychic who worked with the police. Grimacing, she asked, "Do you think he'd mind?"

"No, he won't. Have you got a pen?" He rattled off the number as Kali jotted it down on her notepad. She had Stefan's card somewhere. This was easier.

"Have you spoken with Julie?"

"Not yet."

Kali stared around at the old fir trees on her property. "I'll call her again in a few minutes. I was hoping you had contacted her."

"We're working on it. She was told to check in this morning and hasn't yet. We don't know if she forgot, didn't feel like it or..."

His businesslike tone of voice told her nothing. Did they have any idea where Julie was? What were they doing to try and find her? So many questions. Yet she didn't feel she could ask any of them. He was doing what he could. That things weren't moving fast enough for her didn't mean Grant was sitting on his ass doing nothing.

"Right. I don't imagine she was pleased about last night." Kali massaged her forehead. "She's probably fine. We don't even know if he's after her." And they didn't. She'd latched onto the idea based on her pictures. Stupid. "I can't get rid of the idea that he's targeting disaster survivors. However, that only works if David were a survivor himself."

"We haven't found anything like that in his history so far."

Then why him? She couldn't begin to understand the methodology, the craziness of a killer's mind. Especially a killer like this. "He has to be picking his victims somehow."

"Is there a registry or something for survivors?" The sound of a pencil scratched as he took notes.

"I don't think so. There are support groups where people go to deal with the guilt of being the person who survived." She thought about it. "Both online and in person."

"So he'd have had no problem finding out who belongs to these groups?"

"Maybe initially, but once he tapped it, there'd be a huge supply of victims."

"We can ask Julie about new members to her online group. She's been told to stay in touch, so she's not likely to be too far away. If you reach her, let me know immediately," Grant said, his voice brisk and focused. "Meanwhile, we'll work on finding the connection between these victims."

Grant rang off, leaving Kali to stare at the dead phone. She dialed Julie again.

Julie didn't answer. Again dread rolled through Kali. She'd been out of communication for too long. Even for someone who valued her privacy. She dialed Dan next.

"I can't reach Julie. Do you know if she belongs to groups or associations involving other survivors?"

"She did therapy afterward, and still belongs to at least one online group. I don't know which one." The fatigue in Dan's voice worried her. Dan's health had been slipping *before* this mess. Now…

"Right," Kali said. "Grant wants to talk to her. This killer has to have a way of selecting his victims, a pool to choose from. It could be a support group."

"Oh, God."

She hung up.

Tension ran through her and into everything she did. Like fine wire tightened too far. She knew that anything more and she might snap. She straightened magazine stacks and reorganized her almost empty bedding closet to keep busy.

When the phone rang, she dropped everything. Maybe Dan had good news for a change. Unknown caller. She frowned.

"Hello."

Laughter answered her. The same voice punched her in the gut. Shit. Anger burned away the shock. "Stop it. Quit calling me and quit killing people, you asshole."

Kali slammed the receiver down. Grant's men should have picked that up, too. There. It rang again. She thought it could be the same monster but she hadn't written down the number of the last call. She did this time and refused to answer. Then doubts crept into her mind. "Shit."

She snatched up the phone and answered it.

The same laughter answered her.

"What do you want?" she screamed into the receiver.

"You missed one."

"What?"

But Kali was talking to a dead phone.

"Shit."

Fingers trembling, she had to dial twice before she punched in the right numbers. Grant answered on the first ring. "He just called. We missed one." She started crying. "He said we mis-

"What?" Sharp tension shot through the phone. "Kali, calm down. Take a deep breath."

Choking back a sob, Kali released a shuddering breath. She wiped her eyes.

"Sorry," she whispered. "Just a second." She wiped her eyes on her sleeve and sniffled back the tears.

"Better? Now again, slowly, please."

After a slow deep breath, Kali repeated what he'd said. "I've been trying to reach Julie; I'm only getting voicemail." Kali glanced over at the clock, frowning, her stomach knotting. "It's early. I want to believe her cell phone battery is dead, but..."

"Now you're afraid she won't be coming home." His grim voice added to her queasiness. She could hear him talking to someone in the background, asking for a copy of the call. She vaguely remembered him saying he'd put a trace on the phone. Good, maybe they'd catch this asshole after all.

"I don't know what to believe," she whispered. The horror of the previous night rose to clog her throat with tears again. She walked outside into the early afternoon sun. Her slippers clicked on the cedar slats. Shiloh joined her, nudging her nose against Kali's bare legs. Bending down, Kali hugged her close, needing the comfort as much as giving it.

As she straightened she looked surreptitiously across the property. "You're sure there's surveillance on the house? I'd hate to have to stay inside, but it feels weird out on my deck."

"Go in and stay in when you're alone. We don't want to give him any opportunity." His voice sharpened. "And yes, there's a team watching. Twenty-four hours a day."

That helped. Rotating her shoulders, easing back the tension, she could look around without tearing up again. It truly was a beautiful day. Sun, blue sky and a warm breeze... She took a deep breath of the salty, tangy air. That helped, too. Now she'd follow orders and go inside. Refocusing, she asked, "I'm really hoping he's referring to the round two victim. I'd hate to think there's another one we don't know about."

His silence was agreement enough.

Soberly she asked, "What now?"

"We're working on it."

"Great. The waiting game." Kali couldn't stop the sarcasm from slipping into her voice. "Please call me if there's any development."

Kali hung up the phone. This asshole had to be stopped. A thought glimmered in the back of her mind. She didn't know if it would work or not, but she needed to try. Gathering her art stuff, she poured herself a cup of coffee. This might take a while.

What she really needed was Grant's friend. What was his name? Stefan? Yes, he could be a big help.

***

Stefan leaned against the front grill of his beamer and watched the seagulls floating on the wind. The sense of freedom from the physical plane, achieved through an out of body experience, was a sensation like no other. He'd come to crave it after all these years. Being a sensitive, a psychic, meant he was often buffeted by factors other people couldn't imagine.

For some, it was all hocus-pocus bullshit. For others, like him, it was a strange hidden world coexisting in the same time-space continuum as theirs. For him, the rest of the world appeared to be sleeping. They didn't see what he saw. They didn't hear what he heard. They definitely didn't know what he knew.

It was lonely in the ethers. Probably why he'd started to build a network of friends who were like him. With the world being as judgmental and disbelieving as it was, anyone struggling to understand his abilities had nowhere to go. No one to talk to.

He'd been there with hellish results.

Leaning back, he tilted his face to the sky, letting the sun beam on his skin. He hated traveling. Being in traffic with all those tempers and personalities put him in a maelstrom of other people's emotions.

They were like children. They let everything out, verbally, physically, and for him almost worse was the endless blasting they did mentally.

Keeping his shields in place was automatic, but in rush hour especially, he needed a suit of armor to repel the energies. He loved the water. It held a life force that drew him, calmed him.

Sitting there watching the waves, enjoying the respite, he heard his name whispered. Opening his eyes, he considered the speaker.

Kali.

And what did he want to do about it?

Checking his watch, he smiled slowly. "I know exactly what I'm going to do."

The real question was, should he tell Grant?

***

Kali opened up her sketchbook, stared at the old picture for a few moments, then turned to a clean page toward the end of the book. The two previous pictures had come about as a result of exhaustion and mental overload.

"Neither of which applies here," she muttered to Shiloh.

Kali stared at the blank page, hoping for inspiration. None came. Frustrated, she realized she didn't know what to do. She knew the desired result but not the methodology.

Just when she was ready to throw her sketchbook down in disgust, the doorbell rang. Shiloh jumped to her feet, barking crazily.

She followed Shiloh to the front door where she stopped to look through the small peep hole.

"Holy shit," she whispered. It was Stefan, Grant's psychic friend. There was no forgetting that face. He was tall, and his golden hair had a hint of a curl, just as she remembered. He stared down at her, amusement glinting from liquid chocolate eyes.

Double shit. She looked behind her toward the kitchen where she'd been when she'd wished he could be here with her...and here he was. Coincidence? Surely he couldn't know she'd been thinking of him. Could he? She opened the door and her brain hitched. *Christ, he was beautiful.*

She stared as something else triggered. His energy was warm and soothing, captivating...yet contained. It didn't reach for her. It didn't tease her, attract her...it wasn't for her. And hers didn't respond to his either.

His lips curved. "Hello, Kali. Remember me?"

Stefan, Grant's friend.

Grant.

Her world righted itself.

She sighed happily. "The artist in me would love to paint your face. The woman in me is glad I have other interests."

He laughed with honest humor. "Thanks. I'm glad for Grant, too."

Heat washed her cheeks. She gave an embarrassed laugh. "Oh, that's great. You can read minds too."

"Only wide open ones."

"And mine is? Ouch." She didn't like the sound of that.

"It was when you opened the door." He said. "You've slammed it shut now."

"Yeah, duh. Do you always have that effect on women?" She opened the door wider for him to enter. With her own perspective back in balance, she took a closer look. He really was male model material. "It must be quite a burden for you."

He cocked a brow her way.

"I'm serious."

As if just realizing she was speaking to him, he nodded. "It can be. Few people look beneath the surface."

Not nice. She wouldn't appreciate that herself.

As she led the way to the kitchen, she tossed a curious look at him. "Did Grant suggest you come by?"

"No, I'm here because you were looking for my help. The question is for what?"

Amazed, she stopped in her tracks. "You're saying you're here because I was thinking I'd like to have your help with something?" She couldn't quite get her mind wrapped around it. "Surely you don't hear every time someone thinks of you or says your name? It would drive you crazy."

Some of the light in his face dimmed. His voice deepened; a weariness entered. "That's quite true. I have to keep guards in place for just that reason."

"Christ." She was almost bereft of words. "That is so not nice." Back in the kitchen, she motioned toward a seat beside her

154

own. "Take a seat. Can I offer you a drink of some kind? Coffee?"

A boyish grin whispered across his face. "You do like your coffee, don't you?"

She couldn't help but laugh. "You don't have to be a mind reader to pick that up." She lifted her mega-sized cup from the table and took a sip.

"I'm fine for right now." He motioned to her sketchbook lying open on the table. "What type of help are you looking for? Artistic or psychic or both?"

She winced. "I'm sure Grant told you a little about me." She sent him a questioning look. At his nod, she quirked her lips. "The thing is, even though I'm doing this stuff, I don't know how to do it. If that makes any sense. My drawings always just happened – usually when I'm horribly exhausted."

"Meaning your abilities just happen when they will, without you having any control? As if you're along for the ride instead of being in the driver's seat?"

"Exactly! And now that I'm trying to consciously connect to these abilities, I can't."

"That's because your mind is getting in the way. When you're exhausted, your subconscious can shut your conscious mind down easier as it's too tired to fight back."

Her confusion had to have been evident, because his lips curved and he pulled the sketchbook closer and picked up her pencil. Looking sidelong at her, he raised an eyebrow in question.

"Go for it." Kali hitched her chair closer.

"When you draw, you look at your page, determine where you're going to start and then you start. When you're draw psychically, you don't follow the mental process. You've shifted, for whatever reason, into another consciousness that controls how your drawing looks. It's not that you don't know how – it's that you're working with the wrong part of your brain. You need to let the subconscious have control."

She grappled with the concept. "So I need to draw with my subconscious to tap into the psychic side of things? How do I do that?"

"That's where practice comes in." He wrote a series of numbers down on her sketchbook. "I do have a few techniques for you to try. These aren't things you can go to school and learn. Practice is required. It's the only way to gain control."

"And presumably, I'm not going to get it right off the bat?"

"Most people require some time. It depends on the wrestling match between the two consciousnesses. Some people have no trouble switching from one to the other."

"Like you?"

Stefan glanced up, warm eyes twinkling. "Like me, yes. And you will get there."

He wrote quickly and, before she realized it, he had made a list. His hand moved smoothly across the page. She could see the artist in the simple movements. The sure confidence on the paper, the hand positioning. He was comfortable with who and what he was.

Finally, he tossed the pencil down and turned the page so she could read his notes.

1. Start by turning off all distractions and find a place to be alone.

2. Next – go into a meditative state – by whatever means works for you – soft music, candlelight, yoga position.

3. Relax. It's only through relaxation, that we free the mind.

4. Pick up your pencil and sketchbook and wait in this same relaxed state.

5. An image will form, at least this is how it works for me. I draw what I see.

6. If you are distracted, feeling pressured, or try to force it, the image will disappear.

"Disappear? Really?"

"Absolutely." He waited while she reread the instructions. "It's simple to understand, much harder to do…damn near impossible to do well."

"I have no doubts about that." As she glanced his way, she saw he'd risen. "You're leaving?"

"You need to draw. I can see the energy around you. And what's the first thing on that list? Be alone, if you can." Snatching the pencil up again, he quickly wrote his name and number below the instructions. "That's if you need to contact me." His mischievous smile flashed. "Now you have my number for the third time."

His fingers brushed hers as he handed the notebook back to her. His gaze met hers as he said, "You are not alone."

For the first time she understood some place deep inside her psyche. He was right. She wasn't the only one dealing with these abilities. He was, too. Her heart eased. He wasn't deserting her.

"And there are more of us. One lives not too far from here. She's unfortunate enough to connect with murder victims *as* they are being killed. A skill that damned near killed her as her body would manifest the same wounds as the victims during their attacks."

"Oh no. That's horrible." She couldn't imagine having to deal with more than one murdering bastard…and to physically be harmed in the process… That was just wrong.

He nodded. "It is indeed. But Sam is learning to control that ability and her many other gifts. The more you open yourself up to this…" He motioned toward her sketchbook. "The more your abilities will be enhanced. They can strengthen, and new ones can develop. We really don't know what the limit is."

"That's enough to make anyone think twice."

"Exactly. Like Sam, you will find a level of satisfaction and self confidence you can't imagine, as your abilities let you see and understand more about how the world you live in operates."

She couldn't help asking, "Sam… Is she okay?"

"She is now. She's found a partner, a cop in fact, who understands and accepts her for who she is. He helps her to stay grounded. I'll have to introduce the two of you. You have a lot in common."

Before she'd realized it, Stefan had reached the front door with her trailing behind. She hated for him to leave. "I'm glad for her."

"Be glad for yourself, too. That's one of those things you have in common." Without a backward glance, he walked out to his car, leaving her sputtering in his wake.

She couldn't even form the right question in her mind before he was gone.

Light shone and left. Like sunlight going behind a cloud, her world dimmed. Then she remembered his words...she was not alone.

He was something else. And what the hell did she have in common with Sam? Psychic abilities? Being at the learning stage...a cop who understood and accepted her? She couldn't go there right now. That he was comparing the cop in Sam's life to Grant seemed obvious on one level and ludicrous on another. She forced Grant from her mind.

One thought lingered as she wandered across the deck. Even with all the pain she was going through right now, she wouldn't want what Sam had gone through.

She returned to her kitchen chair, the sketchbook open in front of her. She didn't know if his instructions would work, but couldn't wait to try.

Her house was being watched. That gave her a vulnerable, almost invaded sensation.

Collecting her art materials, she moved into the living room. After lighting several cinnamon scented candles, she gave Shiloh a chew treat, then sat on the recliner. The candles weren't needed for light, but their warm glow added a comforting mellowness. Kali shuffled her chair closer. She reopened her sketchbook, ripped off the sheet with the instructions then turned to her old picture for a few moments. Shaking her head at the artistic skill, she picked a clean page in the middle of the book.

Letting herself relax, she freed her mind. Pictures flowed. She watched and observed but never engaged. After a few minutes she could feel the tension in her spine easing. It drained from her toes, leaving a limp weakness behind. Staring out the big bay window, she watched the clouds above swell in brilliance. The entire sky shone in rings of pearls above her. A stunning display. A deep sigh worked through her, shaking her to the core, and adding to the limp feeling.

Such an odd sensation. Kali stretched, her pencil coming off the paper as she relaxed after. What had Stefan said at the end? Relax and step outside your mind. Right. Easy for him to say.

Leaning back, Kali slipped into an altogether different state. Peaceful, floating, free of cares and worry. Happy. The last couple of days had been tough. She now realized how much stress that had been on her body. Aches and pains had shown up in places she barely recognized.

She shifted into a more comfortable position. A heavy sigh worked its way up and out.

A tiny picture formed in her mind. With her art pencil in hand, she drew what little she could see in her mind's eye. Within minutes, another tidbit showed up. She translated it to paper. By the time that had been completed, a little more appeared. Slowly, step by step, she pushed back the fog. Still unable to see the whole picture, she focused harder. The fog immediately moved in.

Kali stopped.

Aha. Forcing the picture wouldn't work; she had to relax to let the information flow.

Kali leaned back again and took several deep breaths.

And closed her eyes.

There. A tiny twig of the picture emerged again. Her pencil moved at a furious pace. Kali lost herself in the process.

The crazy pace continued for fifteen minutes. Then everything stopped. Kali's pencil stilled.

Drawing blind? Who'd have considered that as an artistic system? Not her.

She opened her eyes.

And couldn't see anything. The soft light sent a weird flickering glow over the black lines. She turned on a pole lamp beside her. Laying the sketchbook down, Kali sat back and studied the drawing.

It was a picture at least. Not a messed up series of scribbles on top of each other as she'd feared.

But what a picture. A tiny woman or child lay curled up in tight ball, surrounded by intense darkness and almost nothing else. A few sharp lines set the scene and a minute bit of shading finished the job.

Another victim.

Kali stood up to look at the picture from a different angle. Grim foreboding hit her in the gut. The picture had a very different look than last time. Was it the missing victim, a new victim or a figment of her imagination? *God damn it.* If her mind could produce the image then it could damn well produce some parameters.

So how?

Kali studied the picture and then backed off and closed her eyes. The information had to be there. She just had to access it somehow.

Closing her eyes, she relaxed into the picture. Out of the bubbling cauldron of emotions and self-doubt came a day. Friday.

Letting the information roll around inside, she sat quietly to see if anything new came to mind. Studying the picture, so dark and black, it was hard to imagine any hope existed for her. *Her?* Then like she had with her painting, she turned to study the room round her and then glanced back. Yes, it was definitely a woman. So dark and depressing. Almost as if devoid of life.

That was it. This victim was dead. She'd died several days ago. Alone and unknown.

Kali's heart broke.

She reached for the phone.

CHAPTER FIFTEEN

The doorbell rang as the coffee finished dripping. Two hours. Not bad. Grant had made decent time, considering he'd had to conclude a meeting before he could leave. Kali rushed over to let him in.

"Hi. Thanks for coming so quickly." Behind him, a second car arrived. *Dan's*. She frowned. "I wonder what he wants?" Motioning in the direction of the kitchen, she said, "Please, go ahead. Dan has no idea about my pictures. I don't want him to see this one, either."

Grant headed obediently into the kitchen while Kali plastered a welcome on her face and waited for Dan to reach her. "Hi, Dan." At his worried expression, her heart sank. "Are you all right?"

"No. No, I'm not. I've been driving aimlessly, hoping to spot Julie. I don't know why, but it seemed like something I could do." He glanced up, an almost blank look in his eyes. "Somehow, I ended up here."

"I've called her several times, but got no answer. Grant's got people looking for her, too." She tried to keep her voice positive.

"I left her a message on both her cell phone and her home phone asking her to meet me at the center this afternoon. She never showed up."

"Maybe her phone isn't on. Or her battery could be dead. Not everyone remembers to keep phones charged. Hell, she might not want to talk to you or me, for that matter."

Dan stomped his feet on the outside mat and stuffed his hands in his pockets. "I'm worried, Kali."

"I was worried last night," she muttered. "Grant's here. Come in and we can ask him what he knows."

"Oh good. I hoped it was his car." Dan bolted for the kitchen. Kali followed at a slower pace. The late afternoon heat had dissipated and the early evening brought a chill as the sun descended behind the hills. Kali detoured to her bedroom and snagged a sweater. Pulling it over her head, she walked into the kitchen.

In the middle of the kitchen, Dan stood wringing his hands, his gaze switching between Kali and Grant. "Grant, I can't get rid of the feeling that, this time something bad has happened."

"I hate to be the voice of reason; however, we also need to consider other possibilities," Kali interjected.

Both men turned to face her.

Kali threw up her hands. "Sorry, I'm worried, too. I also remember searching in a mad panic for her last night, only to find she'd made a trip to the hospital."

"Would she get a nosebleed two nights in a row?" Dan pulled his cell phone out, checking for a message. He put it away again. "Surely, she'd check her messages."

Kali eyed Dan. Flushed and on the point of weeping, his frail build appeared even more fragile. Kali glanced over at Grant. "Have you heard anything?"

Grant sighed. "No, nothing. Dan, we're looking for her. There's nothing you can do but wait for us to call. We'll let you know as soon as we find her."

"Thank you." Dan's face crumpled, fatigue morphed into despondent acceptance. "I'm too old for this shit. I'm heading home. Call me if you find out anything. I won't rest until I know Julie's safe. First Brad, now Julie." Shaking his head, Dan walked out, his steps slow and shuffling. Poor Dan. His world was crumbling.

Kali's shoulders slumped. She knew how he felt. She walked over to Grant. Shiloh passed her, heading to a patch of sunlight on the deck. "Now that he's gone, did the team have anything new to add about Julie? And thanks for coming alone."

"No. They don't know anything yet. And you're welcome. I considered bringing Thomas along, as he's fairly open, but decided I'd hold off a little longer, for your sake." He watched her, his eyes level, his voice steady. "Why so tense about Dan?"

"I didn't want you to mention my sketches to him." Kali brushed past him as she led the way to the deck. "Dan is a staunch Catholic. I don't think he'd see them as a gift from God."

The sketchbook lay closed on the table where she'd left it.

Grant followed. As she reached for her sketchbook, he noticed the page with the instructions for relaxing. His gaze locked onto the name and phone number on the bottom. "Stefan was *here*?"

She paused. "Yes. And what a weird visit that was."

"You're lucky to have seen him at all. The man's a hermit." He hesitated. As if the question was dragged from him, he asked, "What did you think of him?"

Kali studied his face, sensing but not understanding the insecurity that colored his energy when he asked. "I think he knows his stuff. He arrived out of the blue. He said he 'heard' me call. I'd planning on phoning him when the door bell rang and there he was."

"He's very powerful."

"And gorgeous." She shook her head. "He should be a cover model."

"I believe he's been asked. He's a very private person. You should feel honoured that he came here."

That made her pause. She thought about Stefan's visit and the sense of urgency she felt to practice his instructions. "He could have called me. Or waited until I phoned him. He didn't. He came here to talk to me. To assess me, maybe?" She looked up at Grant. "It was a good – but really weird visit."

Grant's face turned grim. He didn't offer any comment on Stefan's behavior. "He obviously helped you, since you called and told me you'd drawn a new picture?"

"Right." Opening the sketchbook in her hands to the proper page, Kali studied her sketch. Next she flipped to the first picture she'd drawn. The one they'd followed to find David. Grant's curious gaze followed her every movement.

"I believe this first picture depicts Julie and that it's precognitive in nature. So it foretells the future."

Grant stepped closer and studied the picture with her. Kali flipped to the new one. "In this one, I think the event has passed and the victim is dead."

"Julie?" His voice was so neutral, she wanted to kick him. She wasn't sure what she'd expected. The drawing screamed at her. From his reaction, he could have been looking at a sunset scene.

"No, I don't think so." Neither the lines of the face nor the body fit.

"Why do you think this victim is dead?"

Again, the neutral tone. Did nothing get to him? Or had he so much experience with psychics drawing weirdo victim pictures that nothing fazed him?

"The blackness, the absence of light – of hope," Kali explained as she flipped to the first picture. "Here, for all the horribleness of this one, there exists a lightness or sense of life." As she flipped to the latest picture, she said "On this one, it's dead, buried, empty, the picture...lifeless. The woman depicted is dead." She took a deep breath. "I think it represents the other victim. The one we missed."

He raised his gaze to lock onto hers for a long moment. Had she said neutral? There was nothing neutral in his eyes. Determination, hope and fear burned deep in those gray eyes. She realized he feared she was right, yet hoped that she was onto something. She wanted to hug him, tell him that everything would be fine. Odd. They both knew it would never be okay for the missing victim.

His eyebrows came together at a fierce angle. "Why wouldn't you have done a precognitive of this woman instead of seeing the event afterwards?"

She laid the sketchbook on the table. "I thought about that. I think it's because I was in Sacramento or sleeping off the exhaustion from that trip at the time."

He considered her point. "No sketchbook, time or energy."

"More than the lack of time and energy, my focus was on helping those people right in front of me. I might have picked up on this victim if it hadn't been for that disaster but..."

Grant reached for the book, flipped between the two pictures. Finally, he said. "I can see what you're saying, based on the pictures."

"Obviously, it's all interpretation – guesswork, if you will."

"So yesterday was all about locating Julie, but instead, we found a different victim. And today is about finding the 'missed' victim who may or may not be Julie."

Kali blinked several times, processing his statement. "Sounds bizarre when you put it that way." Studying the new picture, she added, "The problem here is...nothing speaks to me. I have no idea where she's buried."

Reaching for the sketchbook, she returned to the old Julie picture. "I really thought we'd find Julie last night."

"At least we found David. Could the second picture represent David?"

Kali studied the sketch, slowly shaking her head. She dropped the book on the table. "No. This person is smaller yet again and slightly built. Female." Hands on hips, she turned to face him, her chin on an angle. "I'm beyond confused. Why so many victims in such a short time span? Has a time line been developed?"

"We're listing the Sacramento victim as the beginning of the time line. Unless you can offer a different one." He studied her. "With all the deaths you've seen, have any others been similar, connected even in the smallest way? Other murdered victims that have been buried?"

Bralorne. Kali stared at him in shock. How had she missed it? She blinked, sinking into her chair as she thought it over. Speaking slowly, trying to focus her thoughts, she said, "I don't know. Maybe. I hadn't considered it before. Everything surrounding the other victim was different. I didn't connect the dots."

Grant crouched in front of her. "What victim? Tell me."

Kali filled him in on the murder victim she'd discovered in Bralorne. "The man had been buried. There didn't appear to be any attempt to keep him alive. No oxygen tank." She swallowed hard, trying to remember details. Guilt plagued her. Why hadn't she made the connection? "This guy had survived the disaster with only a broken arm and bruises. He'd been one of the lucky ones."

"That connects." At her nod, he continued, "A very distinctive MO. Potentially, he's our first victim. Possibly the one that set this killer on his path. That's huge. Each victim gives us information about the killer. We need to run the lists of suspects. See who was at Bralorne and in Sacramento." He withdrew a notepad from the back pocket of his pants and jotted notes. "What else can you tell me about that event?"

Kali's cell phone rang. Shiloh whined. She got up and walked over to Kali, butting up against her leg. Kali frowned at her reaction, dropping one hand on the dog's head. Picking up the phone, she checked the number. She didn't recognize it and displayed the number for Grant. He wrote it down.

"Go ahead and answer it."

She put the phone close to both their heads. "Hello."

The same damn laughter.

"Still trying to figure it out, huh?" His voice had the same tinny sound as before. "You're not making this much of a challenge, are you?"

"Why the poor trucker? What did he do to you?" she said, her voice tight and controlled.

"David? Oh, David never did anything to me, except live. No, David was supposed to die years ago during the San Francisco quake."

"Wait, you mean you killed David because he had the gall to survive?"

Laughter floated through the line. God, she hated that sound. She held the phone a little away from her head so Grant could hear.

"An interesting way to put it. God called him home, David refused to answer. It's my job to make these people show up for their appointment, even if they're a little late."

"And Julie? What could she have done to you?"

A heavy silence took over the space between them. An ugly silence.

Tight anger threaded his voice. "That's good. That's very good. Julie's a survivor. I'm sure she'll survive for a while."

The killer laughed again, a more normal laugh than earlier. If anything, that terrified her more. Then he hung up.

Kali very slowly, very carefully closed her cell phone. Taking a deep breath, she said, "All our fears were correct. The asshole has Julie."

Grant, already punching in numbers on his cell phone, disappeared inside.

Kali dropped her head to her arms. Everything hurt. Her head ached, her heart wept, her soul cried for this to stop. God, she was so tired. Her adrenalin and excitement were long gone. Her eyes drifted closed. A minute or two of respite, that's all she needed. Just until Grant finished making the necessary calls.

And she fell asleep.

***

Julie opened her eyes; blinding pain stabbed the back of her eyeballs. A moan escaped – the sound barely audible. She shifted her head, confused. Scared, she tried to move, only couldn't. Where was she? What had happened? Darkness surrounded her. Blinking rapidly, she struggled to clear the black spots before her.

She couldn't see anything.

Her eyes drooped, her head sagging to one side. She tried to swallow. Sandpaper scraped the delicate tissues of her throat in a futile search for saliva. Cloth filled her mouth. Panicking, she struggled to push the material out of her mouth with her tongue. Managing to get it out far enough to breathe easier, she got her first swallow. Several attempts later, her throat eased. A shudder of relief worked up her spine and she sagged in place. Carpet scratched her cheeks. Where the hell was she? What the hell had happened?

Weird shapes formed in the darkness.

Squinting, she tried to focus. Nothing changed. Shifting her position, she gasped. Her shoulders hurt, her back ached. Her hands were constrained. Every movement brought her up against a wall.

A wall?

No. She blinked as reality seeped in. Consciously, she moved experimentally.

She'd been tied up.

As that understanding filtered in, the odd look of the area surrounding her made sense. She was in a small, enclosed space of some sort.

Kali had been right.

Someone had been after her. She'd been kidnapped.

Julie screamed.

***

Hidden in his bower deep on the neighbor's property, Texan adjusted the binoculars so he could see the drama playing out in Kali's house. He could hardly contain his glee.

Plans, plans and more plans. He'd jumped into this scenario a bit recklessly and a little quicker than normal. Now adjustments had to be made. Anticipation rippled through him.

The phone calls…well, he really enjoyed them. Except this last one. The smile dropped from his face.

They knew about Julie. How?

Even though he knew about Kali's black magic, it had been a stunning blow to hear Kali mention Julie. Still, knowing he had Julie wouldn't help Kali find her. Not this time. He'd stashed her for the night and would move her tomorrow. He couldn't contain the ripple of excitement. Finally, Kali was in the game.

She probably thought she was safe, her evil strong enough to go against anything. So naive. A contented sigh washed over him. Evil aligned with evil, but good always won out. It had just taken him awhile to understand his true mission and how SAR rescues were negatively impacting the Lord's wishes.

And Kali was the queen of the infidels. She had to be stopped. First, though, she had to learn the error of her ways. He owed her that. They'd been friends once. She'd be given a chance to turn the devil aside…to fess up to her black magic before he returned her to her Maker.

Slipping from the bower, he wandered to the edge of the woods and a favorite tree stump. The leaves crackled, dry and crisp under his feet. The summer heat had baked the earth. Surprising for this time of year. The undergrowth usually kept the ground dank, if not actually moist.

Tilting his head back, he beamed a smile into the night, his eyes closed, almost in benediction. His soul walked lighter these days. He was grateful.

He hoped Kali slept well tonight.

She'd need it for the challenges that lay ahead.

She had to prove herself worthy of salvation.

CHAPTER SIXTEEN

Kali's head snapped up. *What the hell?* Dusk had started to settle, giving the sky an odd half light. She searched her surroundings, groggy and disoriented. Rubbing the sleep from her eyes, she frowned. Surely, she'd only closed her eyes a second ago.

"Hi. Feel better?"

Grant's face came into focus. "Hey." She cleared her throat and tried again. "How long did I sleep?"

"Ten to fifteen minutes."

Her mind struggled to put the foggy pieces of reality back together. She massaged her stiff neck. "Julie?"

"No news yet. We're waiting for update from our profiler. We tracked the phone number to a disposable cell phone."

He dropped a piece of paper on the table in front of her.

Kali yawned, her brain fuzzy. "What's this?"

"The short list of names."

Her brain clicked on, and she was suddenly wide awake. "Of potential suspects?"

She picked the sheet up and peered closer. And blinked. The first name listed caught in her throat before shocked surprise took over. "Brad? *Are you serious?*"

"Not really, but we have to consider it. He was at the site where the first victim was found."

"So were many other people. He's gone missing, remember?" She was outraged that her best friend was being considered.

"Kali, this isn't about personal feelings, it's about who had motive and opportunity. Please. Take a look at the names and cross off the ones you don't feel could have done it – just give me a reason." He held out a pencil.

She glared at him, snatched the pencil from his hand and with a thick bold stroke knocked Brad's name off the list. "If you put him on *this* list, you might as well add him to the list of potential victims."

Silence. "I did."

She winced and turned her attention to the other eleven names. She knew four from the center. Francoise, a Frenchman, was a good man and a close friend of Brad's. Briefly, she wondered if anyone had told him about Brad's disappearance. Then she remembered, no one was to know yet. "Francoise works with several centers, so I'm not sure where he is right now. You'll have to check on that. I haven't seen him in years."

She crossed the third name off the list. "Sam had a back injury two years ago on a site. He can't do any heavy lifting."

Grant raised an eyebrow and jotted the reason in his notebook. He'd probably double-check everything she said. Then again, he had to... Didn't he?

"Johnson was supposed to go to the Sacramento site but pulled out at the last minute when his wife went into early labor. His name would have been on the original manifest, which probably has yet to be updated." She put a line through his name.

"Good. Keep going. "

Eight names left.

All male.

All white.

All young.

But not all single. That surprised her. "I can't see anyone who is happily married doing this." She glanced over at Grant, but his face was a blank slate. Did he suspect anyone here more than any others? She didn't want any of them to be the killer. She knew them all, friends, coworkers, people she depended on at disaster sites.

Kali swallowed hard and studied the other names. "I saw Zane and Ron from the San Francisco center at Sacramento, but didn't have much to do with them. I've worked with them on various sites. They're both good hard workers."

She put question marks beside two names. "Allen and Joe are both happily married, a half-dozen kids between them and are heavily involved in community affairs. I can't see them having the opportunity to kidnap and murder these people."

"Strike them off and I'll make a note of them here."

Six names remained.

"As much as I want to, I can't find a reason to cross these guys off."

Grant accepted the list. "We'll check them over."

"Ask Dan, too. He knows stuff about everyone – way more than I do."

"Okay. I'll turn this over to the team to start on."

Kali frowned. "So what's next? How else can I help?"

"Rest. Do laundry."

She glared at him. "Aren't you funny?"

Tapping his thigh with the rolled up list, he tilted his head and considered her. "Draw?" His face turned earnest. "We need any and all help possible. I know that's not FBI policy, but I know what Stefan can do. And Stefan hasn't connected to this guy. You have. Let's see what you can do."

Kali considered him. "We need tangible leads, not more conjecture. I may have been right once or twice, but I can't count on being right all the time."

"Leads are good; yes. But as we're lacking those, we have to consider everything. And we don't expect you to be right all the time – we won't know what you can do though, unless you try."

Giving him a disgusted look, she agreed.

"I have to go inside and make these calls, as much as this area is under surveillance and this deck isn't accessible from the ground, I don't want you out here alone..."

Kali blinked. Then shuddered. She'd never given it a thought. She followed him inside and locked the door behind her.

With the sketchbook open to a clean page, she sat under the golden halo of the light in the living room and pondered the strange turn of events in her life. How had her only constructive input become her psychic art, when she excelled at searching for victims, especially murdered victims?

She sat back, stunned.

Could she find the missing victim?

And if she could, then why was she sitting here?

If the victim was dead as depicted by her sketch, she could find her if she managed to get close enough. But what did 'close enough' mean? She had no idea. It was as if she'd accidentally fallen over the energy of the various victims before this. More or less. Pursing her lips, she considered the concept.

She went to locate Grant and test it out. She located him in the kitchen and she said, "I need to go out."

Grant frowned. "Where?"

Kali sighed and wouldn't meet his gaze. "I don't exactly know."

Grant's gaze narrowed. "Explain."

This time Kali met his gaze, calmly. "I need to try something." She waved toward the sketchbook. "It occurred to me that my specialty, up until now, has been *finding* not *drawing* people." She came to a stop, not knowing how else to explain. With a defiant toss of her head, she added, "I want to give it a try."

"I'll go with you."

Kali stared at him, nonplussed. If nothing came of her attempt, she'd feel like an idiot. Who needed an audience to that? "You don't have to. I can go alone."

The niggling sense prodded her. *Go. Now.*

"No." Grant placed a hand on the small of her back, propelling her forward. "It's with me or not at all. There's a killer loose, remember?"

"Fine." Kali hurried to the front door. At the familiar sound, Shiloh bounded toward her, her tail wagging. Kali bent to cuddle her. "We're just going driving for a little while. We won't be long."

"You don't want to bring her?"

Kali paused, frowning. "What I'm trying to do tonight isn't something I've tried before. I don't want to be distracted or influenced by Shiloh and her energy. As we're only going to drive around for a bit, I think I'll leave her behind. She could do with a rest, too."

Opening the door, she stepped into the cool night to check the temperature. Turning back, she snagged a jacket from the hooks by the door. Glancing at her slip-on shoes, she opted to change into sturdy hiking boots...just in case.

Grant waited for her on the gravel path. Stern, patient, professional, he was never really approachable. No, that wasn't quite true. With a casual glance his way, Kali blurted, "You rarely smile. Why?"

He raised one eyebrow and frowned. "That's not true. I smile a lot."

She hid her smile and said lightly, "Really, have I seen you smile?"

Shooting her a look, he added, "Yes, you have. Besides, there isn't much to be happy about right now."

That was a great conversation killer.

Grant continued to his car, opening the door for her. "We'll take my car. You can tell me where to go."

"Love to." She smirked and slipped into the front seat. Grant started the car and pulled up to the edge of the road.

"Which way?"

Kali closed her eyes and let the sensation roll over her. When she followed one of her twinges, a fuzzy bristling would usually nudge the back of her neck, sending her in a specific direction. She felt no such sensation this time. Knowing that Grant watched her, she closed her mind and opened the door to her alternate senses and relaxed. Since he'd witnessed odd behavior from her before, surely this wouldn't throw him.

"Left," she whispered. Kali slid into a relaxed state and blocked out the world. She kept her eyes closed for a while as they drove onto the main road. Sitting blind gave her an eerie insight into the bizarre world of darkness and trust.

She trusted Grant to keep her safe.

Her mind hiccupped. Her eyes opened. What the hell did that mean? Safe in the car? With her life? With her body? Oh God. She couldn't do this right now. She couldn't do energy work with all the unanswered questions. She had to focus. Slamming her eyes shut, she forced herself to draw on Stefan's instructions. Calm down. Relax. She was so caught up following his instructions, that the twinge on the back of her neck came out of the blue, making her flinch.

"Whoa!"

Grant hit the brakes.

Kali opened her eyes as they passed a road sign. They were on the outskirts of the city. "Left again."

Grant glanced at her, but obliged.

The road curved through hillsides and wooded areas. She searched the region. Now where? She waited for a couple of minutes. Nothing. She settled into the seat and closed her eyes again. Bringing thoughts about the victim to the forefront, she imagined her lost and alone and needing to come home. Kali concentrated on the fear, pain and horror of her last days, then brought in conscious awareness, a willingness, a need to find her.

Nothing crystallized. Frustrated, she set up a map in her head, waiting for the next step to appear, only to find herself blocked. Of course. Like her drawing, she'd tried to force the information highway to give up its secrets.

Kali relaxed the building tension, releasing a heavy sigh, shutting down her mind.

"Problems?"

Kali shrugged. "I don't know where to go."

"You knew the last two turns. They came clearly, didn't they?"

"Yes."

"So, let's not doubt the process. We'll keep driving in this direction until you say otherwise."

"Fine. But that's an odd attitude for a black and white FBI agent." How disconcerting to have him so amiable. Contrarily, she wanted to prod him out of the reasonableness. "What if I'm wrong?" she muttered. "What then?"

"Then we drive home and...no harm done." He shot her a curious glance. "How did you get the idea that I am a black and white kind of guy? Haven't we spent most of the last few days living in a gray area?"

Kali addressed the first comment and chose to ignore the rest, stymied for an answer. "I was wrong last time."

"No. Don't say that. You might have been wrong regarding the identity of the victim, but you weren't wrong about there being a victim or where he was located."

"It might be different this time."

"Relax. The inklings won't come if you don't give them a chance.

"Maybe, but it's never worked like this before."

A pregnant pause.

"Before."

"That's something I haven't mentioned yet." Kali stared out at the window. Christ, she'd look like a certifiable nut case when this mess was finally over.

"Explain?"

"Shiloh makes a great rescue dog because she finds people that are alive. Finding dead people upsets her, but she can do it."

"Can she tell the difference?"

Kali glanced at him. "Definitely."

"And you're saying you can do the same thing?"

"No, not quite." Kali answered slowly, considering her words carefully. "Shiloh uses her nose and I...well, I use the Sight. With it I can find cadavers, but a certain type stand out for me. Shiloh can find them all."

"Cadavers come in types?"

"Yes." Kali took a deep breath, bracing herself. She'd never told this to anyone. "I see dark, seething energy in ribbons. They are always attached to people who have died violently, especially people who have been murdered."

***

Grant continued to drive, even though he had trouble processing her statement. He'd known about her psychic talents, but this? Could she mean it? Years ago he'd have run like hell to get away from such a concept. It had taken Stefan to open his mind.

Now this woman continually surprised him, too.

He gave her a sidelong glance. The information might not scare him; still he had to wonder how she could deal with it all.

With every new tidbit she revealed about herself, he became more fascinated and alternately, more disturbed. This was heavy stuff. She'd turned out to be a complex myriad of witch, siren and philanthropist. Impossible to ignore.

Grant snuck a glance her way again. Returning his gaze to the road, he shook his head. He had it bad.

His lips quirked. Here he was working through his feelings and she was staring at him, wondering at his lack of reaction. Her abilities disturbed her, while he found them fascinating. It was his concern for her ability to *handle* them that disturbed him. That didn't say much for his state of mind.

A sigh escaped. He was an idiot.

***

The silence in the car grew to deafening proportions. Kali stared out the window, anywhere but at him. Had he taken the news with his usual stoic attitude or had he decided to drive her to a mental hospital?

"Hmmmm."

"That's it?" She glowered at him. The dark interior of the vehicle couldn't begin to hide his knowing look.

"Sure. There's not much I haven't heard after working with Stefan all these years, you know. And 'hmmm' means I'm thinking."

Kali couldn't believe it. "Good. Fine." She waited a beat. "You know, you may have *heard* a lot from Stefan, but I've never told anyone, ever."

"Right. A little too mild a reaction, huh?"

"Ya think?" Kali couldn't believe it. It would be the last time she shared a secret with him.

Grant glanced at her, a light shining in his eyes. "So tell me how you really feel."

"Ohh. Ohhh, you...you," Kali stuttered to a complete stop. Her fists clenched and unclenched. Closing her eyes, she focused on deep breathing. In the silence of the car, she heard a sound. One she'd never heard before. No way. She turned to look at Grant. He was sputtering. Sputtering for Christ sake. Unfreakin' believable.

He caught her staring at him. His lips quirked. His smirk widened to an outright smile. Before her astonished eyes, he broke into a guffaw, his laughter infectious.

Good Lord. She hadn't thought he had it in him. She laughed. "Wow."

Grant shook his head, a goofy grin decorating his face. "I'm not that bad. Surely?"

"Yeah, you are." Kali bolted upright to stare into darkness. "Where are we?

Grant pointed at a sign up ahead. "We're heading north to Portland. Remember?"

"We've been out for a while."

"A bit. Any more directions?"

Kali dropped her head against the headrest. "No. What a stupid waste of time."

"Not necessarily. Now you know I can laugh."

Smiling, she answered, "There is that. Maybe we should just turn back." Endless darkness surrounded them, with only the beams of the headlights to light their way. A prophetic sign maybe. Her eyes drifted closed under the hypnotic influence of the steady hum of the engine.

Her neck throbbed; she reached up to massage the muscles, but the pain worsened. Kali twisted her head to the right. Sharp, stabbing pain shot upward. She moaned softly.

"Are you okay?"

"Yes. My neck started hurting."

"Your neck or your intuition?"

Raising an eyebrow, she glanced over at him. "I don't know. Maybe?"

"Yes or no?" Grant raised an eyebrow, sending her a sideways glance.

"I usually get a funny prickling at the back of my neck, not sharp pains." And normally, she wasn't deluged in weird colors. This time her normal mental state of lavender blended with a dark blue, becoming almost black in color. She sensed the anger building in the seething morass.

"Maybe we aren't supposed to go back yet. There's a turnoff ahead. Tell me if you get more twinges." Grant pulled the vehicle up to the corner, edging the vehicle slightly off the road.

The pain stabbed into the back of her brain. Her stomach heaved. "Ouch."

Grant stopped the car. He looked at her, then turned the steering wheel, directing the vehicle onto the side road.

Immediately the pain eased. "Ahh, much better. Not perfect, but not stabbing at me either." The dark energy also eased back to a dull purplish black.

They hadn't driven more than a few hundred yards when the pain and the angry colors bashed into her consciousness.

She gasped. Bile crawled up the back of her throat, bringing a sick taste to her mouth. She coughed slightly.

Grant hit the brakes, peering in her direction. "Well?"

The stabbing stopped. Kali sighed in relief. "It's gone."

They peered through the window into the gloomy surroundings. A dirt road loomed on Kali's right. Even in the dark of night she could see the ribbons twisting toward her. Her neck twitched. "Turn here. She's up here."

Kali no longer had any doubts. Images slammed into her. Children playing, a family gathering, laughter and arguing combined as faces and places flashed too quickly to catch as the impressions kept rolling on.

Grant shook his head as he drove the car onto the dirt road. "We are going to have a talk after this. I can't believe that even after seeing your sketches, you didn't tell me about this."

The visions receded, letting Kali catch her breath.

"Shiloh is my cover. To make it look like she's the one finding the bodies." Kali leaned forward, peering through the windshield. "The paintings and sketches are a new development. Not expecting them, I didn't have a cover story ready."

"Anything else you've hidden from me?"

Shearing pain stabbed through the back of her neck. The colors throbbed.

"Stop!"

Kali held her breath, waiting for the pain to ease as the vehicle rolled to a standstill. Kali pointed to his window in the direction where angry ribbons twisted in the night sky. "She's over on the crest."

"God."

Kali hopped out.

Grant exited the car, flashlight in hand and walked over to stand at her side. "There's nothing here."

"Yes, there is. I wish I'd brought Shiloh now. She'd have picked up the decomp." Closing her zipper against the chill of the night, she pointed at storm clouds off to the north. "We need to hurry to beat the storm."

Grant lifted his head to study the horizon. "Why didn't we bring Shiloh, again? If we find anything, I'll have to get a team here fast."

"We didn't bring Shiloh because she's tired, because I didn't expect to actually find anyone and besides...we don't need her," Kali said, her tone grim. "The victim is just a few yards up." Sand and loose gravel grated under their feet. The hoot of an owl sounded far off in the distance. With the stormy weather coming in, the air practically crackled with static.

"How'd the killer expect you to find her way the hell out here?"

"I have no idea. No one, and I mean no one, knows about my weird psychic skills." She thought about that for a moment and realized it was no longer true. "Except you and Stefan."

"The killer may have suspected it anyway. Even if only as an explanation for your successful record," Grant said.

She glanced at him, his face a pale circle in the dark. "Except these skills are relatively new. That reputation was established long before these weird twinges showed."

Grant frowned. "But this person wouldn't know that."

"Christ." The killer could be putting her years of success down to otherworldly reasons instead of experience. By being forced to play the killer's bizarre game, Kali could actually be proving the killer right about her 'mad skills.'

The clouds separated, releasing the moon from its shadowy hold to highlight the violent energy twisting and churning at one spot.

"Why don't we do this stuff in daylight?" Kali asked, knowing there was no answer, but wishing there was anyway.

Grant strode forward, passing her slightly. "You tell me. This is your show."

"No, this is the killer's show." Kali stumbled in the dark, caught herself and carried on. The terrain leveled off. They angled around a crop of bushes and stopped. They were at the top of a knoll with the ground dropping off on the other side.

Kali stopped, hands on her hips, to catch her breath. "Right, she's here. At least I think she is. Normally, I have Shiloh to confirm something like this."

Grant walked closer. "The dirt is loose and the slope accessible on the downward side." As he shone the light over the surrounding area and the big evergreen in front of them, Kali saw some of the dirt had fallen away. Moonlight highlighted the skeleton roots, exposing huge hollows underneath. The dirt pile underneath suggested something was buried here.

She bent over, scraping up a handful of soil, before letting it slip through her fingers. "It's sandy. With the dry spring and summer we had, interspersed with heavy storms, this is a perfect burial place begging for a crazy killer."

"I need to call a team."

"And if she's not here?"

"Is she?" His gaze locked on hers.

"I think so. But are you willing to call out a team without confirming there's a crime scene?"

"How much information can you get about her? Can you show me a spot where there is less dirt that I might be able to brush away enough to confirm what we have? We have to make sure we disturb the area as little as possible though."

Grant rested the flashlight on a root where it cast a yellow light in the gloom. "And I'll try to grab a couple of pictures before we touch anything." He pulled a camera out of his pocket, surprising, and momentarily blinding Kali as several flashes went off.

When he was done, she suggested, "You're at her feet. It might be better to try for her face?"

"You can tell?" Poor light or not, she could see her statement had thrown him. He studied the ground.

Kali stepped forward. "Yes. She's in a relaxed fetal position with her head here." She pointed out the correct layout. "She's facing us." She placed her hand gently where the woman's head lay hidden. A large chunk of earth slid down. "Try there. The layer is thinner now."

Pulling thin gloves from his pocket, he bent to where she pointed and scooped one handful of dirt away. Sand slid into the newly created space. He worked gently for a few minutes. Kali was mesmerized by his gentleness as he brushed the dirt away from the pile. He treated the area with deference. Her heart warmed. He believed her. And he cared about the woman beneath the ground. An odd euphoria swept over her. Followed by doubts. What if she were wrong?

"There." Kali cried out. "Stop. I think I see something."

Leaning back on his haunches, Grant reached for the flashlight.

"I need more light." He flashed the light down on the spot – and reared back.

She crowded beside him. "What? What did you find?"

Eerie flickering light shone on the exposed surface. A small delicate nose blended into the grains of sand. A gold earring with an emerald starburst twinkled in the dirt. Kali sucked in her breath, tears gathered at the corners of her eyes. Although expected, nothing prepared her for the reality of what she faced.

And nothing could camouflage the eye that stared out –
accusing them both.

Recognition slammed into her. Kali jumped back with a
small cry.

Grant spun, reaching for her. "It's okay." He laid a gentle
hand on hers. "We found her. That's why we're here. To bring
her home." He tugged her trembling frame into his arms. "Take a
minute. Breathe."

She shuddered. Closing her eyes briefly, she leaned into his
comforting arms. Nothing could stop the image from burning
into her memory, where she knew it would stay for the rest of
her life. Sorrow washed over her. Pulling back slightly, she gazed
up at him.

Pain speared her heart. "I know her. She's a regular at
Second Chance. Her name is Melanie Rothschild."

CHAPTER SEVENTEEN

Grant stood on Kali's front doorstep. He should have let someone else make this call. Dan maybe. It would have been easier. But it wouldn't have been right.

The news would hurt her regardless of who delivered it. Maybe he could at least give her a few answers to go with it. Even worse, no one who knew about this was going to be able to talk about it. Not until the killer had been caught, just in case it *was* case related.

He rang the doorbell before stuffing his hands in his pants pockets. Inside the house, Shiloh barked. Kali's voice murmured softly. He loved the soft caring in her voice. Her voice took on an almost sing-song tone when she spoke to the dog.

He didn't want to break her heart today. But his news would. He glared at the low-lying clouds. Rain could break before he made it back to town. He didn't have this window of time but had made it happen anyway. He'd yet to make it to bed. Talk about a shitty night. He rubbed his whiskered chin, wishing he'd had time for a shower and shave first. Still, he was here. He could find an hour for her.

The door opened.

Kali's face lit up with surprise...and he hoped, with pleasure.

"Kali, may I come in?"

The surprise dropped away, a hint of dread slipped in to replace it. Wordless, she opened the door wide enough for him to enter. "I have fresh coffee. Would you like a cup?"

"Thanks."

She led the way to the kitchen. "I presume you have news about last night. I have to admit that I didn't sleep very well. Just the thought of—"

"I didn't come about last night." He hated to see her step falter, her back stiffen. Her shoulders hunched as if fearing a blow, but despite that, she slowly turned to face him.

"I'm sorry. I wish I had better news."

She swallowed. "Just tell me."

Shit. Still, straight out was best. "We found Brad."

"What?"

"He's dead."

Kali closed her eyes briefly and bowed her head. Her hand climbed to her neck as she sagged into the first chair. She tried to speak, but no words came out. Shiloh came to her side, whining deep in her throat. She laid her head on Kali's leg.

To give her a moment, Grant walked over to the coffee pot and poured her a cup. Returning, he placed it on the table beside her. He walked to the open porch doors and stared out at the sky that couldn't make up its mind.

"What happened?"

He walked back, pulled out a second chair and sat down in front of her. Reaching over he picked up one chilled hand and warmed it in his. "We don't have all the details at this point. His body was found a few hours ago. Apparently it had been there for a while."

"Where?" she whispered, her other hand buried in Shiloh's ruff.

"In Sacramento. He never left. The authorities are working on the theory that he stumbled into the cordoned-off area after a night of drinking. The area was unstable. Part of the building shifted, crushing him under a heavy load of concrete."

Kali placed her second hand over his and squeezed tight.

"Poor Susan." She stared at their clasped hands, but he doubt she saw them.

"Kali? Kali, I'm so sorry."

"When?" Clearing her throat, she asked in a hoarse voice. "When did he die?"

Grant stroked the side of her hand on his. "Don't know yet for sure. He was found in sector four at the site." His thumb moved gently back and forth. She watched the movement for a long moment, then lifted her head to face him. He didn't have much more information to give her. Except one thing. "He would have died instantly."

Her eyelids slammed shut. He could only imagine she knew exactly what condition of Brad's body when it had been found. She had a wealth of images to draw on for that. Her bottom lip trembled as she struggled for control.

He admired her even more when her lips firmed, but his heart broke when she asked the next question.

"How do they know it was him? Could there be a mistake?"

Her shoulders hunched against his answer. There was no way to make it easier on her. He turned her hand protectively then squeezed her hand gently, bracing her. "I'm sorry. The victim's DNA is being tested to be sure, but there's little doubt. The victim had on a SAR vest and Brad's wallet was on the body. Everything else fits too."

Her shoulders slumped. "Oh." She produced a sad smile. "Being buried alive is every rescuer's worst nightmare, you know. It's something we see too often. Something that sits in the back of our psyche and festers." Kali closed her eyes, hot tears meandering downward at the corners. "It really hurts that he died alone."

"A couple of the locals said he'd stayed around for a while, drinking heavily."

Kali nodded. "He sent Sergeant home to Susan and stayed behind to drink away his demons alone." Tugging her hands free, she stood and walked to the railing. Shiloh followed to lean against her leg. Several sniffles sounded. He wanted to walk over and take her into his arms, but she'd walked away. A part of him understood. She needed to find her balance in a world that had suddenly shifted. As he watched, she wiped away her tears on her sleeve before turning her face to the breeze

"Is there anything I can do?" she asked after a moment.

Grant joined her at the railing.

"I don't think so. Susan's mother is arriving tonight. Brad's body will be shipped home in the next few days. I'll keep you up to date on arrangements when they're made."

"Please do. How's Sergeant?"

"According to Susan, he's fine."

Kali cringed. "Sergeant will be lost. Brad raised, trained and worked him from a young pup."

Grant didn't have an answer for that.

"I wonder what she'll do with him."

"I doubt she knows at this point."

Kali sniffled, releasing a heavy sigh. "So much death."

"I told Dan. He said he'd be here soon." Grant checked his watch. "I can't stay. I'm meeting with the profiler, then I'll try to grab a few hours of sleep."

"Oh, I never thought. You've been out all night on the scene, haven't you?" She rubbed her eyes. "Any news on last night's victim? Do we know if it was Melanie, for sure?"

"Not yet. The coroner has her now."

She sighed. "I came home instead of hanging around, but I didn't sleep. It gets harder every night."

"It's difficult to rest knowing this killer is out there, isn't it."

She stopped. "Damn, this is hard. Could Brad have been a victim of the killer?"

Grant's heart ached. "No, Kali. All indications say it was an accident."

With a tremulous smile, she nodded. "Thanks. It does make it easier. I don't think I could have stood it otherwise."

"It's tough enough to deal with, as it is."

"Dan and I are both going to miss him." New tears formed at the corner of her eyes. She wiped them away. "I relied on Brad's laughter, his compassion and, most of all, his support. My world has become a darker place." She forced a tremulous smile through her tears.

He couldn't stand it. Stepping closer, he opened his arms.

And she drifted into them.

Enfolding her close, he held her while the tears poured. He'd be late. Too damn bad. Sometimes schedules had to adapt. He closed his eyes and rested his head against hers.

It surprised him how quickly the storm burned out. Finally she lay with her head resting against his chest, staring out toward the ocean. He just held her. When she made a move to retreat, he forced himself to drop his arms, allowing her to step back.

"Better?" He searched her eyes, beautiful deep blue, awash in tears. But, thankfully, not so lost as before.

"Thank you. It's going to take some time, but I will get there. Brad wouldn't have wanted me to wallow. He'd rather I open a bottle of champagne and celebrate his life. I'll talk to Dan, maybe plan something like that." She retreated another few steps.

He hated the widening distance, but the moment was over. "Hold off spreading the news. We've asked Susan and Dan to keep a lid on this for a few days. Try to avoid any interference in our investigation. Just for a day or two."

She attempted a smile. "Right. We still have a killer to catch. You need to go. I'm fine. Dan will be here soon and that will help. I want you to make your meeting with the profiler, then please get some rest. This madness needs to stop."

She hooked Grant's arm and ushered him back through the house to the front door. She opened it and damn near pushed him out.

"You're sure you're all right. I hate to leave you alone."

This time her smile had real humor. "I'm fine. Go. And..." she reached up and kissed his cheek. So gently, so tenderly, he almost snatched her back into his arms.

It was the first physical move she'd made toward him.

With that, he left. But in his car, driving down the highway, he couldn't stop grinning.

Progress.

***

Kali stood looking out at the empty driveway long after Grant left.

She hated that sense of loss as the distance between them widened. Could he see the energy, the colors vibrating between them?

Even through her grief and tears, they'd been hard to miss. It gave her hope. Something she badly needed today.

Her eyes burned from the tears already shed, and she could only imagine how they'd be by the end of the day.

God. Brad, her staunchest defender and best friend since forever was never going to come home again. With this psychic murder stuff consuming her, she hadn't had time to really worry about him. She hadn't allowed herself to consider such an outcome. She'd been expecting him to show up out of the blue with that sheepish look of his. Instead he was already dead. And no one had known.

Picking up the phone, Kali dialed Susan's number. If Brad's death was painful for her, she could only imagine what Susan was going through right now. Her heart ached for the widow. Susan and Brad had been married for over ten years. Kali had lost a beautiful friend, but Susan had lost her partner.

"Hello?"

The ravaged voice made Kali's stomach clench in sympathy. "Susan, it's Kali. I just heard. I'm so sorry."

"Sorry?" Susan's voice had a dreamlike quality, as if she wasn't fully hearing Kali's words.

"Yes. I know how difficult Brad's death is for you. It's hard on all of us. These rescue missions can be dangerous, but we don't really expect anything bad to happen to those we love."

"Love?" Susan's voice sharpened. "What do you know about love? Brad was *my* husband. He was down there because of you. Because *you* needed him. This is your fault. Yours. He's dead because of you." Her voice cracked with tension; her blistering words singed Kali's heart. "Stay away from me. Don't call me again — ever. I hate you!"

Kali sat frozen. Logically, she could rationalize away everything Susan had said. Susan was upset, grieving and angry at the world. Kali knew that, but her heart didn't care.

It hurt.

Brad had been her friend. She'd loved him, too. And it hurt to know that to a certain extent, Susan had been right.

A couple of times, Brad had mentioned quitting, staying home with Susan because she wanted him to, instead of gallivanting off at a moment's notice. Kali knew Susan had made sacrifices. She'd endured missed birthdays, messed up plans, long absences. These had only gotten worse with Brad's increased drinking bouts.

Kali had always persuaded him to stay. Brad was good at what he did. Very good. The rescue world needed him.

But at what cost to Brad?

Guilt sat heavy on her heart.

Her world would never be the same again.

Sitting there, she heard the crunch of gravel as a vehicle drove in. Dan. At least she hoped it was; she didn't want to see anyone else.

Getting up, she walked to the front door and watched Dan park his car.

Her spirits lifted at the sight of him...until she saw his expression.

Grief had ravaged his face, wrinkles appearing where there hadn't been any. Skin folds deeper, but thinner, like all the substance had drained from him.

"Kali?"

She teared up. "Oh Dan."

They held each other for several minutes. Holding Dan's frail body, her grief receded as concern for him grew. Dan couldn't handle much more.

She pulled back slightly, gave him a sad smile and ushered him toward the kitchen. "God, I can't imagine not seeing Brad ever again."

"I know." Dan hesitated, as if wanting to ask a question but not daring.

Tiredly, she glanced his way as she automatically gravitated to the coffeepot. "What?"

With a heavy sigh, he asked softly, "I wondered if you had any news, preferably good news, about Julie?"

Kali blinked, her forehead creasing. What was he talking about? Good news. There wasn't any left in this world. "News? Julie? Oh, my God." She spun around. "That's right, you haven't heard."

"What? What did you find?"

"We found the other victim."

"What?" Dan grabbed her by the shoulders. "Where? Was it Julie? Please, tell me it wasn't." Kali, surprised by his outburst, didn't answer fast enough.

"Kali, please. Tell me." Agony threaded his voice.

She closed her eyes. She didn't want to tell him. They had too much pain now. Death surrounded them. "It wasn't Julie."

"Oh, thank God." Dan searched her face, but what he read made his shoulders slump. His arms dropped to his side, while dread hooded his eyes. "Who was it?"

Pain shattered Kali's calm once again. "The FBI people have to confirm it." She took a deep breath. "But I think it's Melanie."

This time tears washed Dan's rummy eyes. "Melanie? Little Melanie Rothschild? She's just a girl. A teenager."

"She celebrated her twentieth birthday a couple of months ago, I think." Kali's voice choked. "Not even twenty-one."

"Oh, my God! Why? What could she possibly have done to this guy?"

Kali had no answer.

Dan stepped through the glass doors into the sunlight shining on the deck, one hand over his face, his head bowed, his shoulders shaking. Kali gave him a few moments. She poured coffee and took her time carrying the cups outside. She sat down in her favorite chair and waited. The air was fresh and clean. There was no sign of the horror and pain going on in the world. There was no fear, or sense of threat out here. Maybe, because she knew about the surveillance team...that she wasn't alone. She didn't believe the killer was after her...yet. But neither did she want Dan to be a target.

Dan turned to face her, one last sniffle sounding. "I saw her at the center a couple of days ago." He screwed up his face. "Wednesday, maybe? I can't be sure until I check the schedule."

"Do you remember who else was there?"

Dan wiped his eyes with the back of his hand and frowned. "I remember a class had started, I'd escaped to my office and she stopped in to say 'hi.' Although, I admit my memory is a bit faulty lately."

A ghost of smile kissed Kali's lips. Dan's memory had long been an issue, but particularly this last year.

"Jesus, Kali. What kind of evil has found us? We have to close the center until this is over. He can't have any more of our people. Let's cut off his supply."

"I think it's way past that point. He already knows many of the people. We can ask Grant about closing the center." Kali dialed his number, hoping to catch him between his meeting with the profiler and his planned nap.

"Ask him about Melanie, too." Dan collapsed on the kitchen chair and rested his head on his hands. "Maybe it's a mistake."

As she waited for Grant to pick up, Kali turned to look at Dan. "What about Melanie's family, wouldn't they have missed her? Have they called her in as a missing person?"

"They've gone east for a couple of weeks. Melanie's in college part-time and didn't want to miss classes."

The mention of schooling twigged Kali's memory. "Right. She'd worked part-time in a vet clinic for years and wanted to become one herself."

"Yeah. I can't believe she's..."

"Let's find out for sure."

Grant's tired but welcoming voice filled her ears, easing some of the hard knots from today's series of shocks. "How are you?"

She understood what he was asking. "I'm okay. I'm adjusting. Slowly. Dan is with me."

"Good, I'm glad he made it. It's better if you're not alone right now. Probably better for him, too."

She glanced apologetically at Dan and moved her conversation into the kitchen. "Did you confirm ID of last night's victim? Was it Melanie?"

"It appears so, but we haven't located her next of kin. Also, I wondered if you knew if she'd been a survivor of some kind? If she had been that would help to cement the link with the others."

"Melanie lived at home, but her parents have gone back east for a couple of weeks. Dan says she was a student here at Rosewood College. As to the other...I'm not sure. Hang on." Kali turned and asked Dan.

Dan's eyes clouded over and stared at her, thinking hard. Then he nodded. "Oh Shit. In New Zealand. Remember?"

Kali shook her head. "I don't think I ever heard about it. What happened? And how would the killer know?"

"She'd spoken of it several times. They were caught in a big rock slide. Her family survived, but a couple they were traveling with didn't. "

She turned back to the phone. "Grant—"

"I heard. Let me talk to Dan for a moment."

"Yes, here." Kali handed the phone to Dan.

With raised eyebrows, he accepted the phone, clearing his throat before saying in an almost normal tone of voice, "Grant? What can I do for you?"

Kali slumped in her chair, letting the conversation drift around her. Too many shocks, too fast. Christ, she hated this. Her neck throbbed as she let her mind wander. She wanted to do something for Brad – and didn't know what. She'd wait until those at the center heard. Brad had been well-loved. Maybe shutting the center down until this craziness was over and the killer caught was the best idea. She couldn't bear it if anyone else was taken. Melanie and Julie were already too many.

Dan interrupted her musings. "Kali, they're putting cameras and some men in the center. They're operating on the assumption he's a regular and don't want to close the center in the event it might scare him off. It's been well over twenty-four hours. I know they have Julie listed as a missing person and there's an APB out there, but it doesn't feel like enough."

That made sense. She thought of something she'd meant to ask him before the bad news had chased everything else from her mind.

"Dan, do you know any religious-fanatic types at the center?"

His eyes narrowed in consideration. "No one comes to mind. Don't know about the groupies though." He shrugged.

Groupies formed and dissipated on a regular basis. Year in and year out there'd be a half dozen core members and a dozen that rotated between the various centers. For the most part, they were harmless, only wanting to belong, to be cool. To remember them all would take a miracle, as they came and went with regularity. Kali eased deeper into her seat, slowly rubbing her thigh muscles. Everything ached today.

"What's on your mind?" Dan asked.

She gave him a dispirited smile. "The loss of innocence."

He stared. "Huh?"

"We've been naive. Cavalier with people entering and leaving the center at will. Our records are dismal, mostly covering payroll and expenses." She looked over at him. "We assumed nothing could go wrong. That because we worked to help people, we'd be protected. Instead, we've left ourselves wide open for this."

Dan hunched his shoulders. "Grant made a similar comment."

Kali shuddered. She could just imagine. "I don't understand. Why is this guy doing this? It's almost as if he sees himself as an angel of death, correcting the balance like in that movie, *Final Destination,* where Death comes after everyone who escaped him." Shivers rode her spine to her hipbones, making her consider the theory a little longer.

Dan's eyes widened. "These people are given a second chance by surviving a disaster. Their lives are changed forever. Many suffer the aftereffects every single day." His words burst out as if his frustration and emotion had finally boiled over.

"I know that, and you know that, but this guy isn't thinking with a full deck."

The conversation waned on that note.

Kali studied Dan's face, the fatigue, the dullness of his gaze. He'd been through a lot already. Did she dare ask him about something painful? Taking a deep breath, she plunged in. "Dan, I called Susan today to offer my condolences. I've actually phoned several times, but she wouldn't return my calls." Kali took a steadying breath. "I know she's hurting right now, but she sounded like she hated me. She blames me for Brad's death. I understand that. But something about the phone call, her words, her voice, made me think there was something else going on."

Dan shifted uncomfortably, his glance sliding away.

Uh-oh. Kali frowned. "Dan what aren't you telling me?"

His sorrowful gaze brushed her face briefly before flitting off again. "I don't want to spread rumours, Kali. Brad's dead. Leave the past where it belongs."

"But that's the problem; he's dead. I can't ask him. And I'd like to understand her behavior."

He ran a tired hand through his thinning hair. He stayed silent for a long moment, then his shoulders drooped. "Susan believed you and Brad were close, too close."

***

The hacksaw moved back and forth with swift sure strokes. Good thing he'd come prepared. The PVC pipe was just too long. But he would fix that. The cut piece fell to the ground as the blade sliced through the last edge. This time he'd planned ahead. Once again, things had fallen into place. The industrial cardboard box had been tossed in a dumpster close to the center. It was big enough for Julie and yet small enough to carry into the woods. It should be a breeze to bury. Good thing she was a little bit of a thing. She'd be fine for several days in here. And he really did want to visit with her for a while.

She'd made it easy for him. Almost too easy. No challenge. Of course she hadn't appreciated his efforts. No, she'd screamed at him something fierce. He grinned. The fighting spirit might keep her alive longer than his other victims. None of them had presented a challenge. Melanie had been docile and David, well, he'd gone out like a light after that blow to the head, never even whimpered. He frowned. Unexpected, that. Something must have been wrong with David in the first place. The guy had really let himself go.

At least it made it easy to send him home. If he'd been conscious and in a fighting mood, David had been wiry and strong enough to have caused him hell. Instead, he'd collapsed after one blow.

Not like Julie. She was a fighter.

He picked up the large PVC pipe sitting off to one side. At six feet long, the pipe would deliver air from the surface directly inside the box to Julie. The bottom of the pipe had been cut off at a long angle to let in lots of air at the bottom.

Turning his attention back to where Julie lay unconscious and trussed like a Thanksgiving turkey, he repositioned her head where she'd have instant access to the fresh air. Closing the heavy lid, he snapped the interlocking tabs in place then used the commercial staple gun to secure them closed. With the pipe positioned inside, he cut a hole on the top of the box. Perfect. He secured the pipe to the box with duct tape, letting it stand straight. Julie moaned from inside her makeshift coffin. He grinned. Her voice was barely audible now and with a hill of dirt on top she'd never be heard.

That ought to give them some time together. And give Kali a chance to figure this one out. Not too long though. Maybe, a day or two? Julie would hold for that long. He could even 'up the ante.' Another phone call maybe? How about a letter? Or another gift? He doubted that she appreciated his last one.

With one last look around, he started shoveling dirt on top of the box. Julie moaned again. He smirked. A perfect time for her to wake up. She'd understand what was happening. On cue, the box shifted slightly as Julie struggled inside. A kick resounded at the bottom end then another. But with both hands and feet tied, her attempts weren't doing much. He laughed.

What was that old saying, 'do what you love and love what you are doing?' Yes. He'd finally found a service that he could enjoy.

Perfect.

With a light-hearted whistle, he lifted the next load of dirt.

CHAPTER EIGHTEEN

"Too close? As in more than friends close?" she asked cautiously, trying to wrap her thinking around Dan's words.

Dan's wrinkles scrunched before relaxing in defeat. "Yeah."

"But we weren't...we never...I mean...It wasn't like that between us." Outrage sparked. "Dan, we were friends and coworkers but nothing more."

He held up his hands. "Kali, I believe you. But I doubt you'll convince Susan."

"But why? We were never...never..." She leaned forward and emphasized the next word. "Lovers."

He squinted, considering her words. "Did you really *not* know how Brad felt?"

Memories crowded in on her. Brad finishing her sentences. Brad delivering coffee when she'd hit exhaustion. The caring hugs during emotional, overwrought times. The constant comforting presence at her side.

"I loved him," she whispered, hating the paradigm shift in her world. "Like a brother."

"And he loved you."

Dan said it simply, eloquently, and Kali accepted the truth. How could she not have known? How well had she known him, really, on the inside where it counted? Her chest hit lockdown. She couldn't breathe. Brad had cared; he'd wanted more from her and she hadn't noticed. She closed her eyes against the tears threatening to fall and slumped back. "I didn't know. Oh, God. I'm so sorry, Brad."

For several moments, Kali couldn't speak as regrets clogged her throat. Finally, Kali leveled her gaze at Dan. "How did Susan find out?"

"I think she probably suspected something for a while, but Brad asked for a divorce before leaving for Sacramento."

"He what?" Kali straightened in her seat. She needed the shocks to stop. "He never said a word to me. I knew they had some trouble but not divorce-sized trouble."

"He wanted to wait until everything had been finalized. Susan had said no, not wanting to change the status quo in her life."

"Status quo?" Kali blinked. What an odd thing to say. "Didn't she love him? Want her marriage to work?"

"Brad told me before he left that he needed time away and his wife needed time to think, to decide what to do. She'd asked him to stay home this trip and work things out. But he left – with you."

"Poor Susan. Oh, Dan. I never wanted to break up their marriage. I was happy for them. Proud to know someone in this day and age who could make marriage work."

"That's why you felt safe getting close to him."

Confused, Kali glanced at him. "What do you mean?"

"Kali, you haven't had a serious relationship in – what, five, six years – or dated for at least eight months. You've been emotionally locked down since Mexico," he said, talking right over her spluttering, "Brad shot to the top of your best friend list years ago because he was married and you thought he wanted nothing more from you. He was safe."

Kali winced. "Ouch."

"Brad understood, particularly how you'd changed these last six months. He felt that, once freed of Susan, he'd slide into a 'more than friend' relationship with you."

"Crap." Kali's mind bordered on overload. Safe and complacent, yup that was her motto. Except in Brad's case, she'd been blind and stupid.

"No wonder Susan won't talk to me." Kali struggled to compartmentalize the new onslaught of guilt. She'd failed everyone lately.

"Right."

Silence ensued. Hurting, Kali whispered. "I didn't know. Honest."

Dan placed a hand on her shoulder. "I believe you."

Kali offered him a wan smile, more exhausted than if she'd come from a three-day rescue with no rest. Done in. "Do I say something to her? Do I leave her alone? What?" And why was she asking him?

Because she no longer trusted her own judgment.

"Let her alone. Give her time to heal."

A common sense attitude, but one that offered no closure for Kali. She wasn't sure how to live with that.

"You might want to consider your relationship with Grant for the same reason."

"I'm not going to think about Grant." Not now. Maybe never – considering Dan's latest bombshell.

"Do you want a relationship?"

Kali quirked her lips and slunk lower. "I hadn't thought so. My life is chaotic enough."

Dan's steady gaze showed years of wise living. "And now?" He raised one eyebrow at her. "Grant is seriously interested. I've known him for years. I know how his job has changed him. But being around you takes years off his face."

"No." Dan was just being sweet. Then again, Grant's energy reinforced Dan's words. There'd be no blending of their energies if Grant wasn't interested, if being together wasn't right on some deep level. That didn't make this the right time or place. "He and I are all about the victims."

"No," he corrected. "That *is* your relationship. You see things the same way, think the same way and do the same work. With so much in common, you haven't realized you're working and growing together. *Growing together.* Did you hear it the second time or do I need to say it again?"

Kali hated the squirming child inside, as if she'd been caught in a lie. He was right. She knew it, but...she didn't know what she wanted to do about it. And what did Grant want with her?

"Right." Dan stood up. "I'm going to head to the center. I want to be on hand in case some of this news sneaks out so I can put a stop to the talk. I doubt they'll release Melanie's name yet. It's going to be hard to keep a lid on this for long. And you, well you need to think about what I said."

Kali gave Dan a good-bye hug at the front door. The phone rang. Hurrying into the kitchen, Kali answered it.

"Hello."

"Found another one, did you? Too late, again. Here, I'd hoped you'd be a decent challenge. Instead, you can't even get into the game."

Fury and pain exploded through her. "What have you done with Julie?"

An ugly silence filled the phone line.

"Julie is fine – for the moment. I've given her a fighting chance as you appear to need the extra time." The voice cackled once before ringing off.

Fingers shaking, Kali struggled to dial Grant's number. Her words tripped over each other as she tried to explain. "He just called... He has Julie...something about a fighting chance... I don't know; he said something about I needed the help?"

Grant fired several questions at her. "Think. Did he say anything specific to help us find her? It's been recorded but give me what you remember right now."

Kali repeated the conversation the best she could.

"I hate to ask, but Julie's life is at stake. Will you please sit with your sketchpad and try to get another picture?"

"There's no guarantee," she warned.

"No. I know. But everything helps and at this moment, you're the best hope Julie has."

***

Ha. Stumped them this round. Damn straight.

A breeze slipped through the branches. He adjusted his stolen jacket, grateful for his foresight in lifting it off the neighbor's back deck. Anything to throw Shiloh off his scent.

Leaning forward, he adjusted the focus on his binoculars to peer through his heavily treed bower directly at Kali's deck. Kali leaned over the railing, her face, a picture of pain. Perfect. Let her stew.

The killer opened up his granola bar, ripped off a piece and popped it into his mouth. This was better than dinner and a show. He vaguely remembered evenings long past, spent in theatres. At a time when he believed in ever-lasting love. Right, those were his young and stupid years. His face puckered. He washed the granola bar down with lukewarm coffee from the thermos. Not a great meal. Still he wasn't ready to leave yet. The sun would be hot soon. Here in the trees, with a breeze blowing in off the ocean, the heat had yet to penetrate.

A great day, which promised an even better evening. He chortled. Later, once darkness fell, he'd go visit Julie.

She'd be waiting for him.

He didn't want to disappoint her.

***

Kali reached for the sketchbook and turned to the sketch that was supposedly of Julie. In the drawing, a pipe brought fresh air in for the victim, extending the person's chances of being found alive. Julie, therefore, had to be restrained in some way that prevented her from digging herself out. The fresh air supply meant the killer assumed she'd be buried for a while. If, and it was a big if, regardless of what had happened so far, the picture was viable, this could be the fighting chance the killer had talked about.

Or he wanted to lull her into thinking Julie was still alive.

"Who exists in Julie's world? Friends? Lovers? And who would know?" she muttered out loud. She laid the sketchbook on the table. "Brenda might." Brenda held a unique position at the center. Not a dog owner or a rescuer, she neither worked nor volunteered but she knew so many that did, she'd become a regular herself.

Picking up her cell, Kali called her. "Hey, it's Kali. Brenda, I have a weird question for you. Do you know if Julie has a current boyfriend?"

"Hi, Kali, how are you? Nice to hear from you. Aren't you wonderful about returning your calls. And why don't you ask Julie yourself."

Kali forced a snicker at her friend's sarcasm. "I would if I could, but she's not answering her phone. And maybe I'm arranging a party for the center and want to know if she has a 'partner' she might like to bring." Kali rolled her eyes at the lame excuse but it's all she could create on the spur of the moment.

"Oooohhh. Am I invited?"

Exasperated, Kali said, "Of course. I'm hardly going to call you about this and then not invite you, too."

"Oh, in that case. As far as I know, Julie does have a new man, but a married one. So I don't think they go out in public."

Not good. A married man meant a clandestine affair. No one would know the details. "That's too bad. I guess I'll have to wait until I get a chance to speak with her then."

And how else could she find out?

"So are you going to ask me?" Brenda's bubbly voice piped up.

Kali rolled her eyes. "So, Brenda, do you have a new man in your life?"

"I dated one guy off and on last month, but that fizzed out." Brenda giggled, obviously not terribly upset over that relationship. "Speaking of losers, I stopped in at the center early last week hoping to find you. Instead, I met a real weirdo. I never did get his name. He called me a couple of days later but I wasn't home. Thankfully."

The hair on Kali's neck quivered. Casually, she asked, "What made him weird?"

Brenda's voice dropped to an eerie whisper, "Fanatically religious."

Religious. Now the hairs on her neck bristled. Taking a deep breath, Kali tried to inject a casual tone to her voice. "How could you tell?"

Brenda's tone sharpened with disgust. "He kept arguing with himself, for God's sake, about how God meted out His own justice." She huffed. "You know me. Any talk of justice and I break out in hives."

Kali knew it well. Brenda avoided all conversations on morals and any mention of right and wrong. She'd enjoyed more than a few married men herself.

"He called and left a message on my machine, suggesting a date with a heavenly experience – a date with destiny." Brenda giggled. "Isn't that the corniest line ever?"

Kali's eyes widened. This guy had possibilities. "Did you erase his message?"

"Absolutely. Think I wanted to keep that?"

"How old is this guy?"

"Who knows – who cares?"

Kali understood. Brenda loved men. All ages, races, and normally, religions. "This guy must have spooked you?"

"It was weird. He called me at home even though I hadn't given him my number. Where'd he get it?" Brenda's voice dropped again. "He had a weird accent – like a bastardized

French or Portuguese or something. Who can tell anymore?" A sigh worked through the phone. "The message kinda freaked me out."

"Would you recognize him again?"

"Absolutely."

"Brenda, I'm going to call you right back. Sit tight for five minutes."

"Wai—"

Kali didn't give her a chance to argue, shutting her off mid-sentence. She immediately called Grant. At this rate, the poor man wouldn't get any sleep.

"Grant," she said without preamble when he answered. "I just spoke with a friend of mine from Second Chance. She met an odd religious guy at the center who called her at her home when he shouldn't have had the number."

"Who?" His voice sharpened, cutting through the line like a knife.

"She doesn't know his name. We can ask Dan, but I don't know if he'll know him from her description either, Grant. I'm wondering about a police artist?"

"I'll call you back."

Kali clicked off the phone. Five minutes later, Grant called back.

"Can you two meet me at the office on Waterston Street?"

"Sure. When?"

"About half an hour. There's an excellent artist who works out of that office. Do you need the address?" Without waiting, he rattled it off. Kali grabbed for a pen, then stopped as she recognized the address. "I know where it is."

Kali hoped Brenda didn't have plans. A half hour didn't give either of them much preparation time. But Julie had no time. She dialed, relieved when her friend picked up on the first ring. "Brenda, I can't explain right now, but I need you to trust me on this. I need you to go with me to the police station and work with a police artist. I can come and pick you up and drive you home again afterwards."

Brenda's gasp came through loud and clear. "The police?"

"Yes, I need you to help me with this."

With a groan, Brenda said. "We've been friends for a long time, but this is just weird."

Kali chewed her bottom lip. "Please, trust me. I have a good reason."

"But why can't you tell me what's going on?" Worry fussed through Brenda's voice. "All right. I don't like it, but I'll do it."

Kali closed her eyes in relief. "Thank you."

CHAPTER NINETEEN

The heat in the small room at the police station made Kali melt. She sent Shiloh to a corner to lie down. After being away most of last night, she hadn't wanted to leave the poor dog alone today. Or maybe Kali didn't want to be without Shiloh. Today had already been hell. Thank God it had been a fast trip to the station. Brenda had peppered her with questions the whole way. Kali stalled her until she could confirm with Grant what she was allowed to say.

Kali removed her light sweater, draping it over one of the chairs before sitting down. "Hi, I'm Kali. This is Brenda. She's the one you'll be working with."

"Hi, I'm Nancy. Brenda, take a seat and let's get started."

Kali hid her grin at the trepidation on Brenda's face. Still, her friend willingly turned to Nancy's fancy computer program.

Once seated, Nancy got straight to work. "Brenda, start by closing your eyes and think back to when you saw this person. Block out all else and focus on his face. Do you see him in your mind's eye?"

"Yes."

"Good. With your eyes closed, give me your impression on the shape of his face? Don't focus on the details, let his face blur into giving you the shape. Round face? Squared off? Perhaps it's more triangular or maybe a heart shape?"

Kali watched as they worked through the various aspects of the face. The artist in her found it fascinating to watch. An irresistible process. A stack of paper sat to one side, with pencils sitting on top. At an opportune moment, Kali snitched one of each, a questioning look on her face as she caught Nancy's eye. Nancy nodded.

Listening to Brenda's answers, Kali sketched the oval face, the large oversized nose, followed with the deep-set eyes. She followed the conversation, understanding the insights as they surfaced. Somewhere along the line, she slipped from awake and aware into something else.

Her hand moved at an incredible pace, filling in, shading, adding a detail here, thickening a line there.

As if a switch had been thrown, she came to an abrupt stop. She leaned back with a deep sigh and rotated her stiff neck. A deafening silence alerted her.

The other two women stared at her.

Kali frowned. "What?"

Brenda spoke first. "You're an artist?"

"It's a hobby of mine." Kali shrugged. "I paint more than I sketch but I'm comfortable with both."

"That's obvious." Nancy spoke up for the first time. Flipping her laptop around, she showed Kali the artistic rendering.

Kali couldn't help but stare. There was something about him she half-recognized. Like someone she should know. The picture, although clear, had a generic look to it. It needed something. But what?

"Now compare the screen to this." Nancy reached across the table for Kali's sketch. She held the sketch up beside the monitor so the other two could see the pictures side-by-side.

"Oh my God."

She'd drawn the same male face. Except her drawing was almost terrifying in detail. "I just followed along with your instructions and her answers."

Brenda peered closer. "How bloody freaky, Kali. You're my friend and I love you, but that drawing is plain scary."

Shooting Brenda a quick glance, Kali returned to analyze the sketch. Hot, fervent eyes stared out at her. A zealot peeped out. The large nose and thin lips represented a simple verbal description that translated into a hawkish nose and a cold angry mouth that promised retribution.

"Maybe my imagination just went wild." Kali avoided looking in their direction. These women had no idea of her weird talents. And Kali didn't want them asking for an explanation.

The door opened. Grant walked in. In the small room his energy surged her way. Tired and pale, it blended with hers – that very act strengthening his. Kali had never seen anything like it as she watched Grant throw off some of the fatigue that had been weighing him down. He even stood straighter.

Casting a surreptitious look at the other two women, she was relieved to see them focused on the drawings.

"Good; you're done?"

"Yep, we're done, but it turns out you didn't need me. Take a look at what Kali sketched while we worked on the digital version."

Kali watched Brenda's reaction to her first glimpse of Grant. Brenda was a notorious flirt. Nothing. Not even a smile for him.

Stepping closer, Grant peered at the paper and digital sketches. "Brenda, is the sketch a good likeness?"

"No, it's a freaking awesome one. Kali nailed him." She shuddered. "Christ, he gives me the chills."

Grant picked up the paper sketch. His eyes met Kali's and held.

Shivers slid down her spine. She understood what he was thinking. She couldn't help but wonder the same thing. Was this the killer?

Speaking slowly, she said, "I think I've seen him around. But this is like an exaggerated version of what I remember. I feel like I know him, but it's not quite right. Dan will know." She gave him an apologetic look. "I've spent too much time away, or hidden in my office at the center."

"Then let's go. We'll have him take a look before I circulate this as a 'person of interest.'"

Kali pulled out her cell phone and dialed Second Chance.

Reaching for her bag, Nancy asked, "We're done, aren't we? I'd like to head out."

Grant reached out to shake her hand. "Yes, thanks for helping. We appreciate it."

"You should convince her to go into the business." Nancy gestured at Kali.

"Nope." Kali shook her head. "Not for me."

Brenda snorted as she stood up. "Sure, you'd rather find dead bodies."

Ouch. Kali ducked the truth. "No, Brenda. I'd rather find live people."

"I say it like I see it." But she smiled at Kali, softening the words. "Can I leave too?"

Kali rose. "I'll take Brenda home, then meet you at the center afterwards, Grant."

"Good, and on the way maybe you can explain what the hell's going on?" Brenda stuck her chin out. "I've been patient Kali, but now it's time for answers."

Grant held the door open for them. "I'll need about ten minutes to finish up here."

Rain drizzled from the gray clouds overhead, forcing Brenda and Kali to make a dash for the vehicle. Shiloh beat them to the car. Kali fired up the engine and drove in the direction of Brenda's home.

As soon as she pulled onto the main road, Brenda bubbled over like a water pipe that had popped a cap. "Now that we're alone, what's with you and Grant? He couldn't take his eyes off you. How come you didn't tell me you had a dish on the side?"

Kali shot her a disbelieving look and changed lanes.

"Typical. You didn't even notice," Brenda said wryly.

Really? Another quick look at her friend confirmed it. "Seriously?"

"Yeah, girlfriend."

"Oh." Warmth bloomed in her chest. Maybe there was something solid there. Good. She could work with that.

Brenda giggled.

She pulled up outside Brenda's house. "Home. Thanks for helping this afternoon."

Collecting her purse from the floor, Brenda commented, "You never did explain what's going on. I got that it's all hush-hush. Grant did give that whole thank you for coming...your cooperation is appreciated line. But still...a little more, please. You know my curiosity – it's going to kill me!"

"Several people have been kidnapped and two, possibly three have been murdered. This guy could be a suspect." Kali stared out the front windshield. "Don't go out with anyone you don't know really well."

"Good enough." Brenda shuddered as she opened the door. "The same warning applies to you. Thanks for a unique afternoon."

"Stay safe." The door slammed shut as Kali repeated the words to the empty interior as her friend disappeared into her house. Checking her mirrors, Kali reversed her car, and drove toward the center. She'd forgotten to call Dan. The traffic thickened but hadn't reached the critical point of no forward movement. The picture she'd drawn dominated her thoughts. She should know him. She did know him. She just didn't recognize him. How sad was that? She'd spent so much time hidden away from the public, she couldn't even place a new look on an old face.

Driving with deft skill, she maneuvered the Jeep forward, taking the next left and then the long stretch leading to the center. She hoped the news of Brad's demise hadn't made it here yet. It shouldn't have, but bad news always traveled. The more secretive the better. She didn't think she could deal with that kind of conversation right now. Tomorrow would be soon enough. Several vehicles pulled out as she pulled in. A class must be finishing.

Kali waited for a car to pull out before she took its spot close to the front. She checked out the lot but didn't spot Grant's car anywhere. She strode through the front doors, propped wide open as always.

Once again, the center was a mad selection of dogs and people. It seemed like Dan's plans to bring in more business were doing well. Laughter and conversation filled the air punctuated by barks and woofs from the many different dogs. Everything was so normal looking. How could the rest of the world carry on, oblivious to the danger that stalked them?

Needing a touch of normalcy herself, Shiloh enjoyed making the rounds, catching hugs and scratches from friends, old and new. Kali waved at a couple people she knew as she made her way to the coffee pot. Empty as usual. So what else was new? Dan could probably use a cup. She took a minute to make a fresh pot.

"You're gonna share, that aren't you?"

"Jarl." Kali gave him a big hug. Stepping away, she peered into his tired face. "Wow, where were you? You look like hell."

His weary face creased into a grin. "That feels about right. Been doing graveyard work. Hell's been a prime topic lately."

She laughed. "You realize the workers are supposed to do the digging."

Jarl tugged on his scraggly beard. "But I like playing in the dirt."

She shook her head at him. "What type of project this time?"

"Moving an old graveyard." His face scrunched at the memory. "When the land was resurveyed, the old one was outside the church's property lines."

He took a sip of hot coffee, watching as Kali filled two mugs.

Nodding toward the cups, he asked, "Thirsty?"

"One's for Dan."

"I didn't know he was here." Jarl checked the field outside the window where a class had started. "I searched earlier but didn't find him."

Kali smiled at the familiar line of dogs and owners. The owners tried to get the dogs to pay attention and the dogs tried to get the owners to let them do their own thing. "He's probably in his office. I'm trying to bribe my way in." Kali held up the two cups. She needed to make an announcement to let everyone know about Brad, but first she should see if Dan had mentioned it to anyone and what they needed to do for a memorial. Brad had been well-loved here. Everyone would want to say good-bye.

"There's a mess of things to catch you up on. First though, I have a few of the details to sort out with Dan."

"Perfect. I'll talk to you later." Jarl joined the long table of people on the veranda. A hue and cry rose at the sight of the fresh coffee and a stampede headed her way. Kali escaped.

Kali set the coffee cup on the large bookcase in the hallway beside Dan's door and knocked twice.

No answer. "Dan? It's me, Kali. Can I come in?"

Silence. Kali tried to the knob. The damn thing was locked. Shit. Kali pounded on the door. No answer. Something was definitely wrong. Checking her pockets, she realized she only had her car keys on her. She didn't carry the spares for Second Chance if she didn't need to.

Could he have gone home? Pulling out her cell phone, she speed-dialed Dan's number. His voice mail played immediately. Shit.

Kali jumped back when the strip of light showed under the door. Shiloh barked, sensing Kali's distress.

"Kali?" Grant walked toward her. "What's wrong?"

"Thank God, you're here." She motioned toward the door. "Dan's door is locked and he's not answering his cell phone. Something's wrong. I need to get in." She jiggled the doorknob again, despite her shaking fingers. The sense of urgency slammed through the roof.

"Step aside." Grant reached into his rear pants pocket, opened his wallet and slid out a thin metallic tool. Kali watched as he fiddled with the lock, then turned the knob. It opened under his hand. Kali pushed the door open and rushed inside.

The office light shone on the old scarred desk piled high with tumbling stacks of paperwork. There was no sign of Dan. Perplexed, Kali strode to the other side of the desk and gasped.

He lay in a crumpled heap on the floor.

"Oh no, Grant…he's hurt."

Kali fell beside the older man, but Grant beat her to him. "Thank God, he's alive." She reached for the phone and called 911. With so many SAR members at the center, she couldn't think if she'd seen anyone on her way through. They all had medical training of various levels, as she did. Some of her panic eased with Grant crouched at Dan's side. His movements were swift and sure. He opened Dan's shirt and ran his hands over the prone body, searching for injuries. When he withdrew his hand from beneath Dan's head, it was covered in blood.

"Oh, no!"

Grant gave her a sidelong glance but said nothing.

Dan's desk drawer sat open a couple of inches and his computer hummed. Odd, his monitor was off. She frowned. Using a pen, Kali clicked it on. The desktop appeared right away but showed no open documents.

Puzzled, she asked, "Grant, there are no open files on his computer, so why would the monitor be switched off if he was in here working?"

Pulling his attention away from Dan, he sent a fleeting glance toward the screen. "I don't know. Sometimes I shut off my monitor when I'm not using it. But don't touch anything, just in case."

"Do you...suppose someone attacked him?"

Grant countered. "Can you find anything he might have hit his head on?"

Kali walked around the office. The wall behind the office chair held a large map taped to its smooth surface. The corners of the desk showed no blood stains and the filing cabinets were on the other side of the room.

"Not that I can see."

"Thanks. Can you direct the paramedics here, please? Don't discuss details with anyone and no one leaves. My team's on the way. They'll want to question everyone."

Kali raced out.

***

Julie pressed her face against the rough edge of the pipe, sucking in the fresh air. Hot tears seeped down her cheeks. She didn't know where she was or what she was trapped in. It felt like paper under her fingertips but had to be something stronger. She'd tried kicking her way through, but the cord keeping her ankles together hadn't given her much freedom for kicking. Not only had she not made a dent in what trapped her, but with her knees snuggled up to her waist, she could hardly move.

Asshole.

Her mouth was so dry she had trouble swallowing. She wanted a drink of water badly. And a blanket.

The experts said time passed quickly when you floated in and out of consciousness. That a person wouldn't be aware of his surroundings. That he'd have no understanding of what was happening.

The experts were wrong.

Julie did drift in and out of conscious. She did float on a timeless vision of the reality she found herself in. But she fully understood what had happened. Somewhere in the mist, the fog wadded around her, holding the understanding close to her, just not sharp and in focus.

The pain did that.

Julie moaned again.

"Awake again? Lovely."

Julie opened her eyes, blinked against the falling dirt, before focusing on the small circle of light above her head. The pipe she'd found last time she'd awakened had become her symbol of hope. Anyone could find it anytime, accidentally or by design. Find it and her.

Julie struggled to remind herself that she'd survived once. She'd do it again. Then she'd show this asshole the reality of being buried alive. Julie closed her eyes, tears streaking her muddy cheeks. God, she wanted to go home. Home. Where Kali had searched for her, had arranged to have an officer waiting for her. And what had she done? Gotten mad. She'd worked herself into a full blown hissy fit and hadn't done what she'd been told to do. She'd been pissed at them all. What a hell of a time to come to her senses. When it was too fucking late.

Through dry lips, she whispered, "Bastard."

Laughter floated through the pipe.

A small surge of anger whipped through her. Where the fuck was Kali?

***

Kali burst outside through the front door; sirens were already audible approaching along the main road. People ran behind her.

"Kali, what's wrong?"

"Hey, what's going on?"

Kali shot them a frantic glance as the ambulance pulled into the lot. "Dan's collapsed."

"Oh, no!"

More people joined in the commotion. As soon as the EMTs emerged, Kali led the way to the office. There she blocked the stream of curious onlookers. The arrival of Grant's men shifted the crowd back.

Several moments later, Grant strode toward her. "They're stabilizing him now for the trip to the hospital. Do you want to drive or will I?"

She closed her eyes briefly. "You drive."

The paramedics were fast. Dan was wheeled out and loaded into the ambulance within minutes. Kali grabbed her keys and purse, locked up Dan's office and raced to the parking lot. Shiloh ran at her side.

Grant drove from the lot amid cries and good wishes to Dan. Kali waved to them through her tears. Dan was deservedly proud of what he'd built over the last decade. If anything happened to him, he'd be sorely missed. Kali immediately castigated herself for the negative thinking. Dan had hit his head, not collapsed due to a heart attack. His injury could be minor. It had to be.

It wasn't.

After almost an hour in the waiting room, Kali learned Dan suffered from a skull fracture complicated by intracranial bleeding. The doctors were monitoring his condition. Grant had explained the procedure the doctors planned to do if the bleeding and swelling didn't stop. Kali refused to contemplate anyone drilling a hole into Dan's skull. The idea of him with his lifeblood dripping away made her cringe.

Stay positive.

Kali rotated her neck to ease the ribbons of tension knotting her shoulders. She knew she should leave, but still hoped to see Dan – if only for a minute. Sitting there didn't help her mind-set. It gave her too much time to think. So much heartache. So many losses. David. Melanie. Brad. Julie. No, damn it, not Julie. Kali jutted out her chin. Enough was enough.

Her shoulders sagged. But what could she do? Grant and his team were questioning everyone at the center right now, according to what he'd said after she'd updated him on Dan's condition. The team had run the list of names she'd given them. The police report had arrived on the Bralorne murder. The profilers were expecting to have something soon. And then there was the sketch. According to Grant, the FBI was working on that.

Kali felt distanced from it all. For those minutes, her life had shifted, narrowing to a single focus – Dan. To lose him...well, she hadn't even dealt with the other recent losses. Emotion flooded her heart and salty tears welled. The losses had come so fast, there'd been no time to grieve. Time was a luxury she hadn't been afforded. When this hell finished, when there was time to honor her friends the way she should, then she'd say her good-byes.

If she were lucky, she'd have sorted through her bewilderment and a growing sense of betrayal, whether right or wrong, about Brad by then. How dare he have those feelings for her and not let her know? If he'd mentioned it, hinted at it just once, she'd have explained her position. Let him down gently. Hiccups happened in friendships. They'd loved each other – just differently. God, she missed him. Tears ran down her cheeks. Kali sniffled, wiping tears away with her sleeve.

As she sat there, her tears shifted to deeper frustration, then to anger. Something good needed to happen soon. She'd about had it with this bad news bullshit. Had the FBI found anything on Dan's computer? Or in his office? Attacking Dan didn't make sense. It was a dumb move, an obvious mistake, and she had no doubt that's what had happened. If the killer had been there, someone saw him. And if the killer had made one mistake, maybe he'd made another.

"Miss Jordan?"

Kali stood up at the arrival of the older man. He wore scrubs and just stood there, worry rising to the forefront. "Yes, I'm Kali Jordan." She wiped her eyes on her sleeve.

The man held out his hand. "I'm Dr. Poole. Dan is doing slightly better. The bleeding in his brain has slowed." The doctor offered her a gentle smile. "We're monitoring the swelling. If he continues to improve through the night, we'll be able to upgrade his condition by morning."

"Thank God for that." Kali beamed as the good news set in. "Is he awake?"

"No, and he won't be soon. We're keeping him in a drug-induced coma."

Kali's heart sank. She shoved her hands in her pockets, to stop from wringing them together. A coma didn't sound good. "Can I see him, please?"

He motioned down the hallway. "I'll let you in for just a moment. Come with me."

"Thank you." Kali grabbed her purse and coat then followed him. "I appreciate this."

"Hospital policy states only relatives are allowed in, but the FBI tells me that you occupy a similar position in this gentleman's life."

Sad but true. Kali knew of no relatives, close or otherwise, in Dan's life. His wife had died years ago.

The doctor led her into the intensive care room where Dan lay, covered in blankets, with tubes running in all directions.

"Oh, Dan," she whispered. The injury had aged him. His heavy wrinkles should be smooth in sleep. Instead, they looked thin and flat, as if piled up on top of each other.

"The swelling has distorted his facial features. But that's a temporary situation."

Seeing him lying like this, hurt Kali. He used to have so much vitality, so much to give. Lately he'd slowed down and his memory wasn't as good.

His skin was now the color of plaster; lifeless. "At least that's something." Kali walked over to Dan's bedside. She placed her hand over Dan's cool, still one. Beside him machines hummed with smooth efficiency.

"Yes, but head injuries are tricky." The doctor returned the clipboard to the bed. "He's not out of the woods yet." He met her gaze straight on, a small smile in place. "Not to worry. We're doing everything in our power to make sure he pulls through."

She hoped it would be enough. Dan looked so ill. "I know you are, but that won't stop me from worrying."

"Caring does that to a person. Everyone deserves to be loved."

True. Kali's heart ached. After she lost her dad, Dan had stepped in as a replacement. He'd become that father figure to talk to, to visit with and to offer well-meaning advice – regardless of how wrong it was.

"Can I sit here for a few moments? I promise I won't disturb anything."

"Just a couple of minutes. No longer."

"Thanks." She appreciated the bending of the rules. Dan deserved to know someone cared. Kali barely heard him. "You're going to be fine, Dan. It's okay. You're safe. Honest."

For five minutes, she whispered to him. It didn't matter if he heard her or not but she needed to talk to him. To reach him in some way and to hope that he heard her.

"Excuse me."

Kali turned to face the newcomer. A young nurse stood in the doorway, smiling apologetically at her. "I'm sorry, but it's time for you to leave."

Kali sighed. The nurse was right. It was time to go. On the way she smiled at the officer standing guard. Thank heavens for that. She had put aside her worries about Dan, in order to find Julie and catch a killer.

She'd almost reached the outside the front exit when her phone rang. "Hi, Grant. Any chance of a ride?"

"Good timing, I'm on my way. We have a face on the camera through the research center. Thomas is working on cleaning it up right now." His voice was sharp and businesslike. "I'm hoping you can identify him. I need you to come back to the station."

Walking out the front entrance, Kali tried to put a face to Thomas. She knew she'd seen him before through this case, and that Grant appeared to have a good rapport with him, but things being the way they were, she'd glossed over all those men. And that was wrong. They were working hard and she couldn't even put names to faces.

An oversight she'd have to fix.

Grant pulled up a few minutes later, Shiloh's head hanging out the window. She barked once at the sight of Kali, who laughed. Obviously Shiloh hadn't been upset by staying with Grant. She gave Shiloh an extra cuddle before getting in beside her. Minutes later they were on their way.

"You have a face from the center?"

"Yes, going into your office."

Kali frowned. "You realize it's not *my* office, right?"

The police station loomed ahead. She let Shiloh out after her, then waited for Grant to lock up the car before walking toward him, and the station. Shiloh danced around her. Kali called her over, bending slightly to put a calming hand on Shiloh's head.

Crack.

Pain burned in a fiery streak along Kali's shoulders and back.

"Ohhh." Kali's knees buckled. What happened? She glanced up, confused. Shiloh whined, her face nudging against Kali's cheeks. She tried to stand only to cry out before collapsing back into position.

"Stay down," Grant snapped, standing over her. She barely heard him for the agony burning her neck and head. Kali wrapped her arm around Shiloh's neck, huddling close. Her stomach really didn't feel well. Grant shifted, circling her, searching the surrounding area. Why wasn't he helping her? He should be, shouldn't he? What the hell had happened?

Unaccountably, tears collected in the corner of her eyes. Whatever the cause, he shouldn't have yelled at her.

She burrowed her face in Shiloh's side. Shiloh whined, nudging her cold nose against Kali's hand. Kali scrunched tighter. Somewhere in the background she heard Grant talking on the phone. What a time to socialize. Didn't he see she needed him? She heard him walking toward her.

"Kali, talk to me. Don't you faint on me? Buck up girl."

Lifting her head, she gasped with outrage. "I've never fainted in my life." She tried to shift onto her knees, only to fall forward. Her stomach knotted in a sudden fierce movement. "Ohhh, God, it hurts. Make it stop, please, Grant."

Grant bent, trying to lift her to her feet. "I will, honey. Let's get you inside. The attacker might still be here."

"Attacker?" Kali shifted upward into a half crouch before making it all the way to a standing position, with his help. "Someone attacked me?" Shiloh leaned against her.

Men poured from the building, spreading out to search the surrounding areas. Grant kept her snuggled tight against his chest while he yelled, "He bolted over there." Grant pointed toward the far back of the lot. Guns at the ready, officers fanned outward.

Kali tried to watch, but black spots kept getting in the way. She blinked, trying to see around them, but they moved with her.

"How bad is it?" One officer ran toward her. Kali turned her face into Grant's chest. Sweat dripped along her side. It tickled and bugged her at the same time. Irritated, she swiped at it. And cried out.

"Shhh. Take it easy, Kali. Don't try to move." Grant whispered against her ear, his arms loosely holding her in place. Through the haze of pain, she caught part of the conversation happening…caught the new arrival's last comment.

"I've called for an ambulance."

Kali lifted her head, pulling a frown at the men. "An ambulance?"

The two men glanced at each other, then at her.

In a soft gentle voice, Grant responded, "Kali, it's for you. You've been shot."

CHAPTER TWENTY

Shot?

Pain blasted through her system tenfold with his words. "You shouldn't have told me," she said peevishly. "Now it really hurts."

Grant hugged her close.

Bile floated up her throat at the movement. Kali closed her eyes and clenched her teeth. A moan escaped and she rested against his chest. A whine first, then the gentle paw on her thigh, caught her attention. Shiloh sat beside her, her huge chocolate eyes focused on Kali. Reaching down, Kali tried to reassure her…but damn, it hurt.

"It's okay, sweetheart." Grant's words were calming and he rested his chin on the top of her head. "You're going to be fine. Appears to be a flesh wound, maybe scraping through the layer of fat on your back."

"Ohhh." Kali reared back and slugged him. "How dare you?"

Grant stared at her in astonishment. "Whoa! What's wrong? What did I say?"

Kali snorted at the glint in his eyes. "I don't have *any*," she said, emphasizing the next word. "*Fat* on my back."

A telltale shaking rumble ran through his chest as he wrapped his big arms around her – her fists tucked up tightly against his chest. With a voice thick with mischief, he added, "If you say so."

"I do," she mumbled, burrowing deeper in his arms. Only the pain dug in deeper, grabbed on tighter. "I don't need an ambulance."

"No, maybe not," he whispered, his cheek resting against her hair. "But I might."

"What?" she gasped, pulling free to pat his chest and shoulders. "Where? Did you get shot too? Where does it hurt?" Damn the stupid male psyche, always having to play the big strong role.

With a tug, he pulled her back more securely against him, cuddling her closer. "I'm not hurt. You are."

"But..." Kali stopped fighting to free herself, trying to understand.

"But nothing. I want *you* in an ambulance."

"Why?" She slugged him once more for good measure then collapsed against his chest.

"Ow. What was *that* for?" Grant asked.

"For making me worry."

Grant shook his head at her. "You're making me crazy."

Sirens sounded in the distance.

Pulling free, Kali ran her fingers through her hair to smooth it down. A wave of intense pain bent her over double. She crumpled to her knees. Shiloh whimpered, nudging her nose against Kali's hands. Gasping for breath, she rocked in place.

"Stay with me Kali. Focus on your breathing."

Kali heard him, only that irritating trickle deluged into a stream of wetness. She slapped her hand over the spot. As she pulled her hand away, blood dripped freely off her fingers. *Christ.* Her stomach revolted; she wavered. Digging deep, Kali struggled to remain conscious. Lord, she hurt. Grant's face appeared in front of her. His forehead creased with worry.

Kali drew a deep breath. "I'm okay. It's just blood." Attempting to reassure him, she patted his hand while ice trickled along her spine. Pausing, her hand mid-air, Kali cast a puzzled gaze at Grant. "Something's wrong."

Ice pooled in her tummy. Kali gazed at her belly. The warmth drained from her face, converting her cheeks to frost. Grant's face blurred. Kali opened her mouth. The words froze inside.

She pitched head-first toward the pavement.

***

"Kali!" Grant caught her before she hit the ground, immediately checking for a heartbeat. It pulsed slow and steady. Several other men joined him. Shiloh twisted between them, getting in the way. Her nose pushing against Kali whenever she could reach her.

"Where's the damn ambulance?" The sirens screamed louder.

"They're here, Grant. Take it easy."

The ambulance peeled into the parking lot. Two men hopped from the vehicle. One ran toward them, the second one opened the rear doors of the ambulance and withdrew a gurney.

"Move aside, please. Sir, please stand aside."

"Grant." Thomas placed a heavy hand on Grant's shoulder. "Move buddy. These guys need to do their job."

As if shaking free of a mental hold, Grant allowed his friend to pull him back. It was obvious Shiloh was anxious as the men worked on Kali so Grant stepped forward and tugged her toward him. "Come on, girl. Sit over here with us." He crouched, stroking her beautiful coat. Finally, the overwrought dog calmed enough to lie down. He straightened to speak to Thomas. "There was such an odd look on her face when she collapsed."

"Shock."

"Maybe." The two men watched the EMTs work on Kali. Grant puzzled over the shooting. "It doesn't make any sense. There's no reason to have targeted her."

"How close were you to her at the time? Any chance you were the target?"

Grant closed his eyes, picturing Kali walking toward him with Shiloh at her side. God, he hoped not. He didn't want to live with that for the rest of his life. As he thought on it, he realized the direction had been wrong. With a decisive shake of his head, he said, "No, she was the target."

Thomas shoved his hands in his pockets. "I wonder if the killer is changing the game. Or maybe he wants to end it?"

Grant shook his head. "Doesn't feel right."

"Then what the hell is going on here?"

The EMTs already had Kali on the gurney and were loading her into the ambulance. Grant moved forward. Thomas placed a restraining hand on his arm.

Frowning, Grant pointed to the ambulance. "I should go with her."

"No. Two men are going with her to stand guard. We'll check on her in a bit. Give the doctors time to do their thing. The best thing you can do is bring this to an end."

The ambulance peeled away, sirens blaring, leaving a parking lot of law enforcement officers staring after it.

Darkness settled on Grant's face. "Let's go. We've got an asshole to catch."

Grant strode toward the entrance, Shiloh at his side and the rest of the men scrambling behind him.

At the door, Grant turned back for one last glimpse of the pool of blood drying in the early morning sun. Fury spiked through him. "I want this asshole caught. Today."

"We'll get him. Don't doubt it."

With jaw clenched, Grant gave a clipped nod before heading inside.

***

Kali moaned as she tried to shift her position.

"Damn, we're almost done. Just need another moment."

Metal clattered, weird sucking sounds and soft squishy noises penetrated Kali's conscious. Sharp pins stabbed her repeatedly. Dimly, words registered. They didn't make sense. Nothing did. So much pain. What had happened to her? Her back burned with pain, making her twist away. "Hurts."

A hand soothed her shoulder. The movement blended into the confusion of sounds and sensations.

"Easy, sweetie. We're done. It's going to be okay."

Kali moved again, desperate to stop the deep aching pain. Her mind fogged. Why was she here? What were they doing to her?

"Try to stay still."

"Nooo," she moaned in protest as something jabbed her again.

"Let's go, people. We're not quite done. Put her under so we can finish this. We can't let her tear out the stitches before we get this closed."

Bright lights flashed in strobe symmetry as Kali blinked rapidly. Stitches. Injured? Hospital? Kali struggled to make sense of the distorted words and images interspersed with the pain. Then none of it mattered. Clouds and soft white cotton batting closed in.

Sighing with relief, she drifted under.

***

Grant parked beside several other vehicles at the front of Second Chance. A couple people wandered the large lazy veranda and there were less dogs than he'd become accustomed to seeing here. Shiloh woofed deep in her throat.

"That's right. This is a second home for you, isn't it, girl?"

"It's a busy place. So how do you want to play this?" Thomas studied the layout of the center and its adjoining fields.

Grant wanted to throw his cover and let everyone know he was FBI and meant business, damn it. And that could cost someone else their life if the wrong person figured we're closing the net on him. "I'd love to go pound heads and get answers, but—"

"But we can't. No one here knows about your FBI connection, at this point, and we need to keep it that way. I wonder if anyone noticed the cameras."

Grant opened his door, "And I wonder who's in charge while Dan and Kali are out of commission." Not that anyone here should have heard the news about Kali yet. Dan yes. Hell, this place would erupt when the news of Melanie and Julie trickled through. Another day. That's all they needed.

The two men exited the car and walked toward the fields. Two classes were going on in the yard. Grant recognized Sam working the left side of the field with a group of owners, their dogs at their sides. Sam was putting Colossus, a brindle-colored Great Dane through the paces. Grant checked the opposite end of the field. There, Caroline, her diminutive stature almost obscured by the attendees, demonstrated obedience training with her Jack Russell terrier. His admiration went up a notch. Anyone who successfully commanded a Jack Russell had skill.

Returning to the white clapboard center, they walked into the general lobby. Shiloh raced over to Maureen. She bent and cuddled Shiloh. "Grant, any news on Dan? The place has been crawling with cops but no one's talking."

Good. Grant responded to the question voiced and not the palpable curiosity in her voice. "He's doing better."

Joseph spoke from behind the two men. "That's great. Fresh coffee is dripping if you're wanting a cup."

Turning to watch the younger man approach, Grant said, "Great. I could use one. The day's been a little rough." And that was the truth. He'd caught a power nap earlier, but sheer adrenaline was keeping him going at the moment. Later he'd crash and burn but only after he had answers and knew Kali was safe.

"Were you two here this morning during all the chaos?"

"No. We teach on afternoons, evenings and weekends and drop in the odd time during the week," Joseph answered. Grant glanced over at Maureen, who nodded her agreement.

Walking over to the still-dripping coffeepot, Grant thieved a cup for himself. "Thomas here," Grant motioned in Thomas's direction, "is trying to identify a couple of men. Maybe you two can help."

Thomas obligingly held up the first picture they'd recovered from the new cameras installed at Second Chance.

Joseph piped up. "Jarl. Jarl...Blackburn. He's worked here since forever. I heard he just returned yesterday or the day before."

"Any idea from where?" Thomas wrote Jarl's name on the back of the picture.

"Oregon, I think. I heard he moved part of a graveyard or some such thing – for a church."

Thomas paused, pen in mid-air, a blank look on his face. "Uh?"

Maureen grinned. "Bizarre, huh? The longer you hang here, the more normal the bizarre becomes. The story I heard was the church lost a parcel of land when the area was surveyed for a new development. The land held old graves. However, some of the markers were gone, so Jarl located the bodies for removal and reburial on the new graveyard."

Grant raised an eyebrow. "He can do that?"

"Jarl specializes in it."

How did that fit into his investigation? They'd have to confirm the dates, but it sounded like the timing, if what

Maureen said were true, gave him an alibi for the early kidnappings and murders. So many of these people were experts at digging and burying bodies. Kinda creepy.

Thomas spoke up. "Do you know how we can reach him by any chance?"

Joseph stepped up to answer. "He'll be on the contact list in the office." He motioned toward the hallway heading to the offices. "If you can't find it, contact Kali. She'll know where it is."

Figures. Neither Dan nor Kali were in a position to help.

Holding up the second image, the sketch Kali had done at the police station, Thomas asked, "What about this guy?"

Maureen frowned. "I've seen him but don't know his name. I think he's one of Brad's friends."

Thomas adjusted the angle of the sketch so Joseph could get a better look. He studied it for a moment, then shrugged. "No. I'm not sure I've ever seen him."

"No problem. Thanks for helping us identify the first one."

"Anyone else here have access to the office?" Thomas studied the almost-empty center. "Someone who might be here now so we don't have to disturb Kali?"

The two instructors exchanged frowns. "I don't know. Those two run the place. A couple of us have keys but only to this common area and the bathrooms, not the offices."

Grant exchanged a glance with Thomas. "Okay, I'll ask Kali. Thanks for the help."

Thomas and Grant reached Kali's office a moment later. Reaching out, Grant tested the knob. Locked. Pulling out his pick from his wallet, Grant opened the door in seconds. Glancing at Thomas first, he stepped inside.

The room appeared normal, untouched.

Grant walked to the far side of her desk and booted up her computer. While they waited for it to load, both of them perused her desk, drawers and bookshelves. Unlike Dan, Kali's workspace was sparse and clean. Cold.

"Hardly looks lived in."

"Kali mentioned she didn't come in often, but when she did she mostly worked."

"Obviously." Thomas paced the small room, checking for anything of interest.

The computer requested a log-in and password. Grant frowned, sat down and entered several possible log-ins. None of them worked.

"No luck here."

"Head to the hospital and Kali?" Thomas asked.

Grant sighed and rubbed his eyes. His cell phone said four o'clock. Time to try the hospital again, for at least the fifth time that day.

This time, Grant reached the nurses' station and as luck would have it, the doctor. "Hi, Dr. Sanderson. Have you an update on Kali Jordan? The shooting victim from the police parking lot this morning?"

"Jordan? Oh, right. That's one lucky lady." The doctor coughed several times, clearing his throat.

Grant waited for him. "How's she doing?"

"I've put in close to thirty stitches. The bullet's path scored the trapezoid and triceps muscles. The skin will take the longest to heal, however everything's been repaired. Time will heal the rest."

"That's good news." He straightened as the load of worry slipped off his shoulders.

"Yes. If that bullet had gone in at a slightly different angle, she'd likely be dead."

"I understand." Grant didn't dare dwell on what-ifs. "Is she awake? Can I speak with her?"

"Maybe in an hour or so."

Grant finished the call to update Thomas. "She's still under. We won't be able to talk to her for a bit."

"Then let's try to identify this second man, then find Jarl."

234

CHAPTER TWENTY-ONE

"Hey?"

Kali turned her head, rising up slightly onto her arms so she could see him. Lying on her stomach gave her a limited view. "Grant?"

His footsteps sounded first, then the sound of him moving a chair up to the front of the bed. He added a second one.

She twisted for another look, only the second person stood just out of view.

"Don't try to move, Kali. I brought Stefan."

"What?" Great, she couldn't even turn to sit properly. At least she wore a gown, though her back lay exposed, the blankets covering her lower half. She'd been so looking forward to seeing Stefan, again. She must look awful.

She swallowed hard before saying as nonchalantly as she could, "I'd say hello except it's a little hard to see you. Grant, can you give me a hand, please?"

Grant's strong arms grabbed her below the ribs and he lifted her free of both bed and bedding.

Kali shrieked as the world spun in a chaotic movement before righting itself. She snagged the blankets to cover herself as she settled down in a sitting position. "Unorthodox, but effective." She smiled up at him. "Thanks."

Arranging herself cross-legged on top of the bed, she looked up and lost her breath again. "Good Lord, I'd forgotten. You're too gorgeous to wander loose, Stefan," she exclaimed. Satan's angel stared at her, a barest smile casting a wicked glint to features already too stunning to assimilate.

His grin widened, his eyes flashing with appreciative humor. "And why would you say that?"

That made her sniff in disgust. "My mom didn't raise any idiots. And my Dad would've bought a shotgun after meeting you."

Stefan laughed outright. "I'd have liked them both. My face was a gift from God. My heart and soul are my own. We're obligated to do all we can to be the best that we can be."

Grant stretched his long legs out in front of his chair, drawing attention to his presence. "How profound."

With a quick glance at Stefan, Kali turned her attention on Grant. "Must be tough to watch the women fall all over your friend, huh?"

His eyebrows beetled together as he studied her. "Sometimes. How are you doing, Kali?"

The subject change gave her pause. Maybe her words had struck home. Tucking the information away for later, she answered, "Fine. I'm learning a new appreciation for drugs." She couldn't resist asking, "Did you two come to bust me out? And how's Shiloh?"

"You'll leave when the doctor says so and not a moment earlier. And Shiloh is doing just fine. I'll bring her when I pick you up – later."

Her face fell. "Bully," she teased gently, remembering how concerned he'd been this morning. Realizing she was staring, she glanced over at Stefan to find he'd been watching their byplay. Heat washed over her cheeks. He already knew where her heart lay. Stefan's looks might blindside initially, but it was Grant who made her heart jump.

Grant's stoic voice interrupted her thoughts. "So, who's Jarl?"

She refocused on his question. "He's a big hearted goof who volunteers at the center when he's not out relocating grave sites."

"A big goof?"

"Yeah. In a good way."

"Dangerous?"

Kali frowned. Why was he asking that? What did he suspect? And was Jarl dangerous? She pondered what she knew of him. "Personally, I believe anyone is dangerous given the right circumstances. Jarl loves very strongly and I would imagine he hates just as strongly."

Stefan nodded, a curious approving light in his eyes. "As do many people."

This time Grant made no attempt to hide his exasperation. "We'd like to talk to him."

"Then do so," Kali responded lightly. "He lives a couple of blocks from the center."

"Where?" Grant pulled out his notebook, tugging a pen free from his shirt pocket.

"I've driven him home several times. Let me think." Kali mentally traced the trip. "Turn left as you leave the parking lot. Jarl's house is two blocks ahead. I don't remember the number. It's a two-story, cedar shingled bungalow hidden behind a six-foot plus high cedar hedge along the front."

"Any idea if he's struggling with any particular problems lately?"

"Not that he's shared. I know he's happily married with two full-grown sons."

"Money problems?"

"I don't know." Kali shrugged, then hissed in pain. "Stupid move." She gasped.

Grant leaned forward, concerned. "Do you need a nurse?"

"Hell, no." Kali breathed deep, then exhaled slowly.

With a frown, Grant sat back, sending a quick questioning glance at Stefan. "That sounded emphatic."

Stefan never moved, except for the knowing grin on his face. He appeared content to watch and listen.

Kali twisted her lips. "Nurses poke and prod and do nasty stuff. I'll skip it, thanks." Kali studied Stefan who studied Grant, a smirk on his face. Puzzled, Kali's gaze bounced between them.

Understanding struck. Grant was jealous! And Stefan knew it. Okay, she was dense. Had to be the damned drugs.

Her lips twitched at his male stupidity.

Grant kept the conversation on track. "Okay, so there's no financial or family problems that you know about? What about competitiveness? Does he like to be the top dog?"

It seemed impossible to imagine Jarl in that type of role. She shook her head. "I don't believe he does. I've never seen any sign of that. He teaches a lot and is well loved – has a great sense of humor, but...I'm not always sure what's going on inside. He's very private."

Grant scratched down notes while Kali watched curiously. "Why the interest? Surely you don't think he's a suspect?"

"The cameras shot him trying to access your office."

"So? That means nothing. It's *the* office, not my office. Dan could have asked him to go in and get something or do some work on that computer. Anything's possible."

"Only Dan lay unconscious in his office at the time we've clocked Jarl's entrance attempt into your office."

"Maybe Dan asked him before he was injured? Jarl was at the center before we found Dan."

"What? He was?" Grant lifted his gaze to stare at her in surprise.

"Yes, I remember giving him a big hug. He'd been away for several days."

"I need to get into your computer."

"There's nothing worthwhile on my account but you're welcome to my login." Kali rattled it off.

"That's not very sophisticated." Grant glared at the number and letter combination on his notebook, his voice sharp. "You need a more complex password than that."

"Why?" she asked reasonably. "Apparently, even the difficult ones are hackable within hours anyway." What could Jarl want in her office? The shelves held a selection of books, and her desk held the financial files for the center. Then again..."

Straightening, she added abruptly. "My computer is the server."

Grant leaned forward. "What? Why your computer?"

"The budget didn't allow for a standalone server and Dan continually crashes his."

"So you use the server instead? That's not smart."

Kali grimaced, barely withholding a shrug. Since lying in the hospital bed, she'd realized how that one simple movement dominated her expressions. Maybe the injury had a benefit after all. She realized Grant was waiting for a response. "Dan's motto is 'do whatever works.' Speaking of Dan, how is he?"

"Still unconscious but stable. The bleeding has stopped altogether."

"And Julie," she whispered, petrified to hear the answer. "Any progress?"

"We're on it, Kali. The FBI does function even without you." Grant's voice was even...almost too even.

Kali shifted, her butt noticing the long stretch in that position. "Sorry, where's Shiloh?"

"I drove her and your Jeep home, then came here with Stefan. I'll head over there and feed her in a bit."

His words pinched. Shiloh was hers. She'd been the only one to feed her – ever. Stupid. She should be grateful that Grant was capable of caring for her.

"Grant." Kali stopped.

"What?"

"If you're going to my house anyway, would you mind bringing my art stuff?"

Stefan sat up. He and Grant exchanged glances. "Are you picking up on something?" Grant asked, hopefully.

Not wanting to get his hopes up, she compromised. "I'm not sure. My dreams...wow! But the drugs are problematic. Are they putting the pictures in or have they opened my mind up further?"

"It could be either or both," Stefan said, his liquid voice soothing her doubts. "We'll get you a sketchbook. You get the images down and then we can take a look. When your mind is overwhelmed with images it's hard to separate real from imaginary."

"Exactly." She stared at him in delight. He understood. Stefan smiled as they shared a conspiratorial look. Flashing Grant a look, Kali found his gaze narrowed on them both. She rolled her eyes.

"We'll head there now." Pushing his chair back, Grant stood, prepared to leave. At the end of the bed he stopped. "I have to ask, are these images related to Julie?"

Stefan had reached the door, but at the question he stopped to hear her answer.

"I can't be certain until I've drawn it," Kali said soberly. "Maybe."

"Back in forty minutes." He started for the door.

Stefan winked at her before walking out of the room.

"Grant."

Almost at the door, he pivoted and raised one eyebrow in question.

Crooking her finger, she motioned him closer. When he stood at her bedside, she reached up and tugged him to her level. Staring him in the eye, she said, "Your friend *is* gorgeous. That does not mean I'm nuts over him. Okay?"

A fine flush worked over his face, highlighting his strong features. "Ouch. I'm that obvious?"

"I understand, really I do. I'm sure women fall all over him. However, and get this straight, I am not other women."

His eyes warmed. Grant bent and dropped a kiss on her forehead. "I'll be back soon."

Kali listened as his footprints faded away. Time for help. She reached for the call button.

A nurse arrived within minutes. "How's the pain, dearie?"

"Liveable. But I have to go to the bathroom."

"Good." With efficient practice, the nurse pulled the blanket back and tucked it over the bed. "Now, on your feet and let's see how steady you are."

A disappointing try, as Kali wasn't as steady as she'd hoped. Eventually, Kali wove her way back to her bed with the nurse's help. Then, bone-weary exhaustion invaded her limbs.

The bed loomed in front of them. Three full steps and a baby one. Climbing up onto the bed, she collapsed onto her belly, then buried her face in the pillow. Oh Christ, she hurt. Flames burned along her shoulders, tremors vibrated along her limbs. There'd be no more lifting her head. "Ohhh," she moaned against the crackling hospital pillow.

"Painkillers?"

Kali twisted her head sideways. "No, thanks. Do you know when I can leave?"

"Nope, but I can tell you going to the bathroom on your own is a definite requisite."

"Right. Failed that one." Kali closed her eyes and waited for her breathing to calm down.

She woke up an hour later and felt so much better; it was hard to understand how that was possible. Had she missed Grant? She frowned, searching her room. There was no sign of her sketchbook. A hospital tray waited for her with a large metal dome hiding its contents.

Kali pushed herself up and attempted to sit sideways on the bed. Awkward, ungainly and painful, but it worked. Kali sighed with relief as she settled into a more comfortable sitting position, her legs swinging over the bed. The blankets reached the floor when she tucked them around her lower body. The over-the-bed table was accessible too. Perfect.

The largest of the plastic domes held a bowl of tomato soup and a grilled cheese sandwich. Cold and greasy. Kali shuddered, dropping the lid. A small salad and a bowl of Jell-O or possibly plastic, wobbled in a small bowl at the back. Well, that wasn't happening.

Depressed and hungry, she was trying to shift back onto the bed when Grant walked in, sketchbook in hand.

"It's good to see you moving about."

Kali glowered. "You may enter if you brought real coffee; can't say a muffin or sandwich would go amiss either. It's supposed to be dinner time, but the meal here can't be classified as food. No Stefan?"

His lips quirked, his gaze switching from the tray to her. His eyes lit with amusement. "Stefan will stop by later, if he can. Here's your sketchbook and pencils, and I'll find you something to eat." He dumped his armload on the bed, dropped a quick kiss on her cheek and left.

Kali stared after him, shock rippling along her spine, her fingers pressed against the ghost of his kiss. He was getting very comfortable with those. She kinda liked it.

To take her mind off her hunger and Grant's behavior, Kali opened her sketchbook to a clean page. Julie had been missing for a full day now. Depending on her condition and the amount of oxygen available, her time was running out. Kali's thoughts turned dark and dreary. Depressed, she worried about how to end this mess. Her mind flipped from one possibility to another as she doodled. What if she went on TV and publicly admitted this killer had her beat hands down? It wasn't as if her ego cared. His ego needed the satisfaction. TV? Newspapers? Radio? Hmmm. She would mention it to Grant. Kali's hand moved aimlessly as her mind pondered the problems.

"That's a face to photograph and me without my camera."

Kali looked up as Grant entered the room carrying two takeout coffees and a paper bag.

"Oh yeah, food and coffee." Kali threw her sketchbook to one side and tossed her pencil on top. "The table is cleared and ready." She shifted, to sit over the edge again, taking her blanket with her. "What did you bring?"

Her mouth salivated at the rich aromas wafting from the bag. She opened it then pulled out two warm oversized muffins and below it, a small container of fruit salad followed by two large Kaiser bun sandwiches. "Perfect. Thank you." She broke off a piece of the muffin and popped it into her mouth. The banana nut flavor filled her mouth. She closed her eyes and moaned with pleasure. After several more bites and a long sip of her fresh coffee, Kali knew she'd survive. She turned her attention to Grant.

"Bring me up-to-date on the progress with the case. Did you talk to Jarl?" In-between mouthfuls, Kali listened, but her hope quickly sank to despair. For all the legwork, phone work and man-hours, they hadn't found much. No idea who'd shot her. No sign of Jarl. And no leads on locating Julie.

Not great dinner conversation. Pushing the table away, she leaned back and massaged her belly. "Okay. I'll survive a little longer. What about the police sketch, any luck identifying it?"

"Your sketch you mean?" Grant dropped his muffin wrapper to the table then reached for one of the two sandwiches he'd brought.

"Nope, the credit goes to the police artist. Her skill dragged the information out of Brenda. I translated the answers to paper."

"So did the police artist, but your picture hit the mark. We showed it to several people at the center and he's been tentatively ID'd as Christian LeFleure. No one seems to know much about him. The team is running a background check on him."

Kali tilted her head. "Christian. Hmmm. Sounds familiar but I can't place him. Dan will know him. We can ask him when he wakes up." A yawn worked up from deep inside. The warm food and drink, not to mention the drugs, were making her sleepy.

"Mind if I go through your sketchbook again?"

Kali glanced to the book at the end of the bed. "I did a bit of doodling while you were gone, but not much." Shifting slightly, she stretched out on her left side, tugging the blanket up to her shoulder. With the pillow crunching under her head, Kali felt lethargy take over. "I need to close my eyes for a just a moment," she murmured.

With eyes drooping closed, she watched as Grant picked up her sketchbook and started flicking through the pages. Snuggling deeper, she drifted off to sleep.

***

Kali's 'doodle' socked Grant in the gut. It also didn't make sense. He turned it sideways and still couldn't get the clarity he needed. "Kali? What's—" Catching sight of her, he smiled gently.

She slept, sprawled like a child, her breathing slow and regular. One blanket rested precariously on her shoulders with a second crumpled at her feet. Grant lay down the sketchbook, stepped over and pulled the second blanket over her prone body. Walking to the other side, he straightened the gown up to her shoulders. The gauze bandage gaped, showing the string of black stitches surrounded by red puffy tissue.

"Shit." Grant whispered softly, his heart aching at the damage. The good doctor had spoken true. She was damn lucky.

His gaze dropped to her sketch.

Kali had incredible talents, whether she believed it or not. Both as a psychic and an artist. Sitting again, he took his time to study the two sketches. The first one of Julie that had led them to David and he presumed the second was of her as well, but he didn't know that.

They needed something useful, landmarks, terrain – to lead them to her location.

Frustrated, he studied the sketch. The close-up showed only the underground hell with little to no above ground markings.

He had the weird sense of missing something important. "Damn it. What's the missing link? Where the hell are you, Julie?"

"She's there."

Grant turned to face Kali. "Did I wake you? Sorry."

Kali's soft voice had an odd flatness to it. "Julie's so scared."

Grant studied her face. She appeared half asleep, half awake. Studying her face, he whispered, "Kali? Do you know the location in your sketch? It looks odd and I can't quite figure it out."

"What sketch?" she murmured, her eyes still closed.

"Kali, this is important. Open your eyes." Grant leaned closer, holding the sketchbook above her face.

She blinked several times, struggling to focus. With a big yawn, she shifted slightly and looked at the picture in front of her. "That's an underground stream."

"Underground stream? Huh?" Grant stared at the picture. With her explanation, he could identify the lines depicting water a distance beneath the body.

"Roystan Park. It's well known for the underground stream running through the length of it. Julie has to be at Roystan Park."

Grant wasn't familiar with the area, had never been to the park and knew nothing about underground streams. One thing he did understand, underground waterways like above-ground ones usually ran for miles. "That's a lot of territory to cover, Kali. Can you narrow it further?"

Kali didn't answer, her eyes drifted closed. She needed her rest, but he needed answers and Julie needed help.

He sharpened his voice. "Kali."

"What?" she answered, her voice groggy, her eyes flickering open briefly.

"Where on the underground stream is Julie?"

"Look at the tree from the first picture. There's a recently disturbed hill."

Snatching up the sketchbook, Grant flipped to the first Julie picture. The first picture showed a unique tree. Christ. "I need to borrow your sketch book, Kali. I need to copy these pictures."

Kali yawned, her eyes drooping closed. "Nurses' station."

"Back in a minute." Grant bent over, dropped a hard kiss on her forehead, only to hear her slow even breathing. She was asleep.

CHAPTER TWENTY-TWO

Kali shifted her position gently, wincing at the tugs on her shoulders and spine. Hospital beds weren't comfy to begin with but for the injured, they really sucked. Opening her eyes, she watched the shadows stretch across the room. She yawned. The afternoon had long disappeared. With a sense of relaxation permeating her soul, Kali realized despite all the aches and soreness, she felt better. Less like she'd been hit by a bus.

The table and her sketchbook, slid into focus. Tidbits of conversation with Grant came back to her. Her curiosity spiked.

Shuffling upright, she stretched out a hand for the pad, flipping to the last picture she'd done. Bold, stark lines stared at her. What had she said? Roystan Park. Kali bolted upright, moaning from pain at the sudden movement. Damn it. Then she caught sight of her cell phone. Her pain forgotten, she reached for it. Yeah, connected again. She dialed Grant's number.

"Why aren't you asleep?" he growled.

"Hi, how are you doing? Nice of you to call," she said, her voice snapping in irritation. She threw back the blankets.

"Sorry, how nice of you to call. Niceties done, why the hell aren't you asleep?"

Kali slid off the side of the bed and walked over to the window. "Because I woke up. Cut the attitude and tell me what's going on. I remember something about Roystan Park."

"That's where we are right now."

"Good, what handlers have you called in?"

Silence filled the phone.

Kali's heart sank and she closed her eyes. "You didn't call any, did you?" Kali couldn't believe it. "Jesus, Grant. You need a canine team and preferably more than one. You'll never find her otherwise."

"I didn't know who to trust," he said, simply.

She paused and closed her eyes in acquiescence. What a nightmare.

"There are forty men here. I'll call you when we find her. Bye."

Frustrated, Kali stared at the dead phone in her hand. He was wrong to believe men, regardless of how many, made up for a canine unit. She lived that world. She understood just what these dogs could do. Yet, he was also right. Who could they trust? She doubted everyone, and no longer trusted those she knew.

Who could help?

Shiloh. And therefore Kali.

Grant would never let her...if he knew. But...was she capable of going out and searching? If she couldn't physically do the job, she'd slow them down – or worse, take valuable man-hours away from the search for Julie. Testing, she rolled her shoulders. A few tugs and a few pulls – and actually it wasn't that bad. Okay, she was lying. Still she felt so much better than she expected. Amazing what a paradigm shift could do.

Encouraged, Kali considered the situation. Julie needed her help. She was out of time. They had a potential location, and all the stops needed to be pulled to make the most of the next few hours.

Kali?

She stilled. Spun around. The room was empty.

Kali, it's Stefan.

"Stefan," she whispered. "Where are you?"

Warm laughter filled her mind. *At home.*

She smiled. *Damn. You're good.*

The same laughter wafted throughout the room. *So are you.*

He was speaking in her mind. And she was answering. A mess of questions rose to the surface, but even the concept of telepathic communication seemed too much right now. She shook her head. *Later. Right now. I have to help Julie. I need to search for her.*

Interesting. Why can't Grant's team handle it?

She needed him to understand. *He hasn't got a SAR dog! Shiloh and I easily replace forty men.*

A deep hum filled the air. Kali turned around slowly, finally laughing as she realized what it was. Stefan...thinking.

"I *have* to go." If heavy painkillers worked and allowed her to function at a safe level, she might pull this off. If she fell and ripped her stitches...well, better to not go there.

Definitely don't go there. I'll help. We will find her.

Kali walked experimentally around the room then attempted to twist and bend slightly one way and then another. Painful, but not agonizing – sore yet doable. She could do this. First, she needed to get the hell home, grab Shiloh and head to the park. Ticking off her mental to-do list, she didn't see any of it happening short of an hour. That meant starting her search and in the dusky light. Damn.

"What are you doing out of bed, Kali? I know you didn't want to stay overnight, but it is for your own good."

Kali smiled with relief. Her doctor had perfect timing. Quickly, she explained what she needed and gave a brief explanation why.

He frowned and shook his head.

She interjected before he could refuse her. "I know this isn't your recommendation. I understand this is a really bad idea. Except a woman is dying. I have to find her."

Thankfully, her doctor had dealt with survivors of several local disasters. His frown deepened and he pursed his lips. "Why can't someone else go?"

"Everyone who can – is. I understand the damage I could cause again, however, the bottom line is that even if I rip out the stitches, the damage won't kill me. If I stay here, Julie will die."

"Overdramatizing, aren't you?"

"No," Kali said softly, sadly. "Julie is out of time. We have to find her soon."

The doctor studied her face then made a decision. "Get dressed and come down to the nurses' station. I'll give you something for now. When you finish tonight, you're to return here. Not home, not the boyfriend's house, but here. Agreed?"

When she didn't answer immediately, he added, "That's the condition. Take it or leave it."

"I'll take it. I'll meet you at the station in five minutes." Kali turned away, opening up the locker at the far wall, searching for her clothes. The cargo pants, although blood stained, were serviceable. She pulled on what clothes she found, realizing belatedly she had no shirt and there was no sign of her sweater. Damn it. The doctor must have cut it off when she'd been brought in.

A nurse walked in. "I guess you don't need my help getting dressed. You've done just fine."

"I'm okay so far, but I can't find a shirt or my sweater. I'm presuming they were destroyed?"

The nurse walked over to look in the locker. "Possibly. But there's a pile of clothes in the Lost and Found. Give me a moment."

What a relief. Kali hadn't relished the idea of walking out topless. There was no way she was going to attempt to wear a bra. In the small bathroom, she washed up and ran her fingers through her hair. Dried blood clung to the ends. More blood dotted her arms and chest. Using the washcloth, she did a quick wipe, removing the worst of the mess. The pain made her shudder, yet it was the change in awareness that made it possible. Knowing Stefan was there, helping, made her stronger. She paused...or was he? She couldn't sense his presence any longer.

"Here. Try these on."

The same nurse held out a black tee shirt and a hoodie in royal blue. Perfect. The nurse dressed her as if Kali were a two-year-old with her arms in front sliding the tee shirt close to her chest before slipping it over her head. "Let's wait until the doctor gives you a shot, then put the hoodie on."

Then Kali tackled her shoes, a much harder proposition. Biting her tongue, she finally finished and stood up again. "Okay, let's go."

She walked out of her room.

And came face to face with a guard – one of Grant's men. Easily, six-foot-four, with steely eyes and linebacker build, he didn't look like compromise was in his dictionary. He raised one eyebrow and stared down at her.

"Oh shit."

The eyebrow went higher.

She sighed, and considered. "It would be so much easier if you overheard my conversation with my doctor." She waited a beat. "Did you?"

He nodded his head.

"Oh thank heavens. Sooo, I'm hoping, that like the good doctor, you'll understand? I have to do this? A woman's life is at stake?"

Again silence, then a clipped nod.

Were all Grant's men so taciturn? She brightened. "Then you'll let me go?"

"Yes. But I'm going with you."

She brightened. "Actually, I'd be pleased to have you. But...I can't have you telling Grant. He's not going to let me go or allow you to let me go."

The guard narrowed his gaze as he stared down at her and sifted through her words.

"I have to do this. Julie's dying. I might be able to save her."

One final clipped nod of that closely shaved head and relief flooded through her. "First stop is home to collect Shiloh, my SAR dog. Then to the site. We're out of time."

She raced to the nurses' station, where she signed papers and waited for the doctor. The guard, Scott – she'd managed to drag his name out of him – drove. She leaned forward but every bump in the road jostled her spine and threw her backwards. At her house, she headed inside where Shiloh waited, wiggling in excitement.

"Hello, sweetheart. Did you miss me? I'd love to cuddle, but we need to go to work." Kali walked into the kitchen and filled her pockets with granola bars and energy drinks. Water bottles had to be filled, dog bones collected and, what else? Another five minutes and Kali decided they were ready to go. Flashlights, rescue bag, snacks, drinks, warm vest and a blanket for Shiloh. At the last minute, Kali snatched up Shiloh's teddy bear. Shiloh understood and waited at the door.

You had to love a dog that gave her all, no matter where or when.

Stefan? No answer. *Stefan?*

Still no luck. Neither could she still feel his presence. As long as he showed up when she needed him...

Scott backed out of the driveway and headed in the direction of Roystan Park. Kali had to push her seat to the furthest setting and sit on the edge to avoid hitting her sore back with every bump. Chewing on her lip, she wondered how much ground Grant had covered. Then she snorted and laughed a little grimly. It didn't matter. She'd have to go over the same miles to confirm they hadn't missed Julie. Shiloh could pick up a human scent within a quarter of a mile and track it forward.

"Have you any idea where they are in the park, Scott?"

He shook his head. "Haven't had an update."

Kali called Grant. "So?" she asked. "Any news?"

"No, nothing yet. But it's early yet."

"How many miles do you think you have to cover?" Kali pointed and Scott turned the Jeep to the right. It should take her another five minutes to reach Roystan Park.

"About ten. The hydrogeologist gave us a map of the underground creek. It's on the west side of the park, running parallel to the back fence."

Her heart sank. Ten. That was likely more than she could do.

"What do I hear?"

Kali heard the frown in his voice and lied without a qualm. "The nurse's trolley is coming."

"Oh. You rest and heal. I promise I'll call if I hear anything."

"Okay. I'll talk to you later." Kali clicked off before he had time to ask questions.

Shiloh knew the park relatively well, as they'd spent many a happy day roaming the area, although, Kali didn't remember seeing a fence along the back. By the time they pulled into the parking lot, they'd already driven in several miles. The kidnapper could use the access roads to go wherever he wanted to, but she couldn't take the chance of missing Julie. She'd start this search in an orderly fashion. There were a couple of FBI vehicles in the parking lot; she could only presume the rest were using the service roads. There should be a dozen vehicles here.

"Scott, I'm going cross country." As she went to give him instructions, a group of FBI came out of the woods, powerful lights shining in eerie patterns in the sky. She needed to be gone before they saw her.

"Scott, grab the others and come behind me. You should be able to see my light easily to catch up. I'm going up this fence line." She pointed it out to him.

Unloading what she needed, Kali clipped Shiloh onto her lead and headed off, the adrenaline pumping, giving her a shot of energy. Feeling good and feeling strong, she let her body settle into a steady stride.

He'd said the underground creek surfaced south of here. The park was a huge rough rectangle but the entrance led to the parking lot in the center of the park. Left and right were the options. The left would offer an easier route with a slight downhill slope, but the creek traveled closer to the surface if she headed right.

Shiloh would decide.

"Shiloh. Go look. Let's find Julie."

Shiloh barked once, looked at Kali then took off left.

Of course. Right would have been the easy answer.

***

The wind had picked up, causing a brutal chill. The sun had long gone. It was the middle of summer and Grant couldn't believe he was zipping up a fleece vest and feeling cold.

Blame it on Roystan Park. Heavily wooded, neither sun nor heat reached deep or stayed for long.

He checked his section of the map again. The geologist had showed him which side of the park to search and the approximate width of the long strip that held the most potential. He'd broken the men into several teams and each had taken an area.

Kali had to be upset at missing this but she'd been through too much already. With any luck, they'd find Julie soon. If luck was on their side she'd be alive. What were the chances? Grimly, he returned his attention to the long red strip on the map in his hands. They'd be lucky to cover half this area tonight. Forty men weren't enough.

"Hey, Grant. Let's get these men moving."

Grant passed over the spare sheets in his hands. "Here are the maps. Let's go."

The hard work began.

***

The cold had settled deep under her skin. Julie hated the endless dark. Exhaustion had set in. Not enough, though. Her body still screamed with pain from the unnatural position every time she twitched.

How much longer? Surely, someone would notice the pipe in the ground soon. She wasn't done yet. That bastard could gloat all he wanted but she wouldn't give him the satisfaction of dying in this underground hell. She fanned the faint flames of anger. It kept her warm at night. Endurance had stepped in. Replaying memories of happy times kept her mind busy, which helped but reminded her of those people already gone from this world.

And that she might join them this night.

She was so cold. A part of her was ready to die.

Kali and Shiloh, Dan, all those SAR specialists probably didn't know she was even missing. How ironic. She'd been pissed at them for entering her home before and now she could only hope they were still concerned enough to check on her again.

Typical. You never knew the value of your friends until it was too late. Or the value of law enforcement; she hadn't even been nice to the guard waiting for her at home. She booted him out so fast.

She was a fool.

Closing her eyes, she twitched slightly. Nerve endings jumped to life like a thousand hot needles throughout her body. Julie spit the grime from her mouth but couldn't do anything about the hot tears streaming in rivers down her cheeks. Who'd have thought she'd end up like this – again?

She'd been saved once before. What were the odds of being saved a second time?

Kali, where are you?

CHAPTER TWENTY-THREE

Kali thought she caught a faint voice on the wind. Not likely, but she picked up speed, giving Shiloh a long lead. She couldn't afford to slow the pace or allow Shiloh to take off. Whatever the doctor had given her allowed her to maintain a strong steady pace. Kali didn't want to sprint in her condition, if not required. Who knew when the shot would wear off?

Or when Stefan would show up?

She figured Scott would be behind her, possibly with one or more of the other men, but the pace had been brutal so far and the night was far from over. She couldn't waste time looking for him. He should be able to follow her light and catch up.

The twilight resembled a gray fog, blurring light and dark. Not a street lamp in sight. No, this wilderness park deserved its name. It housed many long-lived species of trees and plants. The tree canopy was full and heavily covered in green leaves, leaving the moonlight to illuminate pathways to the under layer. It was also cold.

Kali kept an ear tuned for Grant's group as she raced thirty feet along the fence. Gratefully, the stuff the doctor had given her hadn't smothered her other senses. The tingle at the back of her neck stirred, keeping her focused and moving forward.

Thank heavens for commercial flashlights. Hers scanned the woods in a continuous movement, adding a weird glow to the night. Nothing like adding gloomy and creepy to kidnapping and murder. Kali shook her head, throwing off the ugly vibes with determined effort. Julie. She needed to find Julie. Nothing else mattered

As the miles churned under her feet, Kali searched for landmarks, anything that twigged. There were lots of flat heavily treed areas that wouldn't take kindly to digging. A sinking knot settled into her stomach. She faced a huge job, especially in the dark. Scott should be just behind her. This park was massive. People were known to get lost here for days. Tonight, Shiloh's skills came into play, with Kali's as the handler. As she moved through the bush, her mind locked on her weird skills. She'd yet to take the time to study them. She'd always assumed they happened naturally. Lately, though, natural had become wild and weird. It confused, terrified and if she were honest, delighted her on some level. Since she met Stefan she realized that she might learn to control her skills. Skills that had helped them find David and Melanie. Now if only she could find Julie...alive.

"Shiloh, how are you doing?" Kali found comfort to hear the sound of her voice. "Being alone out here is unusual, isn't it? Normally, we're surrounded by people." Although Scott should be here soon.

Shiloh ran toward Kali to say 'hi.' Her ear twitched as she accepted a caress then took she off again, her nose to the ground, her lead stretching a solid ten feet in front. Kali walked faster to narrow the distance between them, but then with the slack in the lead, Shiloh pulled forward.

"Take it easy, girl. We need to conserve energy."

Shiloh ignored her and ran ahead. Kali caught the same sense of urgency and quickly ran up to her, using the powerful light of the flashlight to shine their way. A wind picked up, filling the woods with a chill and odd sounds of dry leaves rustling. Kali pulled the zipper of her multi-pocketed vest up to her neck. The shiver that overcame her was a sign of her lowered health. The doctor's stuff wouldn't sustain her for long at this rate. Kali hunkered deeper in her vest.

The moon peeked out behind the clouds for a brief moment, illuminating the eerie darkness. Branches cast villains and bushes whispered dire warnings. Kali hurried to stay close behind Shiloh. Her watch illuminated the time. An hour had passed. One hour and she'd already reached the cold sweat stage.

Kali's cell phone rang. She jumped at the noise.

"Hello."

"Kali?"

"Hi, Grant." Kali closed her eyes, caught off guard. She struggled to regulate her heavy breathing. Shiloh tugged her forward, forcing Kali to quickly juggle flashlight, lead and cell phone. She shuffled the flashlight to her left hand and picked up her pace.

"Are you okay? Your voice is...shaking?"

"I'm fine, tired maybe." Just a little. "How's the search going?"

"It's in progress. It's weird though, one of the teams thought they saw someone else out here at the same time?"

Kali spun around, searching the woods, expecting someone to burst through the trees at any moment. Had she been spotted? An agent would have approached her, surely? Refusing to be deterred, she plowed forward.

"Kali, what do I hear?"

"What?" Kali glanced at her phone. "What do you hear?"

"You're at the hospital, aren't you?" he questioned, his voice rising. "Those noises make it sound like you're running? Puffing with exertion?" Kali couldn't stop the wince at the aggressive accusation in his voice. He didn't know the half of it.

"Uhmmm," she hedged.

"Kali, where the hell are you?" His voice rose in accusation.

The shit was about to hit the fan. She sighed heavily, and confessed. "I'm probably a couple of miles behind you."

"What?" His roar ripped through the night.

Shiloh whined. Kali slapped her thigh, calling Shiloh over. "It's okay, Shiloh. Everything's fine."

"Like hell it's fine." Grants voice roared his concern. "You're supposed to be in the hospital. God damn it, Kali."

This time, Shiloh barked at the voice thundering through her cell phone.

"Stop it. You're upsetting Shiloh."

Grant sputtered. "I'm upsetting the dog? What about me? What about how upset I am?"

"Get over it," she snapped. "I'm cold and tired and don't want to be out here." Kali shivered in the cool air. She wanted to be in her bed. Julie wanted the same thing and she deserved to have it. Kali wouldn't quit.

"Then don't try; turn around." The phone line crackled with bits of conversation trickling through from Grant's side. "Go home."

"I'd love to," she said, letting her irritation grow. It helped dispel the fatigue. "Except this isn't about you or me. This is about Julie. And I didn't come alone. I brought Scott, the guard from the hospital...except he was supposed to grab another group of men and catch up...only they haven't yet."

"Shit. There are forty good men here."

Kali shook her head, interrupting, "And not one dog team. Shiloh's sense of smell beats your forty men in a heartbeat. And then there's me."

"Where are you?"

"I'm searching twenty feet off the west fence." Kali scanned the gloom to identify a landmark. "A hard walk for an hour plus, I'd guess we're about three miles in. Maybe only two and a half. Hard to say with the rough terrain." Kali tripped and caught herself as she spoke. "Shit."

"What happened?" Grant said, concern overriding the anger in his voice.

She bit back the moan as the burning in her back heated up.

"Damn it, answer me."

"I'm here. Give me a second," she whispered. She took a deep breath, letting it out slowly. "I tripped on a root. I'm fine." And she would be. She had to be...for a while longer.

"Shit, Kali. I'll be there in a couple minutes. Don't move."

Like hell. "Grant, I haven't stopped moving." She searched the gloom for the halo of flashlights. Nothing yet. "Either walk toward me or wait and I'll get there in a bit."

"Jesus, you're stubborn."

Kali smirked. "I've heard that before."

Nearby, the brush rustled. Kali stopped, her hand to her throat. "What was that?"

"What did you hear?"

"Noises. In front of me." Shiloh growled deep in her throat, the sound raising the hairs on the back of Kali's neck. Kali's gaze followed Shiloh's stare. The shadows stilled, blending bushes to trees into a dark silhouette. Clicking off her flashlight, she hunkered close to the ground, one arm wrapped around Shiloh. "Grant. Did you say someone else is out here?"

"There are several teams out here. I have men everywhere, damn it. I don't have an update pinpointing everyone's location. Scott should have stayed with you. Where the hell is he?"

"I'm hoping that's him, but I don't want to call out...just in case." Memories of startling the killer at David's burial site filled her mind. Impatience gnawed at her. She hated the reminder that the killer could be here watching her. "I'd really like to know if friend or foe is in the area."

She did not want a repeat of the last incident where she'd come upon the killer in the dark.

"I can't get the information on the others because I'm talking to you. As I can see just enough to run, I should be within ear shot within five to ten minutes."

"Thank God," she whispered, wishing he'd already arrived. She could hear his uneven breathing on the phone as he covered the ground between them. Kali stayed quiet, hugging Shiloh. She knew Scott would have trouble finding her like this but her light was still on.

Poor Julie, she must be going through hell. Cold, tired, worn out with the effort of staying alive. Survival wasn't for the weak. Kali buried her face in Shiloh's warm fur and waited.

"Kali." *Who said that?*

Kali snapped upright, frowning. Had someone called her name? Grant? No, he'd call out several times. Not in a grated whisper. Her heart pounded. She wasn't alone.

Noises crashed through the underbrush up ahead. No attempt to be quiet. Kali slipped further into the shadows.

And was grabbed from behind.

Kali screamed and struggled to free herself. Shiloh barked and jumped at her attacker, dashing in for an attack before retreating, dancing out of reach of the kicks, then rushing in again.

"Shit." The man grunted, the muffled sound blasting in her ear.

A gloved hand slapped over her mouth. Kali fought, a scream gurgling past his leather-covered fingers. The strong arm pulled her backwards. Fire tore across her shoulder. She cried out with pain, tripping and falling to one side. Her movement broke her free of the one restraining arm. Pivoting, she kicked up at him, screaming at the top of her lungs for Grant.

"Kali?"

The distant shout sounded off to the left. *Grant.* Although she couldn't be sure because of Shiloh's constant yipping. At least Grant would hear her, too.

Her attacker dropped on top of her, trying to pin her arms down, his shoulder shoved against her mouth, pinning her head low. Pain stabbed at her constantly as her stitches argued with the hard ground.

Twisting and kicking with only limited success, Kali managed to slide one arm free. She immediately raked her nails across his face.

"Bitch!" But it was enough to loosen his grip on her mouth.

"Grant, help!" Pain enveloped her entire body. Fire licked across her back and shoulders. Christ, she hurt. Kali ignored her injures as she strove for freedom and still the movements pulled at her stitches. Bile climbed the inside of her throat.

Shiloh added to the nightmare, barking and nipping at any body part she could reach.

Her attacker roared, his arms clamping on hers, pivoting her onto her belly, his knee slammed against her spine as his weight came down holding her there. "Fucking bitch."

Kali gasped for breath, but couldn't get any oxygen. Her spine felt seared and she couldn't imagine the damage to her back. "Shiloh," she whispered.

Shiloh charged. Her attacker screamed again. Suddenly, his weight lifted and Kali scrambled to her feet, bolting into the darkness in her panic.

"Shiloh. Here Shiloh." Kali raced ahead in the blackness of the night.

"Grant," she screamed. "Grant, help. I'm free."

"Kali."

Strong arms reached and grabbed her. She screamed and panicked.

"It's me." Grant pulled her tight into his embrace. "Stop, it's all right. Calm down. It's okay now. It's me."

His words finally penetrated the sound of blood pounding through her veins. "Grant." She burrowed against his chest, her body quivering in fear.

Grant held her gently, careful to keep his arm low and away from her injuries. "Easy. It's going to be okay. We'll get him. Calm down."

Kali twisted to peer into the darkness behind her. "In this light, he could hide out here all night. And there's nothing stopping him from going over the fence."

Grant considered her comment, pulled out his phone and within minutes, he had tapped another team of men.

"Wow," Kali said, pulling back to smile up at him through the tears that had arrived now that she was safe. "A man of action, I like that."

Grant snatched her close again, his chin dropping to rest on her head.

Several more men broke through the brush from the way Kali had come. Scott in the lead. He slowed down, shaking his head when he saw her. "Jesus, when you said catch up, Kali. I didn't figure you'd be sprinting for miles." The men with him dispersed, on the hunt for the killer.

Comforted, Kali closed her eyes and leaned in. Just as tension drained from her spine, Grant tilted her head back so she could see his face. "Why the hell aren't you safe in the hospital?" he demanded in angry frustration. "God damn it. Why the hell can't you stay in one place like you're told to? Do you know how much shit I'm going to give Scott for letting you out?"

"Don't. I begged him to. And it was the right decision. Besides, I'm not a damned dog," she fired back, glaring at him. "Nor am I ragdoll. Stop shaking me. You're ripping out my stitches." Cheap shot, yet effective.

Instantly, he stopped. "Shit. Did I hurt you?" His arms cradled her and rocked her back and forth. "I'm so sorry."

He shifted gears again, pushing her back again, his hands running over her. "Did he hurt you? One of my men will take you back to the hospital right now. Get those stitches checked."

"Stop." Kali placed her hands on his chest and pushed him backwards. "Of course I'm sore, but I'm going nowhere – not until I find Julie. Don't—" She held up a hand to forestall the words as he opened his mouth. "It's now or never for her."

Shrugging free of his grasp, Kali bent to pat Shiloh on her back. "I need a flashlight. I dropped mine when he attacked me. I should have hit him with the damn thing. At least then I'd still have it."

"Jesus." Grant splayed his flashlight across the area. Trampled grass, and broken branches were a testament to her panicked flight. His face grew grim.

Kali watched the hollows beneath his cheekbones deepen. "It's over and I'm fine. Let's get this job done." Before I collapse, she wanted to add but kept it in at the last moment. From the way she felt now, she could use some more of the doctor's miracle stuff – it had long since worn off.

"Take mine. I'm sticking close to you anyway." Grant handed his flashlight to Kali. "Now let's see if we can put an end to this madness."

Kali turned toward the fence line and stepped out. "Shiloh, back to work."

"What the hell, Kali?" Frustration oozed from Grant's voice but he fell into step at her side.

"We're close. I can feel it." It would explain the killer's presence and she had no doubt that's who'd attacked her.

Grant compromised. "One hour. If we don't find her in an hour, you're returning to the hospital and we continue without you."

"Like hell," she muttered under her breath. Hopefully, it would be resolved before that. Kali picked up the pace as Shiloh strained on her lead. She could feel the exhaustion and cold gnawing away at her. Even as she thought of her fatigue, energy surged through her, colors erupted in her mind, bathing her body in a warm lavender energy. Kali didn't dare stop. In fact, she suddenly felt like she could go all day. Then recognition hit her. She laughed inside.

Stefan?

A rumble of warm laughter wafted through her mind.

Thanks. I needed that boost.

You're welcome!

Can you connect to Julie? Tell her to hang on. We're coming.

That same weird humming filled her mind.

I'll try. Not getting much of a reading.

Shit what did that mean?

And he left, leaving a pulsing, throbbing surge of power in her legs and body. She didn't know how long it would last, but she was grateful to have it at all. She hadn't been sure she could go on much longer.

Kali raced now, focused and determined to finish this job before her body, or Grant finished it for her.

For fifteen minutes they raced forward in the darkness. Going left, then right, under trees and around brushes and hillocks as Shiloh tugged on the lead. Kali's determination waned as her energy declined. Her stomach growled. Grant pulled a granola bar from his pocket and handed it over. She snatched it with a grateful smile and devoured it in a few bites. Shiloh's focus had to be intense; she rarely missed a chance at a bite of Kali's bars.

Kali's tingle surged to the forefront, starting a musical beat on her spine. Excitement took over. This was it. She knew it. It had to be...she couldn't go much more.

Shiloh had caught the scent. She barked, tearing off in a flat out run. Kali was jerked forward, her flagging energy gathering for this final lunge. She raced behind Shiloh.

"Kali?" Grant caught up, running easily at her side. "What's going on?"

"We're close," Kali gasped.

Hearing footsteps, she checked behind her, to see a team of men running at her heels. The eerie lights of multiple flashlights in motion, crisscrossing in all directions as the group moved across the rough terrain giving an otherwordly appearance to the landscape.

The knowledge that everyone believed in Shiloh, in her, warmed her heart. And scared the crap out of her. So much rode on this night.

Shiloh ran strong, making for an open area. There. Threads. Dark violent, angry reds and blacks twisting in the night, faint but visible to Kali. "She's here. I can see her."

"Are you sure?" Grant came to a stop beside Kali, walking the area searching for any sign of Julie's presence. "We searched this area already." Grant said. The team with them spread out to search.

Kali walked toward the ribbons, unsnapping Shiloh's lead. "You missed her. She's here."

Shiloh barked once, circling a ten foot radius, stopping at a heavy bush. She sat and barked again.

Excited, Kali ran to her side. "This is it. Shiloh says she's alive." Threads of energy wove through the brush. "Let's get some light over here, please." Men rushed over, flashlights blinding her. More men joined them.

One of the men spoke up. "We didn't spend much time here because the terrain's not right."

Kali circled the bush, making two laps before she spied it. A pipe rose from the ground up into the bush.

Clever.

"Here's the pipe."

The three men ran over to her. "Where?"

"How? It doesn't appear to be a burial site."

The bush had thrown them off. Willow bushes were notoriously hard to kill with their tenacious multiple roots. But had it actually grown here or been planted as a cover? Studying it, she realized none others grew close by. The ground consisted of fallen leaves and moss. Bending, Kali reached deep into the center of the bush, branches snagging on her hair, scratching her face. She grabbed on and pulled.

The bush lifted free easily, throwing her off balance. Strong arms took it from her, tossing it off to the side.

"See." Kali bent to the end of the pipe, shining her flashlight inside. She couldn't see anything. "Julie? Julie can you hear me?"

Silence.

Kali called a second time. "Julie. Julie, can you hear me. It's Kali. We're here to help you."

There. She bent her head closer to listen. She waved the men to silence. "Shhhh."

Everyone stilled, holding their breath.

Kali bent her head and pressed her ear against the pipe. She strained to hear. There. She put up her hand. What was that noise? Kali closed her eyes and focused.

There again.

A slight moan.

"She's here."

A cheer went up.

***

Hidden high above in the leafy bowers of an overgrown fir tree, the killer could see nothing below. But the conversations came through clearly.

"Son of a bitch," he whispered, spit rolling in his mouth. "They found her. That's impossible." How'd Kali pull that off? He'd had trouble finding Julie in the dark tonight and he'd visited the area many times.

His fury grew in tandem with the growing noises below. Were they cheering? How dare they? The assholes figured they'd won. He snorted. He wasn't stupid. Kali might have found Julie, but he doubted she'd survive the night.

He glared at the greenery hiding him from the men searching below. This was not supposed to happen. Not now and not tonight.

In his books, this round counted as a draw. He'd cut his losses and rethink his plan. He must have done something wrong. God had to be displeased with him. But he would sort it through. God knew he was loyal.

Then he could move on.

Kali would have no hope of beating him on the next one. Even with her black magic bullshit.

Good humor restored, he settled down to wait them out.

***

Triumphantly, Kali turned to Grant. "Shovels, men and lights – lots of them."

Everyone moved back several feet looking for the best approach. Everyone but Kali. She sat protectively beside the pipe, not wanting to leave Julie alone, feeling the exhilaration morph into exhaustion. Still her pulse beat a nervous tempo as she watched the team organize Julie's release. Shiloh lay at her side, her chin resting on Kali's thigh. Nothing could dispel the sense of urgency. Julie hadn't made another sound. They had to get her to a hospital, and now.

The hill dropped to a hollow. The men started there. Other teams converged on their corner. A stretcher was carried in and medical equipment. Kali had lost her bearings. She didn't know if the men had found the road access or if they'd hauled this gear for miles. She hoped a vehicle was close by. Walking back wasn't an option.

Feeling moisture gathering on her cheeks, Kali reached up, not surprised to feel tears. She wiped her face on her sleeve. A sniffle escaped.

An odd tingle whispered through her mind.

Nice job.

Kali stiffened. *Stefan?*

Yes. You found her. Good for you.

Thanks to you. I was running low. Might not have made it without your help.

You would have. You tapped into the universal energy all on your own. I just helped to keep everything flowing properly.

Really?

A sensation similar to a warm hug, enveloped her.

Really.

The faint sensation slipped from her mind like it had never been there.

A warm hand squeezed her shoulder. "You did it, Kali. We've found her."

Kali lifted her head to see Grant at her side. She didn't want to mention Stefan's part in all of this – not with their audience. Standing up with his help, she smiled through her tears. "I know. I can't quite believe it." She glanced at the frantic activity. "I won't feel better until she's safe."

Julie had to be feeling the same. Kali leaned over the pipe, speaking down the tube. "It's okay, Julie," she said encouragingly. "We've got lots of men. You'll be out in a couple of minutes. Hang in there, Julie and you'll be fine."

"Kali?" A whisper so soft, Kali almost missed it.

"Julie, I'm here." Kali waved the others to silence.

The men stopped digging.

Her voice, tired and weak, traveled up the pipe. "Kali, be careful. He's here."

"He's here?"

"Yes..." A muffled cough sounded underground.

Kali exchanged looks with Grant. "Julie, who is he?" Several gasping coughs sounded. Kali repeated the question.

The coughing stopped. An eerie silence filled the night.

Grant raced to join the men, everyone galvanized into action. A palpable worry permeated the atmosphere. Kali's stomach knotted. She closed her eyes, repeating a litany of prayers. Shiloh nudged her hand and whimpered. Crouching, Kali hugged her tightly and buried her face in the warm fur. Kali's heart pulsed in tune to the fear throbbing through her veins.

A shout went up.

She surged to her feet. Hands reached out, pulling her back as the front of the hillside slid down, the pipe falling to one side. The corners of a large box slid into view. Men quickly brushed off the last of the rocks and dirt and pried against the crumpled corner. The medical team filled the area and Kali could see nothing but men bending over the opening.

"Is she alive?" Kali called out to Grant, who'd disappeared in the sea of men.

Tense silence worked through the crowd as they waited for news.

Grant stepped free of the crowd. "She's alive!"

The crowd roared.

Shiloh leaned against Kali. She didn't notice.

Kali stood in the cool night air and bawled.

CHAPTER TWENTY-FOUR

Kali drooped in the hospital cubicle, her eyes closed and her body swaying from exhaustion in the overly bright space. As they said in the movies, she'd 'hit the wall.'

"Kali?"

"Mmmm?"

"Kali, wake up. The doctor's here."

Kali struggled to focus until her bleary gaze settled on a familiar face. She gave him a wan smile. "Great drugs, Doctor."

He grinned at her. "At least you put them to good use. I hear you found the missing woman. Good for you."

Kali straightened in her chair. "How is she? Do you have an update?" Memories flooded through her. The medic in the woods figured Julie had spent the bulk of the time sliding in and out of consciousness.

Probably a good thing.

"She's severely dehydrated, and suffering from a head injury. That's what I can tell you at this point. We're running tests now."

"But she's alive."

The doctor patted her shoulder, smiling. "She's alive – thanks to you. We'll do everything in our power to keep her that way."

Kali beamed through the dirt, and gave him a small decisive nod. "I know you will."

"Now young lady, let's see what kind of damage you did to yourself tonight." The checkup didn't take long. Kali was past the point of protesting. She slumped back down, lifting what he told her to lift and showing him what he wanted to see. She never protested at the poking or prodding. She endured in silence. Her eyes drifted closed.

"No new damage. A couple of stitches have torn loose. We can't restitch them. So your wounds will take longer to close. Nothing serious except you're worn out, which will slow your healing. Go home and rest for the next few days and that's an order."

"Hmmm. Sounds good."

"Nurse, bring in that bear of an FBI agent pacing in the hallway…before she falls asleep. Now."

"I'm okay." Kali worked to sit up, her leaden limbs refusing to cooperate. Grant must have been close by because suddenly his face was there, watching her with a grim smile.

"How is she?" he said.

"Exhausted. She needs to go home and rest." The doctor looked down his nose at Grant. "I expect you to see she does."

"Oh, I will. Don't worry." Grant's voice threatened retribution if she didn't do as she'd been ordered.

"*She'd* like to sleep now." Kali slid off the bed and would have fallen to the floor if Grant hadn't reached and caught her.

"Easy does it. Ten, fifteen minutes… Then you can sleep."

She snorted. "Five. You get five minutes and that's it."

Grant raised his eyebrows. "Right. Let's go then." With murmured thanks to the doctor, Kali let Grant help her to his car by the front entrance. Shiloh lay stretched out in the backseat. She gave a tired woof at the sight of Kali. The fresh night air filled her lungs, giving her a small boost of energy. Kali managed to slide into the front seat on her own.

"Home, James," she ordered.

Long minutes later, the house loomed before her. Every muscle ached as Kali made it from the car to the front door. At the bottom of the stairs, she wavered.

"Let's go. Upstairs."

Trembling with exhaustion, Kali grabbed the banister and made it up the bottom set before Grant picked her up and slung her over his shoulder, eating up the last flight in seconds. Shiloh raced to the top beside them.

Grant lowered her to her feet at the base of the bed. She stumbled forward, pulled back the covers and dropped. Shiloh jumped up beside her.

"Kali, wait. Let's get you out of those clothes."

"Too tired," she whispered. Grant didn't leave her alone though. He tugged her shoes and socks off, ignoring her grumbling.

"Typical male." She brushed his hands away as he pulled on the waistband of her pants and tugged her jeans halfway down her legs. "Cold," she murmured.

"I know honey. Come on. Sit up." Sliding an arm under her shoulders, he lifted her into a slumped sitting position. Sliding one hand along her waist, he grabbed the lower edge of her t-shirt easing it over her head. Kali flopped backwards and moaned as the gauze dressing over her stitches pulled on her tender skin. She immediately rolled into a tight ball.

"I'm sorry, sweetheart. You'll sleep better without the heavy clothing."

Kali wanted to comment, only her teeth chattered to the point she couldn't talk.

Grant pulled her duvet up to her chin and tucked it in along the length of her body. Then he left her alone.

Blessed quiet descended in the room

She closed her eyes and sank deeper into the mattress. Grant returned in minutes.

"Just one more thing. Let's wash your face." Soothing warmth filled her as he wiped her face clean.

"Now you can sleep."

Kali sighed as a warm lassitude spread throughout her body. She fell asleep before he made it to the doorway.

***

Sometime in the night, Kali woke up aching...everywhere – tears drifting across her face. Grant's warm arms wrapped around her, tugging her into a comforting hug. The tears poured.

"Shh, it's all right, Kali. Take it easy."

Her shoulders shook as she burrowed deeper. The tears wouldn't stop. She cried in silence. Emotionally battered, her heart ached with the pain, the losses. Tension had knotted her muscles. The relief of finding Julie should have let it go. Instead, fear kept them tight and coiled...prepared.

What if they hadn't found Julie in time? What if there was someone else out there to rescue? Her heart ached too much for sounds to make their way past her throat.

"Shh. Stop crying, please, honey. You'll make yourself sick." Tender kisses landed on her forehead, the top of her head and her temple. His big hands massaged her lower spine, soothing away some of her aches and pains.

Kali's tears finally slowed. Easing her head back, she looked up at him, studying his beloved features. Heat spread throughout her lower body. She realized she wanted – no, needed – his touch. Energy warmed between them, making her realize that lying as they were, their auras had nestled together too.

With a last sniffle, she opened her mouth to speak only to find his finger up against her lips.

"Shhh."

A slumberous warmth slid through her.

Energy spiked, small flashes dancing between them.

What mattered was she wanted him. And had since she'd first seen him. With her eyes smiling into his, she licked the finger held against her lips, caressing the skin upward to the tip.

274

His eyes darkened, deepened – then he shuddered. Kali loved it. Lifting her head, she slid his finger slowly inside her mouth and sucked gently.

"Jesus, Kali," he whispered. Or was that a prayer? "You're playing with danger."

"No, I'm encouraging it." A wicked grin flashed before she closed her eyes and sucked his finger rhythmically.

"Fuck," he whispered, closing his eyes briefly. Tenderly, he placed a hand on either side of her head and stared into her eyes, searching.

She reached up, whispering against his lips, "Yes, please."

Energy blossomed, heat whispering between them, through them.

His hands tightened, cupping her head and holding her fast as their mouths joined. The kiss started out light, tentative, an exploration...then ignited into something deep, intense. Kali felt the answering pulse deep in her belly. A moan slid free. She shifted her position, wincing as her back muscles tightened, pulling her stitches. Sliding her hands over his chest, Kali realized Grant was fully dressed. Searching out the top button of his shirt she moved with delicious pleasure and slid the button through the hole, one finger purposely sliding against the smooth skin of his chest. She reached for the next.

"Christ, Kali, you're driving me nuts." His lips slid across her neck to feast on the delicate shell of her ear. His hands touched her spine and froze. *Her stitches.* Kali sensed his withdrawal immediately, as he pulled back, a protest forming on his lips.

She beat him to it. "It's okay, Grant. We'll be careful."

"God, you're hurt. You need rest, time to heal."

This time her finger stopped his words. "And I will. I need to believe in life again, to believe in love again. I need this. You need this. I need you."

Grant closed his eyes and shuddered. "And I need you...have for a long time."

She smiled, and reached for his lips. "Good. Let's not waste anymore time."

When he took her mouth this time, there was nothing tentative about it. He devoured her, for the first time tasting her, enjoying her, knowing they had hours of pleasure ahead. Sitting up, Grant stripped off his shirt and went to work on his belt buckle next.

But her hands pushed his away and tugged the snap open. The zipper parted as her fingers delved inside.

"Christ." Grant sucked in his breath, backed away from her marauding fingers and stood up. Within seconds he'd stripped and stood nude before her.

Kali, kneeling on the bed, was struck by the male glory in front of her. She feasted on the sight of him, slowly studying his strong muscled body until she reached his hooded eyes. Their gazes locked. His breath caught.

"You're something, you know that?"

Shaking her head, she whispered, "No, you are."

Tearing his gaze away, he looked at the bed, then at her.

She narrowed her eyes, wondering what he'd suggest.

Walking to the far side, Grant stretched out fully. "I guess you'll have to have your way with me, after all."

Kali watched him in confusion.

He opened his arms. "Don't want to tear those stitches…"

Of course – her back. Kali grinned and went into his arms gladly; her kisses joyous and hot. A veritable buffet of manhood lay stretched out before her. She couldn't resist. Her hands stoked and caressed as she dropped greedy kisses down the heavily muscled chest. She explored everything in reach. Grant twisted beneath her, his hands caressing her curves.

He reached out to cup the weight of one breast. Kali shuddered and stopped so he could stroke her hardened nipple. But her need was too great – she couldn't wait. Straddling his body, she bent over and gave him a kiss that raised the temperature of the room. As his arms came up to hold her fast, she slid down his body. She dropped kisses over his heated flesh down to his navel and along the line of hair. Kali caressed him with her fingers and inched downward.

His erection cuddled between her breasts.

Grant's breath caught and held.

"Do I stop?" she whispered, her tongue teasing his belly button.

"Never," he answered in a whispered prayer.

She slid lower to place kisses along the long length of him. "Shit."

Kali found herself dragged upward, her lips seared by his kiss. He maneuvered her back into straddling his body. His hands on her waist, he pushed her downward.

The head of his penis rested at the heart of her. Kali sat back. Her gaze locked on his face, she lowered herself ever so slightly and stopped. His eyes, darkened with need.

"Witch."

His fingers tightened on her hips, digging into the soft flesh. He tugged downward. "Please."

Kali gave him a smoky, languid look. "Is this what you want?" Inch by slow inch, she lowered her body, watching in joy as his eyes closed, his body twisted upward and his face flushed with pleasure.

"Yes. Christ. Yes."

Kali's heart swelled. To tease him and to prolong his pleasure, she paused her descent. Then slowly she slid upward.

"No," he moaned, his fingers digging into her hips. "No, don't leave."

"Look at me," she whispered.

Grant opened his eyes, searing her with his fiery gaze.

She watched him from under half-closed lids then lowered her hips again, taking all of him until he was seated deep inside. Grant pushed his hips firmly against her, sealing their flesh together. A long shudder rippled through them both. Placing her hands on his shoulders, she lifted and lowered, settling into a slow smooth ride.

His hands lifted to cup her breasts, his fingers teasing the hard nipples.

With her head tilted backwards, her hair flowing around her shoulders, Kali lost herself in her own pleasure as her blood heated and boiled. Her breath shortened; her movements becoming faster and faster.

Grant's hands clenched spasmodically on her hips as he tried to stop her from rising too high. He moaned, twisting beneath her.

Finally, his control broke.

Gripping her hips to hold her in place, he took control of the rhythm, driving his hips upwards, driving them both to the edge of the cliff. One. Two. Three hard thrusts and Kali flew, crying out as raw nerve endings exploded with pleasure, leaving her reeling in the intense aftermath.

Energy ballooned, then the boundaries broke, edges dissipated and their auras melted together.

With a long groan, Grant followed her.

Kali collapsed against his chest, her breathing coming in ragged gasps. But her heart and soul flew and soared. Still connected with his body, her breathing eased, became slow and even.

She dropped off to sleep, barely registering the beautiful deep purple aura surrounding the two of them.

Hours later, Kali surfaced to find she was lying on her side, wrapped in Grant's arms. Snuggling deeper into his embrace, she fell asleep again.

***

"Crap." The whispered word barely made itself heard in his hidden perch. What a long night. His neck ached, his back had kinked and he didn't think his legs would extend fully again. Taking his time, he stretched one limb at a time, careful not to dislodge the branches. The assholes continued to work below, walking, talking. He could hardly leave, but damn he needed to take a piss. Damn his back hurt. Men weren't meant to sleep in trees.

Voices floated up to him. The murmurs rose and fell but remained indistinguishable. He still had trouble believing they'd found Julie. Just a little longer and she'd have been lost to them. Then again, he should have killed Kali last night too. She'd been in his grasp. His hands on her neck. And he'd lost her. That failed attempt didn't bear thinking about. And due to his failure – they found Julie.

He pondered on his system. He preferred that Julie had suffered longer. Maybe his design needed adjusting. The pipe provided a great communication link, her suffering a source of joy...maybe it was too big? Allowed in too much air? Then again he'd planned on her living longer.

Kali's success had caught him sideways. She'd been fast. Too fast. He wouldn't hand over a victory to her again. He had to stay on top. Prove to God that he was worthy.

Shifting again, he winced. His stomach growled, reminding him he hadn't planned for hours of hiding. At least not here. The hunting blind at Kali's place had been set up for the long term with snacks and water bottles along with a change of clothes. A couple of sandwiches were there as well. Plus he slept like a baby there.

Close to her.

The FBI were always around but they watched the road entrance whereas he always entered by the beach. With a fat grin, he contemplated the FBI sitting out all night every night – for naught. He hoped they were as uncomfortable as he. Thank heavens for this heavy jacket and work boots.

His jeans had stiffened overnight, but they would loosen as he walked – when he could walk. Hiding in the park overnight hadn't been in the plan.

Still, life was good. Stuck in a tree he might be, but he was also alive and not under arrest. He was free to plan his next step. And the cops had no idea who or when. That's the way he liked it.

Pursing his lips, he hunkered lower and considered his next move.

CHAPTER TWENTY-FIVE

Kali woke to an empty bed.

Rolling onto her belly, she yawned and stretched, wincing at the pain in her back and shoulder. Memories flooded her mind. Julie. Grant. That couldn't help but produce a fat smile. They'd found Julie. Injured and unconscious – alive. Satisfaction wove through her heart. Monday had ended better than it started. Hopefully, Julie would come through this like a trooper. Obviously, she needed to heal, both mentally and physically. And she would, Julie was tough. It would take time but Julie would put this behind her and move on.

Grant was another matter. Kali had no intention of putting that behind her. She looked around her room. No sign of her clothes or his. Hmmm. A knock sounded on her open door. Shifting position, she watched as Grant entered, carrying a large mug. She smiled at the way his soft gentle energy brightened at the sight of her. Being this connected they'd never be able to hide from each other. Their energy would always show the truth of how each felt toward the other.

"Good morning. I just spoke with the hospital."

"How's Julie?" Kali shifted, tugging the duvet over her chest as she struggled into an upright sitting position. Grant passed her the mug.

Kali inhaled the rich coffee aroma, letting the steam float upward to bathe her face in its warmth. With her free hand, she tucked the duvet tighter. Even after a good night's sleep, her exhausted body felt chilled. "Thank you."

"You're welcome." Grant grinned at her as he took a seat toward the end of the bed. "Julie's in critical condition, and has yet to wake up. However the doctors are being cautiously optimistic she'll make a full recovery."

"That's wonderful news," Joy surged through her. "I've been so worried. When the medics couldn't revive her, I was afraid we were too late to save her."

"She's got a long road to recovery." He shifted further back on the bed, crossing his legs at the ankle. "There's more good news. Dan is awake. We can go see him in an hour."

"Wow. So coffee, a shower, food and then the hospital. Sounds great."

"Good, but you'll have to speed it up. Breakfast is almost ready. Shiloh looks hungry but I figured you'd want to feed her."

"Thanks. I do prefer to feed her myself." She appreciated his consideration.

"Thought so." Grant stood and walked toward the door. "You've got fifteen minutes until breakfast. I have a confession to make and I need breakfast to fortify me beforehand. Okay?"

One eyebrow raised, Kali nodded. *Interesting.* "I'll make it quick."

Kali crawled out of bed and headed for the bathroom. Butterflies took flight in her belly. She didn't want anything to mar this morning. What did he want to tell her?

Outside of initial shyness, Kali couldn't help but be pleased at the naturalness of their relationship. It gave her hope for their future. That he wanted to unburden himself could be another positive – depending on what he had to say. Grant hadn't made mention of a future together, but she'd do her damnedest to see they gave it a chance.

Fifteen minutes later, she followed the appetizing aromas into the kitchen, where she found sausages, hash browns and eggs ready for the table.

With a look of disbelief at Grant, she said, "This looks great."

"I dug around in the freezer." Grant brought over two laden plates. "If you pour the orange juice, we can start eating."

Kali obliged, delivering two glasses to the table. "This smells wonderful. I didn't realize how hungry I was until I walked in here." Grant had heaped her plate. Picking up her fork, she took a bite and closed her eyes in bliss.

"Eat up. You're downright skinny as it is. The doctor ordered bed rest for the next couple of days."

She sniffed. "It's hard to keep the weight on when I'm working all the time. Rest will help me regain a pound or two."

"And that is what you'll be doing. One trip to the hospital and then straight back home again where you'll spend the next couple of days resting, eating and doing some serious sleeping."

Kali knew his vision was ludicrous. Not while a killer stalked her. Still, she'd let him play the caregiver role happily for an hour or so. She forked more food into her mouth, concentrating on the flavors. The man could cook. She polished off her plateful. Standing, she refilled their coffee cups and turned to face him. "So what do you need to tell me?"

***

Grant reached for his mug of coffee, studying the pattern of steam as it rose from the hot brew. He grimaced, wishing he'd never initiated this conversation. "Six, closer to seven years ago, you gave a talk in Portland on SARs. I attended that talk."

Kali gave him a wry, lopsided smile. "How did I do?"

He studied the beauty of her face. "You made such an impression I haven't been able to get you out of my mind since."

Kali leaned forward to stare at him. "Really?"

"Yes, really." Should he show her? Why the hell not. Grant reached into his back pocket for his wallet. Flipping it open, he showed her his driver's license on one side and a picture of a woman on the other.

Kali studied the photo. "Is that me?"

Turning the wallet, Grant grinned. "Yeah. I cut it from one of the seminar brochures. How sad is that?"

Amazement lined Kali's face. "That's where I'd seen you before. You looked familiar but I couldn't place you."

"Not surprised. We spoke briefly. You gave your talk, answered questions then left." He didn't add that she'd left with a partner. A boyfriend.

"Seven years ago..." Deep sadness filtered into her eyes. "I lost my parents a few months after that talk. And I'd just realized my fiancé had more than a passing interest in my new-found wealth." With one long finger, she traced her features on the old photo. With the odd quirk to her lips, she handed it back. "How sweet."

"Sweet?" He carefully replaced the picture before putting his wallet away. *Sweet? Was that good or bad?* He wasn't sure. It certainly wasn't what he'd expected to hear.

"I like the idea of leaving an impact profound enough that you thought about me over the years." Kali gazed into his eyes. "A couple of weeks ago, that might have sounded a little creepy because I didn't know you then. But now, well I think it's sweet."

The relief rushing through him made him sit back, his shoulders sagging as they dropped a heavy weight. But her next words made him stop in shock.

"It's a little unnerving though. What if you'd found me wanting after all these years? You didn't know me back then and after getting to know me, what if I hadn't lived up to your memory?" Kali paused. Grant searched her face. She was nervous, afraid even – that the real woman hadn't matched the one in his mind. She couldn't be more wrong.

Confident, caring, compassionate Kali, always concerned about others, lacked the assurance she needed from him. Gentleness whispered through his heart. He could take care of that right now. "You're right. Back then I did have an idealistic view of you. How could I not? I didn't know who you were as a person. When I saw you this time, you were quieter, more withdrawn than I remembered. As if life had dished out some hard years." He studied her face, noting the flash of pain. "Your parents, your fiancé and yes, Dan told me about little Inez, lost in Mexico." He reached across the table to gently cover her hand.

Her gaze dropped to the table, a sad twist playing at the corner of her mouth.

He squeezed her fingers tightly. "Listen carefully. I have never felt disappointed or short changed. You measure up in all ways." With his gaze locked on hers, he pulled her other hand free from its lock on the coffee mug and cradled both in his much bigger one.

"The truth is I didn't know what to expect. I didn't know who you really were, but I couldn't get rid of the feeling I needed to know you. That if I didn't have the opportunity, my life would miss a huge essential element and I'd feel bereft forever." His thumb stroked the soft skin of her palm. "Last night was special," he admitted with a slow smile. "Better than any fantasy I might have dreamed." He grinned. "But in the morning light, I can't be too sure. We'll have to repeat it and see. Often."

The sexiest look he could have imagined slid from her eyes and headed straight to his groin. He gulped.

"Glad to hear that," she whispered softly.

Staring back down at their entwined fingers, he added sheepishly, "My mom wanted me to call you years ago."

Kali blinked, shock on her face. "What? You told her?"

A laugh broke free. "Yes. And she's going to have a great time reminding me. She told me life was precious and if I was really interested, I should call you."

Apparently having trouble with the information, Kali sat back, shaking her head. "Did you tell her you were working with me these last couple of weeks?"

He snorted. "Are you kidding? It was bad enough that Stefan knew. My mom is quite capable of driving down here to meet you if she'd known."

Kali laughed. "A lady after my own heart. I will enjoy meeting her."

"When this mess ends," he promised. He glanced at his watch and raised an eyebrow. "However, if we want to go see Dan, we need to leave – now."

***

They walked through the front entrance of the hospital fifteen minutes later. Grant led her past a set of double doors and into a different hallway. Kali smiled at their clicking footsteps, amplified by the empty corridor. Visiting hours didn't start for another hour, giving the hospital the appearance of a rare serenity.

"I owe Stefan a big thanks for his help last night?" Kali murmured awed by the silence of the long hallway. At Grant's questioning look, she explained.

His eyebrows raised, Grant shook his head. "I had no idea he could do that."

Arriving at a large double door, Grant nodded to a guard standing on duty. Grant showed his ID to the officer who checked it before moving aside.

Kali whispered, "Did you set up security for Julie?"

"Yes, although I doubt the killer would go after her again."

"Maybe not, but she won't survive a second attempt."

"And she won't have to." Entering, Kali saw stark white walls, interrupted only by huge sunflowers standing in a vase beside the bed. Dan lay on his side facing the window, the blanket at his shoulders. Grant walked up beside her. The door snicked shut behind them. When Dan rolled over, Kali caught her breath.

"Oh, Dan." She threw her arms around him in a gentle hug.

"Hi, Kali." Dan patted her arm.

Pulling back, it was all Kali could do to stop the tears from spilling over.

His wrinkled face shifted and reformed into a parody of a smile. "Don't look so worried, Kali. I'm going to be fine."

Sunshine seeped into the room and fell on Dan's beloved face. Kali sniffled. "Thank heavens for that. I can't take much more. Can you please tell us what the heck happened?"

"I'm not sure. I'd been working on the computer when I found something odd. I went to the files to check the information and the next thing I know...I'm here in the hospital."

Studying his face, Kali asked slowly. "Were you alone? Did you fall? Or could you have been hit?"

Grant stepped forward to rest a comforting hand on her shoulder. Kali leaned into him.

Dan noted the movement. A slight grin dimpled his cheeks. "Either case is possible. The office door was open so it's possible someone snuck up behind me." He shrugged. "I'm sorry. I don't know. I didn't see anyone. All I can say is there were lots of people around who had the opportunity."

It hurt Kali to look at him. His face, normally so full and healthy, looked thin and empty. The wrinkles, usually beaming with life, drooped in layers, lifeless. His changed countenance reflected more than a head injury; he looked seriously ill. Kali's stomach knotted at the thought.

"Listen I'm fine. I just need a couple of days to return to normal."

"You'd better." She sniffled and swiped her watery eyes.

Grant took several steps that brought him to the other side of Dan's bed. "You said you found something wrong on the computer and went to check the information. Do you remember what that was?"

Dan frowned, his forehead creasing into more wrinkles – if that were possible. "Not really."

Changing tracks, Grant reached into his pocket and removed a folded piece of paper. "Do you know this man?"

Dan, his shoulders shaking, struggled to sit. Kali reached out and helped him into an upright position. "Take it easy."

"I'm fine." He pulled the bedcovers higher. "Let's take a look."

Dan reached for the picture. Kali and Grant watched him for any signs of recognition. They weren't disappointed.

"Christian LeFleur." Dan took another glance at the picture, his face pinching tight before handing it back to Grant. "Christian pops in now and again. He volunteers for several organizations. He's training a young German Shepherd, with decent success I hear." He glanced up at Kali, his rheumy eyes revealing pain. "Brad and he were close. I imagine he's hurting right now."

Kali frowned. "I don't remember Brad mentioning him."

"He might not have. They were *buds*. You know, they talked about anything and everything, went and got drunk together – guy stuff. Brad mentioned a couple of times how he could be himself with Christian, unlike when he was with his wife. They shared similar backgrounds, interests, even looks. They also belonged to the same church."

Kali's frown deepened as she glanced at the picture.

Dan added. "They used to joke about being brothers. You had to see them together."

Interesting. It didn't help her place Christian in her mind. Nor could she see Brad's features in the sketch.

"Christian's an active SARs member, working disasters for over a decade but he's a loner – and a bit of a ladies' man, come to think of it. Has coffee when he's here, more often than not he takes off with Brad or works alone, if you know what I mean?"

Pondering the picture, Kali shook her head. "I can't really place him in my mind."

A half snort came from the bed. "Of course, you're one narrow-minded person when it involves men."

Grant stepped forward. "What do you mean, Dan?"

Dan cast a sideways glance at Kali. "Nothing bad. It's just she's blind to men. Many try to catch her eye, but she just doesn't see them. The more obvious they are, the more oblivious she is."

With an apologetic look her way, Dan added, "She only remembers men if she has meaningful interaction. Without that, they don't register on her radar. Brad worked for years to be allowed into her inner circle." He reached out to clasp her hand. "Kali doesn't mean anything by it. It's just *her*."

Kali hated the heat rising up her cheeks. "I'm not that bad."

"There's nothing *bad* about it. It's your protective mechanism. If you don't see the men and their advances, you don't have to deal with them."

She gasped in protest. "No one has ever made an advance at me."

Grant glanced between her and a ruefully smiling Dan who held his other hand up. "Like I said." To Kali he added, "And there have been many."

"No way." She shook her head, refusing to believe she'd been that blind. "Let's return to the subject at hand. Christian. What else do you know about him?"

"Not much. When he was with Brad, they loved to debate religious issues. You'd hear them arguing all the time. Both were strong believers but Christian was worse."

"Worse? How?"

"More voluble. The debate I remember was on who deserved to live and die. Restitution, right to life issues. At the time, I'd assumed they were discussing abortion or maybe assisted suicide. I left the room because..." Dan's gaze traveled between the two of them. "Well, I didn't want to know."

Kali understood. Dan hated discussion involving politics or religions as much as he detested girl talk. If any woman opened up on pregnancy, labor or marriage in his vicinity, he bolted. Divorce was the worst topic.

Tossing a glance at Grant, she watched in fascination as his eyes narrowed and he stared straight ahead, as if the room faded out of existence. Even his body stilled.

"Right to life issues fit." She mixed Dan's comments with what she knew regarding the kidnappings and murders. "The survivors cheated death. In his mind they have no right to life. He's helping God by making things right."

"Any apparent competitiveness or jealousy?" Grant continued. "Did he ever ask you about Kali or want to discuss her?"

Dan closed his eyes. Kali watched him in concern. They'd have to leave him to rest soon. His skin had taken on an even grayer tone.

Dan pursed his lips. "He wouldn't have to ask. Her record is well-known."

"Record?" Grant glanced over at Kali before refocusing his attention on Dan. "Is that like a recovery count? Do you people keep those kinds of records?"

"Not official records. Like any industry, some people do. Kali doesn't, but her success rate is often commented on because it's phenomenal. She can't work a disaster without her peers watching, taking note. Many journalists and politicians follow her progress."

Grant spun around to stare at Kali.

Embarrassed, Kali shrugged it off. "I do what I do."

"And she does it very well," Dan interjected. "The industry has noticed. Honestly, her work is a major reason why the center functions."

"You hire her services out?" Grant frowned, his brows forming a v-shape. He stood with his hands fisted on his hips.

Dan chuckled. "I do but she doesn't."

Grant shook his head. "What?"

Kali sighed. "It's not a secret. I mentioned it before briefly. I work pro bono and Dan uses the money to keep the center open and running. I don't need the money, however, the world needs the center. Dan does a lot of necessary work, and on a global level."

Heat rose on her face. She hated explaining herself. She was hardly a philanthropist, but she didn't need the money nor did she want to accept payment for helping people in need. That she gave money on a quarterly basis to the center as well wasn't something she wanted to discuss either.

"Do you get paid to help out when there's a disaster?"

"No. I don't." Clear cut and equivocal her voice left no room for doubt. "There are a couple of paid rescue workers here, for all others the center covers the costs but not wages. Mostly through donations, government subsidies and contract work similar to what Jarl did for that church."

Grant glanced over at Dan, who nodded. "She's right. To stay afloat, we run classes, take on contract jobs. That can be locating graves, missing dogs, people lost in the bush, etc. There's no compensation for helping out on disasters."

Kali jumped in. "It's the same for most centers. The bulk of rescue workers are volunteers."

"Before we leave you to rest, have there been any problems with Jarl at the center or on a disaster site?" Grant's asked.

The question blindsided her. She chewed her lips and snuck a look at Dan. He stared back at her, then shrugged.

"What aren't you saying?" Grant's tone thickened with annoyance.

Reaching over, she patted Dan's hand. "I didn't consider it before but since you put it that way." Kali shifted back into her chair and pleated the folds in her shirt. "A while back, I thought Jarl might have been stealing from the center. I had no proof and honestly I could've been mistaken. I spoke to him about it, and he denied everything. He was quite upset about the whole thing. We had several uncomfortable months before our relationship regained a normal footing." Kali paused. "The thing is...after our talk the thefts stopped."

Dan spoke. "Until recently."

Kali started. "What?"

"I hadn't had a chance to tell you. Just recently I've noticed a few minor problems surfacing. Stuff disappearing, the petty cash empty when it shouldn't be. You know little stuff…nothing serious, more of an inconvenience."

Grant glared at the two of them. "And you're telling me about this now?"

They both shrugged. Kali said innocently, "Why would I have mentioned it earlier? It's not important."

"Christ." Grant threw his hands up in the air. "You do realize this might explain Jarl's presence in your office?"

Kali hated feeling guilty. She ran her hands through her hair. "I wasn't thinking of thefts – there were bigger issues like kidnappings and murders, remember."

"What's the chance he's moved from petty crime to stealing identities or banking information? Presuming, you keep information like that on your computer, Dan?"

"Aye, I do. And I suppose given the circumstances, it's possible."

Both Kali and Grant frowned in sync. "What circumstances?" she asked. As far as she knew, everything was fine in Jarl's life.

"Jarl's wife is seriously ill and their medical insurance won't cover her treatments. It's progressed to the point she can't work, so he's actively looking for ways to cover the bills."

"Shit." Pity hit her. Poor Jarl. She'd have helped him if she'd known. She brightened. Maybe she still could?

Grant, his cell phone already in his hand, headed for the door. "I'm stepping out to make some calls." He strode to the door. "Be back in a few minutes."

Kali waited until he'd left before moving to sit on Dan's bed. "You know we found Julie?"

His eyes lit up. He grasped her hand. "Yes, and thank God you did. The doc said she'll recover. I can't imagine what she went through."

"She's going to need time. Physically and mentally." Sadness pulled at her. No one should have to go through what she'd been through — and never twice.

"She's strong. She'll make it." Dan coughed, his voice hoarse and rasping.

Kali frowned down at him. "Do you need a nurse?"

Tremors wracked his thin frame. "No. They can't help. I'm feeling my age today."

"Is there something you're not telling me?"

A disturbing rattle worked its way up his throat until he coughed and coughed. Kali reached for a tissue and handed it to him. Dan sat, the coughs wracking his thin frame violently. After a few anxious moments, Kali watched his face turned beet red and witnessed sputum spewing. Finally, he could breathe easily.

Dan slumped onto the bed, taking several deep breaths. "That hurt."

Kali hesitated, unsure she should pry. "Have you asked the doctors to check you over?"

"No, they're doing it anyway." He closed his eyes briefly. "The results will take a few days."

The door opened as Grant entered, his face carved in stone.

Kali assessed his features. Time to go. Kali stood. "I'll stop by tomorrow." She dropped a kiss on Dan's forehead. "Rest and heal."

"You take care of yourself." He smiled grimly at the two of them. "Grant, get this guy before someone else is hurt."

"That's the plan," he answered. He opened the door, his hand on the small of Kali's back, nudging her forward. "We'll see you again, Dan. Take care."

Once outside, she asked, "Can we visit Julie?" The hand on her back eased off.

He shot her a quick sideways look. "No, I just checked. She's heavily sedated. And…she's not doing so well."

Kali stopped and stared at him. "Oh," she whispered.

Grant hooked an arm around her shoulders, tugging her into moving forward again. "Her body's gone through a horrible experience. She's injured. She's dehydrated and needs to heal. Her body has shut down to deal with the trauma. It happens and in this case, it might give her a fighting chance."

"I'd so hoped she would have recovered enough this morning for us to be able to talk to her."

They walked past the bustling nurses' station and out to his car. As they walked outside, Kali brought up the one question she'd forgotten to ask. "Why would the killer have been in the woods last night?"

Grant hesitated.

Kali waited until he unlocked the car. After buckling up the seatbelt, she asked, "He likes to watch them, imagine them dying, doesn't he?"

Grant looked at her and nodded before turning on the car and backing out of his parking spot. Once on the main road heading to her house, he spoke up. "Probably something like that. He could have religious reasons for his visits like enumerating their sins or gloating over what was happening. With a twisted mind, it's hard to tell."

"Was the pipe to give Julie fresh air or to talk to her, torment her?"

Surprise lit his face. "Possibly both."

Kali curled her lip. *Yuck.* Thankfully, they were almost home. They pulled into her driveway moments later. Kali hopped out. Grant stayed in the car. Kali bent to look at him through the window. "Are you coming in?"

He hesitated. "I need to go to the office. But I'll be back in an hour or an hour and a half at the most." Grant stared at her. "You be careful. Go in and lock the doors. This guy is a loose cannon. He could come after you next. Remember, the FBI has your house under surveillance but if you leave here you'll be unprotected. Stay smart and I'll be back as soon as I can."

She wanted to put on a pot of coffee, fill her travel mug and head to the beach with Shiloh. Kali switched her gaze from Grant to her house and back again. "I don't have anywhere to go."

"Good. I'll return as fast as I can. I'll bring an overnight bag with me this time." Grant reversed the car and headed down the road.

With a light heart, Kali ran to her front door. She'd have a house guest tonight. Kali laughed and ran the last steps.

Grant had no idea what he'd be letting himself in for.

CHAPTER TWENTY-SIX

Kali hummed in the kitchen as she waited for Grant's return. It had been ages since she'd spent time cooking. She loved to cook, only preparing a meal for one person wasn't the same as for company. She sliced onions and peppers, adding them to the cooking hamburger. Her spaghetti sauce recipe had been handed down from her great-grandma. She'd made several personal tweaks along the way, yet the essence remained the same. She couldn't help but wonder what her mom would have thought of Grant. She'd approve, Kali decided.

Shiloh lay in a sunbeam running across the kitchen floor. They both needed the downtime today. Rest and relaxation was good for the soul. Even with everything going on, Kali felt happy. They'd found Julie alive, Dan was improving and then there was her budding relationship with Grant. She had high hopes for tonight – if this asshole left them alone for that long.

Unfortunately, he was likely searching out his next victim right now. Kali turned and looked outside. The sun had slipped behind a dark cloud. She couldn't help think this was the classic calm before the storm.

Better to not go there now. What would happen, would happen. She'd deal with it somehow.

Kali returned to the kitchen and her sauce. Grant should be here soon. She moved through the mundane chores she'd missed out on recently – like laundry. Shiloh didn't appear to have the same sense of duty though as she lolled about around the house, watching as Kali worked.

Knowing the time was disappearing; Kali strode into her bedroom and quickly dealt with the clothes. As she started to leave, she turned to gaze thoughtfully to the bed. Checking her watch, she made a fast decision. Striding back over, she stripped the bedding off and made the bed up with fresh sheets. Better to be prepared and not have an opportunity than to have an opportunity and not be prepared.

Jamming the old sheets into the washing machine took another few minutes.

"Whew." Kali checked the laundry room over for dropped items. Then she headed back to the kitchen.

She walked around the corner when a hooded figure, dressed all in black, lunged for her.

Kali screamed. She spun and bolted back toward the laundry room. He grabbed for her arm, pulling her off balance. Pain streaked across her back. Kali stumbled, kicking wildly and heard him grunt. Freed unexpectedly, Kali screamed, "Shiloh, help!"

Shiloh barked and jumped. Kali didn't see anything else as she ran for the kitchen, bursting through the glass French doors, onto the deck, jumping the stairs two at a time.

"Shiloh," she screamed at the top of her voice. "Shiloh, come." The trees on the property weren't going to give her much coverage, only she'd take anything right now. She dared to look behind her. He wasn't following her. Shit. Kali stubbed her toe but didn't dare break stride. She could run ten miles without stopping, only right now, worry for Shiloh kept breaking her focus. She'd be running to catch up if she could. That she wasn't, couldn't be good.

She hid out in the woods and paused to catch her breath. Kali peered from behind a tree. Where was he? Kali closed her eyes and leaned into the tree. "Shit. Shit. Shit."

Her legs trembled in shock and she could hardly breathe. She took several deep shaky breaths. *Think. Think stupid. What are you supposed to do now?* Shit. Her cell phone. She slapped her hands over her pockets. There. Her fingers fumbled frantically. Finally, she managed to pull it free but struggled to punch in the numbers. She failed the first time and had to redial. She kept watching for any sign of him

"Hello."

"Grant," she hissed softly.

"Kali. What's wrong? Where are you?" he yelled. Fear leapt through the phone and raised her own panic level. She peered nervously through the brush. Where were Grant's men?

"He's here at the house." She buried the phone in her shoulder at his yell. "I'm hiding out in the back yard at the bushes by the beach access. Grant, there's no sign of your men."

"Shit. I'm on my way. You stay put. Do you hear me?"

"Hurry." Kali couldn't stop the pleading tones. She didn't give a damn. She was scared and being alone was the last thing she wanted. "Something has happened to Shiloh. Either he has her or she's hurt."

"I'm in the car. I'll be there in less than ten minutes. There's two men on surveillance duty – have you seen any sign of them?"

No and damn it, she'd expected them to come to her rescue. Had counted on it.

Instead she was alone.

Cut off. With no sign of Shiloh.

And terrified.

Swallowing hard, she said, "No. Hurry, this is going to be the longest ten minutes of my life."

"Just make sure you're alive by the time I get there. If the bastard comes after you, run like hell."

"Don't worry I plan on it." She chewed on her lower lip, daring to peer around the tree. Her house sat silent and still. She searched the windows looking for any sign of movement...of life.

"Kali?"

"Shhh. I'm here." Kali pulled back behind the tree.

"Can you see him?"

"No." Her voice had dropped to a barely audible level. Kali scrunched up into a tight ball and sank further under the branches. "Hurry."

"Be there in a few minutes."

"Don't come alone." Kali's voice rose and suddenly remembering, she dropped it down to a hoarse whisper. "He's going to be waiting for you. I'm afraid he's hurt the surveillance team."

"I'm pulling into the driveway now. Stay where you are. Be there in minutes."

Kali's phone clicked off. She stared at it, then put it back into her pocket. The silence was eerie and unsettling. She couldn't stop peering behind her, afraid the asshole was going to pop up from nowhere.

It seemed like forever yet it was probably only three to four minutes before she heard the welcome sound of sirens in the distance. "Thank God. Please be okay, Shiloh. Please." Kali prayed for her best friend. Shiloh might be a dog to others, but she was family to her.

There. She peered around the tree, her head barely above ground. Someone was running toward her. Grant. She wanted to run to him but couldn't be sure of his identity. Her heart pounded. She peered out from her hiding place.

"Kali." Grant yelled, his hands cupping against his mouth. "Kali, where are you?"

A noise behind Kali had her spinning on the spot. Her throat constricted. The rustling sound moved in Grant's direction. *There.* A flash. Another movement. A heavy rustling.

Kali realized Grant, his gun at the ready, raced toward her right in front of the tree line. Exposed. An easy target. *Shit.*

And there was the killer…creeping up on Grant.

"No!" Kali bolted toward Grant. She hit him in a flying tackle but he twisted at the last minute – just as a funny spitting sound split the air.

Kali arched as her back hit the ground, tumbling into a mass of limbs. Men shouted and spread out into the wooded area.

Kali moaned and struggled to move.

"Kali? Are you all right?" Grant rolled over and regained his feet. He bent down to help her up.

"I'm fine. That was a rough landing." She smiled up at him. "He's a lousy shot. Go."

"Thank heaven for that. Still, he took out the two men watching the house. I have to find him." He cradled her gently, dropped a quick kiss on her forehead. "Are you sure you're okay?"

"Yes, yes. I'm fine. Go. I need to find Shiloh."

"Wait for me at the house. The rest of my team should be here soon."

Nodding, Kali took off at a run toward the house. Worry for Shiloh dominated – her own injury was forgotten. Maybe she was hurt, hiding somewhere. She burst into the house, calling out, "Shiloh?" Kali went from room to room, hating that she'd taken off without helping her friend. "Shiloh, where are you?"

Walking through the kitchen, she grabbed Shiloh's treat bag and walked into the bedroom, shaking it.

Kali stopped. She closed her eyes and reached out with the Sight. *Where are you, sweetheart? Shiloh?* Kali could feel her. She was alive, but hurting. Shit. Kali broke into a run and headed to the laundry room. The closet was open and on the floor back in the far back corner lay Shiloh, motionless. She didn't make a sound when Kali bent down beside her. Shiloh's fur was warm, except she didn't move when Kali touched her. Kali crawled into the closet and ran her hands over her friend. She stopped when she came to a sticky patch. She withdrew her hand to take a closer look. Blood.

"Oh God. Shiloh." Kali reached into the far back in the closet and slid her hand gently under Shiloh's chest and hips. Awkwardly, she backed out, shuffling on her knees, half-dragging and half-lifting Shiloh. The dog whimpered.

"Easy girl. You've been shot." Kali was already punching in the vet's number. "Oh God, please answer." It took just a minute to inform them that she was on her way.

Keys. Where were her keys? Kali panicked until she located them on the fridge with her purse. She made it through the front door and ran ahead to unlock the back door on her car. One agent saw her and ran to help. With his help, as gently as they could, they loaded Shiloh into the passenger seat. Kali raced around to the driver's side. She hit reverse and tore out of the yard, gravel spitting behind her tires. Grant would be pissed. Too bad. Grant had his responsibilities.

Kali had hers.

***

Kali drove recklessly. Shiloh was dying. Tears clouding her vision, hindered her driving.

"Hang in there, Shiloh. It's going to be all right girl, we're almost there." Kali ripped into the parking lot and drove up to the back door. She pulled the Jeep to a squealing stop and hopped out. There was a buzzer outside the back door. Pounding it several times, Kali raced to the passenger side. Shiloh hadn't moved.

Dr. Samson slammed the backdoor open and raced toward them.

"How is she?"

Kali stumbled in her reply. "I don't know. She's been shot but I have no idea how badly."

"Move over. Let me get her." Dr. Samson stood well over six-foot-four and was built like a line backer. Kali didn't argue, was just grateful he was here at all. An animal gurney arrived at his side.

Shiloh was quickly transferred into the operating room and Kali was left standing alone. She didn't want to leave the surgical room, however the assistants ushered her to a waiting room and left her there. Paperwork had to be done, and her vehicle needed to be moved.

There was one more thing she could do. She leaned against a wall and sent loving healing energy toward Shiloh. She had no idea if it would help, but hoped it would. Could Stefan help? She didn't know how to contact him. Tears pooled in the corner of her eyes. It wasn't fair. Shiloh was family and Kali had lost too many people already.

I am helping her. Continue to send healing energy yourself.

Stefan.

Kali smiled through her tears, her heart full of hope. *Thank you!*

The wait was physically uncomfortable. Kali couldn't lean back and she couldn't sit still. Her phone rang on the fifth lap around the small waiting room.

"Where the hell are you?" Fear and anger sliced through the phone.

"At the vet's. The asshole shot Shiloh. I had to take care of her."

"And you couldn't fucking call me? You know this killer is hunting, right? What the hell do you think I thought when I couldn't find you?" His roar hurt her ears. "I told you to stay at the house."

Anger of her own spiked. "Well you haven't caught him and look at how many people have died. Don't tell me how to protect my family unless you think you can do a better job. And so far, you haven't."

Silence.

Kali cringed. She hadn't meant to be so harsh. "Look I'm sorry. Shiloh is in surgery and...I just didn't think." Kali stopped her pacing and brushed her hair back off her head. "She's been in there for over an hour. I don't even know if she's alive." Pain stabbed through her heart at the thought.

His voice turned soothing. "I know this has been tough on you."

"And, no, you don't understand," she cried out, her voice breaking. "This is your work. This is the stuff you deal with all the time. I don't. I don't want to either. I want this all to go away." Tears collected again in the corners of her eyes, and again Kali brushed them away. "He's hurt so many people. Destroyed so many families. When will this stop?" God. Her emotions were a mess. She sniffled quietly, but Grant still heard.

"I'm sorry, sweetheart. Stay close to Shiloh and I'll call you back in a little while."

Kali put her phone away. Every time she thought about him and his work, she felt confused and upset. Talk about double standards. Her work had put off more than one prospective date. Yet, she was doing the same thing to him.

They weren't dating though. Yeah, right. So what did one call it?

"Kali."

She twisted to find Dr. Samson waiting to talk to her. Kali hastened over to him.

"How is she?"

"I think she's going to pull through. The bullet did some damage on its way through but missed the vital organs. We've patched her up. She'll need to stay here for a few days, under sedation, so we can keep an eye on her to make sure the bleeding has stopped."

Kali closed her eyes in relief. She swayed as every muscle in her body weakened.

"Here, sit down." Dr. Samson's concerned face stared down at her.

Kali smiled back at him. "I'm okay. Just relieved that she's going to make it."

"She's not out of the woods yet," he warned.

"She's a fighter and if she's given a fair chance, she'll do her part to pull through." Her heart suddenly felt lighter. Kali

303

reached up and kissed the vet's cheek. "Thank you. Shiloh deserves to live. She's saved so many lives; I'm grateful you were here to save hers."

"We need Shiloh in this world. As long as she does her part and wants to live then I'll do my part and give her that chance."

The two friends shared an understanding look. "Can I see her?"

He shook his head. "You shouldn't. She's covered in blood with tubes coming and going in all directions. She wouldn't even know you."

It took some convincing but finally Kali headed back out to her car. Kali winced at the sun high and heat. She'd already been through so much today, surely it was bedtime. Before getting into the car, she called Grant. "I'm on my way home. Where are you?"

"Searching your yard. We've got a team sweeping the neighbourhood. I'll be at the house by the time you get back."

"Glad to hear it. See you soon."

Her shoulder had stiffened to the point where she could barely move it. Still Kali figured she could make the less-than-five-mile drive to where her bed waited. She drove slowly and carefully, not wanting anything else to go wrong today. She stopped at a red light.

Her phone rang. She snatched it from the holder. "Hello?"

The same horribly mechanical voice filled her ear. "You're too late...and now your lover is going to die." Laughter filled the Jeep's interior before being abruptly shut off.

Kali cried out in pain and horror.

The killer had Grant.

***

Walking casually along the tree line, visible enough to be seen, hidden enough to not be obvious, Grant closed the phone and tucked it away in his back pocket. He'd been glued to the damn thing all day. His mind raced over the information he'd just received. He was tempted to tell Kali but didn't dare until he'd had his suspicions confirmed. Besides she had enough to worry about.

But he might have just gotten a major piece of the puzzle handed to him. The DNA of the victim found in Sacramento was not Brad's.

"So you think you've figured it all out, do you?"

The cool confidant voice came from behind him. Grant gave a small hard smile. Then something small and hard dug into his back. Shit.

"Hold out the gun, real slow."

Grant's fingers flexed on the gun as he held his hands out. The gun was tugged free. Double shit.

"Now, turn around." Twigs rustled with the leaves as the gunman stepped back.

Tossing his options around in his head, Grant slowly turned to face a tall, muscular brown-haired male. Only by a stretch of a good imagination did it resemble the elusive Christian.

"Brad, I presume?" He narrowed his gaze at the smirk flashing across the other man's face, replaced only for a second by uncertainty and surprise. Brad might have been hiding out for days but he looked to be in peak physical condition. Except the eyes. The fervent glare shining his way looked anything but normal.

"Took you long enough, didn't it. Not so smart, are you? FBI trained and I still have the drop on you." He waved the FBI issue pistol in his hand, while he slipped Grant's gun into his pocket. "I'm going to have a decent collection of these by the end of the day."

Shit. That meant at least one of his team was down. There had to be a half dozen men out here. He cast a furtive glance around. Why had no one seen him?

"I've got a special hiding spot close by. A bird's-eye view of the place, so to speak." His lips might have twisted into a smile, but there was no reflection of it in his eyes. Grant could see the killer who lived inside instead. "It let me keep an eye on Kali. Pick my time to take you out. Or did you think I hadn't noticed how she looks at you, or you at her?"

Grant stared, his mind racing. He needed answers. He needed a way out. He needed to take this nutcase out before Kali got here. "I'm sorry. I don't know what you're talking about."

"Like hell, you don't. Do you know how long I've been trying to get her myself?" Brad snorted, pulling the gun to point at Grant's forehead. "God damn it. I let my marriage disintegrate for her. Did she care? No." Spittle formed at the corner of Brad's mouth as he worked himself into a more agitated state. He waved his gun around as he talked but was always careful to keep it pointed in Grant's direction.

"Stupid bitches. Her and that dog. Witches both of them. She had me cuckolded for years, caught up in her spell. Believing in her. I was an idiot. Not now. Not anymore. I've finally seen through her trickery."

Grant held back his retort, not wanting to slow the flow of words out of Brad's mouth. It might be the only chance he had of getting answers. His team should have them surrounded by now. It wasn't like Brad was making any attempt to be quiet or hidden.

Providing any of Grant's team were left alive to hear.

Brad's face turned mean. He motioned to Grant to turn down a well-travelled path through the trees. Obediently, with an eye to the surroundings and scanning for a way to escape, he wove through the trees.

Thankfully Brad kept up enough conversation for the two of them as they walked.

"I guess I'm not the brightest star around but I prayed to God for help. It seemed like nothing I did ever changed anything." Frustration bubbled through his voice gone hard and angry. "Not with Kali, not with the disasters. If anything, it seemed like the more people we rescued, the more people needed rescuing."

Grant started to turn around to, but Brad nudged him hard with the gun. "Keep moving. We're almost there."

They walked a little further. Kali's neighbour's house was off in the distance on the left – to the right, trees. They were descending slightly. Behind him Kali's house. In front…nothing but cliff and ocean.

Grant said, "Where are we going?"

Brad shoved him hard. Grant stumbled, and recovered. Three more steps and he could see the small clearing, barely big enough for the two of them at the cliff edge.

And a small hollowed out depression.

His stomach sank. Try to take Brad out now and risk a bullet and a fall off the cliff, or wait for the others.

Stall. "Why are you killing these poor people? I thought the purpose was to help all of them?

Snapping the words out, Brad said, "No. That's the problem. I didn't get it. Until Mexico." Brad snickered.

"I had a light-bulb moment. The reason things never changed is that I wasn't doing the right work. God created these disasters to call his people home. Natural disasters …are naturally occurring…as in they're manifestations of God's will. I wasn't supposed to rescue the buried victims. I was *supposed* to help God and finish the job on those people God missed because of interference."

He was crazy. That's the only explanation for the twisted excuse Brad was handing out. This was going to break Kali's heart.

"Then I made one last realization. I was supposed to enjoy my life. I hated to go home to my bitch of a wife, suffering in silence with unrequited love for the witch, and working my ass off to boot. That's no life for one of God's special workers. Not anymore. Life is fun now. This work is a joy." He laughed, pausing to wipe the sweat from his brow. "This is great. I'm dead to the world and you'll be...just dead."

Grant's mind raced. How to get out of this alive, before the madman with the gun started shooting? *Anytime, people.*

They are almost there. Keep holding him off.

Grant's knees almost buckled at Stefan's voice.

Thank God. Am I glad to hear you.

Kali is almost here. Hold on. Stefan's voice was sharp and urgent in Grant's head.

Grant straightened, spinning around. *No! Stop her. Brad will kill her.*

Too late. She's only minutes away.

"No!" Grant screamed, spinning around.

The blow came out of nowhere. It slammed into the side of his head, dropping him where he stood.

***

Brad laughed, waves of power flying through him. He could do this. He'd been off-stride all day. Driven by rage after last night's fiasco. But now things were pulling together... He thought he'd had the Julie stuff under control, but to learn that she'd lived through it had festered, eating away at him all morning.

Then he'd lost Kali in her own damn house. How stupid. By this time, he should have felled her several times over. Shooting Shiloh had hurt but when he recognized Shiloh also worked against God's will, firing had also given him an outlet for his rage.

And, he'd just redeemed himself. Still chuckling, he tossed the gun to the ground and bent over his latest victim.

What could Kali possibly see in this fool?

He dragged Grant the last few feet until he lay in the depression. Christ, this bastard was heavy. But the location was perfect. There was only room for him to stand. The cliff was so unstable here, no one would think about checking this outcrop. The eroded edge was ready to go as it were. Not that Grant would care. By the time the cliff crumbled, he'd be dead.

Brad stopped and took a deep breath; he mightn't have pulled this last one off if God hadn't been on his side.

He had to hurry. Kali could be here any minute.

He wanted to be ready for her.

CHAPTER TWENTY-SEVEN

Kali gasped, "Grant. Oh, God, no. Please, no." She couldn't help the plea that floated around the interior of the car. She grabbed for her cell phone and dialed quickly. Cars honked. Kali hit the gas and sped toward home. She listened for his voice, but the ringing went on and on. Grant didn't answer.

Kali dug furiously through the front cubbyhole for Grant's card. She hit the brakes at the next stoplight. *Christ.* Where was it? Panic set in when she couldn't find it. There. Under several pens. She snatched it up. Good, there were the more formal channels on the card. Kali dialed the first number, wracking her brain for the name of the friend who worked with Grant.

Thomas, that was it. She asked the person on the other end to speak with him – explaining it was an emergency concerning one of their agents, Grant Summers. It took a moment but finally she had Thomas on the line.

Kali quickly filled him in.

Thomas wasted no time. "Where are you?"

"Almost home. I'm turning into my driveway now." She drove in and parked.

Grant's car was there. Along with two other FBI vehicles. Kali sighed with relief. She raced up to her front door and opened it. "Grant? Hello? Are you here?"

Silence. "Thomas, he's not answering and there's no sign of him. I think the killer has him."

"We're almost there. Don't go inside. Get back into your car and leave the property. Do you hear me?"

"Too late, I'm already here. Where's Grant's back-up team?"

She walked through the house checking for signs Grant had been here. There were none. She headed into the kitchen; the lingering aromas of her spaghetti sauce reminded her of their long forgotten plans. Kali walked onto the deck and searched the backyard. She returned to the kitchen. Surely, there should be other agents here? "The bastard must have circled and snuck up on Grant."

"There are several teams there now and I've got another one with me. They'll find this guy. Stay out of their way and let them do their jobs," said Thomas.

Kali surveyed the room. There were papers on the kitchen table. She walked over to check. On the top of the pile, a short ripped-off piece read: "Who's going to help you now, witch?"

"Shit! The bastard left a note on the kitchen table."

"God damn it, stop," roared Thomas. "We're almost there. Let us take care of this."

"As you've taken care of everything else?" Kali snorted. "I don't think so. I happen to care for Grant and I'm sure as hell not going to leave his fate up to you."

"Kali, don't do anything stupid. I know you want to help. So do we. We're only minutes away. Stay there until we arrive so we can at least assist you. This guy wants you to do something foolish. But unless he's huge, he's not going to move Grant too far."

"Not likely." Kali closed her eyes. Grim reality hit home. "That's why he shot Shiloh, so I wouldn't have her help to find the victims. Giving him yet another advantage. He's determined to have me show my true self."

Kali turned as she heard several vehicles roar into the yard. She raced to the front door and opened it. Thomas still had his cell phone and was talking to her. "True self? What do you mean? Don't you need Shiloh?"

"No."

He looked confused when Kali walked up to him. They exchanged grim smiles at each other as they put their cell phones away. The men collected in a group around them. Several stood listening to the conversation. She didn't think Grant would have told any of them about her abilities – except maybe Thomas.

She motioned for Thomas to walk a few steps away for a private chat.

"He thinks I'm using black magic," she said. "He called me a witch in his note."

"Why is that?" He frowned.

Kali was beyond caring about his opinion. Grant's life was at stake here. "Some of you saw Shiloh and me in action earlier. But it's not always Shiloh that does the finding. I do too."

Thomas stared at her.

"Shiloh isn't a rescue dog?"

"Yes, she is and a damn good one. But I often pick up on victims, too. She does well when Mother Nature causes chaos. My specialty is when men are responsible for the damage."

"Because you're psychic?" Doubt and skepticism were evident.

"I'm not really psychic. More a barometer for violence." Kali shrugged. "Shiloh and I work well together as a team. But I *have* worked and *will* work without her if I have to. Like now," she added grimly. "So if you don't mind, park your doubts and leave your questions for later. Let's find Grant before he's buried alive."

Thomas stood beside her, cell phone open, already texting his team. "Any idea where to start looking?"

Kali spun in a circle. She was Grant's only chance. If she could just find that faint trail of violent energy.

A faint sprinkle, like sunlight on dust – only much darker – floated to the right of the house. "Yeah, he's headed to the beach."

"Let's go then."

Kali summoned the Sight, easily picking up the scattered energy. She pointed the way and took off at a dead run. She could see the trail flattened through the woods in her mind's eye but hadn't caught sight of the actual trail in the woods yet. She didn't need to. A few hundred yards took her to the steep stairs. Energy fluttered at the top then continued along the top of the cliff. The stairs had been considered but had eventually been tossed. Opened her eyes she turned left. "This way. Hurry."

Kali crashed through the bush, knowing that sneaking was better than charging like an elephant, but she couldn't stop herself. Urgency rode her hard.

The men crashed noisily behind her.

She came to an abrupt stop. Clouds of energy billowed atop the bushes. She spun around and held up a hand to stop the charge behind her. Thomas walked quietly to her. "What's up?"

She leaned toward his ear, whispering, "He's just up past the bend. I recognize the place. The cliff is very unstable here. There's no space either. Enough for one man, maybe two – but that's all. You'll take the cliff down if anyone tries to rush him. You'll end up killing Grant anyway. And possibly other members of your team."

Thomas stared in the direction she mentioned. "So how do you know he's up there?"

Kali shot him a withering look. "I can see the energy."

He looked at her, a puzzled expression on his face. Then he said, "We'll fan out and come in from several directions."

"Quietly," she cautioned. Kali moved forward ten feet, twenty feet and then thirty. She heard a voice and came to a dead stop.

A pain worse than anything she'd ever experienced unfurled in her heart. Her soul was already splintering with the horror that came with the voice recognition. "It can't be. Please not." Pain and grief clogged her throat as Brad's voice roiled through her defenses.

Kali peered through the brush. She gazed on the face of the man she'd considered her best friend for the last decade. So changed by expression and his words, each one a fresh stab into her soul.

The crazed killer...the one who'd kidnapped and killed so many people, was her best friend...her dead best friend. Oh God, the same person who'd killed little Melanie and almost killed Julie, had been a friend to them all.

Brad.

Kali burrowed her head in her hands. Had Brad killed other people? People he was called to save...how many had he killed? Brad spoke again. Kali strained to hear the words.

"So you're coming around already, huh?"

Kali groaned softly. He had to be talking to Grant.

"Maybe that's good. Not that it will save you. That bitch needs to know my life, to live my old world. Feel that sense of failure. That knowing that nothing she does ever changes anything. Your death will teach her so much."

Kali's heart shattered. Brad's mind had broken. He'd morphed into this bizarre killer. She couldn't even begin to imagine who lay in the morgue wearing Brad's toe tag. His words reverberated in her soul. So much emptiness, so much pain, so much evil. A monster.

And *that* Brad had Grant.

Creeping closer, Kali wished for the first time in her life that she had a weapon of her own. She looked around for something that could do some damage. The sight of the men creeping toward the unstable area made her heart stop.

Rising up slightly, she tried to locate Grant but there was no sign of him. And Brad stood at the edge of the cliff. Shit.

Enough. She had to help Grant.

She stood up, calling out, "It's me you want. So why do you keep attacking everyone else? Brad, why are you hurting all these innocent people?"

All the while talking, she searched the area for any sign of Grant. Again nothing. Except she spotted a gun tossed off to one side. Her heart sank when she saw freshly turned dirt piled against the cliff rising behind the small jutting ledge. If Grant survived the burying, the cliff was poised to fall away at any moment, killing him anyway. Without air, he had only minutes. Who knew if Brad felt Grant rated an oxygen tank this time? Billowing clouds of grey energy engulfed the area. Signs of violence in progress. Kali could barely see through it.

Brad stepped back, his chest heaving, shock evident on his face. "No, you can't be here. Not yet."

Approaching slowly, Kali sought the right words. "Of course it's possible. I'm better than you."

She watched warily as his face turned purple and red, the veins on his temple bulging.

"No. I'm better. I've proved it."

"Proved what? That you're weak and useless and you like attacking innocent people?"

Anger speared his voice. "Innocent? They are not. You don't understand, but then how could you? You don't know I'm doing God's work. But you think these people deserve to be saved. They were supposed to die in the first place." His voice rose until he practically screamed the last words.

Kali stared at him. So that's what a broken mind looked like. Horrible.

"They deserved to die like this? Suffering for days? What disaster did Grant survive? You're only killing him because of me. How many other people have you killed?" She paused, then whispered softly, "You're crazy."

But not softly enough.

"I am not crazy," he screamed. "I'm sending these people home, my way. Sending them back. They were supposed to have died – like all the others. I don't know how many I helped God take home. I didn't kill them, God did. I'm just putting them back into the same situation they shouldn't have gotten out of. God's will must be done!" he yelled at her.

Then suddenly, he stopped talking.

He'd seen the men rise up behind her.

"You're too late. You'll always be too late."

Kali stiffened. "What have you done?" She ran at him, screaming in fury.

Before she could reach him, the pile of dirt shifted in waves and a hand reached out from the grave. And grabbed onto Brad's ankle.

Brad cried out and jumped back, breaking the hold on his leg. Just then a heavy rumble sounded. An odd look rippled across his face as the ground beneath him gave away.

Kali stopped in her tracks as a horrible scream filled the air. She stopped breathing but her heart pounded crazily as her mind filled with an instant replay of what had just happened. And froze on the glimpse she'd caught of Brad's face as he went over the cliff. The disbelief. The fear. The horror.

As if he saw, not God, but the devil.

Then he was gone but his shocked face remained in her mind for a long instant before fading away. Her breath whooshed out.

Brad was dead now. This time – for real.

But Grant... Relief filled her as he heaved up from the grave onto all fours.. He was alive!

Later she'd deal with Brad's betrayal, but right now the only feeling rushing through her was pure happiness.

She raced to Grant as he struggled to his feet. His chest heaved as she threw herself into his arms.

"Christ, Kali," he said, choking on the words.

Kali didn't care about words right now. She squeezed him tight, relief bringing tears to her eyes.

It was over. Held tight in Grant's embrace, Kali's splintered world glued itself back into a cohesive whole. From the bits of conversation going on around her, she understood Brad was gone. The hillside had sent enough dirt and rock on top to require equipment and men to recover his body. Fitting in a way.

As she stood, her face buried against Grant's heaving chest, she came to a realization. The real Brad, her best friend Brad, had disappeared a long time ago. As she'd internalized her pain from the Mexico disaster, the Brad she'd known had fractured, becoming someone else.

She'd mourn the loss of her friend. She could only be grateful for the death of the madman he'd become. Maybe understanding in this way, would give her closure.

Her heart eased. She shuddered as the weight of so many lives slipped off her shoulders. Tilting her head back, she stared up in Grant's warm loving gaze. "I'm so glad it's all over."

"So am I." The glint in his eye was the only warning before he captured her lips in a devastating kiss.

The men surrounding them cheered.

By the time he lifted his head, Kali collapsed against his chest, exhausted, but smiling.

***

Kali gently bent over to scratch Shilo's ears. She lay on the far side of the deck. She'd healed but hadn't fully recovered her strength yet. Kali didn't care; Shiloh had survived. That's what counted. Hopefully, they'd have many more years together.

"How's she doing, Kali?" Julie asked.

"She's doing fine. Although it will still be a few weeks before she's back to her normal bouncy self."

She straightened, twisting against the damn itchiness that was damn near killing her. "At least her stitches aren't bugging her as much as mine are. Damn." She tried to reach the one spot on her right shoulder and couldn't.

A large hand found and scratched the spot for her.

Kali moaned in relief, leaning her head against Grant's chest to give him better access. From the coziness of his arms around her, she surveyed the motley crew collected on Kali's deck. Grant

317

had fully recovered. Julie had also pulled through. Her face could use some more color, yet she looked to be managing her recovery well. Dan on the other hand, looked to be managing his demise. He was dying.

Kali had shed many tears for him. Even now moisture collected in the corner of her eyes. As if sensing her distress, Grant whispered, "Are you okay?"

She tilted her head up and responded softly, "I'm just struggling with Dan's acceptance of his own death. Why refuse treatment. It could really make a difference."

His arms tightened around her. He dropped his chin onto the top of her head. "Because it would only give him a few months. He wants to go peacefully – the way God intended."

Kali flinched. "And that just reminds me of Brad. How could he kill Christian, his best friend, in order to gain a fresh start?"

A heavy sigh worked free of Grant's chest. "Brad brought a lot of pain and torment to many people."

Cringing slightly, she nodded. "True. I'd be happy to take Sergeant. He's a great dog."

"Give Susan a chance. If it doesn't work out then you can suggest it." His deep murmur sent shivers down her spine.

"And Jarl?" She tried to hold her bitterness back.

"You can't fix everything, honey. He shot you. He attacked Dan. I don't care how worried he was you'd finger him for the thefts, attempted murder is going to put him away for a long time."

"Well I hope he gets to stay with Penny until the end. She only has a few weeks left." It had to be hard on her to know what Jarl had done and the penalty he'd pay for trying to fix their situation. Not a nice end to her life.

"You're such a softy." He cuddled her closer.

Rational, sensible Grant. He'd been the stalwart one throughout all this. He'd calmed her when anger had overwhelmed her. He'd held her when despair had taken hold. He'd loved her when she hadn't loved herself.

He'd become everything to her.

Grant returned to gently scratching his hand along her slowly healing wounds. Kali moaned with pleasure.

"That feels so good."

"Didn't you say that very same thing last night?"

She flashed him an intimate glance. "Yeah, I think I did. Maybe it'll be your turn to moan tonight."

He winked. "I look forward to that."

"Hey you two, my old heart can't stand much more of this. Keep it clean." Dan's teasing voice brought them both back to their surroundings.

Stefan added his two bits. "Take pity on those of us unattached and unloved." He'd become a regular visitor as he was enlisted to help Kali develop her skills.

Grant snorted at his friend. "You're alone only when you choose to be."

And if Julie had her way, Stefan wouldn't be alone tonight or any other night. Kali surveyed her group with satisfaction, her gaze landing on Dan, his face alight with knowing laughter.

Grant reached out and captured her fingers in his. "So were you planning to do anything special in the next couple of months?"

She wrinkled her nose. "No, I don't think so. Other than enjoy life."

"Sounds good to me. How do you feel about having company?"

She glanced sideways at him. "I'd love to have some company. Are we talking for a day or two? For a few weeks or a few years?"

Her fingers were squeezed in a death grip. "If we're talking that long, maybe I should ask how do you feel about a house guest?"

Wow. Kali raised an eyebrow. "I guess that depends on whether he's going to be a guest or if he's moving in." Kali gave him a saucy look

Grant's steely gray eyes searched her face. Kali cast a warm glance from her partially closed eyes. His lips twitched. "Is moving in an option?"

"Hell, yeah. House guests are work. Partners share the load." Kali smirked.

"We do make a good team, don't we?"

"Damn right we do.

"Then partners it is."

Dan finally spoke up. "About damn time too."

They all laughed.

Grant squeezed Kali's hand. She smiled. Her future looked warm and bright for the first time in over a decade.

Personally, she couldn't wait.

Psychic Vision Series
Maddy's Floor, book 3

Medical intuitive and licensed MD Madeleine Wagner thought she'd seen every way possible to heal a diseased body...then patients start dying from mysterious causes in her long-term facility.

The terminally ill fight to get into her ward. Once there, many miraculously...live. So when her patients start dropping and she senses an evil force causing their deaths, she calls on her friend and mentor, Stefan, for help. Together, they delve beyond the physical plane into the metaphysical... Only to find terror.

She wants to save everyone, but are some souls not meant to be saved?

Detective Drew McNeil has two family members in need of Maddy's healing care, but his visits to her facility leave him wondering - who cares for Maddy? Bizarre events on her floor raise his professional curiosity. And the more time he spends with Maddy, the more personal everything becomes. When the deaths on Maddy's Floor intersect with one of his cold cases, he realizes an old killer has returned - and Maddy's standing in his path.

How can these people stop something that no one else can see, feel or even believe?

Garden of Sorrow, book 4

Her world is in chaos. His world is in order. She wants to help the innocent. He wants to catch the guilty. But someone is trying to make sure that neither gets what they want.

Alexis Gordon has spent the last year trying to get over the loss of her sister. Then she goes to work on a normal day...and reality as she knows it...disappears.

Detective Kevin Sutherland, armed with his own psychic abilities, recognizes her gift and calls in his friend Stefan Kronos, a psychic artist and law enforcement consultant, to help her develop her skills. But Kevin has never seen anything like this case - a killer with a personal vendetta to stop Alexis from finding out more about him...and his long dead victims.

The killer can be stopped. He must be stopped. But he's planning on surviving...even after death.

About the author:

Dale Mayer is a prolific multi-published writer. She's best known for her Psychic Visions series. Besides her romantic suspense/thrillers, Dale also writes paranormal romance and crossover young adult books in several different genres. To go with her fiction, she also writes nonfiction in many different fields with books available on resume writing, companion gardening and the US mortgage system. She has recently published her Career Essentials Series. All her books are available in digital and print formats.

Books by Dale Mayer

Psychic Vision Series
Tuesday's Child
Hide'n Go Seek
Maddy's Floor
Garden of Sorrow
Knock, knock...

Death Series – romantic thriller
Touched by Death
Haunted by Death - (Fall 2013)

Novellas/short stories
It's a Dog's Life- romantic comedy
Sian's Solution – part of Family Blood Ties
Riana's Revenge – Fantasy short story

Second Chances…at Love
Second Chances - out now
Book 2 - Winter 2013/2014

Young Adult Books
In Cassie's Corner
Gem Stone (A Gemma Stone Mystery)

Design Series
Dangerous Designs
Deadly Designs
Deceptive Designs – fall 2013

Family Blood Ties Series
Vampire in Denial
Vampire in Distress
Vampire in Design - out now!
Vampire InDecision – coming soon!

Non-Fiction Books
Career Essentials: The Resume
Career Essentials: The Cover Letter
Career Essentials: The Interview
Career Essentials: 3 in 1

Connect with Dale Mayer Online:
Dale's Website – www.dalemayer.com
Twitter – http://twitter.com/#!/DaleMayer
Facebook – http://www.facebook.com/DaleMayer.author

HIDE'N GO SEEK